PRAISE FOR THE NOVELS OF A. L. JACKSON

Come to Me Quietly

"As always, A. L. Jackson knows how to tap human emotion. Every word she writes bleeds meaning. *Come to Me Quietly* is a riveting tale of loss, two souls destined to be together, and discovering strength in forgiving one's self from regrets keeping them chained to finding true happiness. Simply breathtaking."
—Gail McHugh, *New York Times* Bestselling Author
of *Collide* and *Pulse*

"*Come to Me Quietly* is raw and real. It's an achingly beautiful story about a man with a ravaged soul and his chance at a life he never thought he deserved. A. L. Jackson has written such an emotionally impactful story that grabs you right from the start."
—Kim Karr, author of *Mended*

"Exquisite, beautiful, poignant—A. L. Jackson is in a league of her own! [She] has a way with words that makes the pages come to life. You'll live with these characters, feel their ups and downs, their loves and losses. You'll bleed *with* them, and *for* them.... Heartbreaking and heartwarming, this book made me ache, made me cry, made me think, and made me fall in love."
—S. C. Stephens, #1 *New York Times* bestselling author of *Reckless*

"A devastatingly beautiful story of love, grief, and healing. Every emotion on the page will grip at your heart, and leave you stuck in the characters' lives for days after."
—*New York Times* bestselling author Molly McAdams

continued . . .

Lost to You

"I was completely hooked from the second I opened *Lost to You* . . . a beautiful and powerful love story."   —Flirty and Dirty Book Blog

"Can A. L. Jackson write anything but excellence? . . . She always finds a way to get my insides twisted into so many emotions that I feel like it is all happening to me. . . . 5-star perfection!"   —Madison Says

"A beautiful, heart-stopping love story. . . . You will sigh happily, swoon, smile, cry, and get pissed off. What a great range of emotions."
—The Book Enthusiast

When We Collide

"A great read. . . . The intensity in the novel is extraordinary and I look forward to reading other books by A. L. Jackson."
—Reviewing Romance

"Reading *When We Collide* was like a slow, agonizing torture, but in the best way. . . . I felt so much love and hope for these characters. It was an amazing read."   —The Book List Reviews

"Books like this remind me why I absolutely adore reading. Books like this that grab me, hold me captive, envelop me in the story, and leave a mark on my heart."   —Aestas Book Blog

"A. L. Jackson delivered another emotionally driven love story. I was captivated from the first page until the last. This book evoked empathy, tears, anger, and hope in me. This is another book that will stay with me for a while."   —Romance Lovers Book Blog

Take This Regret

"Absolutely amazing!...I felt love, hatred, joy, sadness, pain, betrayal....This is truly a great read."   —My Secret Romance

"There are no words that could begin to explain how wonderfully powerful this story is. It wasn't your typical romance. No fluff stuff here! It was an emotional roller-coaster ride from the beginning till the end!"   —Crazy for Books

"Oh this book was amazing. I know I gush like a schoolgirl, but I cannot contain myself when I find a story that leaves me clutching its pages to my heart...or in this case my Nook to my heart....My heart broke with this story, I cried for this story, and I fell in love with all the characters from beginning to end."   —Tina's Book Reviews

Pulled

"There are not enough words that could possibly describe how I feel about this book. It is hands down one of the most amazing love stories I've ever read....Thank you, A. L. Jackson, for allowing me into the world of these characters."
          —Gail McHugh, *New York Times* bestselling author of *Collide*

"What an emotionally intense and addictive story...and I loved every minute of it! This is what I look for in a romance book."
          —My Secret Romance

"A novel that will pull at your heartstrings...[and] leave you convinced that the power of true love can conquer anything."
          —Jersey Girl Book Reviews

"This story ripped my heart right out more than once, and convinced me that I should buy stock in Kleenex. It also warmed me from the inside out!"   —Book Snobs

Also by A. L. Jackson

The Closer to You Series
Come to Me Quietly

COME TO ME SOFTLY

The Closer to You Series

A. L. JACKSON

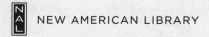

NEW AMERICAN LIBRARY

New American Library
Published by the Penguin Group
Penguin Group (USA) LLC, 375 Hudson Street,
New York, New York 10014

USA | Canada | UK | Ireland | Australia | New Zealand | India | South Africa | China
penguin.com
A Penguin Random House Company

First published by New American Library,
a division of Penguin Group (USA) LLC

First Printing, July 2014

LIBRARY OF CONGRESS CATALOGING-IN-PUBLICATION DATA:
Jackson, A. L.
Come to me softly: the closer to you series/A. L. Jackson.
p. cm.
ISBN 978-0-451-46797-3
1. Man-woman relationships—Fiction. I. Title.
PS3610.A25C68 2014
813'.6—dc23   2014010477

Printed in the United States of America
1   3   5   7   9   10   8   6   4   2

Set in Bell MT
Designed by Spring Hoteling

PUBLISHER'S NOTE
This is a work of fiction. Names, characters, places, and incidents either are the product of the author's imagination or are used fictitiously, and any resemblance to actual persons, living or dead, business establishments, events, or locales is entirely coincidental.

To my mom, who has always been there for me in every aspect of my life. I wish there was a way to tell you how much I love and respect you, but there are no words. You are simply the best.

Acknowledgments

Chad ~Thank you, thank you, thank you. All of this would be impossible without a man like you at my side, constantly supporting me and picking up the slack. I love you forever.

Thank you to Devyn, whom I love with every piece of me. You are incredibly brilliant and beautiful, and having you a part of this every day is something I treasure.

To my little men, Eli and Braydon, for being such amazing boys. I am so thankful I was blessed so much to get to call you my sons. I love you more than you know.

Katie ~ Thank you for being with me every step of the way, through thick and thin, through the good times and the bad. I love you so much, my BFF.

Thank you to Big Rollin' Bitches Rebecca Shea, Molly McAdams, and Kristen Proby for challenging me to stay on task, for pushing me harder and faster and farther! I love calling you amazing authors my friends!

To the team at New Adult Library ~ Thank you so much for your support and dedication to my work.

And I have to mention the incredible authors of Authors off the Shelf. I cherish the laughs and insight, the goofiness and the advice. I love you all.

COME TO
ME SOFTLY

ONE

Jared

Comfort.

I'd gone without it for a lot of years. It was like this hole had been hollowed out inside me, begging for anything to fill it. Like hunger pangs when you're starving and your body eats at your insides, searching for satiety when there's no sustenance to be found. The idea of it'd become a vague memory, there to taunt me with what I could no longer have. Mocking me with loneliness and desolation, reminding me I'd lost the right to be loved.

Leaving me to rot.

Because without love, what's left?

Nothing.

And that's exactly what I'd become.

I'd accepted it because that's what I deserved.

My life as a penance.

A due.

In the hazy morning light, I breathed in the coconut and the good and the girl. Swimming in her warmth, I lost myself in the way it felt to have Aly's perfect little body all tucked up close to mine.

Comfort.

It surrounded me now.

I brushed my fingers through the silken strands of her long, dark hair, so dark it looked black in the silhouettes of the soft morning light that filtered in through her bedroom window.

Did I deserve that comfort now? I had no fucking clue.

Really, I didn't know anything aside for one fact.

I loved this girl.

I was in love with Aleena Moore.

Now that I'd finally admitted it, it was all I could see.

Part of me wanted to climb out of bed and grab my journal, my fingers itching to pour my confusion out in words across the pages, to release the chaos tumbling through my mind. But at the cost of leaving Aly's bed? Not a chance.

A soft sigh slipped through her parted lips, and a little moan of contentment flowed from her mouth as she sank further into the security of my hold. That little sound lit every one of my nerves.

I pressed all my hard to her soft, holding her close against me as I flattened myself to the snowy skin of her back.

Mmm . . . yeah.

I was in love with this girl.

And I wasn't going to let her go.

Not ever. Days without Aly were darkness, and I was done surrendering to it. The seedy shit I always found myself in. The self-destruction. That fucked-up kind of life was over because I had finally come to accept Aly *was* my life.

I'd been lying there in her bed awake for hours. Just thinking, trying to sort it all out while I watched her sleep. Guilt fluttered along the fringes of my consciousness. Pressing in. All night, I'd been asking myself if I was wrong by coming back here to her.

Would she and our baby be better without me? Was I still taking what I had no right to? Was this gorgeous girl curled up in my arms tainted by me? Had I wrecked her good by putting part of myself inside of her? Would I destroy her?

I'd been certain I would. Now I had no idea what to believe. Because Aly had shattered all my beliefs.

Coming back to Phoenix yesterday had terrified me. I had no idea what to expect or what I would find. All I felt was the intense need spurring me forward. One that told me I had to somehow get her back.

Or maybe I'd come here to win her for the first time.

God knew I'd spent so many nights while I'd been staying with Aly and her brother over the past summer, sneaking into her room, that she and I had never really felt real. I'd given us over to fantasy. Figured if I couldn't have her, at least I could pretend. Take a little before I lost it all, before she became just another fucked-up memory.

Turned out she'd always been mine.

I'd just been too much of a fool to see us for what we really were.

Aly and I had grown up together, this girl a part of me for all my life. We grew up living across the street from each other, her brother, Christopher, my best friend, our mothers best friends, too, like our families were one and the same. Until the day I turned sixteen—I'd been so careless. Reckless. My chest tightened as visions flashed. Guilt pressed in as all the air seemed to get sucked from the room.

I killed my mother in a car accident that day.

I was driving us home from getting my license. I'd slipped

quickly after that day, diving into drugs and alcohol, hoping it would cover up the suffocating guilt of what I'd taken from this world. But that lifestyle had never dimmed the shame, that shame growing so much that two months after my mother's death, I tried to take my life. But Aly, this girl, had been there. Saved me.

That act had sent me away to juvie until the day I turned eighteen. My father had shunned me, and I'd thought I had nothing left in Phoenix, so when I was released, I ran. As far as I could, living for four years in New Jersey. But I'd been drawn back here. Should have always known it was Aly, that we were connected in ways I didn't understand.

Six months ago I came back to Phoenix and ran into Christopher, who took me home to stay at his place. He was living with Aly. What grew between Aly and me was intense, and I soon found myself trying to keep from falling for her. But I did. I fell hard.

We kept what was going on between us a secret, mostly because I couldn't accept what we were or what I was feeling. I'd always believed love wasn't something I deserved. I didn't get happiness. But we'd also kept it a secret because of her brother. He knew as well as I did I wasn't good enough for his sister. So when he'd discovered us and everything had come to a head, I did what I did best. I ran. I fled everything I couldn't face and ended up in Vegas for the last three months, once again trying to drown out the pain of my life.

I thought I'd always be running until I crashed my bike one night three weeks ago. In that flash of a moment before I hit the pavement . . . in that singular moment . . . it was the first time I didn't want to die since I'd turned sixteen.

And I knew it was Aly. Even if I had to live with this guilt for all my life, I knew then I had to come back to her. And I finally made it to her last night.

Now her back burned into my chest. As I slowly slipped my hand down to her abdomen, my breath got all locked up inside me. I was filled with both fear and a need I didn't quite understand. My palm came to the flat plane of her stomach, to the place that harbored one of the greatest shocks of my life.

Beneath my touch, Aly's stomach lifted and fell in a slow rhythm, her breaths calm in the depths of sleep.

Pinching my eyes closed, I did my best to imagine what was happening inside her, this little life I had no idea how to manage.

If I'd expected anything, it sure as hell hadn't been this— the news Aly had given me last night when I returned to Phoenix, the new weight that had been added to my shoulders.

Yeah, a weight. I'd admit it. I wasn't cut out to be a father, and the idea of it scared the shit out of me.

But this weight was no burden, and the strongest sense of devotion pumped a new kind of need through my veins. Something overpowering. Something right.

Aly made me want to be better.

I pressed my hand firmer to her belly.

This made me want to be better.

Last night, I warned Aly that I was fucked-up and I was always going to be. I could feel it there, still simmering in my bones, the truth of who I was.

And damn, Aly and I were young. I got that. She was only twenty and I was twenty-two, and I knew that only added to our issues, too.

I buried my nose in her hair and held her as close as I could get her. Because I thought my love for her . . . maybe . . . maybe it was stronger than all of that shit.

God, I hoped so.

I needed to be better, because there was no doubt these two needed me.

What scared me most was how much I needed them.

Aly sighed and mumbled, these cute, muddled sounds that did something crazy right at the center of my chest.

I nipped at her ear, coaxing her from sleep. "Baby," I whispered low. I just needed to see her face. Talk to her. Make sure it was all as real as it had felt last night. "Come here."

In my arms, she slowly rolled over to face me and her eyes blinked open. The intense green slipped all over me, memorizing, searching my face in the shadows like maybe she was needing reassurance of the same thing.

Today was a first for us. Waking up next to her instead of sneaking out of her room in the middle of the night like the asshole I'd been, hiding us away and making her ashamed.

A slow smile curved her perfect mouth, and I couldn't do anything but lean down and brush mine against the fullness, kiss the girl who'd undone me.

My chest tightened. All the months I'd been gone, I hadn't known what to do with what I felt for Aly. The truth of what she was that I'd been fighting for so long. Now it was prominent, thrumming wildly with every pulse of my heart.

"Hi," she said quietly.

Shifting, I wedged a knee between her legs as I climbed over her, hovered close. Damn, she was the most gorgeous thing. She stared up at me, her olive skin all smooth and flawless, her cheeks high and striking, defined.

Still, everything about her was soft.

Good.

I cupped my hand around that trusting face. "Morning, beautiful."

God, how perfect was it waking up next to her?

Soft fingertips fluttered along my jaw. Something powerful simmered in her eyes. "You stayed." The words seemed to come from somewhere deep within her, revealing the fear she still kept harbored inside.

My gut twisted because I wanted to take all that away from her, all the pain she'd been living with during the months I'd been gone. For the longest time, I just looked down at her, a promise held in my stare. "Baby, I already told you, I'm not going anywhere."

My hold increased on her cheek, my nose an inch from hers. Because inside I already knew the answer to all the questions plaguing me.

Aly needed me.

I let part of my weight settle on her, careful not to hurt her, because I was finished with all that hurting shit. I murmured close to her ear, "I need you to believe that. Yeah, we've got some shit to deal with, but we're going to do it together. Okay?"

Leaning back, I let myself get lost in her hopeful gaze. Instinctively, I twisted a lock of her hair with my finger. A bond. My home.

I'm not going anywhere.

Aly blinked like she was absorbing what I'd said. She wound her arms around my neck and buried her face in it. A breath of words flooded out to kiss the skin just under my ear. "I believe in you, Jared. I always have."

Affection pounded against my ribs. God, it felt so good because this girl really fucking got me, understood when no one else could.

"Thank you." I gripped her face and swept my mouth across hers. "Thank you for seeing something in me that I didn't know was there."

I kissed her deeper. My tongue dipped in to taste the sweet and the good, and Aly met me, her tongue all soft and welcoming.

And damn if just that little brush didn't cause every last inch of my body to harden.

Motherfucking trigger.

For so long I'd thought of her that way, provoking all these feelings inside me I didn't believe I had the right to feel.

Turned out I didn't mind this trigger so much after all.

Outside her room, a door slammed, hard enough to shake Aly's walls.

We both froze, eyes going wide, before our attention flashed to her closed door. For so many months, that door had hidden us away. Like some kind of sick, dirty little secret. Instead I should've been screaming out about how much this girl meant to me.

That's how twisted I was. But I never claimed I was right in the head. Far from it. Thought I was doing her some kind of warped favor, saving face when in turn I'd just brought her shame.

Worry flashed in Aly's eyes when the heavy footsteps plodded down the hall. A shadow blinked under the door when her brother passed.

I dropped my forehead to hers, and I suppressed the groan that rose in my throat.

Fuck.

Could anyone blame me for being none too excited at the thought of going toe-to-toe with her brother Christopher? Him finding me here? Dude was not gonna be pleased. But that meeting was inevitable.

No time like the present, I thought sarcastically. *Seize the day and all that.*

Pretty sure it was going to be Christopher seizing my balls.

Last night Aly told me she'd confided in him about the baby

and how important it was to her that he'd been there for her in the time I was away.

"Think I have some business to take care of. Why don't you wait here or maybe grab a shower while I have a little chat with your brother?" I whispered softly, tucking a lock of her hair behind her ear.

Wasn't exactly a question. More like a plea.

Aly didn't need to deal with more of the shit storm I conjured, then fled from the moment it hit land. I wanted her to stay here where I could protect her from what needed to be said. Or maybe I just didn't want her to hear it, whatever Christopher would spew, because in it would be nothing but the truth.

Aly grimaced, like maybe I'd just wounded her.

I shook my head, knowing exactly what she was thinking. "Give me ten minutes, baby, then I'll come back and we'll spend the day in bed. Just you and me."

Knowing eyes peered up at me. The look alone called out my bluff. "You can't start hiding stuff, Jared. We're a *team* now," she emphasized. "We're supposed to do this together."

Old pain twisted my face, and I edged back a fraction. I was so used to handling shit on my own, just dealing, pushing it all aside so I could stay afloat. Really, I'd just been drowning.

And here was this girl, promising she'd stay by me and help me keep my head above water.

I searched for her hand and pressed her palm to my face. I hoped somehow she could feel the sincerity in my words. "This isn't because I want to hide you away, Aly. But I *need* to do this alone. I'm the one who fucked it up and I'm the one who has to make it right. I've known your brother a long, long time, and this isn't just about you and me."

Before I left, I'd lost control on my oldest friend, beaten him bloody, my mind a cloud of rage and agony. It was the night he busted in Aly's door and discovered us together. He'd confronted us, and the tension between us had escalated fast. I didn't even realize how far I'd slipped until it all came back into focus and I realized his body was a heap in the middle of Aly's bedroom floor. After what I did, I had no idea if I even could make it right or if he'd give me the chance. No doubt, I didn't deserve one. But for Aly, I was going to ask for it. Face him. Own up to the shit I still wasn't sure I knew how to control.

I brushed my fingers through her hair. "Let me talk to him, okay? I need to start facing some stuff in my life. It started with you yesterday, coming back here. Now it needs to be him. I can't keep running, can't keep tossing walls up to hide behind. Please understand."

"I get it, Jared. But I also need you to know you're not alone anymore." Tender fingers burned into my skin where she ran them down my jaw. "I want to be a part of whatever you have to face in this life so I can be a part of your future."

Her statement washed over me like a balm. Like overwhelming peace I didn't deserve. But there was no stopping myself from submerging myself in it. I placed a closemouthed kiss to her lips, before I turned to the soft shell of her ear and whispered, "You are my life . . . my future."

Never had one without her.

Aly's fingers curled in my neck as she drank in the words that had been locked up in my heart. I could feel them race through her veins and take hold. Because the two of us?

We fit.

This fucked-up puzzle that finally made sense.

Reluctantly, I climbed from her bed. Grabbing the jeans I'd left in a pile on the floor, I couldn't help but smirk as she watched me pull them on. Those eyes raked down me with pure need. It felt amazing that this girl wanted me as badly as I wanted her.

Her fingers trembled toward me from where she lay on her stomach. I came back to her and brushed my lips over her fingertips. "I mean it, Aly."

"I know," she said, everything I never thought I'd have lighting in her eyes.

Then I turned and headed out her door. Quietly, I latched it shut behind me.

I stepped out of the sanctuary of Aly's room. In one second flat, all my nerves were wringing me tight. My chest tightened, and I could hear my pulse drumming in my ears, this steady progression of unease spinning me up and stringing me out. Harshly, I blinked and squinted, trying to adjust to the bright light blazing in through the sliding glass door in the living room.

I had no clue what to expect when it came to Christopher, but I sure as hell didn't want a repeat of the last time I walked out Aly's door, that argument and fight that ended with me running to Vegas for three miserable months.

Some things were unforgivable. All the fucking deplorable sins I'd committed that would haunt me all my life. I drove my hand through my hair. Pretty sure beating my best friend to a bloodied pulp qualified as one of them.

Figured the fact I knocked up his little sister probably didn't sit very well with him, either.

I drew in a deep breath and pushed all those thoughts aside.

Didn't matter. I made the decision when I came here. I was finished hiding.

Silencing my feet, I inched down the hall, buying a little time, trying to feel him out.

I spotted him over the bar that separated the main room from the kitchen. He was flinging open cupboards and slamming them closed just as hard. I studied him as I passed.

The shock of black hair on his head was a fucking disaster, sticking up everywhere, probably three inches longer than the last time I saw him. He wasn't wearing anything but a pair of holey jeans. Color bled all over his back and arms, intricate tats sketched in beautiful patterns across his skin, the opposite of the horrors that stained mine.

But I didn't miss the way his muscles bunched in his shoulders, his entire being ticking with hostility and his movements harsh. He kept banging shit around, all wound up and fucking on edge. Tension radiated from him as he shoved two pieces of bread into the toaster.

Awareness prickled between us like a live wire, just waiting for the spark, one little movement that could cause us to combust.

With my stomach twisted in about fifteen knots, I rounded the bar, hesitating right between the border of the kitchen and the small, round dining table. He kept his back to me, like maybe I was dead to him, the way I should be.

He will hate me before I'm gone.

How many times had that silent promise made its way through my thoughts? Enough times to know their truth—that was for sure.

Finally, I pulled out a chair from the dining table, turned it around, and sat down facing him. Slumping forward, I rested my elbows on my knees. I rushed my hand over my face and down my chin, as if the action could wipe away all the shit we had to deal with.

Christopher had been my best friend all through my childhood, our tie thicker than blood, the brother I'd never had. Without question, he'd welcomed me in when I'd first come back to Phoenix last summer, the guy cool enough to overlook all the crimes that had sent me away in the first place years before.

And what had I done to repay his welcome? Lied straight to his fucking face, taking advantage of the situation—and his sister—with every turn I made.

Shame. It was thick. Stifling. I hated what I'd done, how I handled things, the way everything had gone down when it all came to a head. The sad thing was I'd known it was coming. It'd been so clear what was building, and I'd just fucking stayed until the situation had exploded.

But it was because of Aly. Because of her I couldn't walk away all those months ago. Because of her I was sitting here today.

Still, Christopher didn't turn around. The toast popped up in the toaster, and he jerked a plate from the cupboard. Utensils clattered when he ripped open the drawer and grabbed a butter knife.

And I just sat there. Waiting. Giving him time to let out whatever was roiling inside him.

When he finally spoke, his voice was tight, laced with disgusted amusement. "Well, well, well, if it isn't the infamous Jared Holt. Figured I'd be seeing your sorry ass this morning. Saw that piece of shit bike sitting in that spot downstairs when I got home last night. Then I come inside and, lo and behold, my little sister's door is all locked up tight."

A hot breath pushed from my lungs, and I tipped my head up to witness the disdain pouring from him when he turned around to meet my face. He crossed his arms over his chest and backed up against the counter. "How ya been, man?" It was all sarcasm and sneer. "Wait . . . let me tell you what it's been like around here first."

"Christoph—"

"Why don't you shut your mouth and listen to what I have to say? Or do you feel compelled to feed me some more bullshit first?"

I sat back, staring up at the venom pouring from his gaze, welcoming it because I knew I had this coming. I mean, shit, I had no defense. I knew what I'd done.

"So how did it feel last night? Climbing right back into my little sister's bed?"

My jaw clenched at the accusation, and my lips pursed into a thin line to keep from lashing out. Dude knew how to hit me where it hurt. I jerked my head with one harsh shake, nausea winding through my being while he stared down at me like I was some kind of bastard traitor. And maybe I was, but I hated the way he saw it, thinking I was taking advantage of Aly. As if she wasn't the most important person in this world. To him, I'd just been fucking his little sister.

"Come on, man," I muttered low. I rushed a shaky hand through my hair and cut my eye to the wall before I found the courage to look back at him. "It was *never* like that."

"Wasn't it?" The accusation dripped from his twisted mouth.

"No." The word grated from my throat with the sound of remorse, and my knee was fucking bouncing because I didn't know how to handle it. That old warning flare was blaring, telling me to grab my stuff and go. I strangled it, silencing that shit because nothing could tear me away from Aly.

Averting his gaze to the floor, he grasped the counter, contemplating something before he angled his chin up. "Did she tell you?"

My nod was slow, filled with understanding of what he was asking. "Yeah." Shame hung my head, and I felt a new kind of guilt wash over me. God, I wished I'd been here for all of it. Wished I'd been the first one to hear Aly's news. Wished she hadn't had to rely on him.

Thank God she had him, though.

Christopher edged forward. Every step was calculated contention, anger, and hate. He worked his fists as he advanced on
me. My chin lifted further with each step he took until he was
right up in my face. "You think you can just come back here and
act like nothing ever happened? Like everything is the same?
Well, guess what, asshole. Nothing is the same."

Aggression spiked, heated in my stomach. A tremor of that
same fucking insanity that had tormented me for years rolled
through my body. My own fists flexed, and I struggled under
the weight of it. He was breathing his bitterness all over me, and
it took about all I had not to shove it back in his face.

He laughed, smug, and his voice dropped lower. "Does me
getting in your face piss you off, Jared? You want to hit me
again? Watch me bleed? Lose control? Will that make you feel
better?"

He was baiting me. I knew it. Maybe that pissed me off the
most. My jaw clenched and I squirmed under the anger blazing
from green eyes that were so much like Aly's.

Something that sounded like fear wove into his words.
"What happens when it's Aly who pisses you off? Are you going
to beat her, too? How about when that baby gets in your line of
fire?"

Every nerve in my body fired—pressed and pulsed with a
crushing pain.

"Never." I blinked hard. My hands fisted in my hair and I
choked over the words. "Fuck, Christopher, I would never hurt
them."

He took a single step back, still glaring down at me like the
piece of shit I was. "Yeah, and you're supposed to be my best
friend, too, and you didn't seem to mind letting it out on me."
Conflict reigned in his gaze, questions and worry and blatant
hurt.

Guilt knotted in my throat, and I found myself trying to explain what had sent me over the edge that night. "I know you didn't mean to, but you hurt her and I just . . . I lost it, man. The thought of anyone hurting her makes me crazy."

Understanding flashed like a bolt across his face before his eyes darkened. The anger from seconds before was replaced with disappointment. "Yeah, well, guess what, Jared. You hurt her, too. You want to know what it was like while you were gone? Her not knowing where you were, or if you were coming back? The pain she's been going through? And guess who was here taking care of her while she puked her guts out for three straight months. Guess who held her while she cried and wondered how in the hell she was going to make it. *Me*, Jared. And now I'm not going to stand aside and let you ruin her. Not after everything you've already put her through."

I ruin everything I touch.

The thought slammed me like a kick to the gut. Air wheezed down my throat as I struggled to pull it into the well of my lungs. That was something I was going to have to come to terms with—the fact that I didn't have the first clue what Aly had suffered while I was away. I only knew my own pain, the fucking misery I'd endured day after day—all those days praying she'd somehow find a way without me, not knowing I'd walked away and left her with the greatest reminder of me I could have. Marking her. Scoring my body into hers.

Even if I hadn't left her with our baby inside her, I'd been a fool to believe she could ever forget about me. As if I didn't feel the honesty in her touch and hadn't witnessed the truth in her eyes.

Aly loved me.

I shot to standing.

Caught off guard, Christopher stumbled back. I began to

pace. I turned back to him, hoping he could feel the truth in my own confession.

"I love her, okay? I'm fucked-up. I'm the first to admit it. But it doesn't change what I feel about her." The words bled from my mouth. That girl, the one lying in her bed down the hall, she was it.

My truth.

"You can hate me, Christopher, blame me . . . because it's my fault. All of it. But it doesn't matter what you say. I'm not going anywhere." My voice dropped in the same second my face did, so that I was staring at my feet. "Before I came back the first time, I hadn't felt anything but hate for a long, long time. It's the only thing I felt until the day you found me in that bar and invited me into this apartment and I came face-to-face with her. She did something to me . . ."

Something terrifying and completely right.

"She *changed* me. And if you spent so much time with her over the last few months, then I know you know Aly and I are supposed to be together. None of this other shit matters. None of it. Nothing except for her and the baby." I met his eye. "You and I have been through a ton of shit, Christopher. I know I messed up. I messed up with you and I messed up with your sister. And I'm sorry. I wish I could change the way I handled everything, go back and do it differently, but I can't."

I saw the hurt bleed through the anger in his eyes, and he shook his head as he looked to the wall. "You lied to me, Jared. Fucking lied straight to my face when I asked if you had something going on with my sister behind my back."

"Yeah, I lied. But you didn't just ask if there was something going on. You told me there couldn't be. Aly and I . . . there was no stopping us. We were going to happen." I swallowed hard. "And I was ashamed of it, ashamed that I couldn't stop myself

from going to her. You think I didn't know I should stay away?"
I touched my chest. "I *did*. But I couldn't. Keeping it from you
was shitty. Wrong. But I didn't know what else to do. I didn't
want Aly feeling any of the shame I was feeling, and I thought
by keeping us a secret, I was somehow protecting her. And that's
all on me."

I looked at my oldest friend, fucking laying myself bare.
"The first night I snuck into her room, I knew I was going to
hurt her, Christopher. I knew it because I wasn't right inside.
And I'm never going to be completely right. You and I both
know that. I've destroyed a lot of shit . . ."

I let my gaze fall, drift, and I slowly shook my head. "But
Aly . . . I'm always going to love her. Pretty sure I have since we
were all little kids growing up together. You can hate me all you
want, but you'd better get used to seeing my face around here
because I'm not going anywhere. And if I do leave, I'll be taking
Aly with me."

My attention darted to the movement at the end of the hall.
Aly was standing there tucked up against the wall, listening.
Dark hair tumbled all around her shoulders, her eyes swimming
with the assertion I'd just made. The girl was staring at me like
I was her light.

I swallowed hard.

But she was mine.

And fuck, it hurt thinking and talking about everything I'd
done, the past I could never outrun, the sins I'd committed, the
destruction I continually left in my wake.

Still, she was there, her eyes flooded with all the love she felt
for me.

I stretched a hand out in her direction, beckoning. She
dropped her head, shuffled forward, and folded herself in my
arms.

"I love you," she mumbled when she buried her face at the side of my chest.

I kissed the top of her head before I ran my hand over it. Holding her close, I looked over at Christopher. He watched us with something that maybe looked like relief, all wrapped up with a ton of distrust that I didn't know if I'd ever be able to erase.

Of course I wanted to fix the damage I'd done. Bottom line, Christopher was my best friend. He'd been my entire life.

But the girl in my arms?

She was the one who really mattered, the one I had to make things right with, the one I was going to love for the rest of my life.

TWO

Aleena

Warmth blanketed my skin, Jared's admission like a balm that penetrated my soul. It filled up the places inside me that his absence had hollowed out, those places that had ached with abandonment and throbbed with the fear that I had to do all of this alone.

Like water to parched soil, that warmth filled me up until I felt it blossom into something else—pride.

I was proud of him. Because I knew how difficult it was for him to stand in front of my brother and say everything he had, to admit all of it aloud.

I burrowed myself deeper into his embrace because while his words soothed and nourished me, what I needed most of all was to feel.

"Thank you . . . for coming back to me. I needed you . . . I need this," I mumbled almost incoherently. Once the words were released from where they'd been locked inside, I couldn't stop them. "You don't know how thankful I am."

"Aly," Jared said almost as if he was rebuking me, shocked by the confession pouring from my mouth. "Baby, it's me who is thanking you. Without you, I don't have anything. And you've given me everything."

"But that's where you're wrong, Jared. I need you, too."

His skin was hot and smooth, radiating the same desire he'd left burning in me since last night. Strength vibrated in his every move, his sinewy muscles corded and tight.

Jared was rough. Hard. The defined angles of his jaw were coated in coarse hair, and turbulence swam in the depths of his ice blue eyes.

But he was holding me as if I were delicate glass, as if he'd just been granted a gift, like I was the most fragile kind of treasure that he would guard with his life. There was something secure and strong and incredibly gentle in his hold.

Even as damaged as I knew he was, this gorgeous man was my perfection.

Almost on instinct, my fingers crawled up his narrow waist to the place where a haunting depiction of my eyes had been etched into his skin. The most intense green stared out from between two wilted petals on the dying rose sealed on the center of his chest.

That rose had always seemed a beacon to me. A key.

Almost every inch of Jared's torso and arms were covered in ink, swirled colors and sweeping scenes of blacks and grays that represented all of his pain twisted across his skin.

But the rose that represented his mother on the center of his chest had always seemed the most profound because it wholly represented his love for her and how much he believed he'd lost when she died.

I'd been undone when I found he'd made me a permanent part of it. Like the moment that had defined him had defined me, too.

And now he'd allowed me to become part of his definition. Still, I hurt for him because I understood that he was a broken man. Last night we'd lain awake for hours in the quiet, me in his arms while he stared at the ceiling and let all the revelations of our reunion seep into his consciousness. He'd murmured into my hair that he'd never be good enough for me, even though he'd spend his life trying to be. He told me it was so much easier admitting he loved me than accepting that I loved him.

I knew he still felt unworthy of love.

Yet I loved him with everything that I was.

That love was enough to crush me.

I knew that from the pain I lived through in the months he was away and recognized it in the devastating relief I felt when I found him sitting at the top of the stairs waiting for me yesterday evening. It'd been blinding.

And God, I'd been so scared, telling him about the baby. But he had to know, even though I'd realized there was a very real chance the knowledge would drive him away once again.

This was no longer just about Jared and me. Now I had a baby to think about, too. And I understood the risk in taking Jared back. How vulnerable it made me.

I'd missed him so much, and I wasn't sure I could deal with him leaving me again.

But it went far beyond that.

The little life growing inside me filled me with so much fear and anxiety, but even stronger was this surprising sense of anticipation. It filled me with love along with my worry, and wonder at the way that my life had been sent down a different course than I'd ever imagined.

So many nights had been spent praying and begging in the dark for him to return, drawing his face again and again in the pages of my sketch pads, those images that came to life in them the only thing I had left of him. Until last night, I'd never shown anyone my hidden drawings. They were so special to me, I didn't think anyone could understand how important the faces I drew inside were to me, and I worried that others might minimalize the way I saw the people I loved as I brought them to life on a page. But last night, I'd shown Jared, because I needed him to know, to understand how significant he was to me and how he'd inhabited my drawings since I'd first picked up a charcoal pencil when I was just a little girl.

I'd desperately wanted him to be a part of my life.

I always had. But God, I couldn't fathom how much I wanted him to be a part of our child's life.

I believed in what we created. With all of me. In the beauty of it.

Last night, we'd talked very little about it. Instead, I'd found Jared's affection in his touch, in the way he kissed across my belly and looked at me with fear and amazement shining in his eyes.

I searched for his left hand and lifted his knuckles to my mouth. I brushed my lips across the tattooed skin that marked the year Jared believed he had ceased to exist.

2006.

Jared had spent his life running from his past.

I thought of his right hand, where the knuckles were stamped with the year of his birth.

1990.

Jared had once believed those sixteen years were the only ones he'd truly lived.

But he returned now because somehow, through all of that, he'd seen a future with me, that he'd seen life beyond the date when he believed he should have died in his mother's place.

I chose to believe in him because I knew no other truth.

I chose to believe in his love, as fragile as it was.

I chose to believe he would be strong enough to face all the demons darkening the goodness of his spirit, the ones he'd etched onto his skin in images of horror, the ones that manifested as tremors that shook him in the night.

Jared had always been a risk I had to take. Risks always involved danger. But the only danger I felt where he was concerned was the possibility of him no longer being a part of me. That was a fate I refused to consider.

He shifted, taking my face in his hands and lifting it to his. He pressed his lips to mine, softly, yet wholly intense. Almost desperate. His large hands covered most of my face. His fingers dug into the back of my head, something that I felt all the way to my heart.

"I love you, Aly." His voice was low, rough with the promise, like maybe he needed to remind himself. Blue eyes blazed as he pulled back and stared down at me. I'd seen his love for me in those eyes for so long.

It was unmistakable.

How amazing did it feel that he was no longer trying to hide it?

"I love you . . . so much," I whispered back.

"God." Christopher cursed from behind us, the sound a mixture of disgust and surrender.

These last months, I'd scared my brother. I knew that. I'd witnessed it in his expression as he'd watched me lying balled up on the couch. I'd seen the worry in his eyes and known he had no clue what I needed or how to help me.

But he had. Just being there and supporting me had helped me. Up until last night when I told Jared, Christopher had been the only one to know about the pregnancy. I hadn't been able to bring myself to tell my parents, who lived so nearby. I don't know what I would have done without Christopher to support me.

My face was still buried in the safety of Jared's chest, but I could feel him and Christopher still staring each other down. Testing. Tension thickened the air, so heavy I could actually hear Christopher swallow.

"You want to stay here? With her?" Christopher finally demanded. "And I'm not talking some temporary bullshit. You know this isn't some kind of fucking game."

Jared placed his warm hand on the back of my head, as if he were shielding me. "It was never a game, Christopher. I already told you that." He ran his fingers through my hair, and I shifted to look back at my brother. "I think you already know that," Jared continued. "I wouldn't be here otherwise."

A grimace twisted Christopher's mouth and he looked to the wall again. He huffed a loud breath. "Guess I'm going to have to get used to the idea of you two."

Jared's heart thundered where I had my ear pressed to his chest. "Yeah, you're going to have to get used it." Jared brought his mouth to the top of my head, and I knew his words were whispered to me. "Because I won't let her go."

"Go," Jared grumbled at my mouth as he bent me back, those strong arms holding me up while he kissed me again.

"I don't want to," I contended with a forced pout, clinging to the back of his neck.

At all.

I just wanted to stay there.

In the safety of his arms.

Forever.

The arms that promised my future. The arms that told me he'd missed me as intensely as I'd missed him.

The exam I spent the last week struggling to study for, the one I had to take to pass my class? It suddenly didn't feel all that important after all.

The thought of leaving him physically hurt.

He pulled back. A smirk lifted one side of his full lips. "You think I want to let you out of my sight?" Tender amusement flickered around his mouth before he leaned in close to my ear. "Not in this century, Aly. I want to spend my life wrapped up in you, wrapped up in that body that has me itching to drag you back to your room and show you just how much I don't want to let you go. Just how much I've been missing you."

His teasing turned serious. "But you have shit to take care of, and I'm not going to be the one who stands in the way of it."

I nodded in acceptance, in understanding of this good heart that I was sure Jared still didn't understand himself. "Okay. But for the record, you dragging me back to my room sounds like a really good plan."

My heart had begged for him. Whispered and pled for him. But God, did my body ever ache for him.

He chuckled through a groan, and a grin danced all over his flirty mouth. Chills slipped down my spine with the expression that lit on his face, with the affection that played in his blue eyes as they played across my face. He caressed my cheek with his thumb.

"Baby, I'm going to be making love to you for the rest of my life. Don't worry about it. Go to class now, and to work. You can be sure I'll make it up to you later." His voice dropped low in suggestion, his promise resonating deep in the pit of my stomach.

I quirked a brow at him. He wasn't helping things.

"Go," he commanded through a closemouthed kiss.

"Fine . . . I'm going." I hefted my bag up further on my shoulder. Tipping my chin up, I met his eyes when I stepped around him to open the front door. I paused in the threshold, caught in the million emotions that seemed to be fighting for dominance in him. Those emotions flitting through him had to be a mirror to my own.

I think we both got it. Neither of us really knew anything beyond the fact that he was here.

Last night, our discoveries had all been too deep, revelations that changed lives. Shaped them. We hadn't gotten into details or plans, and I had no idea how we were going to manage all of this. How our lives would merge. Become one.

But as I stood there staring at him, I knew they would.

"I'll be thinking about you," he promised.

"Me, too," I whispered. I stepped out into the day and shut the door behind me.

Sunlight shined down, fall's warmth a caress to my skin. Yesterday when I'd left for class, the sun had stood so much the same, though it had felt completely different. It'd cast the promise of its rise and then fall, just another lonely day that would give way to another lonely night. Never had I imagined when I climbed into my car yesterday that my life was hours from being rocked, that once again, Jared's return would come as something I couldn't fathom.

An upheaval.

But this was a disturbance I'd been praying for.

I lifted my face to the warmth of the sky. Thin ribbons of clouds rode on the breeze, sweeping out in slow waves.

Thank you, I said, so low it could not be heard.

Jared's mother, Helene, slipped into my mind. And I thought maybe . . . maybe she, too, was filled with joy. Maybe I *had* been heard.

I knew this was the way Helene would have wanted things, for Jared and me to be together, that she'd seen something between us long before either Jared or I could understand what the bond we shared as children really meant. I crossed the lot to where my white Corolla was parked in its spot.

I gasped when arms wrapped around me from behind, then

melted when Jared buried his face in my neck. He spun me around and pressed me up against the cool metal of my car door. His hands were on my face, in my hair, slipping down my sides before he brought them back up to force me to look at him. "Thank you." Desperation poured from him, his hold increasing as he stared down at the shock I felt lining my face. "Thank you for believing in me, Aly. For *getting* me."

A lick of fear flashed across his face. Or maybe it was remorse. He swallowed hard, and his voice hardened with strain. "I'm scared to think of where I'd be right now without you."

The fear that flashed on his face coiled in my stomach. Because I didn't know where he'd been. I had no idea where the last three months had taken him. How far or how low.

I wasn't sure I wanted to know.

"You're here with me now." I had to believe that was all that mattered.

He grimaced. Gripping my face, he leaned down and kissed me, hard and demanding. There was no soft affection, none of the playfulness from upstairs. This was a seal. A branding. He jerked back. A storm raged in the blue of his eyes. "Don't think I can't see all those questions brewing in your mind, Aly. And I may not have all the answers right now, but we are going to figure this out. Do you hear me? I promise you that."

And I saw it all there, the torment that plagued Jared, this beautiful man who had lost direction, the one desperate to find his way home.

"I'm not scared," I promised.

A sad smile wavered at his mouth.

The only thing that scared me was I knew *he* was.

Anxiously, I glanced at the large, round clock hung high on the wall. My exam had gone as well as expected, if not better, and my lunch shift here at the cafe where I'd worked for the last two years had kept me busy. Still, the day had passed too slowly. Hours crawled by. Seconds . . . minutes . . . each willed away because I just wanted to see Jared's face.

I needed to see him again.

Feel him.

Be reassured that it was all real.

It was like the moment that I left him staring behind me in the parking lot this morning, Jared's fear had chased me. Caught up to me.

How the hell were we going to do this?

All I'd wanted was for him to come back.

I guess I'd never really thought beyond that, to what would happen when he did.

What I saw was clear. A family. Jared and me and our baby coming together like a picture of our pasts, the way Jared and I had been raised in houses full of love and support and encouragement.

But how distorted had the idea of family become for Jared? How much of it would be too painful for him to bear?

There had been no deceit when I told him I believed in him. I did, because I believed in the love that shined from him.

Maybe our family was something we would have to define for ourselves.

Finally, three o'clock rolled around, and I stuffed my apron into my bag after I finished up my side work. My stomach knotted in anticipation. I couldn't wait to get out of there.

"Someone's anxious." Clara, one of the other waitresses at the cafe, interrupted my restless thoughts. Even though we seemed an unlikely pair, mismatched, she'd become one of my closest friends. Older by almost ten years, she was loud, bold, a single mom who never hesitated to speak her mind.

A tease lifted her brow, and she smirked at me from where

she tallied her checks for the day. "You've been skittish and fighting both a grin and a grimace since you walked through the door three hours ago. Care to tell me what's going on?"

I laughed under my breath. "God, Clara, do you have some kind of sixth sense or what?" She always knew when something was up. She had an intuition about her, a keen eye and a soft heart. So maybe I'd only told Christopher and Jared about the baby. But Clara knew.

Six weeks ago she'd caught me off guard, completely unprepared for her unsolicited question. "So how late are you?" she'd asked, keeping her attention trained on pouring dressing over two dinner salads and away from the shocked expression her question shot to my face, like she had been giving me time to process her words. That had been before I'd worked up the courage to take the test, back when I'd tried to convince myself it was just the trauma of Jared being ripped from my life that had thrown my body off schedule. Though in my heart, I'd known. Just as clearly as Clara had when she finally lifted her face and pinned me with a meaningful stare.

I'd stopped by a drug store on the way home and taken the test that evening.

In the middle of the night, Christopher had found me crying. Just crying.

Because I couldn't see through sorrow to the other side, couldn't feel anything but the pain and the need. It'd hurt so badly, knowing what Jared had left me with and knowing he wouldn't be a part of it.

I had wanted it and hated it all at the same time.

Christopher had crawled into my bed and taken me in his arms, and the admission had bled free. He'd rocked me for the longest time, promising it would be okay. Then he'd slipped from my room and into his. Seconds later, I'd jerked to sitting, startled by the sound of the first crash, Christopher's curses and chair and feet slammed against his wall, my brother taking all his anger out on his room.

I almost wanted to laugh now.

Jared and Christopher were so much alike, but neither of them could see it.

Violent.

Passionate.

Protective.

Each in their own way.

Now Clara grinned as she gathered her tickets into a pile and tapped the edges to straighten them. "Nah, babe, I'm just really good at reading people. You've been dragging your feet around here every day for the last three months and suddenly you have enough energy radiating from you that you have me contemplating the gym for the first time in five years."

She lifted her chin, probing yet knowing.

I dropped my gaze to the dingy ground. "He came back last night," I admitted quietly. Peeking up at her, I searched for her reaction. I'd come to value her opinion. I saw her as wise, as someone who'd learned the hard way.

She stilled before she tucked her stack of tickets into her front apron pocket and leaned back against the counter. "Came back to Phoenix or came back to you?"

Her question made a smile flutter around my mouth.

"To me . . . he came back to me. I just . . ." I shrugged in bewilderment. "It shouldn't be possible to feel what I felt last night. The relief I felt." It'd been staggering, both terrifying and perfect. "I was so worried about him. Not knowing where he went and if I would ever see him again. And he was just sitting there, waiting for me after I got out of class last night."

"Did you tell him?" she asked.

I bit at my lip and nodded once. "Yeah."

"And he stayed?" The question was weighted, like the answer to it would deliver the ultimate verdict.

"He freaked out at first and took off. But I knew he'd be back. He just needed some time to process it."

I mean, I'd been shocked, too, the burden of it something I didn't know how to carry. I'd known what it would do to Jared, the havoc it would wreak. But when he had finally returned, I knew our worlds had changed because they had aligned.

Jared finally understood what he had always meant to me.

He *remembered*.

He remembered *me*.

Joy and sympathy washed her expression into something tender. "I'm happy for you. You know that, don't you?" Her tone shifted, hardened in emphasis, and I could tell she was about to offer me some wisdom I might not want to hear. "Enjoy it, Aly. Enjoy him. But don't you dare forget these last months. Don't ever forget you made it through when you didn't think you could. Don't forget you're strong and you know what you want from your life." Softly, her head dipped and inclined toward my stomach. "And don't ever forget what's relying on you."

Unease flitted through my consciousness. My hand sought out my belly. "I know what's important, Clara."

"I know you do, Aly." Her voice softened, the same as her eyes. "I imagine things are going to be different between you two now. But that difference is either going to be for the better or the worse. Just make sure he treats you well."

That's what she didn't know about Jared. She saw the outside, the gorgeous, dangerous man. The one covered in a horror of tattoos, those same horrors reflected in the sea of pain that raged in his ice blue eyes. She saw a man plagued by his demons who knew nothing else but to run from them.

I knew that's what others would see, too.

But I saw so much deeper than that. I knew the good that lay beneath the shell of a hardened man.

No. There was not a single worry inside me about whether Jared would treat me well.

My concern was only with how he treated himself.

Still, I promised her, "I will," because my friend only cared and I knew a lot of her worry was with her own insecurities. Maybe our histories were hinting at similar circumstances. Her boyfriend left her with a tiny baby boy, never seeing her son's father again. We both knew there was a possibility my story could turn out the same.

But I had faith Jared and I would have an outcome different from hers.

She grinned to break up all the tension. "So what are you waiting for? Get out of here. Go get your man."

Crossing to her, I hugged her hard. "Thank you, Clara. I hope you know how much I appreciate everything you've done for me the last few months."

"Us girls have to stick together, right?" She grinned a little, repeating what she always told me, just this simple reassurance that no matter what, she was there for me.

I doubted many people knew how smart she really was, the woman who appeared to be nothing more than a sad cliche, the single mom working at the diner just struggling to get by.

I headed for the door, respecting her more than I ever had.

"I expect details," she hollered at me from behind, "'cause that is one crazy-hot man."

I laughed, because that was always Clara's way, a pendulum that rocked from one extreme to the other, from teaching to an outright tease.

I tossed a glance back at her as I pushed the door open wide. "Not on your life," I called.

Laughter broke through her wide smile.

"I'm all finished, Karina," I called to my boss as I passed. "I'll see you this weekend."

She glanced up from the register and smiled softly. "Have a great Thanksgiving, Aly."

"You, too." The door swung shut behind me.

A cool breeze rushed over me when I stepped outside into the crisp fall air. Nerves buzzed in a quiet hum under the surface of my skin. The sun blazed a path westward, casting rays of late-afternoon sun across the canopy of blue, shedding its warmth and promise of a mild winter across the city sky. I lifted my face to it, breathed it in as I started down the sidewalk and around to the employee parking lot.

That breath left me when I saw him leaning up against the back of my car. His bike was angled sideways behind it. Short wisps of blond hair whipped in the breeze, the man absorbed in the hole he dug into the broken pavement with the tip of his boot. Completely lost in thought, he remained unaware that I approached.

I took the moment to appreciate him. My gaze made a slow pass across his jaw and full lips, down his neck to the strength bristling beneath his tight black tee. He lifted a cigarette to his mouth, and his wide chest expanded when he inhaled. My stare got stuck on his hands, the blocked-out numbers bold where they were stamped on his strong, long fingers.

Slowly he lifted his face. Those blue eyes locked on mine. I froze, stuck in them.

Something trembled within me.

Something powerful.

This was my man.

My future.

He dropped the cigarette to the ground and toed it out with his boot. Lifting his face, he pursed his lips and exhaled toward the sky. Smoke curled around his head, climbing toward the heavens before it bled into nothing.

Part of me wanted to deflect it—how beautiful he was, the intense feelings he stirred, the churn of need created with just a trace of his presence.

He looked back at me. One side of his mouth lifted, all sexy and indecent.

Could he know what that one look did to me? Not a chance, because this feeling was impossible.

Crossing his arms over his strong chest, he rested further back on my car, and his mouth spread into a full smirk.

I shook my head at myself. Maybe he actually did know.

"What are you doing over there when you're supposed to be here with me?" His voice slipped along the ground, his intent reverberating against me.

With his words, I all out shook. A rush of red flamed against the cool breeze that caressed my cheeks. I dropped my head, trying to contain my grin as I shuffled toward him. It broke free when I stopped a half a foot in front of him and lifted up on my toes. I pressed my mouth to his.

Damn, it felt amazing to openly proclaim us.

"Hi," I whispered. "What are you doing out here?"

"Couldn't wait to see you any longer." He brought his hand to my cheek and his flirty tone shifted. Everything about him sobered. "I've been missing you for too long, Aly Moore. I'm done with all that shit . . . missing you. No more, baby. I don't want that for us anymore."

He looked away, to the ground, before he brought his attention back to me. "If I'm being honest, maybe I couldn't stay away because I needed to make sure all of this is real. It still feels like a dream to me."

I wrapped my hand around his wrist, and he ran a thumb under my eye.

"It's real, Jared. Us. All of it."

"Yeah?" he asked. The fact he needed reassurance, that he felt compelled to come here to gain it, hurt my heart.

The sad thing was that I needed it, too.

"Yeah," I promised.

He shook his head in disbelief. "Can't believe I'm here, Aly. Can't believe you want me after all the shit I've dragged you through."

I leaned forward, tipped up my chin to capture his gaze, and brought us close. "You think I didn't understand why you left? Do you really think that all those times we hid away in my room together that I didn't understand you? That I didn't understand why? That I didn't *know* you?" I squeezed his wrist. His pulse thrummed wildly at my palm. "Because I did. I *know* you. I was there, too, Jared. I saw what you went through. And I'll never pretend I understand everything you've gone through, but I promise I do *understand* you and I will always be here for you."

Relief left him in a stuttered breath. "God, Aly, what did I ever do to deserve you?"

I pressed myself to him, to his gorgeous body and the power that radiated from his spirit. That warmth covered me whole. "It doesn't work like that. We don't earn love . . . it's a gift we're given."

He pulled back. Brushing his fingers through my hair, he twisted a single lock in his finger. "And what if I want to return that gift?" he asked through a whisper at my ear. "Give it?"

I fisted my hand in his shirt. "You already have."

His head shook. A hint of laughter floated out with his

breath. "See, I was right to begin with . . . I'll never deserve you." He tugged at my hair. "You . . . perfect girl . . . will never see yourself the way I see you."

I slowed. The hold I had on his shirt increased as my unease flared. Because I did want something from him. Or maybe I just wanted it for him . . . for us.

"Do you know what tomorrow is?" I hazarded, taking a chance as I pushed a little. Was I aware I was treading on dangerous ground? Yeah. But I knew we couldn't go on as we had before, dodging what was important.

Jared stiffened. Nerves rocked through him and a rush of air left him on a heavy exhale. Shakily, he raked his hand over the top of his head. "Yeah, I know what day tomorrow is."

Thanksgiving.

These last months had blurred, the holidays approaching with little anticipation. Or maybe I'd approached the thought of them with trepidation. I knew it was coming, and I knew the holiday would be the time I would have to tell my parents everything. Before Jared had returned, I'd planned to finally speak his name tomorrow and admit it all, telling them I was pregnant and I had no idea where Jared had gone.

And I would have done it without shame.

Even though Jared's guilt had been enough to drive him away, I knew it didn't have the power to diminish what we had shared.

Regardless of the circumstances, I loved him and I knew he loved me.

Still, I knew my announcement to my parents wouldn't escape being greeted with anger and disappointment.

No doubt, my parents would be feeling all of it. Anger at the situation. Disappointment in me for what could only be construed as irresponsibility.

But I knew most of the anger would be directed at Jared.

My father kept me on a pedestal, and to him, I'd always been *in the white*. Without blame. Pure. Innocent in his mind, which only saw right and wrong.

And I had no doubt that he would hold Jared in the wrong.

Now that Jared was back, I was counting on time proving my father wrong.

And tomorrow Jared and I had the chance to begin making this *right*.

"I'm going to spend it with my family," I said, intention seeping into my tone.

Grief flashed across Jared's face.

A knot of pain twisted in my stomach. Pain for him. I always promised if he let me bear some of his burden, I would. I hoped I was bearing some of it now.

Taking a chance, I took a small step forward. "You're that now, you know." My voice dropped to a whisper with the declaration, and both my hands cinched tightly in his shirt as I drew him closer to me. "*My family*. Come with me tomorrow. Share it with me."

His throat bobbed heavily when he swallowed. "They know?"

I barely shook my head, my nose so close to his they brushed. I clung to him a little tighter. "I planned on telling them I'm pregnant tomorrow." Emotion pushed at my chest. "I want you to be there, Jared, for you to stand beside me when I do."

"What about me? Do they even know about me? About us?"

The words lodged at the base of my throat. I forced them around the lump. "Just my mom. I finally told her about us just this last Saturday."

Jared jerked his head away, and he gripped the back of his neck as he turned his attention to the sky. "Goddamn it." It came as a wheeze, as fear and another challenge that we had to conquer. He dropped his gaze back to me. "This is all wrong, Aly. I did this all wrong."

"What are you talking about?"

Humorless laughter rolled from him, and he lifted his mouth in a sneer. One directed at himself. "It's backward, Aly. Fucking backward. Because I should have stayed and told them how I feel about you. I should have told them I love you, rather than showing up with your dad knowing nothing about us and announcing to them I got you pregnant. I'm sure that's going to go over really fucking well."

Bitterness bled, and he flung his arms out to the side. Disgust poured from him. "I mean, fuck . . . look at me."

I cupped his face, taking in the sorrow that haunted the warmth I saw so vividly in his eyes.

"Hey . . . don't do this, okay? What matters is what I see when I look at you and what you see when you look at me. Don't you understand that? I know it's going to be rough telling my parents . . . for both of us."

For Jared, just going back to the old neighborhood would be a trial. Three months ago when Jared had left me and run to Vegas, all it'd taken was seeing my mother. She'd shown up at my apartment, unannounced, and just her being there had thrown him over the edge, broken down the walls he hid behind, and brought the words he kept buried inside himself flooding from his mouth.

And all of it had sent him running out my door.

It was like everything had been building and my mother was the boiling point.

I wasn't fool enough to believe any of this would be easy for him.

But I knew it was something we had to do if we were going

to make it, if Jared and I were to have a chance to make a life out of the wreckage of his past.

"I need you to be there with me, Jared. Even if you don't say a word, your presence will say everything."

Dropping his forehead to mine, his lids slipped closed, and his hands dug into my hips. He tugged me closer. "I never wanted to ruin you." I could barely make out the words, he uttered them so low. Still, I felt them all the way to my soul.

"You really believe that?" Hurt bled into my incredulous words. "That you ruined me? Do you know the joy you've brought me? I never thought I'd find love, Jared . . . because my heart always belonged to you. And even though it broke me when you were away, never once did I regret us."

A breath of surrender flowed from him. He pulled me fully into my arms, buried his face in my neck. He inhaled and held me closer. "I just want to make you happy, baby. Do right by you." His hand went to my stomach. His palm trembled there. "Do right by *this*."

"You already have," I promised.

He chuckled a little. The storm from moments before passed, and the traces of joy I'd witnessed so often in Jared's expression made a reappearance on his face. "At least I got my job back."

"Really?"

"Went to see my old boss before I came over here today. I figured he was going to tell me to take a hike, but I walked through his door and he said he'd never been so happy to see anyone in his life. He was in a bind, needed me. He hooked me up with something similar to what I was doing back in Jersey. I'll be the supervisor at a few of the construction sites, plus he wants me to do some custom carving, trims and designs. I start back on Monday."

Weaving my fingers through his, I tucked our connection between our chests. "See . . . we're going to make this work."

He nodded and kissed my nose. "Yeah. We are." He smiled. "Come on, let's get you home."

"'Kay." I stepped back, swinging our clasped hands between us. Was it ridiculous I didn't want to let him go?

A grin quirked up on one side of that full mouth. He seemed as reluctant as I was to let go. Then he released me, swung his leg over to straddle his bike, and kicked it to start.

The engine warbled deep.

Jared stretched his legs out, his booted feet holding up the bulk of metal between his thighs. He teased at the throttle and let his gaze drift over me.

I stood there, breathless. Emotion tumbled through me, pitched through my consciousness and spilled into my stomach as desire and devotion.

I loved this man, the beauty and the heart, and every single flaw.

Forcing myself to turn away, I climbed into my car and started the ignition while Jared rolled out. Backing out, I followed him to the road. He revved the throttle and wound out onto the street. His shirt flapped against his back, his hair striking blond in the rays of sun gleaming down at him, the ridges and lines of his arms flexing as he powered the bike.

God, he was beautiful.

Following close behind him, I felt confident but shaky. All of Jared's reservations were valid, and I felt them, too. But it was time to face them. As I auto-dialed, a tremble of nerves rushed through me.

"Hello?" Mom answered almost cautiously. A din of noise rose up in the background around her. She'd called me numerous times over the last few days since I revealed Jared and me to her on Saturday. Worried, she'd been checking up on me, promising me one day it would be okay.

I guess moms know best.

"Hey, Mom."

"Hi, sweetheart. How are you?"

"I'm good," I answered honestly. For the first time in months, it really was true. "Where are you?" Distorted voices echoed through the line.

"Ugh . . . standing in a line at the grocery store that is about a million miles long. Remind me next year not to do my Thanksgiving shopping the afternoon before. Everyone and their mother is here. I think there was a fistfight on aisle two over the last jar of cranberry sauce." The words were light and funny and good-natured, just like my mom.

I smiled, and I could see her rushing around, trying to cram five days' work into one as she prepared for dinner tomorrow.

"Is everything okay?" she asked. "You seem . . . different."

"Yeah . . . I just needed to talk to you . . . or tell you . . ." I trailed off.

Silence met me from the other end, waiting.

Jared rode ahead of me, a beacon I followed because he'd always been my destination. My best friend and the master of my thoughts, the one I yearned for even when I hadn't been old enough to understand what that yearning meant.

"I'm bringing *him* to Thanksgiving dinner at the house tomorrow."

I didn't even need to mention his name because everything Jared meant to me was wound into that one simple statement. A proclamation.

The silence thickened, and her breaths slowed as realization set in, then hastened in relief. She spoke quietly, "I knew he'd come back to you."

Tears welled in my eyes. Because I was thankful. Thankful for my mom, for her heart, for the support I already knew she was going to give. Thankful for Jared. I stuffed the emotion down and continued, "I want to be the one to tell Dad about us, but I think it'd be a good idea that you tell him Jared is coming so he's prepared."

Tomorrow would shock my dad. At least he could be prepared to see Jared's face.

I could almost see her frown. "Yeah, sweetie, I think you're probably right."

THREE

Jared

God, this woman did things to me that couldn't be legal.

And if they were, they sure as hell shouldn't be.

I paced the hall outside her bathroom door, feeling like the freak I knew I was.

The shower head squealed when Aly turned it on. Metal screeched as the shower curtain was dragged back. Water echoed, pounding into the empty tub.

She'd kissed me at the door five seconds ago and said, "Give me a couple minutes to get cleaned up."

From inside, fabric rustled. She was stripping out of her clothes. I knew it. I was picturing her unbuttoning that white blouse she always wore to work, unzipping the black slacks, removing the silk and lace hidden underneath.

My hands weren't the only thing to twitch.

A low chuckle escaped me. Yeah, I'd done that a time or two for her before, torn those work clothes from her body, back

when we'd slinked and stole, back when I cursed myself every
time I locked the door behind us for taking what I never should
have had.

Guilt taunted me from somewhere deep within my consciousness and wove with the remnants of doubt that weren't
buried all that deep.

I had no idea what was right anymore. I'd spent so much
time berating myself for wanting her, now it seemed almost
wrong that I was allowed to have her.

I paced a little more before I forced myself to sit on the
couch. Either that or break down the bathroom door, and I figured enough doors had been broken down around here.

About ten minutes later, the shower finally shut off. Vague
noises filtered through the walls, the slam of a cupboard, the
rush of the faucet, the thud of a drawer, hints of my girl who'd
left me aching ever since she shut me out just moments ago.

God, I needed her.

A lot of shit had changed since I left, but one thing definitely
remained the same.

The girl made me completely insane.

Fucking certified.

Mad with desire and confusion and every fucked-up, contradictory thought I could ever have.

The bathroom door unlatched.

She was never supposed to belong to me. Yet there she was,
standing at the very end of the hall, peering over at me.

Mine.

My responsibility. *My* life.

Nerves jackhammered my heart into a frenzy.

I still couldn't make sense of it, everything that had been
revealed last night.

Shifting on her feet, she watched me, searched me, like she

would give about anything to dig through my thoughts, to really know what I was feeling. Her expression softened.

And I thought, *No*. Maybe she would just be satisfied to crawl inside me, to sink down into the marrow of my bones and take up residence in any place I'd let her.

But she was already there.

Aly was everywhere. I felt her life in my veins, because she'd breathed hers into mine. All of me belonged to her because before her, I'd been nothing. Nonexistent. Worthless. Now I meant something to someone. Someone was relying on *me*, and that reality fucking terrified me.

I stretched my hand out, and she shuffled across the floor. Unrestrained pleasure fluttered all around her mouth as she neared, and I couldn't help but smile. Her hair was all wet, the long length of it flattened out in near-black sheets from where she'd run a brush through it. Dampened tendrils clung to her bare shoulders. She was wearing a tank top and of course those sleep shorts.

I wondered if she knew . . . if she wore them because she could see right inside my mind, watch my thoughts careen and swerve, skid into a desire that surged through every inch of my body.

I yanked her down onto the couch with me.

Aly yelped, giggling as I flung back and pulled her on top of me.

She wiggled and laughed, and I was pretty damned sure she knew exactly what these shorts did to me.

Warmth rushed through me with the joy contained in the sound that passed through her lips, the weight of her blanketing me in the same comfort I'd woken up swimming in this morning.

She inundated my senses, coconut and the good and the girl. *God*.

How much had I missed that? How much had I missed her?

There was no putting an amount to it, no counting it up or figuring out how much this girl meant to me. Because it was beyond anything calculable. Beyond the rational. Tripping, tumbling, crashing through all sensibilities.

Fear lashed. A rush of bitter bile curled in the pit of my stomach. Because I didn't know what I would do if I lost her.

When I lost her.

The thought knotted my gut and sent a wave of nausea ripping through me. Struggling for a breath, I swallowed it down and buried my face in the haven of her hair. Didn't want to go there. Couldn't.

"Hey, baby," I said, the affection coarse as I forced all that worry back down deep inside where it belonged. Because I was going to be better.

I was going to be better for her.

"Hi," she mumbled into my neck, her lips a tender caress as she kissed along my jaw.

A shot of greedy lust hit me, and I crushed her to me and let my free hand wander up the leg of her shorts. She was always doing this to me, clouding my senses. I cupped her sweet little ass. "You know exactly what these shorts do to me, don't you?"

Aly giggled more, all self-conscious and sweet, and she folded her arms in between us as I wrapped mine around her, like she wanted me to take her whole. Embarrassment colored her voice when she admitted quietly into my chest, "I like what your eyes look like when you see me in them." She risked peeking up at me, her chin digging into my breastbone. "I remember always craving your attention, even when I was just a little girl. But by the time I was thirteen, I wanted you to *look* at me." Redness blossomed on her face, her cheeks blazing with it, yet her voice was completely serious. "I know it was stu-

pid . . . ridiculous to think you'd notice me. But I always wanted
you to."

I chuckled a little, gripped her by the back of the head with
my free hand and pressed the rest of her tight against my body.
"Would've been pretty messed up had I noticed you like that
then."

I felt the smile that took over my mouth, all gentle, one that
could only be given to her. Because it was her hand that soothed
me, her heart the only thing that had ever calmed the rage that
would forever simmer within my soul. I hooked my finger under
her chin so she couldn't hide that gorgeous face. "But this has
been a long time coming, hasn't it?"

Aly wiggled one arm free. Softly, she traced her fingers
along my lashes before she pressed them to my lips.

Affection welled at the base of my throat, right where that
bitter rock of unspent emotion lay with my corruption, like Aly's
touch was chipping away at it.

Fuck, this girl had a hold on me.

"Maybe it hasn't just been coming, Jared. Maybe it was just
always supposed to be. Maybe Christopher running into you
that night he found you at the bar, found you back in Phoenix
for the first time . . . maybe that was supposed to set it all into
motion. Because one way or another, you and I are *right*. Maybe
our situation is messed up. But who is to say it's wrong?"

She wrestled out of my hold, and before I could make sense
of it, I was subject to hers. Fierce fingers gripped the flesh of my
shoulders. "I won't believe anything but the fact that you're supposed to be here, with me. Whatever we have to go through,
whatever we have to face, I've never believed anything so
strongly."

Her green eyes flared with worry, with passion as she looked
all over my face, searching for something. What, I didn't know.

"This isn't going to be easy," she said. "You know that, don't you?" Sharp, blunt nails deepened their hold in my skin, cutting, demanding my attention. Fear latched onto her words. "Promise me you won't run when it gets ugly, Jared. Because life always does, and I can't bear the thought of living without you in mine."

"Hey," I said softly, hoping to calm her. "I know that, Aly. Coming back wasn't easy. But I'm here."

I didn't think she really understood what it took for me to mount her stairs yesterday afternoon, the clash of commitments it caused—my loyalty to my mom and my love for Aly. Those two forces created an all-out war between the demons that owned my soul and that place in my heart Aly had exposed.

A soft breath left her, spread across my face. "Here is where I need you," she said.

I ran my hand down her neck and drew her to me so I could whisper in her ear. "I know, baby."

Aly hummed.

I swore, this girl brought me to edge of sanity. Pushed me off it, really. Straight into a free fall. No doubt that crash back in Vegas had been when I finally hit the bottom, when I'd been slammed with a realization I never thought I'd gain.

That maybe . . . just maybe . . . there was something in this fucked-up world I was supposed to be living for. Last night had only confirmed it.

I was living for her.

Her fingers curled in the neck of my T-shirt. Clinging to me, she lifted her head enough to peer up at me. "Here," she whispered on a throaty sigh.

Groaning, I palmed her bottom, squeezed a little more. "Here," rumbled from my chest as I took over her mouth. The kiss came hard. Demanding. Aly fucking moaned and opened to me, her tongue all inviting as I swept mine across hers. My hands got lost in the mass of her hair, before they stroked down her spine and came to rest on her glorious ass, which had gotten me started in the first place.

A key rattled in the lock and the front door flew open.

I froze.

Heavy footsteps thudded on the floor as Christopher barreled in. I couldn't see him. My vision was obstructed by everything that was Aly, hair and hands and every inch of her perfect body. Still, I could feel him stumble to a standstill at the end of the couch where Aly was sprawled across my body.

"Ah . . . fuck. Are you kidding me?"

Sure as hell could hear him, too.

I tried to nudge Aly off of me, but she just laughed and held me closer, refusing to allow me to push her away.

Instead she lifted herself enough to look at him over her shoulder, her hair falling all around me as she tossed her brother an amused smirk. "Now you know what it feels like," she said. "At least you didn't have to find my ass on the couch buck naked with some random hookup."

I shifted and pushed Aly's hair back so I could see around her. Christopher cracked a smile and ran an easy hand through his unruly hair. He lifted a nonchalant shoulder, but I could tell he was doing his best to keep his laughter at bay. "Hey now, that's hardly fair, Aly. You know that only happened once, and I was nice enough to introduce you to her."

Shaking her head, Aly scoffed, her tone sarcastic but filled with all the tenderness she held for her brother. "And you can't even begin to imagine how much I appreciated being put through that awkward moment. Believe me, I'm scarred for life."

I tried to suppress my laughter, but there was no containing it because this girl was just so damned cute, so sweet and funny.

Smart, too.

I knew what she was doing, making the statement to her brother that we were now an *us*, and he was going to have to get used to seeing the two of us together because there was no tearing us apart. And he had nothing to say about it.

Like my laughter triggered it, Christopher busted up. Apparently he couldn't hold it in, either, and Aly was fucking grinning between us like she'd won some sort of prize.

I guess maybe she had, getting us all to laugh like that together again. It had been a long time.

Christopher shook it off. As if tossing me a casual hello, he lifted his chin toward me. "So I need you two tonight, the Vine . . . seven o'clock." He glanced behind him into the kitchen at the clock glowing from the microwave. "You have twenty minutes to get ready."

Going to the Vine sounded like about the last thing I wanted to do. I hugged Aly to me. "Not up for that kind of shit yet, man. Aly and I have . . ." My eyes drifted over the lines of her face, that perfect body still plastered to mine. Lust curled in my stomach. I was pretty sure I wasn't letting her out this door until I'd explored her body for about the next fifteen hours. ". . . catching up to do." That was about all I could say, because I sure as hell wasn't going to give her brother details on what I did have planned for tonight.

"You're supposed to be my best friend, remember?" Christopher drew out, all cynicism and snark. Funny, he did sound a whole lot like the friend I used to have. "And you don't have to stay long," he continued, nonchalantly tossing his wallet to the bar. "But it's Cash's birthday, and the asshole went and got himself a girlfriend, and I refuse to be third wheel in that fiasco. He wants us to have dinner and a couple of beers to celebrate, then the two of them are heading out. Pretty sure I'm gonna need backup."

Chuckling, I lifted my head to meet his eyes. "What, so you want to play fifth wheel with us instead of third?"

He pointed at me. "Fuck you, dude."

I laughed.

Aly quickly twisted to her side, her thigh burning into mine as she sat up and looked at her brother. "Wait . . . what? Cash has a girlfriend?"

"Ridiculous, right?"

"Poor girl. That'd be about as tragic as you coming through the door and announcing you had a girlfriend." Aly shook her head with the tease. "I'd have to talk some sense into her."

Christopher rolled his eyes. "Ha, like that's gonna happen. Not a chance you need worry about that." He smirked. "I refuse to look at some chick the way this ass looks at you. Don't need all the shit that comes with it." He shot me a mocking glare before he slanted a soft one on Aly.

Disbelieving laughter built in my gut, but I held it back. Fucker was a good guy underneath all the asshole. "Whatever," I said, my smirk just as big as his.

Aly tsked. "I take it back. Maybe a girlfriend to keep you in line is exactly what you need, Christopher." Playfulness saturated her tone, though there was no mistaking the point she was really making.

Christopher caught it, too. "Instead of riding my ass, why don't you get off yours and get ready? 'Cause I'm not leaving here without the two of you. I haven't met his girl yet, Aly, and I need you to run interference."

One side of Aly's mouth lifted in question as she turned to me. "I'm actually kind of hungry and don't feel like making dinner. You up for it?"

"Whatever you want, baby. You know I'm game." Wasn't

really. I just wanted to stay here, curled up on the couch with her. But if my girl was hungry, then I figured we'd better get her fed.

Aly hopped off me, dipped down to peck me on the lips just as fast. Her expression was tender when she pulled back. "All right, then. Let me get ready, and then we can get out of here. Sound good?"

I touched her face. "Yeah, sounds good."

Aly disappeared into her room and reemerged thirty seconds later with a wad of clothes balled against her chest, grinning the cutest grin as she passed back by and into the bathroom so she could finish getting ready.

Sitting up on the edge of the couch, I raked a flustered hand over the top of my head while I stared at the space she'd just inhabited. How could one girl affect me the way she did? Control me? One glance from her was an outright provocation, her barest touch a switch.

Motherfucking trigger.

"You okay, man?" Christopher's voice was low, without even a hint of the contempt he'd directed at me this morning.

Tipping my head, I looked up at my oldest friend. I shrugged, not because it didn't matter, but because I really didn't know. "Don't know what I am, Christopher. All of this is fucking overwhelming. That's about all I know." I lifted a single brow. "That and the fact I love your sister."

He smiled, all cool and casual, the way he always did, as if that was the only answer I needed. "Good thing. That's what she needs. Aly has all the rest of that shit together."

Awe filtered out from me in a weighted sigh as my gaze burned into the wall that separated us, to the place where Aly was changing, the goodness in her presence enough to fill up the entire apartment. "Guess she probably does, doesn't she?"

Urgency clouded his relaxed demeanor. "You know, the whole time you were gone, she just kept telling me she didn't want to do it alone." His throat bobbed as he swallowed, and he shifted his attention to the ground before he lifted it back to me like he was weighing his admission. "I don't want her to have to do it alone, either."

For a flash I turned away and scrubbed my palm over my face, nodded hard. Because I fucking got it, what he was saying. "Wasn't lying to you earlier, Christopher. I won't leave her."

He just pursed his lips in acceptance, then shoved the intense moment off as fast as it'd come. "Gonna get changed."

He headed down the hall. I climbed to my feet, went into Aly's room, and dug around in my bag. Seemed strange, all my shit in here. I pulled on a fresh tee and pushed my hair back with both my hands before I went back out in the main room and plopped down onto the couch to wait.

The bathroom door knob rattled, and I shifted forward at the same second Aly came walking out.

My breath caught. Literally got stuck right in the middle of my fucking throat.

Goddamn.

The girl was gorgeous.

She was wearing black skinny jeans. And heels. Heels I hadn't seen her wear before that made her about five inches taller. The girl was already all leg, sexy as all hell. Pair her body with those jeans and those shoes and she was a goddamned wet dream.

Just because it was Aly, she had to match it with this soft gray sweater, something that made her appear all innocent and shy, the thick woven threads dark and plush. The hem brushed just over the top of her low-cut jeans. She swayed a little, letting her ankle fall to one side as she chewed at her lip, like she was impatient to see my reaction. Or maybe she was nervous. Either way, it was really fucking cute and a little bit infuriating because this girl had not one single clue the effect she had on me. She fidgeted as I rose to my feet, shifting enough that I caught a flash of the creamy skin of her still-flat belly.

I shook and my fingers twitched, 'cause damn, I just wanted to touch.

The sleeves of her sweater were fitted and long, extending down over her hands. She fisted the material in her palms, squeezed her shoulders together, watching me approach.

I edged her up against the hallway wall and took her by the hips. "Baby . . . you are . . . you look amazing."

A self-conscious giggle left her, and she looked up at me with a blush kissing her cheeks. Chewing at the inside of her lower lip, she set the welcome of her green eyes on mine. "I fig-ured since it was our first date and all, I'd dress up for you." Then she winked.

She fucking winked.

Amusement curled one side of my mouth, and I dipped in and took over that nibbling on her bottom lip. "Our first date, huh?" I mumbled at her mouth. "Not sure what you'd call all those times I had you on the back of my bike. How about all those times in your room?"

"I'd call that us . . . getting to know each other," she drew out.

I nudged her chin up with my nose and buried my face in the warmth of the delicate flesh of her neck. "I'd say I got to know you pretty well," I murmured at her skin.

I felt her raspy laughter roll up her throat. "Yes, I'd say you definitely did."

Pulling back, she gazed up at me, brushing her fingertips

down my cheek. The girl just looked happy. And maybe it was wrong, but I couldn't describe how good it felt to be the one to paint that expression on her face.

Christopher yanked his bedroom door open and rushed down the hall. I turned in his direction, and I could feel the joy that witnessing Aly's had pushed to my face, all uncontained and uncontrolled.

Because I was fucking happy, too.

Christopher smiled a little like it didn't piss him off so much, him seeing me there with his sister. As he sauntered toward us, his eyes drifted down Aly. As he passed, he clapped me on the shoulder. "Looks like you're trying to get our Jared here in another fight, Aly."

I chuckled low. Dude knew me well. Something I was going to have to get under control, too, losing myself to the chaos that simmered below the surface, ready to overpower my heart and mind. I'd lose her if I didn't, and I'd rather die than let that happen.

Confusion twisted Aly's mouth into a frown. Her attention darted between Christopher and me.

Figured I'd clarify, though I was pretty sure she had to know exactly what he was implying. Without breaking our connection, I inclined my head toward him. "I think that's your dickhead brother's way of telling you that you look really nice."

Irritation flashed across that gorgeous face. Offense puckered those full lips, and she flung her arms out to the side. "Oh come on, Christopher. I'm completely covered. What do you want me to wear, a sack?" she challenged.

That sounded like a brilliant idea to me, but I sure as hell wasn't going to voice it. The way this girl looked was dangerous, hazardous to my sanity, fucking perilous to any asshole who even thought about moving in on her.

Not gonna happen.

Quiet laughter seeped from him as he stuffed his wallet into his back pocket because he knew it, too. His tone softened. "You look beautiful, Aly. But you always do."

Hers was just as soft. "Thank you."

I wound Aly's hand in mine. "You ready, baby?"

She turned that softness on me. "Yeah, let's go."

FOUR

Jared

Night had taken hold as the shortened fall days threatened to give way to a desert winter. A crush of cars jammed the streets, a string of restless headlights and frustrated taillights as rush hour crammed the city the evening before the holiday. It seemed everyone in the city had someplace to go.

It took us less than five minutes to make it to our own destination. Aly made a left into the gravel parking lot of the Vine. Loose rocks crunched beneath her tires, and she carefully made her way through the overflowing lot to find an open spot. She pulled in between two beat-up pickup trucks, cut the engine, and we all climbed out.

A cool breeze blew through, kicking up loose debris and scattering it along the ground. Dense city lights glowed a foggy haze against the inky dome above. Only the brightest of stars broke through the urban night. In the windows of the square, brick building that held the Vine, neon lights burned with the promise of beer and a moment's reprieve, and a low thrum of classic rock seeped through the walls of the tiny bar.

Aly rounded the front of her car. I snaked my arm around her waist and tugged her to my side, because I just needed her close. It was weird, too, unsettling almost, being able to step out with her like this. To proclaim she was mine and not some dirty secret that could only happen behind closed doors.

I pulled the door open and stepped aside to hold it for the two of them. Christopher entered first, and I placed my hand on the small of Aly's back as I followed them in.

A shot of panic hit me, escalating my pulse. I froze at the threshold as a deluge of memories crashed over me.

And not the pleasant kind.

Three months ago, the day Aly's mom had shown up at the apartment, I'd come here to escape the dread that had taken me over. That night, I'd been propped up at the bar, alone, doing my best to drink away my anxiety, to hide from it. Really just to fucking drown in it. Because the end result was already clear. I'd known destruction was coming. I'd felt the rending, the tearing away that would usher in the ruin.

I swallowed hard as I glanced at the bar to the right.

Sitting there that night, I'd felt it—the fantasy Aly and I had been living getting ready to come to an end. The end had come just hours later.

Roughing a shaky hand over my head, I tried to quell the sudden suffocating impulse that screamed at me to bolt. To run.

I'd been running so long, it was the only thing I knew how to do.

My chest jerked as I sucked in a breath.

God, I was a fucking disaster. A nightmare. I couldn't even

walk into a building without feeling like I might lose my god-damned mind. It was just a building. A place that meant nothing. The only thing harbored here were memories.

But it was memories that chased me. Memories I could never escape. Memories of what I'd done. Every single one of them seemed to lead my mind back to the greatest mistake I'd ever made.

As if Aly sensed my unease, she stilled and slowly turned around to face me. Concern drew her brows together. In the second she turned and caught my expression, it was like she immediately saw inside me, understood the war I'd fought three months ago. Like she knew how fucking badly I'd wanted to stay, all the while knowing the only choice I had was to leave.

Like she knew I'd had to run because I still hadn't come to the place where I fully grasped what she meant to me. The significance of what we were.

Green eyes caressed my face and settled on my gaze.

She also understood why I hadn't run far.

And in the end, I just came running back to her.

Tender fingers brushed down my cheek. "If you don't want to be here, just say so, and we'll go home," she offered.

Home.

Even when I'd destroyed mine so long ago, Aly was willing to build a new one with me.

I pushed the heaviness from my lungs and reached out to twist a single lock of silken hair around my index finger. Anchored myself to her. An unseen connection traveled through it, a bond that tethered us together. My spirit stirred as I looked down at the complete selflessness staring up at me.

And right then, I knew I had to remember I'd run into Christopher here, too, six months ago, the first time I'd come back to Phoenix. That not all the shit that'd happened here was bad. Maybe, like Aly had said, that meeting was supposed to happen and this little bar hadn't just been some random place I pulled into.

I had to believe *she* was supposed to happen.

Aly leaned into me, and I sighed and dropped my forehead to hers. "No, baby, I'm good. Let's get you some dinner, pay those dues we owe your brother, then we'll go home."

I tugged a little at the tuft of wound-up hair.

Relief mellowed the concern that had clouded her eyes. "You sure?"

"Yeah. I could use a beer and a burger myself."

She searched my face again, before she let whatever was worrying her go. Because she could see I'd let my worry go, too.

She smiled and laced her fingers in mine.

"Well, since I can't have a beer, I'm going to have a double burger." She raised a teasing brow, and I chuckled and tugged her around to my front.

I dropped a soft kiss to the top of her head. "A double burger it is, baby."

We headed deeper into the darkened bar. The place was packed, the noise level high. Busier than I'd ever seen it. Dim lights from above cast a faint glow over the crowded room. Televisions flickered from where they were hung high on the walls, subtitles playing along the bottom while music blared from the speakers.

We shoved through, making our way over to where Cash and his new girl waited for us in a large, horseshoe booth.

Christopher slid into the free side first and around to the inside. Aly scooted down beside him, sitting directly across from Cash and the little dark-haired girl tacked onto his side. On a heavy exhale, I sat down beside Aly, didn't give it a second's thought when I immediately draped my arm over her shoulder.

All right, so maybe a second's thought, because I was feeling some kind of fucking pride or some shit, sitting next to her like that.

A contented sigh seeped from her, and she resituated herself to rest her head in the crook of my neck.

Joy pushed at my chest.

"How's it goin', old man?" Christopher tossed out, grinning at Cash.

"Don't even start. I'm only three months older than your lame ass." He wagged his brow and pulled his girlfriend closer. "Besides, what's that they say, men only get better with age?"

Aly rolled playful eyes. "Seriously, Cash, that only applies to men . . . not boys pretending to be men. Ask us again when you turn forty-three."

Christopher cackled and high-fived Aly. "That's my girl."

"You two suck," Cash said, laughing as he got more comfortable in his seat.

I'd only met Cash once when he'd stopped by the apartment during the summer. He was cool enough, a whole lot like Christopher, indifferent, approaching life with outright apathy.

Which I guess was why it surprised me when he introduced us to Fiona. She was tiny. Prim and straitlaced. She waved to us with a shy hand and a blushing face as she burrowed further into Cash's side with just the mention of her name. I could only imagine she was feeling completely out of place and unprepared for Cash and Christopher.

I doubted few people could be prepared for the two of them.

And I suppose I was even harder to take.

A waitress stopped at our table, introduced herself as Holly, and took our drink order. In just a few minutes she was back with a bottle of water for Aly and a round of beers for the rest of us.

Christopher raised his bottle. "To Cash. Happy birthday, man."

A chorus of *happy birthdays* went up and we raised our bottles. Glass clinked as we tapped the bottlenecks where they all met in the middle of the table. Aly shot me a knowing look when she stretched out to tap her plastic bottle against everyone's beers.

Easy conversation struck up between all of us. Christopher and Cash led it, their voices boisterous and loud, while Aly and I laughed, adding to it, usually to call the two of them out on their bullshit. We ordered food, set into an easy pace, the five of us seeming to relax in the casual vibe.

With my girl tucked in close to my side, I took a swig of beer. Ice-cold liquid slid down my throat and settled in my stomach. All the tension that had been nagging at me had drifted away.

I felt good.

Really fucking good.

For once, I welcomed it, and for a few minutes, I refused to let guilt taint my joy.

I just wanted to enjoy my girl and the thought of us having a future. A real one. Not some fucked-up existence where I was just wandering aimlessly through the days.

Even Fiona jumped in on the laid-back banter, laughing as she did her best to keep up with the man who seemed completely wrong for her. She was just so quiet and shy, while Cash couldn't keep his mouth shut for longer than three seconds, the guy larger than life while she seemed content to fade into the shadows.

I glanced down at Aly. She tipped her head up to look at me. Affection shined bright in her eyes. I kissed her forehead.

Guess I had no place making judgment calls like that. I sure as hell didn't have the first clue about who should be with who, because never in a million years would I have thought that someone as amazing as Aly could be for me.

Our food was served and we ordered another round of drinks.

Aly dove into her burger. She planted her elbows on the table and leaned over her plate, shoving the huge burger into her mouth. She slanted an eye over at me and hummed.

God, she was cute.

Soft amusement pulled at my mouth, and I massaged my fingers into the thick mass of her hair at the base of her neck while she dug into her food.

"Starving," she mumbled around her burger as an explanation, and I just laughed and dug into mine.

God, maybe it was stupid, but I had the sudden sense that I *belonged*. Like maybe there was a place for me in this world after all.

I finished my food, pushed my plate away, and tossed my napkin onto it. Lifting my bottle high, I polished off my third beer.

Satisfied.

Cash lifted his beer, downed half of it, and pointed the neck in Aly's direction. "Are you always going to let your asshole brother talk you into being DD, Aly?"

In the middle of another bite, Aly froze. Then her head snapped up, like she'd been caught in a lie. But she wasn't looking at Cash. She was looking at me. All kinds of worried questions played out on her sweet face. Like maybe she was asking for some kind of permission, some guidance on how to proceed.

Are you ready for this?

I shrugged because there were few things I worried less about than what some guy like Cash thought about me. What mattered was how she felt about announcing this to world. Especially before we even got to tell her parents.

Now, telling her parents? That I fucking cared about. I was doing just about everything I could not to think about tomorrow. Going back to the old neighborhood, walking through their front door, sitting down at their table. I didn't know how I was going to handle it. Or if I even *could*. The rock sitting heavily in the pit of my stomach assured me I wasn't ready for all that. But Aly had asked me to be there for her and I was sick of letting her down. So since this afternoon, I'd shoved the thought of it down, buried it, refusing to listen to that voice warning me going back would be straight-up disaster. No doubt, dwelling on it would send me into a tailspin, a nosedive that there'd be no recovering from. So I just filed that shit.

Tomorrow was just another fucking day.

Aly swallowed hard and straightened in the booth. She focused on Cash. "Well, truth is, he didn't have to plead with me all that much. Looks like I'm going to be shoo-in for DD for the next six months or so." Aly tipped her head to the side, the words sharp with the implication.

With his beer halfway to his mouth, Cash stopped dead. Then his attention volleyed between Christopher and me, waiting for some kind of reaction from the two of us. Like he was prepping himself to jump across the table to stop the brawl that was about to break out. No question, he knew if this was news to Christopher, dude was not gonna be happy.

What Cash didn't know was that shit had already gone down months ago. Punches weren't necessary. They'd already been thrown.

Christopher exhaled, his brow lifting to his hairline like one huge shrug. He had nothing more to say about it.

Cash looked back at Aly. "No shit, baby girl," he muttered below his breath. "That is . . . crazy," he seemed to settle on. I got the distinct impression Cash cared more than he'd ever let on, and he was feeling a wave of protectiveness rise up in him over my girl. "You okay with all this? This seems kind of sudden."

He cast me a furtive glance packed with speculation.

As if I wasn't going to notice.

Couldn't blame him, though. I mean, fuck, I left her. For three months. Showed up on her doorstep last night, ready to grovel, to beg her to take me back. When she did, I'd pretty much just held her for all of the night because the thought of letting her go left me physically ill. Truth was, I really hadn't even talked with her about how she felt about the pregnancy. How she *really* felt about it. If she was happy or scared or fucking mad.

But something inside me knew I didn't need her to vocalize it. She'd already spoken it all in her eyes. In the awe that had shimmered, in the anticipation that had burned so bright.

There was no mistaking the affection caught in the soft sigh that had parted her lips when I'd kissed her *there*, right below her belly button, over the place that harbored the thing that terrified me most.

Aly reached for me. Her short nails dug into the back of my hand as she squeezed, searching for reassurance. Or maybe she was giving it to me. Then she turned back to Cash.

"Honestly? I've had a rough couple of months." Helpless, she shrugged, like the right words were impossible to find. She grimaced as she worked through her thoughts. "I was shocked. Scared. *Sad*," she admitted quietly. "I didn't expect this . . . at all."

She glanced over at me. One side of her mouth curved with a small, genuine smile. It was something that should be so insignificant. Still, it twisted me all up inside.

She angled that smile on Cash, her voice soft with the same devotion I witnessed in her last night. "But I can't imagine a greater honor than being a mother . . . bringing a life into this world." She paused, blinked as she settled a tentative hand on her stomach. "I just want to be worthy of it. To love and raise this baby the way it deserves."

Aly knocked the breath from my lungs.

Unworthy?

It was me who was unworthy.

My fingers found the back of her neck, and I nudged her to face me. I dropped my forehead to hers and cupped her cheek. A surprised breath rushed all over my face, her nose touching mine. I didn't give a second's fuck that three sets of prying eyes burned into the side of my face.

The words came out harsh, low, *desperate*. "Don't you dare think for a second you could be unworthy of this, Aly. There's no chance you're not going to be a good mother. Not one. Do you understand me?"

Aly pulled back a fraction, and my free hand went to the other side of her face. I sat there holding her. Aly's cheeks flamed under my palms, searing where they burned into my skin.

An image of my own mother's face flashed, pressing into my consciousness. Pure and devastating, the perfection of her face. Soft. Compassionate. Filled with all the love Aly was hoping for. She'd been a good mother. The best.

God, she'd been the best.

And I wondered if she'd ever felt like this. Scared. Unsure. Not knowing what the future held.

I swallowed around the emotion wedged in my throat. Aly was going to love like her. "This is going to be the luckiest kid in the world, Aly, just because it gets to call you *Mom*."

Aly nodded against my head, her hands coming up to cover mine. I leaned down and pressed my mouth to hers.

Wound myself one notch tighter, climbed one rung higher.

I pulled away and squeezed her a little before I reluctantly let her go.

Christopher was looking at me like he didn't recognize who I was.

Which shouldn't have been that big of a surprise because I sure as hell didn't recognize myself. Not around Aly.

She unlocked something in me I didn't know I had. Revealed it.

Or maybe she created it. Same way this girl had been created for me.

Cash and Fiona were wrapped up in each other, smiling across at us.

I just let my head drop back to Aly's again, wishing we were alone so I could show her exactly what she made me feel.

Christopher slammed his empty down on the table. Smacking his lips, he blew out an exaggerated sigh. "All right, enough of this sappy shit." He pointed an accusatory finger around the table. "You all do realize I'm sitting here, right? I mean, don't worry about the single guy, or anything."

Aly laughed, leaning back in the booth so she could see Christopher. "Ha . . . like that's anyone's fault here but your own."

"Yeah, yeah, yeah, here we go again." His smile was soft on my girl; then he shifted his eyes to me. "I do believe it's time I kicked your boy's ass here in pool, though."

A low chuckle rumbled from my chest. "Pretty sure of yourself there, my friend."

"That I am." Christopher smirked and gestured with his chin for us to get up. I climbed from the booth and extended my hand to Aly. "Come here, baby."

Aly slid that gorgeous body out from under the booth. She was so fucking tall in those shoes, so damned sexy I didn't know how to stop the clash of thoughts that clattered through my brain. Because one second I was picturing her as this sweet mom and the next I was picturing her sweating under me.

Aly looked at me from under those long dark lashes, and bit her lip to contain her blush, like she'd just witnessed the salacious scene I'd just fantasized playing like a reel in my eyes.

She tipped up her chin and stepped closer to kiss me in a way that wasn't exactly proper for a public place. Not that I minded all that much.

I groaned and mumbled the words at her mouth, "You are too much."

"And I will never get enough," she whispered back.

"I'm holding you to that when we get home."

She bumped me with her front. "You'd better," she taunted a little more.

Desire barreled through my veins.

Motherfucking trigger.

Because this girl really was too much, sent my senses spiraling, left me unsure how to deal with the things she made me feel. Like I wanted to hug her until she couldn't breathe. Protect her so she always would. Love her until she couldn't see.

"And again . . . right here, assholes." With his finger, Christopher drew a big circle over his head, feigning offense as he climbed to standing behind us. But there was no denying what lit in his expression, everything about it declaring how happy it made him that his sister was happy.

Emotion fluttered through my chest like a riot of birds.

I had to admit I'd made her that way, at least on some level.

And that shit scared me.

"Come on, let's go grab a table." Christopher wove through the crowd, Cash and Fiona right behind him. I smiled down at Aly, wrapped her hand back up in mine, and placed a quick kiss to the back of her hand.

I zigzagged us through the throng, sweaty bodies pressed in on all sides. People laughed and talked too loud, fighting to lift their voices above the noise. I squeezed Aly's hand, just making sure she was fine. She squeezed it back.

I couldn't help but grin at the little secret conversation we were sharing, like it was just the two of us against the fucking world.

We ducked under an archway into the separate room tucked back at the far end of the bar. Five worn pool tables sat beneath dim lights that hung from the ceiling. A haze thickened the dingy air like a city storm hanging on the ceiling, the faces gathered around the tables little more than silhouettes in the muted glow.

We all stood along the far wall, chatting while we waited for a table to free up.

A waitress came in and we ordered another round of drinks. By the time she returned, a group was finishing their game and gestured for us to take their spot.

"All right, are you ready to make this game legit?" Christopher dug into his back pocket for his wallet and pulled out a twenty. He slapped it down on the pool table.

With a wry smile, I shook my head. "You really want to go there tonight?"

"What, you don't think you can take it?" He squeezed his shoulders together, lifting his hands, palms up. "I mean, if you don't want to play with the big boys, I'm sure Aly or Fiona would be a good match for you."

"Hey," Aly shot out in defense. The insult earned him a smack to the back of his head.

Laughing, Christopher stumbled back, gripping the back of his head to guard himself. "You are a feisty one, Aly. I'll give you that." Then he dug himself in deeper. "Doesn't mean you can play pool."

A taunting grin split my mouth as I finished off my beer, and

I shrugged like I felt bad for him. I sauntered over to the table, every second of this feeling like old times. The good ones. The ones that made me want to *stay*. I tossed a mocking glare at him, all too willing to take the bait. "I think I can handle it. I just didn't want you to embarrass yourself or anything. But since you talked down to my girl, I'm going to make an exception."

Christopher grinned like I just made his fucking day. "Oh, it's on, bro."

"Count me out of this." Shaking her head, Aly walked over to where Cash and Fiona were snuggled up at a high round table set up along the wall, before she tossed over her shoulder, "You two are never going to learn." It sounded like she was scolding us, but she was all smiles because she was just cool like that.

God, I loved that about her. How casual she was. Game for anything. Fun.

Even after all the shit I'd put her through, here we were, fucking enjoying ourselves because of Aly's pure heart.

There was no stopping the grin pulling at my mouth when I stepped up and racked the balls, thinking back on all those days when Aly was a little girl and had done her best to keep up with Christopher and me, how fucking cute she was as a kid, and how she'd grown into the most amazing girl I'd ever met.

None were like her.

No one could touch her.

Christopher leaned over the end of the table to break. He pulled back his stick and hit the cue dead on. It spun as it sped, slamming straight into the one-ball with a loud crack. Balls shot around the table, bouncing off the cushions and setting up the game.

Christopher watched them dance around, scatter, then slowly spin to a stop. One solid ball teetered at the edge of the corner pocket before it found footing on the felt.

I laughed, all raucous and loud.

He didn't sink one.

Christopher groaned and threw back his head, gripping a handful of unruly hair. "Ah, shit. Did you see that? I was robbed. I think you breathed on it," he accused as he tried to hold in his laughter.

"Not looking so good there, Christopher," I said, giving my condolences as I stepped up to take my shot.

"Come on, baby, you've got this," Aly shouted from where she watched. She rested her back on a high round table, her elbows propping her up. At her ankles, one long leg crossed the other, and she rocked on the spike of her heel.

Damn.

Amusement danced all over her face, floated on her words. "Don't let Christopher hustle you out of that twenty."

Christopher's mouth dropped open. "Are you kidding me? After everything I've done for you, *Aly Cat*, you're taking his side?" He shook his head. "Now you two are really ganging up on me. How is this fair?"

I tipped my beer to my mouth, chuckling as I swallowed. I leaned over the table, banked the cue to hit home on the same ball Christopher had left hugging the pocket.

"Oh, dude . . . not cool."

I smirked at him and proceeded to drive in a couple more before I missed and Christopher stepped in to take his turn.

I glanced up. In the same second, my jaw ticked.

What the hell?

The guy who'd been playing next to us was standing there, chatting up my girl.

I turn my attention away for all of two minutes and someone decides to make a move.

Cocking my head to the side, I caught Aly's eye as she looked at me from over the asshole's shoulder. She shrugged a little, all innocent, like she found it funny to see the instant shot of possessiveness that locked my hands into fists.

It wasn't like he was all over her, or anything.

Or touching her.

But he was talking to her and I was thinking that was an automatic foul.

Like Christopher had said. *Not cool.*

I left Christopher to his turn and slipped around the guy talking to Aly. Sidling up to her, I slinked my arm around her waist. I cracked a smile.

And not exactly a welcoming one.

Disconcerted brown eyes jumped all over my face, like he was taken aback to find me standing there. He looked all of seventeen, though I doubted very much he would have made it through the front door if he really was. He fidgeted and took one nervous step back.

"What's up, man?" I asked, lifting my chin. I slanted what was supposed to be an innocuous glance at Aly, though it was so obviously packed with something that looked a whole lot like jealousy. But shit . . . this was my girl and I was not okay with some asshole making a move on her. "This a friend of yours, baby?"

One side of her mouth twitched, and that amusement was back in full force, though this time at my expense. "Oh, this is David." Her eyes widened as she messed with me some. "We just met, so I guess you could call us friends."

"Really?"

David shifted on his feet, no doubt feeling the lurking hostility that would be all too happy to break free if he didn't get a clue and take his place.

But there was nothing aggressive about this guy. He looked more like he was about to piss his pants.

Couldn't blame the poor kid. If I were him, I'd be itching to make a move on the knockout leaning up against the table, too.

Too bad she was coming home with me.

I tugged her a little closer and my toothy grin widened more. "Well, it was really nice to meet you, David."

An uneasy smile wavered on his mouth. "Right, so I'm just going to . . ." He stepped away with an awkward wave. "See ya around."

Quiet laughter rumbled deep in my chest as I watched him make his way back to his friends.

"Was that really necessary?" Aly asked at the side of my face. I didn't look back at her until the kid disappeared into the crowd; then I turned to catch the irritated mirth flushing her sweet face.

"Uh, yeah, it most definitely was." I turned to gather her in my arms, pressed a kiss to her pouty mouth. "You think I'm really just going to stand there while some kid makes a move on what's mine?"

She laughed quietly, biting at her lip like she wanted to laugh and admonish me at the same time. "You could have done that without going all caveman on me."

I scoffed, lowered my voice as I spoke against the sharp line of her jaw. "That wasn't close to going caveman on you, baby. If I wanted to go caveman, I'd toss you over my shoulder and take you back to your bedroom . . . where you belong." I growled the last as I jerked her against me.

It was all a tease. Of course, she didn't come close to knowing how serious I was. I'd just about lost my cool when I found out about that asshole Gabe texting her during the months I was gone. I knew she'd blown him off, was kind and good the way she always was, but she didn't string him along. My girl'd been waiting for me. But hearing about it still felt like Aly was threading a needle through my skin.

Aly twisted her hand in my shirt, couldn't keep back her smile, her words landing in a harsh, hot whisper on my face. "You are unbelievable."

Then I hugged her. I mean, *hugged* her, my arms consuming as I pressed her warm body to mine because I really needed her to know. My voice dropped as I spoke in her ear, serious and severe. "Won't let anyone or anything come between us, even if it's some punk kid who's trying his hand at his first pickup line."

Aly burrowed into my chest and fingers dug a little deeper into my shirt. "I get it, Jared. You're going to have to learn to trust me, too."

"I do trust you."

Trusting her was easy.

Natural.

While I rocked her, my attention roamed over the mass of men filling up the space. It was them I didn't trust. No doubt, most of them were just like me, like I *had* been, assholes out on the prowl.

Guys like Christopher, who currently angled up beside us. He cleared his throat. "Well, now that you've pissed all over my sister, do you think you could finish this game or are you going to stand there all night and suffocate her? I mean, if you were too scared to play against me, you could have just said something."

Laughing, I released Aly and stepped back. My gaze swept the table, counting balls. Christopher had only taken one. "I just was giving you the chance to catch up. Looks like that didn't fare too well for you."

He resumed chalking his stick. "I'm saving it all up for the glorious end. Besides, I was too busy scoping us out an escape route while I waited for you to take out that kid." He grinned and laughed too loud.

I rolled my eyes. "Whatever. Let's just finish this."

Christopher and I went at it, slandering each other like we'd always done. Neither of us took any offense. We'd done it for as long as I could remember. It always seemed the thicker the insults were, the closer we got.

I hated the shit that had gone down between us. But I knew he wasn't going to hold it against me. I thought he'd probably already forgotten. It was me who didn't know how to forget.

I won the game, but it was close. Cash was way too into Fiona to take a turn, so Christopher and I decided to start another round, another twenty on the line.

Balls skidded around the table when I broke, and Aly wandered over while Christopher went in for his first shot. "I'm going to go use the restroom," she said as she placed a quick kiss on my chin.

"You want me to come with you?" I offered, my hand snaking out to tug at two of her fingers.

So what if I didn't like the idea of letting her out of my sight?

No one could blame me.

Lightly she shook her head and stepped back, her smile all flirty. "Pretty sure I can manage."

"I'll come with you," Fiona said as she untangled herself from Cash's arm.

Reluctantly, I released Aly's hand. "Don't be long."

Knowing laughter tumbled from her mouth. "I just have to pee, Jared. I'll be fine."

They walked out, and my eyes trailed them, like the heat of my gaze could carve out a path of safety for her as she went.

Wasn't going to let any of these fuckers get an eye on my girl. She couldn't help it she was the sexiest damn thing that had ever stepped through the Vine's doors.

"What is it with girls having to go to the bathroom together?" Cash cut in as he joined us. "That is some messed-up shit."

Christopher went in for a shot. "It just means they need a private place so they can talk shit about you."

"Really?" Cash said like the thought had never occurred to him.

I shook my head, chuckling low. I took a deep pull of my beer. Poor Cash was clueless.

"You're up, man." Christopher stepped back and I came up to take my turn. Leaning in deep over the table to get the right angle, I caught Christopher's eye out of the corner of mine. "You really think my girlfriend is in there slandering me, huh?" I asked. I drew back my stick, set it free against the cue ball. I pocketed the stripped eleven and eyed my next move. I readjusted my spot.

Christopher stood across the table from me, supporting himself on his cue stick. "No, she's probably in there singing your fucking praises, or some shit. You two are disgusting. And your girlfriend? She'd better mean a whole lot more to you than being your girlfriend."

My shoulders lifted to my ears in a defensive shrug. "What the hell do you think?" Of course she meant more than that. She meant everything. I just didn't know how to define us, what kind of label to put on us. *Us* was all that mattered.

Then the asshole rolled his eyes, because he already knew it and he was just trying to get a rise out of me.

God, he was a punk.

I bent in further to take my shot, but instead my attention

got stuck on how his eyes flashed somewhere behind me, then narrowed. He leveled them on me. I thought he was pissed before I finally caught the meaning of his expression.

It was a warning.

I frowned and started to look behind me when every cell in my body seized. A fucking rock the size of Texas sank to the pit of my stomach when a hand I wasn't all too keen on feeling again flattened in the center of my back and ran all the way down to grab my ass.

What the fuck?

All my defenses kick-started me back into motion. I thrashed as I jerked around. Doing my best to put some space between us, my ass hit the pool table when I came face-to-face with Lily.

Which was really fucking difficult to do when she was all up in my space, pushing, pressing in.

I hadn't seen this chick since I skipped out her door six months ago, back when I was doing just about anything I could to purge Aly from my mind.

Including her.

I'd run into Lily during the first week I came to Phoenix. Hooked up with her once when Aly started getting under my skin and I was still trying to convince myself I was never gonna touch her. I was itching to bury myself in Aly and had sought out Lily instead.

Lily's blond hair now had a pink stripe running down one side, her sweatshirt cut out at the neckline and hanging off one shoulder. A coy smile curved her mouth. She stood there looking at me like I owed her something, like if she played her cards right she was going to win this hand.

She stepped forward, so close her breath washed across my face. "Been wondering when you were going to make your way back here. I've been missing you."

In the handful of times I came back to the Vine after I started things up with Aly, Lily hadn't been working there. I guess I'd figured she'd moved on, left, though I didn't give much thought to where because I really didn't give a shit.

She hadn't even crossed my mind when I came in tonight.

I was too wrapped in the memories . . . the memories that mattered.

And this bitch wasn't one of them.

I felt Christopher edge around the pool table, coming out to my left where I could see him, where he could see me. Urgent eyes were shouting at me, like he was screaming at me to fix this and fix it quick.

Part of me wanted to explain myself, to give Christopher some kind of acceptable reason as to why this girl had me backed against a wall.

But that was completely unnecessary. Christopher already had it all figured out, added it up, surmised the situation. Because he knew the game all too well. He played it all the time.

I'd had her and she wanted more.

She inched forward, came in so close she was almost touching me. She rocked a little and brushed up against me. The movement was an invitation, something intended to tempt.

My fingers jerked. Because the only thing I wanted was to push her back.

Instead I held in the blink of anger that surged through my veins. Really, I was pissed at myself, anyway. I attempted to control the venom in my voice. "Didn't come here for you, Lily. Sorry if you seeing me here gave you that impression, but I'd think six months would be plenty of time for you to figure out I wasn't interested in anything more with you than what happened that one night."

Hurt flashed across her features.

"Really? You seemed plenty interested when you came back looking for me that night." She almost sneered when she plastered an artificial smile on her face. No doubt, it was more in defense of her feelings than anything else.

But it wasn't her feelings I was concerned about.

Like I was drawn, I looked over Lily's right shoulder just as Aly came through the archway. Laughing, completely carefree as she talked with Fiona, her hands were all animated as she talked.

Panic pushed at my chest. I raked a hand over my head, squeezed the back of my neck. I wasn't used to this shit. Relationships. How to handle them.

Wasn't used to caring.

But fuck, I did, and the last thing I wanted was Aly to see this.

I knew the second she did. Her head snapped up and she fumbled to a stop. A deep line cut into her brow. Confusion lit in her gaze as it jumped between Lily and me. It took her less than a second flat to process the scene unfolding in front of her.

Guilt gripped me by the throat. Aly stared at me with outright hurt from across the room. Tension filled up the space between us, slowing time. Every scenario seemed to flip through the green of her eyes, every worry and distrust she'd ever harbored for me clawing to the forefront of her thoughts.

I saw it.

Fucking *felt* it.

Less than half an hour ago, we'd been joking around about the asshole kid, the whole interaction swollen with this innocent playfulness as I got territorial on my girl. No one could blame me.

But Aly sure as fuck could blame me for this.

Because *this* wasn't innocent, that much was obvious. I'd had this girl every which way to Sunday and back again, and here she was, rubbing up on my dick, asking for another round.

Green eyes watched me with some kind of unknown misery and outright disappointment.

But there was no anger.

Just fucking sadness and it broke me a little more, reminded me of the piece of shit I was and why I would never be good enough for her. I hadn't been back but twenty-four hours, and here was my past, already showing up to haunt me.

Motherfucker.

Fiona set her hand on Aly's shoulder, her mouth moving close to her ear. They were too far away for me to hear what was said, but I could tell she was asking if she was okay.

I knew she wasn't.

"You should go," I said in a low threat toward Lily, because I wasn't giving her an option.

Christopher's eyes bored into the side of my face, silently urging me to do something as he tried to inconspicuously gesture at Aly with his chin, like I wasn't already well aware of the fact that my girl was standing there watching this go down.

Aly was fucking trembling.

Goddamn, it was almost like I could feel it, her heart thud and her mind spin, even across the distance of the room. Like all of this hurt was rushing from her and slamming into me. As much as she was trying to hold it in, to rein in her reaction, witnessing Lily all over me was too much for this innocent girl to deal with.

Lily splayed her hand across my chest. "What do you say you let me change your mind."

Shame belted me just as hard as the anger. I grabbed her wrist and flung it off me. My attention fastened on Aly and I seethed out the hardened words, "Stay the fuck away from me, Lily. I'm not going to tell you again."

Like she'd finally caught on, she tossed her chin over her

shoulder, searching out where my eyes were trained on the center of my world.

The world that was threatening to crash around me.

I wasn't about to let that happen.

Lily turned back to me, shaking her head. She cocked her chin in an attempt to be cute and coy. "Well, it looks like you already had your good time all lined up for the night. Don't mind me."

Then she stepped back, bowed out, and crossed the room. She made sure to knock her shoulder into Aly's when she pushed passed.

Harshly, I shook my head. *Stupid bitch.*

Aly cringed, and I was staring at her, silently begging her to realize that girl didn't matter.

Fiona took Aly's hand, tugged it, prying her away from the spot where she'd been glued to the floor. Aly shuffled forward, her eyes bouncing all over the room, anywhere but my face, unwilling to look at me as Fiona dumped her at my side and took up her spot at Cash's.

She fidgeted, looked to the floor.

Fuck, I couldn't stand this, Aly hurting, thinking whatever goddamned thoughts she had running through that sweet head of hers. I had to get her out of there. Explain. Let her know there was no reason for her to be shaking and falling apart because there wasn't a chance in this godforsaken world I could even consider being with someone else than her.

Like I'd ever trip and fall into that trap.

I nudged her chin with my index finger and whispered, "Come on, baby, let's get out of here."

She shrank back. The space she put between us was minimal. Still it was completely unbearable. Profound. She glanced up at me with a forced smile, the edges of that gorgeous mouth trembling. "It's okay. Finish your game."

Was she kidding me?

She was not fucking okay.

Frustrated, I grabbed my stick and sank the eight-ball when there were still seven others on the table, throwing the game. I tossed my cue stick on the top of the table. Wood clattered against the remaining balls. "There, game over."

I shot a pointed stare at Christopher. *We're out of here.*

He tipped his head toward the entryway to let me know it was cool and he'd find his own way home.

FIVE

Jared

I grabbed her hand and towed her outside.

Cold air pelted us, the night deep. Dull lights seeped across the lot, and Aly sucked in a breath as she withdrew her shaking hand from mine. She fumbled through that huge-ass purse for her keys, distracting herself, doing her best to pretend that everything was okay.

She clicked the fob. The running lights flashed. I stood at the passenger door and watched her walk around the front of the car. She climbed inside and started the ignition.

Fear constricted my chest. This was the first time I'd seen Aly this way, pushing me away instead of begging me closer. Exhaling a heavy breath from my lungs, I finally unlatched the door and sat down in the seat.

Silently, Aly put her car in reverse, backed out, and pulled out onto the street.

The ride home was short and still the fucking longest of my

life. Aly didn't say a word, just kneaded at the steering wheel, while her chest rose and fell in spastic quakes. Like she was struggling. Struggling not to cry. Unspoken words strained between us, fighting for release. But the truth was, I didn't know what the fuck to say because I didn't know what Aly wanted to hear.

She parked and got out, and I followed her upstairs.

Inside, the apartment was dark. Empty. Cold.

Aly dumped her purse to the floor and went straight for her room. I swallowed hard as I trailed her, three steps behind. I stopped in the doorway. She flipped on the small lamp on her dressing table. Dull light climbed up the wall, spread out in a subdued glow across the ceiling.

She kept her back to me and hugged herself across her middle.

I fidgeted, shifting uneasily on my feet. Aly was just so goddamned beautiful, it caused me physical pain to look at her. It was an ache that started in the center of my chest and spread out to saturate the deepest places in my body. It throbbed in that hidden place that'd been made for her, the one she filled up when I had no idea that was really where she was supposed to be.

Pressure built up in the stifled air.

Suffocating.

I wanted to reach for her, break through it.

I fucking hated it. Hated hurting her.

I took a step inside and locked the door behind me. Hesitation stilled me before I finally found my voice and whispered, "Aly . . . baby . . ."

Crossing to the middle of the room, I stretched out my hand with the intention of touching her, comforting her, but Aly whirled around, stumbling back.

Wetness streaked down her cheeks and glistened in her

eyes, that gorgeous face a mess of tears. My gut twisted into the tightest knot.

She blinked rapidly, fighting some kind of internal war. She fisted her hands, clutched them like a shield at her chest. "Did you fuck her? When you were with me?" The words were chopped and broken.

They cut through me like a jagged knife, bleeding me dry. "What?" was all I could gasp.

Disbelief shook my head, and I wet my lips as I roughed a hand down the back of my neck, dropped it to my side, and took one anguished step forward. "Goddamn it, Aly ... you really think I'd be with her when I was with you?" I asked, incredulous, my head pitched to the side. "You think you weren't the only fucking thing I could think about, night and day?"

More tears slipped free, and Aly blanched as she gasped for air, hit by another wave of pain. "I don't know!" It came out as a tormented cry. She held her fists closer, tighter, her voice cracking as it lowered. "I don't know, Jared, and that *scares* me. I feel like I know you better than anyone else in this world and there's still a huge part of you I don't know at all." The words tumbled out in an agonized confession.

Emotion slammed me, shame and guilt and the fucking insane amount of love I had for this girl.

Aly's eyes went wide when I rushed in and gripped her by both sides of the head. Waves of soft hair were all bunched up between my fingers, her smell and her sweet and her heart washing over me in a breaking wave. I forced her to look at me, my hold intense. Desperate. Just as desperate as the admission that flooded from my mouth. "I will never lie to you, Aly. And, yeah, I fucked her."

A sob tore up Aly's throat, and she thrashed, struggling to break away.

But I was not letting her go.

My fingers dug into the back of her head, my thumbs on her soaked cheeks. "It was before I ever stepped through your bedroom door. The first week I was here."

A sharp breath wheezed down Aly's throat, and she wrapped her hands around my wrists, like she didn't know if she wanted to push me away or pull me closer.

I made the decision for her, tugging her close enough her nose was touching mine. "Even then . . . *even then* . . . I felt fucking guilty because somewhere inside me, I already knew I belonged to you."

Aly whimpered and dug her fingers into the skin of my wrists. She winced, the words rough with her own insecurities. "I can't stand the thought of you being with someone else. Not knowing who you were with or what you did while you were gone these last three months. It kills me, Jared . . . *kills* me to think of what you were doing while I was here worrying about you. When you came back, I tried to pretend like it didn't matter, that it was in the past. But seeing you with that girl . . . it hurt."

My fingers twisted in the mass of her hair. Shame sliced through my consciousness, flashes of the dirty hotel room in Vegas where I'd wasted away, where I'd begged for death to come. Where I'd missed and hurt and gave in to the demons that would forever plague my mind.

"You want to know what I did while I was gone, Aly? *Fine.*" I squeezed her tighter, lifted her higher as I forced her to look at me, to *see* me, to see the part she was scared she didn't know. The part I didn't want her to see because it was the part she *should* be scared of. The side that harbored the foul, where the vile held my soul captive.

"I fucking filled my body with everything and anything I

could find to cover up the ache that was left without you in my life. I started using again, Aly. Day after day, night after night, I tried to drown out the memory of you. Then I almost got myself killed. I should have died out there on that deserted road when I crashed my bike. But somehow there was still something keeping me chained to this world. Last night I found out what that was. It was you. It's always been you."

I cupped her face. My whisper intensified as I stared down at the fervent green eyes begging up at me. "I never touched anyone while I was gone. No one. I couldn't. Not after you." I brushed her tears away and shook my head. "*No one.*"

With my words, Aly snapped. She gripped me by the back of the head and dragged my mouth to hers. She made a desperate play to bring me closer, pressing the length of her body to mine as she tore at my shirt. Her kiss came urgent, like she was dying and I was the only one who could save her.

Heat surged into the confines of her room, drowning us in need.

I wrapped her in my arms and lifted her off her feet as I kissed her hard, welcoming the warmth of her tongue as it slipped along mine. I staggered forward. Aly's back hit the wall next to her window with a low thud.

"Jared." It was a plea. Persistent fingers dug into my shoulders, raked down my back, gripping at my neck as she did everything she could to bring me closer.

Between our frantic kisses, I mumbled at her mouth, "Aly, baby, I'm so sorry . . . so sorry . . . I never wanted you to witness something like you did tonight. I hate that it hurt you. You . . . it's you." I repeated her words from months ago, when she promised she belonged to me.

The night I took her.

The night I took it all.

It scared the hell out of me that the same promise now bled
so easily from me.

But I knew it was always going to be her.

That I belonged to her, heart and soul.

Because I only existed in her.

Aly yielded to my kiss, gave me all of her while I devoured
the good and the girl. Blood thundered through my veins, my
pulse pounding so hard I couldn't see. Nerves rushed as an un-
found need crashed through me, and tripped my sanity.

She set me on fire, lit me up. Every inch of my body tightened. I was fucking hard, straining.

God, I wanted inside her.

To bury myself in beauty.

To get lost there.

Forever.

My hands found her waist and I crushed her against me so
she would make no mistake of just how fucking badly I wanted
her. So she'd know exactly what she did to me.

Aly moaned.

I kissed her deeper. Her weight was pinned to the wall with
my hips. I ran my hands up her sides, over the soft fabric veiling
the perfection beneath. I dragged them up her arms, grasped
her hands, pinned them over her head.

Aly writhed, rocked against me, and wrapped those long
legs around my waist.

Fuck.

How was it possible one girl could feel so good?

"You." The word was hard. Rough. My spirit's demand.

She slipped down my body and settled on her feet, her hands
frantic as she ran them under my shirt. Her hot palms flattened
on my stomach. My muscles jerked and ticked, twitching in anticipation. Her hands were all smooth and soft as she dragged

my shirt up. Still, they burned, leaving a trail of fire in their wake.

I took one step back and leaned down, and Aly ripped my shirt over my head.

For a second, we stood there, staring, our breaths heaved into the thick air. My gaze traveled down the glorious curves of her body, rushing over the softness of her sweater, the slim black jeans that had me itching to get inside them, and down to the heels that just about left me undone.

Then she crashed back into me in the same moment I crashed into her. I pressed her into the wall, like I could consume her.

She whimpered, clutched my shoulders. She dipped down and covered the dying rose in the center of my chest with her mouth and her love and all the fucking belief in me I'd never deserve. The blunt edges of her nails raked over her eyes that stared out from behind the wilted petals.

"You," rumbled out in a slow breath from my mouth as she touched her mark.

The one who'd given me something to believe in, the one who discovered something in me that had been buried for so many years.

The blameless one amid all my sins.

"You," she whispered back at my skin. She scorched me with her touch, her palms sliding up and over my ribs; then she changed course, splaying her fingers wide as she slipped them down my sides. With trembling hands, Aly yanked at my fly and ripped the buttons open with one firm jerk.

Need thundered through my veins, burned as it sped, stoked the need for this girl that was never going to let me go.

"Ugh . . . Aly . . ." I fisted my hands in her hair as she kissed a trail across my chest. Her mouth was wet, hot as it blazed a path down my stomach.

Aly dropped to her knees, dragging my jeans and underwear down my thighs as she went.

Air punched from my lungs and I gripped her tighter. "Oh shit," I wheezed. My cock sprung free, fucking begging for this girl who was on her knees, staring up at me.

Trust and fear collided on her face, merged into this tentative hope.

She took me in her hand.

I jerked. Pleasure rocked down the back of my thighs.

Slowly, she stroked me as the severity of her gaze kept me pinned. Her expression left her exposed, vulnerable. A thousand insecurities played out in the depths of her green eyes, worries and fears and needs. Like this was some kind of surrender.

Or maybe acceptance.

I hissed when she took me in her mouth. "Oh . . . shit . . . Aly."

That sweet mouth felt so fucking good, it nearly brought me to my knees.

I gripped her head, fucking straining as she took me whole.

This sound reverberated from her throat as she looked up at me, like she was trying to convey something she was too scared to say. Like she was pleading as she pleasured me, her mouth so fucking hot as her lips pressed down my length, taking what she could while she gripped and stroked the rest of me with her hand.

My spirit thrashed, expanded and danced and writhed.

Because I saw something there I'd never seen before.

Something that sent a chill rushing through me in the same second every cell in my body flamed in praise of her.

Aly had always been a treasure I'd placed on the highest

pedestal. The girl was my perfection. But maybe that foundation had its own fissures, cracks that could widen, cause her to crumple.

It was something that was so difficult for me to grasp—meaning something to someone.

But there was no doubt she needed me too. Aly was fucking scared, and maybe she didn't have this all figured out, either. We were in this shit together, and together we had to figure it out.

The second she saw I understood, she whimpered and quickened her pace, taking then releasing. Winding me up, ratcheting me higher.

"Fuck . . . Aly . . . baby," I groaned. "Baby, stop. I'm gonna come."

One hand dug into my ass and she pulled me closer, refusing to let me go. She took me as deep as she could.

Pleasure pulsed as I came, careening through my senses.

I roared.

Tremors rolled through me, and I looked down at the girl, her face steeped in emotion, her eyes squeezed shut, her perfect lips wrapped around me.

It lit a frenzy in me.

Motherfucking trigger.

I gripped her under the arms and yanked her from the floor. Aly wrapped her legs around my waist. Sharp heels bit into my ass, and goddamn, if I wasn't hard again because that's just what this girl did to me.

With my jeans twisted around my knees, I stumbled to the end of her bed.

Her mattress was a tangle of black sheets, and I fell over her, desperate to get her closer. I kicked out of my shoes, twisted out of the rest of my clothes.

Her chin tipped up to meet my face, her hair brushing the

bed as I crawled over her. I dragged her up the bed as I climbed higher.

Aly rocked, her body arching, seeking mine. "Jared, need you . . . need you so bad."

Good thing, because she was about to have me.

"Is there anything I can do to hurt the baby?" I asked, just needing reassurance because I couldn't stand the thought of doing something stupid, of giving in to the recklessness as I sought a second's pleasure.

Frantically she shook her head, maybe just as frantic as I was to get her sweater over it. "No. You don't have to worry."

I tossed her sweater to the floor. Her olive skin glowed in the dim light. Redness swept up her belly and came to rest on her cheeks as I laid her against her pillow. I sat back and took her in.

"Please." She lifted her hips with the appeal. I flicked the button free on her jeans, dragged down the zipper, slipped them from her hips.

Aly ran her hands down the flat plane of her stomach like she didn't know what to do with them, released a soft moan of satisfied anticipation when I tugged her heels from her feet and ridded her of her jeans.

She squirmed under my stare as she lay there wearing nothing but silk and lace, her chest rising in spastic quakes. Everything about her was soft and slender and curved. Delicate and strong. Just like my girl's heart.

"You're beautiful, Aly," I murmured, feeling those words strike me deep.

The rosy buds of her breasts pointed through the thin meshed fabric, fucking straining as painfully as me. I wound my hands under her back and unclasped the hook of her bra, spread my fingers wide and slipped them up her back and over her shoulders, capturing the straps as I lifted her arms and dragged it free. Climbing onto my knees, I watched her, my gaze intent. I edged her panties down those long legs that did insane things to me.

I grasped her by the knees, spread her wide.

"Fucking perfect," I muttered, the words scraping like gravel from my throat.

And shit, I didn't want to be disrespectful because this was *my girl.* But my girl was unreal. She was like the perfect pinup with her perky ass and even perkier tits. Like one of those girls on the pages of a magazine. Intangible. Make-believe.

A fantasy.

But Aly had become my reality.

I dove into the sweet of her body with my mouth. My tongue explored the folds of slick flesh, kissed and suckled and roamed. She was so warm, so wet. And this girl tasted like heaven.

Aly panted, begged my name. Fingertips trailed across my face and brushed along my lips where I kissed that body senseless.

I grabbed her by the thigh. Splaying my fingers wide, I palmed her and slowly dragged my hand down her leg to her knee. I hooked it over my shoulder, tugged her tighter to me, sucked her clit into my mouth, teased her with my tongue.

Ruptured cries escaped her in an incoherent tumble of pleasure, utterings from deep within that tickled at my ears, pricked at my chest. Tremors rolled across the surface of her skin and jerked her hips from the bed.

I took that as an invitation.

I slipped one finger inside her, then two, fucked her with my fingers while I caressed her with my mouth.

A rattled groan rumbled in my chest, reverberated from my mouth because I was thinking how good it was going to feel to be all tucked up inside her.

Aly lifted her hips higher. "Jared . . . oh my God . . . please."

I increased the pressure, increased the pace. Loved the sounds she was making, loved that I was making her feel this way.

I felt it hit, the crashing wave that broke over her. She whined, all the muscles of her body constricting as she tightened on my fingers.

Consumed, I rushed up her body and drove inside her because I had to ride that out.

Both of us cried out, grasping at the other. Aly convulsed as another tremor tore through her.

Struggling to find a breath, I climbed to my knees, scooping her up and taking her with me. At the small of her back, I supported her, held her, and Aly wrapped her long legs around my waist. With my free hand, I gripped the top of her headboard. I lifted her and slammed her back down on me.

Aly wheezed, raked her fingernails down my back.

We began to move. Frantic, our bodies rocked, finding this frenzied rhythm, something that struck some kind of pitch-perfect chord between us.

Sweat dampened her skin, her body straining as she moved over me, working me right back to where she had me not ten minutes before.

My hand slipped up her spine and I grasped her by the back of the neck.

Aly's eyes locked on mine. Emotion swam in their depths. Devotion and fear. Adoration and need.

I rocked into her hard, my body demanding. I felt consumed, agonized in this pleasure. Because she felt so fucking good, so fucking *right*.

I always thought I'd be her ruin. But right then, I was pretty sure she'd be mine. My faultless demise. Because I'd suffer for her. Bear all her burden and her blame. Would gladly die for her.

The most terrifying part of it all was that I was willing to live for her.

Aly arched. Her hands burned into my shoulders where she braced herself on me, wisps of her hair falling all down my hand and dipping down onto the bed. Every inch of her was stretched tight, tension wound in her muscles. Her stomach flexed and bowed, the cut of her arms and shoulders defined. Her full, round breasts pushed up in my face as she rolled back. Her nipples were all taut and pouty. As pouty as her mouth, her lips parted as her jaw dropped lax.

I captured one in my mouth, laved and lapped.

Soft moans fell against my ear.

My fingers slipped down her ass and brushed over the sensitive skin.

Aly gasped, rocked as she rolled over me. I lifted and strained, pressed and pushed.

And I took.

I took and took and took. For once, this taking was right.

Because maybe I had something to give back.

I was consumed, desperate for this hunger to be quelled when I knew there was no possible way to get my fill.

There was no stopping the storm building inside of me. A flicker of rage. A flash of fear. I quaked with the thought of not having her, of losing her, and I grasped at her skin, my fingers digging in.

Wanted to dominate and devour.

Harsh breaths panted from her mouth, and my heart beat so fucking hard, slamming around in my chest.

The sick part was I'd been running so far and so fast from that trigger. Now I was fucking desperate to keep it near, to hold her safe. I couldn't lose her.

And I craved.

Wanted.

Needed her so badly I thought I would lose my mind.

But this time I wasn't searching for numbness. Wasn't begging for the blackness to invade. Wasn't looking to block it out.

Feeling lit through my entire body and overtook my senses. Every nerve fired, every inch of me alive.

I cried out, "Aleena," my arms hugging her tight as I crushed her to me.

Motherfucking trigger.

Aly had become my drug.

I buried my face in her neck, my grip like a vise at her waist as I buried myself in her.

Completely.

Wholly.

Aly threw her head back and cried out my name. Her nails burrowed deep into my skin, just like she'd burrowed somewhere deep in my soul.

Ragged breaths palpitated from my lungs, and I just held her, Aly's body limp when she collapsed against me.

I lifted my head, kissed her softly.

Aly stuttered a sigh.

Gently, I pulled out. I shifted, laying her across the bed. "I'll be right back."

I pulled on my underwear and slipped out her door. I made my way into the bathroom and flipped on the switch. Bright lights burned my eyes, and I blinked as I shuffled inside.

Turning the faucet high, I waited for it to warm.

I caught my reflection in the mirror. Colors dripped and bled across my skin, the sins I'd committed glaring in the glow. Green eyes glinted out from them, striking like a flare.

Aleena.

Shaking, I ran my fingertips over them, like I was searching for some kind of answer, like maybe I could discern if any of this was really right.

Because how would I ever really know?

I stared at my eyes. They seemed much too bright. Too alive.

Flames of fear licked through my body, kindling the madness Aly created in me, and my gut twisted into the tightest knot.

What happened when I lost it all?

I slammed my eyes shut and shook my head.

Stupid shit.

Couldn't go there.

I grabbed a washcloth from the cabinet under the sink.

Just as I was wetting it under hot water, Christopher appeared in the doorway.

He lifted a sarcastic brow. "Looks like you two made up."

"Fuck you, dude."

God, he was such a smartass.

Chuckling, he leaned against the doorway with his arms crossed over his chest. In thought, he pursed his lips. His voice was softer than I expected. "You know my sister isn't one of those girls who holds grudges, Jared."

I lowered my face and shook my head. I wrung out the washcloth. "You think I don't know that? That's the only reason I'm here."

Didn't deserve to be. He and I both knew that.

Sighing, he roughed his hand through the mess of black on his head. Somehow he managed to make it stick up even worse than it already was. "You've gotta be honest with her, man. Let her in. Tell her about whatever shit your past has gotten you into because you can't leave her unprepared for it. She loves you enough to forgive you for it, whatever it is."

I nodded, swallowed hard as I straightened. I looked at him seriously. Honestly. "I just wish I could erase the mess of it."

Guess I was more scared of repeating it.

Humorless laughter seeped from him. "Don't we all."

I rubbed my palm over my face and blew a breath from my lungs.

He inclined his head toward Aly's door. "Go on . . . take care of my sister . . . you know she's waiting for you."

SIX

Aleena

A soft sigh hit the back of my throat as I watched him go. Or maybe it was a whimper. My bedroom door slowly closed behind him. Loosely it came to rest on the jamb. I turned and faced the ceiling. Lying there, I tried to catch my breath, to slow my thundering heart. Tried to make sense of what had just happened between us.

It had been uncontrollable. Turbulent. Explosive.

Exhaustion sagged my entire body into a useless puddle curled in the middle of my bed, but his touch still fired along the surface of my skin, burned beneath it. Below me, the sheets felt both hot and cold, glowed with the remnants of heat from the impassioned fury that had taken us over. I flattened my palm out over them, over the place where he had had me. Where he had found me.

Deep satisfaction penetrated into the marrow of my bones. Above that satisfaction, my nerves skittered with unease.

Only one other time had I witnessed Jared like he was to-night, control slipping and something wild flaming in his eyes. It was the morning that had begun so intensely, when Jared had locked us away behind my bathroom door, the same day my mother had discovered him in our apartment.

It was the day fear and shame and self-contempt had driven him away.

Every time Jared touched me, there was something power-ful in it, something overwhelming. Something stunning.

Breathtaking.

Lost in the deepest reaches of that connection, I'd felt the disturbance. Like I was so close to him I could feel his anguish as his body became one with mine.

Like I was partner to it.

I'd felt it again tonight.

But there was something distinctly different.

That day, three months ago, I knew Jared was trying to push me away.

Not tonight.

No, tonight he'd sought, hunted, like he would do anything, give up anything, to be closer to me.

And it was almost frightening, how close we were.

Maybe it was my reaction that scared me most, the one at the bar and then here in my room.

When I saw him with that girl at the Vine, I'd been shocked by my reaction. It was violent. Vicious. One glance and the deep-est ache had seized me, left me gutted, splaying me wide open.

Left me *questioning*.

Worries I had tried to suppress had pushed their way to the forefront. Those months I'd spent alone in this room, miss-ing him, mourning him, crying out for him, I couldn't stop myself from imagining what he was doing and who he was with. Every time my mind would go there, it would break me a little more.

But when he'd returned yesterday, I'd made the decision that it was in the past. He'd left, without obligation to me, and he had made no promises other than the one that he would forget about me and I would forget about him.

He'd broken that promise because forgetting each other was an impossibility. I think we both knew it, even though I'd struggled and prayed that one day I would accept he was gone and move on instead of pretending he would find his way back to me.

But he had. He came back to me, and I wanted to believe nothing else mattered.

Until I'd seen that girl rubbing all over him. A swell of possessive envy had collided with my love of him, and all of those worries had come flooding back.

Maybe it was because we were at the Vine. It was the place where Jared would go to unwind when he wanted a beer. It was the place that had become his excuse, where he'd tell Christopher he'd been when he was really hidden away in my room. Maybe it was the proximity to our apartment that made it so real. That made it *matter*.

One look at the way she was touching him, one look at the panic on his face, and I knew.

I just didn't know when.

Part of me wanted to keep pretending whatever had happened didn't count, to assign it to the past and focus on the future.

But I couldn't.

Because it hurt.

I once believed I'd take whatever piece of him he was willing to give.

That was no longer good enough.

I wanted it all.

As hard as I tried to hide it, it crushed me to think he'd been with someone else during the months he'd been living with us, stealing into my room and into my bed. When he'd hold me and love me and make me whole.

I'd flinched away when he touched me back at the bar, thinking those hands had strayed. I'd tried to forge on with the night and force my worries back inside.

But Jared knew, because he knew me.

Relief had floored me when he brought me home, promising there had been no one else.

Only his true admission had been so much worse.

His confession weighed heavily on my mind and even heavier on my heart. He told me once he would always be an addict because he knew how easily he could slip. He'd also said he'd never go back there because slipping into oblivion was the easy way out and he didn't get easy.

But somewhere inside me I already knew Jared had fallen. I'd seen the newfound shame dimming his blue eyes, the way he'd hung his head as if he believed himself even lower than the day he'd fled out my door.

I knew it the first time I saw him when he returned and I ran my fingers along the coarse, jagged scar that snaked around his head.

I just hadn't wanted to see how bad it had actually been.

And I hurt for him. Was scared for him.

The truth was, I was scared for myself because I didn't know what this new information meant.

Rough, distorted voices traveled through the gap in my door. I trained my ear, listening.

Jared and Christopher.

They were speaking too softly for me to hear what they

were saying, but their tone was mild enough to assure me no ill will was happening between the two of them.

I'd already seen it on my brother's face.

Forgiveness. And maybe even relief.

A couple seconds later, the door swung open. A halo of light silhouetted Jared's frame, his presence thick and overwhelming.

He stood there, gazing at me from across the room.

Under his stare, I squirmed, fisted the sheets at my sides.

When he stepped forward, he slowly he came into view. He towered over me. As he approached, my eyes caressed the sharp angles of his face. My attention jumped along the deformed, warped story played out on his chest and down the deep lines cut into his rugged stomach. His hips jutted out above his tight underwear, something so tempting in the way he moved. Sinewy muscle bunched and flexed beneath the color of his strong arms, bristled in the corded strength of his powerful legs.

A tremor rolled through me.

He was indescribable. Devastating.

So hard, every inch of him, callused from the wounds that had marred his life, this terrifying beauty that held me captive, tying me somewhere to the darkest places of his soul.

But his eyes . . . they were soft. Bright. Filled my own darkness with light.

"Hey," he murmured quietly as he drew near.

"Hey," I whispered back.

He knelt at the side of my bed and leaned in to brush back the matted hair stuck to my dampened forehead. "Are you okay?" Concern tightened his brow as he searched my face. "Was I too rough?"

Softly, I shook my head, unable to look away from this gorgeous man. "No, not at all." I trailed my trembling fingers down his face. "You don't need to worry about me so much."

"How can I not? I just want to take care of you."

I jumped when he placed the warm, damp cloth between my thighs, then hummed when he gently massaged it over me, deliberate, soft, because taking care of me was exactly what he was doing.

Complete acceptance nodded my head. "I know that."

He finished cleaning me and tossed the washcloth into the hamper. Slowly, he crawled into bed. Rolling onto his side, he pulled me to him. "Come here."

I snuggled into the security of his chest, and he drew the covers over us, wrapping me in the safety of his arms.

Warmth spread over me, contenting every fiber in my being. I buried my face in his chest, brushed my lips across the rose, breathed him in.

Jared exhaled as he pulled me closer. And I could feel the shift. Tension clotted the already heavy air. He gathered my hand and wove our fingers together. He held it tight between us. In the dim light, his blue eyes met mine, wholly tender, yet fierce and severe.

"I need you to understand something, Aly. You don't ever have to worry about me stepping out on you." He squeezed my hand tighter. "I can promise you that."

For a flash he averted his gaze, before he leveled the force of it back on me. Vestiges of shame swam in the depths. "But I think you already know I left a whole mess of that behind me in Jersey."

Jealousy bit at my consciousness, and I squeezed my eyes shut as if I could block it out. I didn't want to be that girl, the one who let things that could not be controlled affect her life.

The one who let insecurities invade, fester, and destroy. But I had to be honest and admit it hurt. Thinking of him with other girls the way he'd been with me left something inside me uncovered, abraded and raw.

Tonight had only proven that.

It had revealed a weakness in me.

Because I'd only ever belonged to him.

I knew it was foolish. Wrong. But I couldn't help the way I felt.

He jerked at my hand, demanding my attention. My eyes flashed open. "Four years were spent that way. There were a lot of them, and I can't promise you something like what happened tonight won't ever happen again." He blinked like it caused him physical pain. "Seeing your face tonight, how much it hurt you to see me with her . . . God, that killed me, Aly. I don't ever want to see you hurting that way. If I could go back and change it, you know I would. But I *can't*. But you need to know none of them ever meant anything."

He edged back, released my fingers, and pressed my palm to his chest right over my eyes marking his skin. "You did this, Aly. You made me feel . . . really feel. None of them did that. Not one. I told you once I used girls just as shamelessly as Christopher. I'm not using you. You have to know that."

Discomfort needled through my senses and embarrassment rushed to my face. But I refused to look away from him. I chewed at the inside of my cheek, searching for the courage to speak. "I do know that, but the thought of you with someone else, touching them the way you touch me . . ." My voice dropped. "I only want you to belong to me."

Like a testimony, my naked body burned against his, the way I'd given myself to him.

Only him.

Jared pulled back so he could see my face better. Knowing laughter seeped quietly from his mouth, and he softly ran his fingers through my hair. "I've only belonged to one person, Aly, and that's you." His mouth was suddenly at my ear. "And believe me, I've never touched anyone the way I touch you."

A shiver raised goose bumps across my flesh.

He chuckled more as he sat back and took in my expression. "You understand?"

I hid my face in his neck, feeling all flustered and self-conscious and completely adored. "Yes."

"Besides, have you looked at yourself in the mirror? Do you have even a single clue how beautiful you are?"

I lifted up onto my elbow, smiling down at him with the tease. "I'm going to get fat here pretty soon. What then?"

Jared turned away to look at the ceiling. A wistful grin tugged at his mouth. He turned back and that grin widened. His hand came flat to my belly. "I seriously doubt that. I can't help but picture you just like this with a little round ball *right here*," he emphasized as he palmed my stomach.

It was sweet, playful.

"What happens if you're wrong?" I contended.

Mischief glinted in his eyes. "Baby, I'll take you any way I can get you."

I bit at my lip, feeling an unsettled rush of nerves travel through my body, anticipation and love and hope. I covered Jared's hand and looked up at him. "I can't wait," I said honestly.

It was the first time I really realized it was true, when the fear of the future, the fear of the unknown, became so much less important than my hope for this *life*.

The playfulness faded from his face. "I can't believe we're going to have a baby. It's so hard to imagine what's happening inside you right now."

He swallowed hard and increased his hold.

My eyes darted all over his face because it told a million truths, fears and shame and the misguided belief that he could never deserve a gift like this.

But I also saw the longing.

I clung to it.

"Everything about our lives is going to change, Jared," I whispered seriously, urgently. "I . . ." I tripped over what I wanted to say next, my face suddenly pressed to his neck because I was scared of what haunted him, of what would stalk him in the darkness. Tempt him and trap him. "What happened in Vegas . . . Jared, you can't—"

Jared jerked back and gripped me by the face, cutting me off like he couldn't bear to hear it come from my mouth. "I know that, Aly." Tremors rocked his chest and he drew in a ragged breath. "I know."

His voice softened, though his eyes darkened as he stared me down, baring it all. "After I woke up in the hospital this last time, I knew I was coming back to you, but I wouldn't allow myself to come back here for *three weeks* because I had to make sure I was well enough to be here. Well enough to stand in front of you with a clean mind and a clean body. But I can't change who I was in my past, Aly. That's always going to be a part of me, something that is never completely going to go away. I'm fucked up. I warned you last night. But I promised you then you make me want to be better. That you *make* me better." He splayed his hand wide across my stomach. "*This* makes me want to be better."

"Do you . . ." I shook my head, grasping for anything to say that might convince this man that he deserved it, that this baby and I deserved it. "Don't you think you should talk to someone?"

But the question held so much more than that, asked so much more of him, like a silent plea straight from my heart.

You have to get help. Find a way to heal.

Still, Jared heard it.

He stiffened. His voice trembled as he forced out the words. "I'm okay."

Reluctantly I nodded and settled my head on his shoulder. I knew he'd come so far. But still it scared me he may not ever be ready to get better.

Gentle fingers played in my hair. Softly Jared wound a thick lock in his finger. He tugged a little before he pressed a kiss to the top of my head. "I love you so much. I need you to believe that." It was his own plea.

And I knew he wasn't ready.

Shifting, I moved to straddle him and Jared rolled to his back. I dipped down, kissed him across his heart, hoping he could feel my belief in him. "I do."

Tender hands flattened on my back and he pulled me down to him.

This time, his kiss was slow.

My eyes flew open to a heavy blanket of darkness. Anxiety clawed at the walls and spilled out across the floor. Panic thundered through my veins, spreading like wildfire along the surface of my skin.

But this panic was not my own.

Jared's arms and legs twitched and jerked as he held me pinned to his side. Sweat slicked his clammy skin, and he groaned incoherently from the horrors that kept him under.

Tremors rocked through him in a rolling wave as he slipped along the fringes of sleep, an uncontained frenzy in his fingers, desperate in their search. They dug deep into my sides, and he burrowed his face into my chest in a pained embrace, as if he were searching for some kind of solace from the torture that ruled his spirit.

Jared's entire body jolted with the nightmare that was his reality.

Frantic, I wrapped him in my arms. "Shh . . . shh . . . Jared. It's okay . . . I'm right here . . . it's okay." I swept my mouth across his forehead and brushed my fingers through his dampened hair, clutching him to me, murmuring reassurances again and again to the man shaking in my arms.

Sharp breaths wheezed from his lungs, and he struggled to draw in air.

Grief traveled his throat in a sharp gasp and blurred with the anger I could feel radiating from his pores.

I took his face between my hands and forced him to look at me. In the darkness, wide blue eyes stared, completely lost.

There were no tears. Just pain.

Nausea pooled in my stomach.

"It's okay," I whispered again, knowing it was a lie.

Because no matter what I said or what he claimed, I knew Jared was not okay.

The next morning, I stood in the kitchen at the bar, peering out the sliding glass door to the apartment balcony.

Jared was there. With his back to me, he stared out over the low stucco wall to the parking lot below and the city extending out far beyond his view, though I knew he was lost to the thoughts in his mind. Twitching, he lifted his hand, and his back expanded as he inhaled the cigarette that burned between his fingers. Smoke curled over the top of his head, evaporated in the sharp gusts of wind that whipped short pieces of his blond hair into an uncontrolled frenzy.

Dark jeans hung low on his narrow waist, clinging to his hips.

But he was shirtless, leaving the canvas that continued his story exposed.

Bold marks of suggestion cut across his wide shoulders and spiraled in a shifting whorl down his back. Distorted faces flashed in a tumble of color, some appearing demonic. Others angelic.

Of all the ink covering his body, this was what terrified me most. It screamed confusion and chaos, an unsound spirit lost in a daze of disorder, something begging to break free from its chains.

So much like what I witnessed in his eyes last night when I woke him from his nightmare.

I lifted the glass of orange juice to my mouth and sipped at the cool liquid, my eyes refusing to lose sight of the man I loved with all my life, willing him to recognize it.

To see through it.

This morning, he was agitated, but I knew he was doing his best to make this okay.

Today was going to be rough.

He and I both knew it.

Christopher barreled down the hall, breaking up my thoughts as he came around the bar and into the kitchen. He planted a quick kiss to my temple. "Happy Thanksgiving, little sister."

He grabbed a mug from the cupboard. The coffeepot clanked as he pulled it out and poured a cup.

My attention slid to him, and my mouth lifted with sincere appreciation. "Thank you, Christopher." Clearly, I was thanking him for so much more. He'd supported me through the last three months when I was scared and alone.

For a second he just looked at me, serious, like he knew how truly grateful I was for everything he'd done for me. "You don't need to thank me, Aly. You've always taken care of my sorry ass."

Mild laughter seeped from me. "No . . . I just nagged at you enough to make you think I was taking care of you."

"Ha . . . now that you have." He winked. Leaning back against the counter, he held the mug between his hands and took a tentative sip of steaming coffee. "You still planning on telling Mom and Dad today?"

I nodded. "Yeah. We are."

Christopher looked at his feet. A sympathetic snort escaped his nose as he glanced up at me. "You know Dad's going to lose his shit."

"I know." I wasn't defensive, just sad, because I knew my dad so well and I felt like he knew so little about me. I knew he loved me, how much he cared about and hoped for his children. He wanted us to be happy and strong and live good lives.

I just wasn't sure he understood what having all those things really meant to me.

And I wasn't a child.

But I'd always be my dad's little girl.

Christopher and I stood in silence for a few minutes, scenarios running through our heads on how things might play out today.

I finished off my orange juice, doing my best to ignore the anxious nerves that nagged at my heart and mind.

Christopher blew out an exaggerated breath. "Well, we'd better get a move on. Mom's going to start calling and asking where we're at if we don't get over there soon."

I inclined my head to the balcony door. "Give us a few minutes to finish getting ready."

"Not a problem. I need to finish getting ready myself."

He dumped his mug in the sink and brushed his fingers across the side of my hand as he passed by, leaving me with a silent show of encouragement.

Walking out into the main room, I stopped for a moment to appreciate Jared from behind, before I went into my bathroom to finish my makeup and hair. Five minutes later, I headed out of the bathroom and turned the knob to my bedroom.

I smiled a little, correcting myself.

Our bedroom.

Was it ridiculous that the idea of that made me giddy with joy? The thought of Jared and me as a family? That the man who held all of my dreams had become my home?

And I thought *no.* There was nothing ridiculous about us, about this love that was always supposed to be.

That's what I was giving thanks for today. For this start, this beginning, as rocky as it was. But really, I couldn't even think of it as a beginning when Jared had forever been my always.

I swung my door open. Jared stood in the middle of the room. He fumbled with the buttons of a dark blue, long-sleeved dress shirt.

From under his brow, he glanced up. He stilled when he caught sight of me.

Something that looked like awe and disbelief filled the blue of his intense eyes as I stepped inside and shut the door behind me.

The truth written on his face sent a flood of emotion rushing over me. Just the look thundered my heart, pounding it with affection for him.

"God, you're beautiful," he murmured.

I smoothed out the deep plum dress I'd put on for Thanksgiving dinner. It had a fitted V-neck bodice with three-quarter sleeves, and the tailored skirt came down to just above my knees. Black stockings kept my legs warm, and I'd paired it with black ankle boots. My long hair was pinned up into a messy, chunky twist, and pieces fell down around my face.

Thanksgiving dinner at my parents' was never fancy, always a house full of laughter and easy conversation and comfort. And a strong current of thankfulness.

But we dressed up a little just to honor the day. The dress was simple but pretty, and my parents had given it to me last Christmas, so I thought it was fitting.

Jared slowly crossed the room, each step unhurried, like he relished each one that brought him closer to me. As he approached, he tipped his head to the side in slow appreciation. "Keep telling you, baby, but every time I look at you, you knock the breath right outta me." Something significant flashed in his eyes. "Still can't believe you're my girl."

My fingertips fluttered down the hollow of his strong neck, trailed down his chest to take over his job. I slowly worked through the remaining buttons of his shirt as I gazed up at him. "I've always been your girl. You just didn't know it."

His expression was all over the place, sexy and sly, this cocky quirk lifting just one side of his mouth, an expression that hammered my heart and sent my stomach tripping with desire. But it was the soft creases at the corners of his eyes that stole my own breath.

I straightened his collar, murmuring close to his mouth, "Thank you for doing this with me . . . for me. I can't tell you how much it means."

One arm slipped low around my waist, and he tugged me flush to him. "I'm not ever going to leave you alone to deal with shit again, Aly. We're in this together."

A surge of joy pushed at my ribs. I bit my lower lip as I

melted into his embrace, trying to contain how happy he made me. I rested my cheek on his chest. "*Together*. I like the sound of that."

He wound me a little tighter, rocked us as he held me in the middle of the room. "Me, too," he murmured at the sensitive skin just below my ear. An errant lock of hair strayed down the side of my neck, and Jared brushed it back with his nose, kissed beneath it, before he wound it in his finger. "I like anything that ends in you and me." The suggestive words fell into my room like a promise.

I sighed and shoved all my worries down because none of them mattered when I was in Jared's arms.

Two loud raps rattled my bedroom door. "Let's go," Christopher called.

Jared pulled back. Something mischievous and sweet played all over that gorgeous face. "God, your brother is a pain in my ass."

Softly laughing, I laced my fingers with his, thinking how the two of them had hardly changed, how they fought and warred and seemed once again forever the best of friends.

"Come on. Let's go celebrate." The words were soft, filled with my hope for the day.

With my hope for us.

Yeah, today might be difficult, fraught with the glaring obstacles Jared and I knew we'd eventually have to face, sooner rather than later because we'd been tossed right in the middle of them.

We would have to contend with his past that would forever trail every move he made, the lurking shadows that chased him in the day and haunted him in the night.

But today that past wouldn't just linger in the recesses of his mind.

I'd asked Jared to go back and stand right at the doorstep of the ghosts that ruled his world.

To step into them.

And we'd have to deal with all the assumptions born from the trouble Jared had been in, the faulty ideas bred in my father's mind, and the inevitable disappointment that would come along with them.

A shiver of nerves raced through me as Jared squeezed my hand.

But Jared and I were doing this together.

In response, I gripped his hand tighter and let the deepest peace settle over me.

Yes, today was a day to celebrate.

SEVEN

Jared

Crisp, cool air floated on the light fall breeze. Across the desert sky, the ice blue canopy seemed to go on forever, the sun casting rays of warmth across the heavens.

Aly ambled ahead of me, balancing in these cute little chunky boots she wore with that dress. The slight lilt of her hips struck up a cadence with the rest of her body. It left me all itchy and anxious. My fingers twitched as I followed her across the parking lot. Wayward pieces of dark hair spilled down from the mass of locks twisted on the top of her head, dripping down to kiss the back of her luscious neck, which I was pretty damned sure she'd done with the sole purpose of driving me out of my mind.

Aly tossed a glance over her shoulder. Something like welcome and peace flashed in her eyes when they washed over me.

I roughed my palm over the top of my head and ran it down to grip at the tense muscles in my neck, doing my best to shove down the nerves that spiked inside of me.

This girl. I swear to God, she was something else. So fucking sexy and unbearably sweet.

I'd be damned if I didn't do this for her. For once in my miserable life, I needed to stand up for something that was right.

I mean, shit, I didn't just need to. I wanted to. I wanted to be the man who stood at her side, to declare this beauty that had been bred because it was bred of her.

Still, a slow dread simmered under it all, marching like an army of ants beneath my skin, burning a fiery path as they worked their way out.

Never had I stepped back into the old neighborhood. Drawn, I'd gone what seemed too many times, sitting across the road while those simple houses seemed to taunt me from afar, a picture of the life I'd been erased from because I'd been the one who destroyed it.

But that empty field . . . it'd called to me, the place that echoed the memories that both comforted and crushed, begged me closer the night when the memories trapped in the deepest recesses of my mind had finally been cut free. Where they had run rampant, challenging, changing everything I'd ever believed.

I climbed into the front passenger seat of Aly's little car, and Christopher slid into the backseat behind me.

I watched Aly slip behind the steering wheel. She turned over the ignition, put the car in reverse, and carefully backed out, craning her head around to make sure all was clear.

I swallowed down the terror that was building steadily, born somewhere in the darkness places of my spirit.

It had always been her.

Now I'd do this for her.

No turning back now.

The old neighborhood was only about fifteen minutes away.

Buildings and stores and houses whizzed by in a distorted haze, grayed-out flashes of nothing as we flew past. No words were said. Instead we just let the tension steadily build in the confines of the car.

It was like Aly and Christopher knew how difficult going back to the place where we all grew up together would be for me, and the short trip was given as a moment of silence.

She turned right onto the wide, three-lane road that carved through the center of the city.

I sucked in a ragged breath.

Aly reached for my shaking hand over the console, weaving her fingers through mine. Uncontrollably, my knee bounced. With every second that passed, anxiety ratcheted me one degree higher.

As a kid, I'd been down this road what seemed a million times. Just a stretch of common, innocuous pavement. Until it became the place that meant the most, where stupidity and self-ishness had reigned. God, I'd felt so powerful when I traveled the short expanse of road for the first time, thinking myself such a man. In turn, I'd learned I was just a foolish little boy.

That hollow place inside me throbbed and tremors crawled in a creeping wave through my body, like they slithered out from the darkest places in my spirit.

God, I didn't know if I could do this.

I felt the power of Aly peering at me, searching me through her worry. In the same moment, she was comforting me with the promise of what I never thought I'd have.

She turned her attention back to the road, flicked on her blinker, and eased into the left-turn lane.

Fear tightened my throat, cinching off the air that fed my lungs.

Aly squeezed my hand.

And she knew.

God, she knew.

She knotted her fingers with mine, then she turned left and cut over the spot where I had ruined the good, where I had permanently snuffed out the life and light.

I choked over the ball of unspent emotion.

Two nights ago, I'd crossed the same spot on my own.

Now I was crossing it with her.

To the left, the old neighborhood rose like a smoke signal sent to warn me away.

Still, she clung to my hand, reinforcing the lifeline that somehow tied me to this place.

Even though its height was inoffensive, in the shimmering daylight, the chain link fence that blocked off the empty field where we had spent so many of our days playing now seemed so out of place. Wrong. It gave way to the wooden fences that harbored the homes in safety.

Aly again flipped on her left-turn signal. I couldn't stop shaking, couldn't relax, couldn't come up for a breath as she slowly eased onto the street where we'd all grown up together.

Flashes of light overwhelmed my senses, pictures of moments lost to time. A torrent of memories pummeled through my brain, beat and crashed and consoled.

Because so many of them were good.

Aly as a child, black hair flying, that little girl who had always held me in the palm of her hand. Christopher and I laughing too loud, fighting like brothers, living too free.

My father.

My sister.

My *mother*.

Pressure squeezed my chest, almost as tightly as Aly clung to my hand.

She inched up the road. On the left, her parents' house came into view.

But that was not what held my attention. It was fixed across the street and one house down.

I exhaled a pained breath from my lungs.

The little tan house seemed so much the same, though somehow entirely unfamiliar. The blue trim was now brown, muting out the face of the home. What had once been a staggered trail of flagstone had been completely reworked with a sidewalk and widened driveway.

I swallowed down the lump that formed in my throat.

Her flowers . . . they were gone. The colorful beds that had always grown so tall, so proud, what she'd tended and nurtured and loved beneath the windows of that little house were now a wasted desert of rocks and dirt.

I squeezed my eyes closed because I didn't want to see.

"Fuck," fell as a muffled breath from my mouth, and it took about all I had not to jump from the car.

What the hell was I doing here? Showing my face around here when it should have been wiped clean from this place. Just like *hers*.

But Aly was holding on to me. Even though she said nothing, I could still hear her whispering, *Stay*.

Carefully, Aly pulled up beside a small red truck parked in her parents' driveway. She killed the engine. All three of us just sat there. None of us knew how to move on from here because I think we all knew I didn't *belong* here.

Christopher set his hand on my shoulder and squeezed it. His voice was low and rough, muttering words that were the opposite of what I felt. "Welcome back, man. This place was never the same without you."

"Thanks," I forced out as I stared ahead, unable to look at

the face of my friend who occupied so many of the memories battering me now.

Wrenching the back door open, Christopher climbed out. He left Aly and me to drown in the murky waters holding me under. Maybe I was just a fool, because I'd always been a prisoner to them. I had always been facedown, head under, just on the cusp of death. The feeling that I was suffocating had become a mainstay in my life.

Was I just pretending now? Pretending I could come up from it? Survive?

My chest heaved, and I struggled to take in a cleansing breath, trying to rid my head of all the bullshit ravaging my brain.

God, I was sick of it.

Aly's voice was strained as it broke through the flood. "Are you okay?"

I shook my head and stared down at where she had her hand clenched in mine. Together our skin bore such a striking contrast, the smooth, flawless flesh that spoke of her innocence wrapped up in the horror marking mine.

I chanced looking up at her. Sympathy dimmed the vibrant green of her eyes and darkened them with concern. But they were free of all the bullshit pity I'd come to expect from those who feigned knowing me, like they could really understand what it was I was feeling. In them was just this unending outpouring of love and awareness.

"Fuck, Aly . . . I don't know what I am." Blankly, I stared out the windshield. "I knew it'd be hard coming back here . . ." Pain twisted up my face as I experienced it all, this overwhelming sense of what I had lost and the fear of what I had gained.

What I'd gained in this girl who sat there listening with that pure heart.

"But I had no idea it would feel like this. And I just keep thinking I shouldn't be here. I fucked it up, Aly, I ruined this place, and here I am, coming back. It feels like I'm disrespecting her memory showing up here."

Aly leaned across the console. "Look at me," she demanded.

I turned toward her and she pressed her forehead to mine. She reached up and held one side of my face, her tender fingertips brushing against the faint scruff that roughened my jaw.

"You can do this, Jared . . . you belong here . . . just as much as I do. This street is a part of your life. *Our* lives." As she stressed it, she increased her hold, as if she could breathe those words into me and make me believe them.

And I wanted to.

I wanted to trust in that belief as much as she believed in me.

I inhaled the satiny skin of her neck, let this girl saturate my senses as I forged on, opened myself up to answer her honestly. "I came back here that first night when I found out about the baby . . . to the empty field," I clarified, the words scratching up my throat. "It felt different that night, like I could feel you everywhere, like I was supposed to be there. Maybe it was because the field was where we spent so much time, but being here, in broad daylight . . . I feel like I'm trespassing. Invading something that's sacred. Crossing some line into a place where I shouldn't be."

"Anywhere I am, that's where you're supposed to be," she said, resolute and without question, like it was the only thing that mattered. Gentle fingernails scratched down my cheek like she was somehow fastening herself to me, her mouth so close to mine. "I need you here, Jared . . . with me."

On a heavy breath, I tipped my head and kissed her, my mouth firm as it sought out hers. I reveled in the feel of that sweet face resting between my hands. I pulled back and searched for understanding. "You're the only reason I'm here, Aly."

Aly leaned back. Her green eyes shined with all I'd run from for so long. "Maybe that's the only reason you need."

Then one side of her mouth quirked up, all soft and playful, like she was tossing all the heaviness aside. Because my girl was just cool like that, like she knew exactly what I needed and when I needed it. She grinned. "Besides, we get to have Thanksgiving dinner together. Can it really be all that bad?"

I laughed a little and dragged my fingers through my hair. "Um, yeah, Aly, it might just be that bad. You do remember what we have to tell your parents today, don't you? Pretty sure your dad isn't going to welcome me back with open arms after we deliver our little piece of news."

"I do remember. And I also remember I'm not twelve any-more," she countered. Her eyebrows disappeared into her bangs, her eyes widening as if she was trying to tell me just how ridiculous she thought I was being, worrying about her parents' judgment, when really, this was just about us.

But she had to know better than that.

I'd done some foolish shit in my life, but I was no fool, and Aly was just acting naïve. I hadn't seen her dad, Dave, in years, not since he caught me sneaking out my father's door in the middle of the night. I'd been off to find my next fix, just a couple of days before it'd all completely gone to hell and I'd been sent away. He made it clear then I'd never be welcome in their house again. Hatred had poured from his mouth as disappointment and disdain, giving me a warning to stay away from Christopher . . . to stay away from the rest of his family. He almost spat when he told me I was no longer considered a part of it.

That was almost seven years ago.

How much had changed since then?

Subtly I shook my head and unbuckled my seat belt. I seriously doubted his perception of me had changed all that much—that was for sure.

"Come on," Aly encouraged, cracking open her door. "Let's go hang out with my family. I think you might have forgotten how great they really are."

I opened my door and began to climb out. "I haven't forgotten, Aly." Ducking down, I captured her gaze, looking at her seriously, hoping she would see she was taking this a whole lot more lightly than was wise. "But you can bet they haven't forgotten about me, either."

I followed Aly up the sidewalk. Christopher was waiting for us at the door. He cocked a single brow at me, like he was asking me if I was ready for what was about to happen.

I shrugged, because I was about as ready as I'd ever be.

He rapped once at the wood and opened the door. "Happy Thanksgiving!" he sang all off key and obnoxious as he swung the door open wide.

Aly glanced over her shoulder at me. Joy sat prominent on her features, softened her eyes, and parted her lips, and a tiny giggle seeped from her mouth, like maybe she appreciated her crazy brother just as much as I did for breaking up the tension, for trumpeting our arrival like we were ushering in a celebration rather than stepping into a field of land mines like I was pretty sure we were.

From somewhere inside the house, Aly's mother, Karen, squealed. Five seconds later, she came barreling around the corner. She yanked Christopher into her arms, squeezing him and rocking him almost violently side to side. "There you are!" She pulled back, all this mischief running through the brown of her warm eyes. She fanned herself. "I've been slaving away in the kitchen all day. It's about time you all showed up to give me some help."

I stifled a chuckle.

Maybe I really had forgotten she was that way. Funny. Casual. Kind like her daughter and roguish like her son. Laughter from years ago rang in my ears, the way she and my mother would sit for hours and just laugh and talk about what seemed like nothing at all while we played away our days.

Something strong pushed out from the inside, and my heart beat a little too hard. I stepped away, awkwardly hanging back at the door as she playfully swatted Christopher's chest and turned to drag Aly into her arms. This hug was both tighter and softer than the one she gave Christopher. Something serious passed between the two of them while Karen Moore held her daughter in her arms.

I shifted on my feet, doing my best not to lose my shit as I watched the tender affection transpiring in front of me.

The last time I had seen her, Karen Moore had sent me over the edge. All the forgiveness and love and relief she'd poured out over me had been far too much when it'd been the last thing I wanted.

Now I stood on her threshold, treading dangerous ground as I walked headlong through her front door.

What the fuck was I thinking? Coming here?

That was the problem, though. I no longer knew what was right, my fate, where I was supposed to end up—because somehow I'd received a pardon from my penance and I still didn't know what the hell to do with it. Was it right I was accepting all this goodness or was I just adding another check mark to my sins?

But how could Aly be that? How could she be wrong? All I could see when I looked at her was a gift.

Karen ran her hand over the back of Aly's head and down her back, staring at me over her shoulder when she did. Wide brown eyes spoke to me, glistening with all the same welcome she'd showered me with on the day I'd run.

Or maybe there was even more there, like she saw all the questions running through my mind and she was telling me this was *right* and this was exactly where I was supposed to be.

Slowly she untangled herself from Aly. She never took her eyes off me as she stepped closer. Her movements were almost tentative, though filled with all this cautious purpose as she edged in my direction.

Then Karen Moore wrapped me in her arms.

With her gentle touch, a blink of agitation lit in my nerves, sparked that shame and remorse always lying in wait. But I held it in and let her hold me.

And shit, maybe it seemed impossible that I could, but somehow I forced myself to return it.

Truth was, I had always cared about her. She'd been like a mother to me, never hesitating to encourage me when I needed it or to set me straight when I was stepping out of line.

Closing my eyes, I just let her rain that old affection on me. With it came a downpouring of all the old memories of her and this house and everything that had taken place behind its walls.

Some of those memories I welcomed. Others I shunned. Because I just wasn't ready to go there yet.

Didn't know if I'd ever be.

"Welcome home," she whispered near my ear, like it was our greatest secret, like maybe she knew if she said it aloud it would cause me more pain than I could handle. "You don't know how happy I am you're here . . . that you came back to her."

Her words fell on me, causing confusion and comfort, because I was thinking Karen should be mortified I was with her daughter, and she was singing it like praise.

She edged back a fraction and took me by both hands, her

grip fierce and her gaze unwavering as her eyes traced my face. I just stood there staring at her. None of this made any sense, Aly's love for me and this woman who'd been closer than a sister to my mom giving me the same. Had that love always been there? Had I just been blind to it?

Just as she pulled away, Dave and Aly's little brother, Augustyn, came in from the back of the house.

"Hey guys, Happy Thanksgiving." Aug was all dimples and smiles when he approached, although he wasn't so little anymore. Already sixteen, the boy wasn't as tall as Christopher, but he was pure muscle, bulk and brawn. His appearance was so different from Christopher and Aly, you'd never guess they were siblings. Except for the fact he looked just like his mom, light hair and brown eyes. Christopher and Aly looked a lot like their dad. But Aly? There was something about her and her mom that just fit. They didn't resemble each other a whole lot, but when they stood side by side, there was no mistaking they were a pair.

Aug and Christopher shook hands, pulling each other in for a swift hug and a short clap on the back. Dave basically took Christopher through the same motions, though I could feel the weight of his eyes on me, even when they seemed to be doing their best at avoiding me.

Aug came toward me, completely casual like he always seemed to be. "Hey, Jared." He stuck his hand out, and I took it. The hug he gave me was just as short as the one he gave Christopher. "How's it going, man? It's so cool you're here."

"Yeah, great to be here," I was quick to agree, although I wasn't exactly sure I did.

Besides, I felt like I was quickly wearing out my welcome.

Karen looked at her husband, tipping her head in an almost imperceptible nod toward me. No doubt, she'd told him I would be here. And by the way he warily turned his attention to me, I had no doubt she'd given him a warning to behave, same as she'd always done. The man was wrapped around Karen's finger just as tightly as I was wound around Aly's.

If I wasn't watching so closely, I would have missed the subtle search of his eyes, like he wanted nothing more than to inspect me in the same second he could barely look my direction. Ultimately that search landed on the back of my hands where the color bled out from under the cuffs of my shirt. The green of his eyes locked on the numbers stamped across my knuckles. He flinched when he caught onto the meaning, and he turned away just as fast as he'd latched onto the sight.

Reluctantly, he took a step forward and stretched out his arm to offer his hand. "Happy Thanksgiving, Jared. Glad you could join us."

I accepted it, my hold firm as I shook his hand. "Thank you for having me."

Why are you here and how long are you staying? All these questions played out on the lines twisting across his face.

It didn't take long for Dave to get his answer.

From just inside the foyer, Aly paused and looked back on us from where she was embracing her little brother. She stared at me with outright affection. Then she extended her hand, beckoning me to her side.

My eyes shot to Dave. I just couldn't help it. It was like I had this impulse to see his reaction when he realized why I was really here.

And fuck, did I wish I hadn't seen.

White blanched his face, before a rush of redness hit his cheeks. The hand that just seconds before had been shaking mine flexed into a fist. There was no question he was about as repulsed by the idea of Aly and me as I had been with myself the first night I'd fed from her beauty. When I gave in and slipped into the sanctuary of her arms, giving myself over to the fantasy.

But what Dave didn't realize was he was witnessing our reality.

This was the aftermath of all that sneaking. The outcome of all the hiding behind closed doors and all the lies that had been told.

This was what happened on the other side.

I stepped up and took Aly's hand. It was warm and fit perfectly into my palm.

Yeah, Dave was seeing that Aly really was mine.

Aly led me down the entryway hall that led deeper into the house. The entire place echoed with the memories of our childhood.

The hallway walls were proud with pictures, photos of all three kids and the family displayed exactly the way I remembered Karen had showcased the images, except there were some new ones that added even more honor and love to the story they told. Both Aly's and Christopher's smiles shined bright as they posed for their high school graduations, a ton of Aug's football pictures were put on display, and a family picture I could only assume was taken sometime around last Christmas took precedence among them all.

I was quick to drop my attention when I saw that we were still there, too—a fucking picture of the family I'd shattered was set on display right smack dab in the middle of the Moores' story. It was the same one that had taunted me at my mother's funeral, the one that had cast its insults at me as they'd laid her in the ground.

My pulse thundered and my pace slowed, and Aly was tugging at me like she *knew*, like she was removing me from what she knew I couldn't face.

When we passed through the curved archway into the kitchen, I realized not much of this house remained the same. It'd been remodeled, and only the main walls of the basic structure were unchanged.

A modern kitchen had taken the country kitchen's place. The bar we'd once sat at now was a large granite island with a row of low barstools taking up the end. A small table was still tucked in the bay window, but the windows were now larger and offered a better view of the backyard. Natural light shined in, reflecting off the pool, basking the entire space in the comfort of the fall sun. The wall that had blocked off the family room where we'd spent so much time hanging out had been gutted, making for one large room.

Still, it all felt so much the same, the same gentle warmth clinging to the walls.

And this smell . . . this fucking delicious smell that reminded me of the days we'd spent here. Us kids running around, clamoring through the cramped kitchen, our moms yelling at us to take it outside.

God, how much did I miss those simple days?

Aly glanced up at me. A wistful expression framed that gorgeous face. "I'm so glad you're here," she mouthed, like she somehow knew I was experiencing all of these emotions I didn't know how to process, a disorder of disgrace wrapped up with this fucking irrational feeling, something that felt like I'd somehow made it home after I'd been lost for so long.

But it was her.

I knew it.

It thrummed a steady beat within me. This girl had brought me home.

The one who had breathed life into a blackened spirit and a deadened heart.

Right behind us, Karen clapped her hands once. "Okay, we need to get busy in here. Dinner will be ready in about an hour, so things are about to get hectic."

Karen was wearing this granny apron that covered her whole front, and these tight little black ankle slacks and heels almost as high as the ones Aly had been wearing last night.

She'd always been a knockout, not that I'd ever thought of her that way, but damn, I wasn't blind.

All of mine and Christopher's friends were always calling, wanting to hang out at our houses because they wanted to get a look at our moms. Funny, 'cause it was kind of gross but kind of made us proud at the same time.

Aly released my hand and stepped toward the stove. "Just tell me what to do, Mom. That's what I'm here for."

Karen lifted a lid and poked at the boiling potatoes inside with a fork. "The green beans need to go into this pot here," she said, pitching her head to the side to gesture to it. "We can probably mash these potatoes in about twenty minutes, then we need to get the gravy going and the turkey out, and then we need to get the rolls in the oven." Her mom rattled this all off like she had the whole thing mapped out in her head, this organized chaos fueling her energy as she moved so easily about the kitchen.

"I'm on it," Aly said as she washed her hands in the sink and went to work.

"Anything I can do to help?" I offered, standing there with my jutted hip resting up against the counter. *Awkward* didn't quite describe what I was feeling. My emotions were in such conflict, I couldn't begin to describe them, this unrelenting distress that nagged at all my senses and this comfort I wanted to sink into.

"I think we have it under control for now, but all you boys

are on standby," Karen commanded with a wave of her hand, drawing a line in the air with her pointed finger indicating the end of the island, like we weren't allowed to step foot out of the kitchen's boundaries.

Aly tossed me a knowing glance, one that just said we should go with it, and everything would be fine.

Aug pulled out a barstool and sat down, and I figured I'd best to do the same.

Christopher clapped me on the back as he headed toward the refrigerator. "Hey, man, you want a beer?"

"Uh . . . sure."

If I wasn't feeling so damned uncomfortable, I might have laughed at being here this way, because the last time I'd had a beer at this house Christopher had snuck us a couple when we were fifteen.

It seemed crazy that so many years had passed. That so much had changed and still these people were completely the same.

Good.

Christopher opened the large, stainless steel door of the fridge. Disappearing behind it for a couple of seconds, he came out bearing two beers. He slid one my way.

"How about you, Dad? You want one?" he asked, twisting the cap free from his and tossing it across the room and into the garbage, completely nonchalant.

Appearing to be feeling just about as uneasy as me, Dave hesitated.

Couldn't blame him all that much. I kept thinking Aly should have warned him, given him some kind of indication of what to anticipate. Poor guy didn't deserve this double blow.

If our roles were reversed?

I couldn't help but imagine the baby, what it would be like, if it'd be a little girl or a boy. If it were a girl, this kind of bullshit would definitely not fly.

I wouldn't stand for it.

Not my little girl.

Not a chance.

I twisted the cap from my beer and drained half of it, fucking overcome by the thought, because I hadn't truly allowed my mind to go there. Those thoughts had always been an impression of what seemed an impossibility.

I looked up to meet Dave Moore's face. Blatant distrust saturated every inch of his expression. He was graying now, just a hint around his ears and at the back of his neck. But he was a whole lot like Karen, looking so much younger than he actually was.

"Yeah, sure, son," he said, keeping his attention trained on me, this slow simmer of anger burning somewhere in the depths of his eyes.

Christopher passed his dad a beer before he plopped down in the stool next to me and ran a hand through his unruly hair. Would have thought he'd have attempted to tame it for today. Dude was such a slob, but he was just acting like himself, and I realized that's just the way he was. There wasn't a whole lot of pretense obscuring what was happening inside of him.

Had to respect him for that.

Christopher tipped his beer to his mouth and took a long pull, smacked his lips, a clash of glass and granite as he set the bottle down too hard on the bar. "Damn, Mom, I have to admit, that turkey smells delicious."

Karen smiled a little. "You think so? I hope it turns out well. . . . That thing has been sitting in brine all night. I researched about ten different recipes."

"Oh yeah, for sure. So much better than the turkey we had

when we were ten," he pressed on, slanting a knowing eye in my direction.

I sputtered over my beer and swiped the back of my hand over my mouth, trying not to bust up laughing, but that had to have been about the worst damned dinner I'd ever eaten.

Should have known from the tone of Christopher's voice he was getting ready to razz his mom. That'd always been one of his favorite pastimes, messing with her, because she was just so unsuspecting.

Offense stopped Karen midstride. Her eyes narrowed when she set them on her oldest son. But the frown carved on her face fluttered with amusement, like she was about three seconds from busting up at the memory, too.

"I have absolutely no recollection of that," she finally answered in defiance, lifting her chin as she finished her pass from the oven to the island. Metal clattered as she picked up her whisk and began whipping something in a large silver bowl.

"No . . . no . . . I'm sure you don't remember that Thanksgiving at all," he prodded, ribbing her more. "I'd have wiped that from my memory, too, if I'd tried to cook a completely frozen turkey."

Aly flicked a bean at Christopher's head. "You're such a jerk. You leave *my* mom alone." She punctuated her words by widening those expressive, green eyes.

Christopher exhaled an offended breath. "Are you kidding me, Aly Cat? First you're taking sides with this ass over here . . ." He hooked his thumb in my direction. ". . . and now you're gonna turn against me when we're talking about Mom's cooking when we both know how terrible it is?" He placed his hand over his heart. "You wound me."

Aly waved her knife. "Yeah, I'm going to wound you if you don't leave *my* mom alone." It was all tease and affection, the two of them always at each other's throats in the moments they weren't having the other's back.

Aly smiled at me, all cute and sly, and I couldn't help but smile back. Because it'd always been like this here. Casual, easy, safe.

Somehow both frenzied and fluid, Aly and Karen moved about the kitchen, as if they were enjoying every second of creating this meal together.

"Hey, Mom," Christopher called, "looks like you have a little issue over there. Not that I'm surprised or anything." He laughed as Karen flew around from what she was whisking on the bar to find the pot of potatoes boiling over. A tower of steaming water bubbled up from under the lid, racing down the side of the pot and hissing as it splashed onto the stove.

"Oh my God," she said. She grabbed a potholder and yanked off the lid. She quickly stirred it, mumbling profanities under her breath, all of them directed at Christopher.

Her son cocked a sarcastic brow. "You sure you have that under control over there? Because it definitely doesn't look that way to me. The whole kitchen looks like a war zone."

Karen's grin was wide and mocking. "Oh no, my sweet boy, I'm sure everything's fine. Because you'll be the one doing dishes."

Christopher floundered at that. "Ahh ... shit, Mom, I was just playing around, and now you're going to go and punish me?"

"Um, yeah, I am, because you deserve it. And watch your mouth before I wash it out with soap," she scolded, pointing her spoon at Christopher.

Middrink, I cracked up, because Karen was just really fucking cool. When Christopher punched me in the shoulder, I spit out the mouthful of beer I was trying to hold in. I was doing my best to cover it all up with my hand, but I couldn't stop myself from laughing, couldn't stop myself from feeling like I wanted to *stay*.

I caught Aly's eye from where she was rinsing off the green beans at the sink. A hint of a smile played at her mouth, something that said *I told you so* and *Things are going to be just fine*.

But her eyes said so much more. They were welcoming me home.

Guarded, Dave watched the whole scene from where he rested back against the far counter. Really, he was just watching me, maybe warning me.

I dropped my gaze, dreading what was in store. Because if he couldn't accept me now, he sure as hell wouldn't accept me when he found out what was coming.

Close to an hour later, we all gathered at the table, Aly and I wedged on the inside near the windows, Christopher to my left at the end, and Aug directly across from me. Karen sat across from Aly, and Dave sat at the head in between her and Aly.

Maybe Karen had screwed up dinner twelve years ago, but she sure as hell had perfected it since. A moan rumbled somewhere deep in my chest when I took my first bite. "This dinner is unbelievable, Karen," I said, not because I was kissing her ass but because it really was true.

A chorus of agreement rose up at the table.

An appreciative smile kissed her mouth, and she lifted her wineglass to me. "I'm just thankful you're here to share it with us."

"Thank you." My voice came rough and quiet, but I really meant it, too.

Because God, it felt amazing sitting here. Sharing this with Aly. With her family.

Being with her.

I searched for her hand under the table and pulled it onto my lap, because I just wanted to feel her. Warmth sped through my veins, lighting a fire in my stomach and in my mind because as I sat there, I couldn't stop myself from dreaming of what could be.

Through the large windows behind us, the sun began to sink toward the horizon, the early evening encroaching as the day slowly slipped away. It dimmed the room and thickened the mood, that same joy that sat so prominent on Aly's face hours before now radiating from her entire body.

Conversation was light and the banter was high, like it had always been at the Moores', though Dave had said few words the entire day. I knew Aly felt the tension from her father, but this girl just chose to enjoy the day that we had, forging on with the celebration like she'd promised when we left her room this morning.

It's what mattered to her, so I made the choice for it to matter to me, too.

I just ate and enjoyed and forced down all the worries plaguing me.

Christopher chewed, swallowing before he spoke. "So, Aug, I hear the big game is coming up in a couple of weeks?"

Aug's face lit up. "Yep, two weeks from tomorrow. Can't believe we made it to State. It's going to be a tough game, but I think we have a really good shot at winning the championship."

"Proud of you, man," Christopher said, lifting his chin in his younger brother's direction. "You led them to it."

"Thanks, Christopher." Augustyn's attention bounced around the table. "You all are coming, aren't you?"

"I wouldn't miss it," Christopher immediately said.

Aug gestured to me. "What about you?"

"Of course." It fell from my mouth without hesitation. No question, Aly would want to be there. Her little brother was the star quarterback, and this was going to be the biggest game of his life—so far, at least. And shit, I hadn't gotten the chance to know him all that well, and I was happy to sign up for something that made the kid happy.

A crash of metal and glass halted the easy conversation. All eyes darted to the end of the table, where Dave had thrown his fork to his plate. He pushed his chair back from the table. "Goddamn it." His voice resonated as a low growl when he muttered the words, just loud enough for the table to hear.

The man stared back at me with unmitigated hate.

"Dave," Karen whispered urgently. Outright worry creased her forehead.

"What?" he shot back, unfazed, his anger escalating. "You want me to just continue sitting here, pretending like I shouldn't be concerned with what's happening?" His glare made a pass over me and Aly before he jerked it back to his wife. "Because it's pretty damn clear I'm the only person sitting at this table who is taken by surprise that there's something going on with these two, and I don't exactly appreciate being made the fool."

"Dad, no one is trying to make you out to be a fool," Aly said, her tone almost pleading as she leaned toward him.

Hurt knitted up his brow. "Then what are you trying to do, Aly? Because I'm sitting here feeling like the brunt of a sick joke."

Sick joke.

Guess Dave didn't feel like keeping up pretenses, either.

To my left, Christopher stood, stripped of the easiness he always wore. "Come on, Aug, let's go shoot some hoops out back, give these guys a minute to talk."

Aug seemed reluctant. His gaze slid over the mess of faces, over the worry on his mother and the sadness on his sister. It finally settled on the hostility emanating from his father. Slowly he stood. "Yeah," he said awkwardly, "would be good to burn off some of this dinner." He placed a hand on Karen's shoulder and kissed her on top of the head. "Dinner was great, Mom. Thank you."

Silently, she nodded and patted his hand before they turned to leave.

We listened to their footsteps retreat, like they were a silent marker, a bell.

Fire struck in Dave's eyes as he leveled them on me before he set them on Aly. Waiting.

Waiting on an explanation I knew he was going to be none too happy to receive.

Closing her eyes, Aly tightened her fingers on mine where our hands were still clasped on my lap, like she was looking for some kind of strength from me. I squeezed her back, ran my thumb over the back of her hand, not knowing what to say, not knowing how to take this away from her. Because no matter what, I knew this conversation was not going to go well.

Finally, she lifted her face back to Dave. "Dad, I'm sorry. It was never like that. I knew we needed to talk, but I wanted to wait until after dinner. I just wanted us to enjoy the holiday. Enjoy dinner and our family."

"Enjoy dinner?" he asked, incredulous. "This has been about the least enjoyable dinner I've ever had. Your mom tells me Jared is coming to dinner yesterday, but she doesn't say a word about the two of you, instead making it seem like he's in town visiting. Sure doesn't look that way to me. How long has this been going on?"

I gritted my teeth, because he was sitting there talking down to my girl, like she was some ignorant child who had no idea what she was doing. But I saw it in his eyes. Concern. So I swallowed it down, holding in the shiver of nerves that tingled through my limbs, the adrenaline spike I knew so well.

Fuck.

Almost apologetically, Aly glanced at me. Unshed tears blurred her eyes. "This summer—"

"What?" The mention of months gone by had Dave cutting her off before she even had a chance to start. He leaned forward in his seat. Obviously that bit of information pissed him off. His shoulders bunched up like he was trying to contain his own aggression.

"Let her talk, Dave," Karen demanded, low, almost as intense as what had shot from her husband's mouth.

A burdened breath seeped from Aly, and she chewed at her lip, like she was gauging the best way to lay this on her dad.

When I was a kid, I'd always thought Dave was a good guy. But even back then, I'd always been a little fearful of him. He'd never let anything get in the way of protecting his family, and he'd be damned if he let Christopher and me play him in any way.

Keen. Quick to judge.

And that was the thing—he'd cast his judgment on me years ago, and there was nothing Aly or I could say that would sway it.

We just were getting ready to seal it.

"At the beginning of this past summer," she continued, her nails cutting into my skin, "Christopher ran into Jared. Jared ended up staying with us for a few months . . . and he and I . . ." Aly trailed off. Suggestion colored the words. Clearly, she wasn't going to fill her dad in on all the little details she didn't exactly relish elaborating on.

Thank God for that, because I was already sitting there fucking squirming on the hard, wooden chair, feeling all those eyes boring into me, searching for my intent.

The fucked-up thing was Karen looked like she wanted to squeeze me in her arms until I couldn't breathe, and Dave just looked like he wanted to squeeze the life out of me.

Couldn't blame him.

He knew it, saw it written all over me. He knew I'd been buried in his daughter, feasting on every ounce of pleasure that this girl could bring me.

But what he didn't know was how it made me feel, what *she* made me feel. He had no clue that this wasn't just some game I was playing with her.

He had no idea how Aly had changed me. Despite all the hate I harbored inside, this girl still managed to make me love her. She'd poured so much of it into me there was no chance I wouldn't feel it back.

"What do you mean *for a few months*?" Dave frowned, putting the fragmented pieces together, trying to make it all add up, because the guy wasn't stupid and he knew he didn't have the full story.

A soft sigh flowed from Karen as she watched Aly with sympathy, because she knew all about the pain I'd brought down on her daughter. But really, she didn't know the half of it. She didn't know how badly Aly had been hurting, how scared she'd been while I'd been away.

"He stayed with us for a few months. Some things happened and he left."

"He left." It was a statement. Dave Moore had just found his sum.

Frustration and hope tumbled from Aly in a flood of words, and she leaned across the table, flattened her hand against it in front of him, trying to create some kind of connection with him, imploring with him to listen. "Dad, I know you can't understand all of this, or maybe you just might not want to, but things happened between me and Jared that he wasn't ready to deal with. And, yes, I was hurt when he was away." Honesty poured from her. "But he came *back* to me. For good. We're together and we're going to be."

She said it like it was the simplest thing in the world when everything between us had always been so complicated, every emotion that flushed through my body complex, the joy hinging on the hate, this reckless balance that could so easily tip and spin us out of control.

But I wasn't going to let it.

As if he knew it, Dave watched me, like he could somehow see through me, inside me, deep into the darkness that possessed so much of my blackened spirit. And I knew it scared him because he was scared for his daughter, and it was the exact same shit that scared me, too.

"So that's it . . . he's just here and you're together?" Dave shrugged like it didn't matter all that much, but there was no mistaking the rage boiling his blood. "And I guess it's safe to assume he's back at the apartment with you and Christopher."

Slowly, Aly nodded, carefully wetting her lips, buying time. Dread radiated from her pores, panic thick as it locked up her throat. She fought to get the words through. "Yes, he's staying with us. But no, that's not all." Her voice cracked on the last word.

Everyone stilled. A dense silence thickened in the stagnant air.

Dave stared at me with unfaltering hate while Aly dropped her attention to her lap, like she could find the courage bundled there. "Jared and I . . ." Determined, Aly lifted her face. Her eyes darted between her parents. "We're going to have a baby."

Every nerve in my body lit in searing pain and gutting shame, because I was never supposed to be allowed this. It was followed by a flood of all the love I felt for this girl and this insane sense of pride.

Fidgeting, I raked my free hand though my hair as I clung to Aly's with the other. I searched for something to say to cover up this fucking insufferable stillness that had taken over the room.

But no one said anything. They were just staring, wide-eyed and in shock. Both of them. That stagnant air suddenly dropped, strangling us like a fucking noose as Aly and I tried to breathe around all this bullshit and judgment.

Then that silence came crashing down.

Dave shot to his feet and threw his plate across the room. China shattered as it hit the far wall. It rained down, and pieces scattered across the tile floor.

Aly cringed, her shoulders coming up. She turned her face toward me, ducking from her father's reaction.

Karen Moore started to quietly cry.

I rocked in my chair, that warning system blaring in my ear, screaming at me to get my shit and go.

Motherfucker.

And Aly was just sitting there, tears streaming down her face.

All I wanted to do was grab her, wrap her up in my arms, and get the hell out of there.

Fight or flight.

I was really fucking good at both of them.

But fighting with her dad seemed like a really bad idea.

And I knew I wasn't going anywhere.

Dave pressed his hands into the table as he glared at me. "How dare you come here ... into my house ... after you did this? I told you years ago you weren't welcome here, and here you sit with that smug look on your face."

Aggression stirred, simmered in that place where hostility and anger always seethed and smoldered inside of me. Unstoppable, my hands curled into fists. Adrenaline pumped like fire through my veins, the malice from within my blackened soul spurring me forward, urgent as it begged for release.

I couldn't stop it, couldn't control it, and I pushed to my feet. My jaw clenched, the sound of my teeth grating in my ears as I tried to contain it, hold it back.

Because this was Aly's dad who was staring me down, getting all up in my face. I knew he was just trying to protect his daughter from what he saw as a threat.

The same threat I'd been trying to protect her from for all those months I was hiding away in her apartment.

And was that threat any less real now?

I gripped the back of my head, doing all I could to try to calm myself, to hold in the rage that built and spread.

The thing that pissed me off the most was there was no self-satisfaction, nothing smug about what was playing out on my face. Yeah, there was pride, but that pride was all wrapped up in this amazing girl who'd shaken my world.

I tried to get control of my thoughts, to put them into words, because Dave Moore thought he had me pegged. "You have no clue how I feel about this . . . how I feel about Aly."

Disbelieving laughter rocked from him. "Do you think I care about how you feel? What I care about is my daughter."

Aly pushed up to my side. "I'm not a little girl, Dad. . . . You know that. And I know you're disappointed, but this is what I want."

"This is what you want?" he spat at her. "You want to ruin your life? Have you even thought this through? You've worked so hard, getting accepted into nursing school, and now you're going to settle for this?"

Aly recoiled, leaning back as if she needed to put space between them. "You think I'm settling?" Sadness flooded her admission. "I never even wanted to be a nurse . . . tell me when you ever heard me dreaming of that, Dad? *When?* Deciding to go to nursing school was *settling.* Do you even know anything about me?"

Remorse flashed across his face and mixed with the anger. "Of course I know you."

Aly's voice trembled. "You obviously know very little about me if you think a child is going to ruin my life."

"I'm not worried about you wasting your life having a child, Aly. I'm worried about you wasting your life with him. He destroyed his family. Don't let him destroy yours, too."

The words speared me, the sharpest possible knife driven straight into my soul, splitting me wide.

Pain seized my heart.

I destroy everything I touch.

Voices and faces and memories pressed in too close, clouding my mind. Bitterness roiled. I stumbled back.

Aly gasped. "Oh my God. Jared."

I pushed around the table, all this fucked-up world too much for me to take.

Aly scrambled over the chairs, trying to get to me, her face all pleading and filled with the fear I knew she harbored inside, the one that told her one day I would leave.

"Jared," she whispered.

Karen stared wide-eyed at me, sadness swimming in her eyes, while Dave glared at me like the piece of shit I was.

"Just need some air," I forced out because I couldn't walk out of this house with Aly thinking I was walking out on her.

Rapidly Aly blinked, stepping away, giving me space.

Because this girl knew me.

I rushed out of the house and into the night. Cold air clashed against my heated cheeks, and I gripped my hair in my fists.

"Fuck!" I roared.

I stalked up the sidewalk, struggling to draw a breath into my constricted lungs, trying to forget the words that had just been spoken inside.

Because in them, I knew the truth. I knew what Dave Moore saw because I saw it in myself.

I froze when I lifted my head and caught sight of the little house that harbored so many memories.

Images of *her* face beat against my consciousness. Conflict ate me alive, tearing me down and at the same time building me up.

I hated it, knowing how those walls once held her presence, how she'd lived and breathed in them, filled them with laughter and joy and the warmth of her love.

Tonight darkness blanketed the face of the little house. It screamed of emptiness, of a hollowed-out vacancy that could never be filled.

I hated it, knowing I'd destroyed it.

Hated knowing I'd destroyed her.

That I'd destroyed beauty.

And now again I held beauty in my hands, and I didn't know how I was supposed to handle it. How did I protect something so fragile. What if I broke her?

But I knew in my gut that walking away from Aly *would* break her.

As if I ever could, even if I tried.

Because there was no walking away from her.

Not now.

Not ever.

EIGHT

November 1995

"*Jared, where are you?*" *Christopher bellowed from down the hall.*

Jared ran on his toes through the small family room of his house, keeping his footsteps light. No way was he gonna let Christopher find him.

He slipped into the kitchen. Steam spilled from the pots on the stove, and the smell of heaven filled his nose.

His stomach growled, but his mom, Helene, told him it was still going to be a couple of hours before they ate. She'd offered him a snack, but he wasn't going to waste any room because he was saving it all up for pumpkin pie. It was his favorite, especially when his mom let him put on his own whipped cream.

He tried not to make any noise when he maneuvered around the butcher block island that sat right in the middle of the kitchen.

Both his mom and Karen stood around it, talking and laughing while they chopped and prepared, just like they always did. Jared's mom's belly was big and round, like a ball. It looked so funny, but his baby sister was in there. He was getting her for Christmas, at least that's what his mom told him, but he wasn't so sure that's what he really wanted.

"No fair, Jared!" Jared heard Christopher shout from somewhere in the living room over the roaring noise of the football game their dads were watching on the television. "I've been looking forever. It's your turn to hide."

Jared snickered. Christopher had it comin'. He was always cheating and Jared was determined he was gonna win this time.

Listening to Christopher's footsteps approach, Jared got onto his hands and knees and scrambled to the other side of the island. He hid in the long sway of his mother's skirt.

Christopher burst into the kitchen. "You seen Jared in here?" he asked. Jared peered through the baskets and bags piled under the island. Red sneakers peeked out from just the other side. Christopher shifted his feet.

"Nope . . . he must have disappeared," Karen teased. Jared held in his laughter when Christopher turned away and opened the pantry door, sticking his head inside. "You in here, Jared?"

Jared's mom sneaked him a playful glance before she looked back at Christopher. "Well, I bet he's around here somewhere. You're just going to have to keep looking," she encouraged, her face all soft and caring.

Jared's belly felt warm as he rested against her leg.

He loved the smell of the turkey in the oven, but he loved the way his mom smelled best.

Soft fingers fluttered in his hair, and Jared leaned into them. His mom was the best person in the world. He was sure of it.

Christopher took off through the archway, running toward the back of the house.

"Whatcha doin'?" The little voice beside him made Jared jump. He fumbled back and met the wide eyes of the tiny girl crouched beside

him. *Her face was all round, her cheeks as chubby as her little fingers. He should tell her to shoo, to get away before she gave him away and her brother found him, but Jared liked her best, too.*

He lifted his index finger to his pursed lips, pushed out a low, "Shh. I'm hiding from your brother."

Her green eyes grew round with delight as she caught on to the game. Aly grinned, showing off her tiny teeth. "I wanna play with you, Jed."

She always said his name wrong too, but that didn't make him mad, either. She was only three, and all her words came out funny.

Softly he wound her hand in his. "Okay, but you have to be super quiet."

She nodded vigorously, stringy locks of dark hair flying.

Jared got to his feet and tugged at her hand. "Come on, Aly Cat."

Aly giggled, scrambling to keep up with him as he led her by the hand.

And Jared liked the way it sounded, like the softest song, just like his mom sang to him at night.

NINE

Aleena

I watched in horror as Jared escaped out of my parents' house. Every part of me wanted to run after him, but I knew he needed his space. He needed time to process what had just occurred.

The door slammed behind him.

A charged silence took over the room.

Slowly, I turned back to my parents. Trembling, my mom climbed to her feet. I knew she'd been shocked into silence, her own disappointment and worry so clear. But above it all, I could feel her compassion. Her worry for Jared was just as thick as mine.

I took a single step toward my dad, who still stood there glowering over the table. Although maybe it was he who now appeared smug, like he was satisfied with the outcome.

I was so angry I wanted to pound it off of his face.

"How could you?" I whispered, taking another step toward him. "How could you say something like that?"

"Aly . . ." My name was uttered like a harsh appeal, like he was trying to get through to me, to make me see.

But it was my father who was blind.

"I just want what's best for you. Don't you know that? That's all I've ever wanted it." It was said as if it could excuse him from what he'd just done, from the pain he'd inflicted.

I glanced away, at the floor, wetting my lips before I forced myself to look back at him. "I can't believe you could be so cruel." Disappointment rushed from me in the quiet accusation.

He flinched.

I stumbled over the emotion in my throat, feeling those tears I couldn't hold in earlier resurfacing. Because I knew they'd be disappointed, that they'd envisioned a different path for my life, and I could accept that. But I wouldn't stand for him treating Jared this way.

"Maybe I let you down, Dad, and you can be angry over that. I get it." I placed my hand on my stomach. "I didn't expect this, either, and there were some nights when I didn't know how I would handle this all. But this is what *I* want. Jared is what *I* want. I love him. He is a good man, and what you just said to him . . . I don't think you have any clue how much you hurt him."

"Aly, that kid has never cared about anyone but himself."

I pounded my fist at my side, every cell in my body straining for control. "You are so wrong."

"What happens when you find out I'm right?"

I backed away, unable to grasp my father's reaction, the spite that bled from his mouth.

"Aly," he begged, starting around the table, "sweetheart, I'm just protecting my family."

Putting my hand out in front of me to stop him, I swallowed hard. "And I'm just protecting mine."

Unwilling to stand in his presence any longer, I turned and headed for the door.

In the hall, footsteps clamored behind me. "Aly, wait." Tears coated my mother's plea as she jerked at my arm.

I spun around.

When she pulled me into her arms, I burst into tears. I couldn't hold them in any longer because I was so angry and so *sad*. What had been said couldn't be taken back, and those were the exact words that Jared definitely did not need to hear.

"Oh, baby, I'm so sorry," she murmured at my head.

"I can't believe he'd do that . . . say something like that," I mumbled into the fabric of her shirt.

Gently, she ran an errant lock of my hair between two fingers, her voice low and sincere. "He just loves you . . . he doesn't know how to see anything else."

The conversation blinked through my mind, the hardened expression he'd worn so pronounced on his face. "That doesn't make it okay."

"No, it definitely does not. But I know your father very well and all of that came from fear."

I struggled to force down all the resentment and see that, because I knew it was the truth.

But I also knew it didn't make it right.

She edged back, holding me by the upper arms as she explored my face. "Are you okay?"

She was asking about so much more than the outburst that just played out in the dining room.

I blinked through my blurry vision. "Yeah, I think I am."

Tumult tripped across her features, played in her eyes. "God, Aly, when you were here last week, I knew you were hurting so badly, but I had no idea how much you were dealing with. How could I not have known?"

"Mom, you can't blame yourself for any of this." Remorse coursed through the words that scraped from my throat.

Compassionate brown eyes searched me, and a jolt of shame worked its way through me because my mother had never been anything but supportive. "I should have told you . . . I should have told you a lot of things. I kept my feelings for Jared a secret my entire life, and there was no reason for me to continue doing it. I just didn't know how to tell you . . . especially when I was still trying to figure out how I was going to manage all of this by myself. It wasn't because I was ashamed or because I didn't trust you with knowing about it, it was because I didn't have any answers. I didn't know how I was going to do this alone."

"Sweetheart . . ." Her brow pinched in emphasis. ". . . you don't ever need all the answers to talk to me . . . or to live your life, for that matter. A whole lot of it we have to figure out along the way. But no matter what, I am always here for you. I don't want you to ever think I'm not here for you or that I would ever judge you."

A wistful smile arched her mouth. "Probably should have mentioned that a little earlier in your life, huh?"

"Mom . . ." Regret shook my head. "I've always known that. None of us knew how to handle Jared . . . how to handle what happened."

A knot traveled up Mom's throat as she swallowed, and she inclined her head, her eyes narrowing as if she were trying to see inside me. "Are you happy, Aly? *Really happy?* Is this really what you want? You want to start a family with him?"

"Yes." I said it without hesitation because it was the truth. "I've loved him my whole life, Mom. And no, we haven't worked out all the details." There were so many things we needed to decide, to figure out because so much had changed in such a short time. In my mom's tone, I heard so many of those questions, how would I continue with school, would we get married, how would we manage? There were so many things I wanted, to call Jared my husband, to be a normal family with him. But I knew he needed time and needed to adjust to this new life.

"But we are going to make this work." That was the one thing I knew. Nothing else mattered.

Her smile was soft, knowing, and she reached out to push back the lock of hair stuck to my cheek. "I know you will." She laughed a small laugh. "Can't believe you're going to make me a grandma."

Fidgeting, I looked to the wall covered in pictures of the past, across the faces of the people I loved. There was a tiny snapshot, the color faded with age, Christopher and Jared and me with mud smeared all over our faces, grinning at the camera. There was so much joy there . . . and I'd found that joy again.

I turned back to her. "I know things aren't always going to be easy with him. But he's worth it."

"Then that's all that matters." She stepped back, wiping under her eyes and sniffling. She tipped her head toward the door. "Go and get him, Aly. He shouldn't be out there by himself."

"Thank you, Mom."

I started toward the door, and she reached out and stopped me. Over my shoulder, I looked at her. Lines deepened on her forehead and the words dropped in a quick whisper. "I love him, too, Aly. I want you to know that. No matter what has been said, he has and will always be a part of this family."

Thankfulness thudded my heart. And I just nodded, my small smile saying everything that both of us wanted to say.

I slipped out the door. Night had chased away the muted warmth of the November sun, and a chill pebbled on my arms as I stepped out into the darkness. I crossed my arms across my chest to block out the cold. Quietly I edged down the sidewalk leading away from my parents' front door.

The night was heavy and quiet. A gentle breeze whistled through the trees. Branches rustled, creaked as they brushed against the side of the house.

My footsteps were light as I walked down the driveway and past my car, to the sidewalk lining the street.

To the left, he was there, slouching where he leaned his lower back against the top of the short, wooden plank railing fence that edged the boundary of the neighbor's yard next to my parents'.

Directly across from his old house.

His long legs were stretched out in front of him with his feet planted on the ground. Staring ahead, he lifted a half-spent cigarette to his mouth. The red glowed bright as he drew it in. His hand fell to his side, twitching, his head dropping toward the ground in the same movement. Seconds passed before he turned his face to the night sky. Smoke curled above his head as he slowly blew it out. He seemed to watch it dissolve into nothing as it floated away.

Sadness poured from him.

God, I hated seeing him this way.

Cautiously, I slipped forward, never looking away from him as I approached. I wrapped myself around his back. Pressing my face into his spine, I fastened my hands around his stomach. The wooden fence bit against my thighs as I flattened myself to this beautiful man.

I wanted to sink into him, to search for all the guilt and shame inside him. Rid him of it.

Because when he fled from my parents' house, it was the only thing I could see.

Jared released a weighted breath. He dropped his cigarette to the ground and toed it out. For the longest time, silence took us over. We swam in it. Tension thickened in the crisp fall air.

I knew he was hurt. Those words had cut him deep. I wanted to shield him from them, protect him, but this was just another obstacle we had to face. All I could do was support him, hold him the way I was now, my touch a promise that I didn't believe the accusations my father had spewed.

Finally, he spoke, the words a strained groan. "Fuck, Aly." Harshly, he shook his head. It seemed in surrender. "I knew I shouldn't come here. I don't belong here. Your dad is right." He slumped farther forward in a blatant attempt to move away. "Every fucking word of it . . . he's right."

His pain pushed into my spirit, and I wound my arms tighter around him, unwilling to allow him to drive any distance between us. The words came as a muted whisper as I begged at his back, "No, he's not. He doesn't know you, not the way I do. He's just surprised." I blinked into the darkness, trying to make sense of what had just gone down inside. "Shocked," I added. "There's a big difference."

Even though my voice lowered, my tone strengthened. "And even if he really believed what he said, it doesn't change anything." I hugged him closer, my cheek pressed flat against his shoulder blade. "Do you remember what I told you the night you came back? I love *all* of it, Jared. I love *all* of you. And what I think is what's important, not him or anyone else. It's just you and me. Nothing else matters."

Jared brought both his hands over mine that were clasped in his shirt, and we fell back into silence.

I didn't say anything, because I could feel it bubbling inside of him, a swelling of thoughts and emotions brimming at the surface. Fighting for release.

Plastering myself to his back, I hugged him closer. Stood *behind* him. Holding him. Giving him whatever support I could.

A palpable tremor rolled through him. "How long have they been gone?" The words came on a stuttered breath, on all the pain it took him to force the question from his mouth. Immediately I knew he was asking about his father and his sister.

I didn't know how I managed to pull him closer, but I did. "Jared," I said, wavering on what to say because this was something I didn't know, something I hadn't even really considered because it'd happened so long ago. But Jared had been estranged from his family for longer. "Did you . . ." I chanced through a whisper, "Did you know about your grandma?"

Jared gripped my hands harder. "Yeah," he said, sorrow weaving through his tone. I felt him quake before he continued to speak. "They brought me in to see this social-worker lady when I was in juvie . . . I'd been in there a long time . . . I don't know . . . like a year and a half or something. Had been in another fight the day before and I figured I'd done it that time and they were finally going to give me a real punishment, send me away for good, but instead she sat me down and told me my grandma was gone. Said she could arrange to get me to the funeral." His voice cracked. "Fuck." He ran a shaky hand through his hair. "I just couldn't go, Aly. I couldn't. I didn't belong there, either."

A sob thickened in my throat. Jared had been through so much. Lost so much.

I pushed around the sorrow. "It happened during the second summer you were gone. Your sister had been living with your grandparents after the accident, but when your grandma passed, your grandpa brought your sister back here to your dad. I guess he didn't think he could take care of her without your grandma.

Two days later, the house was for sale. They moved about a month later."

I could hear him gritting his teeth, like he could grind away the panic that came with talking about his family. "You know where they went?"

I shook my head against his back. "No. He still didn't have much to do with my parents. He promised my mom he'd be in contact, but he never was."

Remorse tightened Jared's voice. "I haven't seen my sister since she was nine." He looked away, his head bobbing like he was calculating. "God . . . she has to be like fifteen now."

Terror filled me with the assertion I had to make, but I was more terrified of what would happen if I didn't voice it. "Jared, you *need* to find your father."

My gut burned with this truth. Jared needed to face his father, face the *past*, if he was ever going to heal.

"No." The word came harsh and fierce, with a brute force that knocked loose the breath in my lungs. He squeezed my hands like he was trying to soften the blow. "No, Aly," he said again through a ragged murmur. "I told you before, I ruined his life. Not going back there. What's done is done."

"Jared, I—"

His hands clamped down on mine. "Please . . . Aly . . . you need to let it go. For me, I need you to let it go."

"Okay," I said with the greatest reluctance, because nothing inside me agreed. Ultimately Jared would have to face his family. I knew it.

I thought maybe he did, too. He just wasn't ready yet.

A heavy sigh puffed from his lips, before he slowly turned around to face me. Chills rushed through my body when he set his cold palm on my face. I leaned into it, welcomed the freezing burn.

"I'm sorry, Aly," he whispered, running his thumb under my eye.

"What are you apologizing for?"

"For being me . . . for not being better for you. You deserve someone you can bring home without it ending in a war zone in your house."

"You are the *best* thing for me." There was no being *better*. "Remember it's just you and me. Nothing else matters."

His strong hand spread out against my still flat belly where our child grew. Blue eyes flamed when they locked on mine. "Just you and me and *this*."

Everything softened, the tension, the worry, the shame that had seethed through his veins.

It was Jared's own promise. An oath.

We wouldn't let any of this stand in our way.

"Just you and me and *this*," I promised back.

Jared glanced toward my parents' house, before he settled the questions on his face on me. "What you said back there . . . about being a nurse. Were you serious about that?"

"Yeah."

He frowned. "You never wanted it?" he asked again. Confusion tipped his head to the side.

I shook my head. "No. I mean, it'll be a good job, it's just not what I really want."

"Then what do you want?"

Redness rushed to my cheeks as embarrassment set in, and I dropped my forehead to his chest to hide my face. "It's stupid," I mumbled.

He ran his hands up and down my arms, warming me up, inside and out. "Baby, nothing you say could possibly be stupid."

My face was still buried in his shirt when I let the admission bleed out. "I want to draw." I almost choked over it. And I hated it, wanting something so desperately and knowing it was an impossibility, a foolish idea floundering through my mind. One that had been there since I was a child.

I almost wished I could take the statement back.

Jared didn't say anything. He just kept rubbing his hands up and down my arms.

I chanced peeking up at him. "See, it's stupid, right?"

His expression was tender, his voice just as soft. "No, Aly, it's not stupid. Not at all."

In thought, he glanced away, before he brought his attention back to me. "We should get our own place, yeah?"

An unexpected thrill raced through me. I chewed at my lip, trying to contain it. I probably shouldn't be so excited over the prospect, but I was. The thought of Jared and me having our own place, sharing our lives. Growing it. Well, I couldn't think of anything more appealing.

A blush crept to my face when I thought of what we'd get to do with all that privacy.

I fiddled with a button on his shirt. "Before you came back, I was thinking I needed to get my own apartment or something. I figured a baby running around the apartment might put a cramp in Christopher's style."

Jared chuckled, pulling me closer to keep me warm, wrapping his strong arms fully around me. "Oh, I'm sure that asshole would find a way to use it to his advantage, sucker in a few more girls with a cute little baby."

I couldn't help my laughter. "Yeah, he probably would, wouldn't he?" Sobering, I splayed my hand across Jared's firm chest. "But I like that idea . . . like, a lot."

Jared nuzzled his face into mine. "That's good . . . because I think I really like the idea, too."

And I was grinning, loving everything about this man. How could I not?

Stepping back, I took both his hands in mine. "Come on. Let's go back inside. Warm up and get a piece of pumpkin pie. I know it's your favorite."

He pulled away. The grimace that lined his face was full of regret. "I'm sorry, Aly, but I'm not going back in there. Your dad doesn't want me here and I can at least give him that amount of respect."

Sometimes Jared shocked me with how truly good he was inside. The amazing man hiding beneath all that shame. One day he would see it. He had to. Jared needed to see himself the way I saw him.

Of course, my father's hatred didn't help things.

And it really sucked that it had to be this way, but for the time being, I could accept that it was. My father was my father. I couldn't change him, sway what he saw. He was the one who was missing out, the one shutting Jared and me and our baby out of his life.

I pushed off the heaviness that weighed in the air and on our chests. "I think I have a much better idea, anyway," I said with a smile touching one side of my mouth.

Jared smirked, and a salacious grin spread across his face. "Oh, you do, huh? And just what would that be?" Suggestion rode on his voice, his fingertips flicking up to brush along the bare skin exposed over the neckline of my dress.

"You'll see." A tease filled my words. Jared was so obvious. And I was thinking *Not a chance,* because it was really stinking cold out. This boy was just going to have to wait until we got home.

I gathered his hand and lifted it high, leading him down the length of the short fence to its end at the Schmidt's driveway. As soon as we were free of the barrier separating us, I tugged him behind me, running ahead. I dragged him up the sidewalk to the old rickety fence backing the neighborhood.

Over my shoulder I tossed him a wide smile, before I ducked down, maneuvered around, and wedged myself through the hole in the wooden fence, all the while still hanging on to his hand while I whisked us away to our special place.

A throaty chuckle rumbled from his mouth and floated out to embrace my senses in an inundating swell of joy. My heart pounded as he squeezed himself through the hole that led to the center of our world, where our dreams had been bred, we're we'd discovered and grown into the people we were.

Tall, dead grasses grew up in the field. They swished and snagged at our clothing as we passed.

I led him right to the base of our tree. Dropping his hand, I wedged my boot onto the first rung of wood that had been hammered into the trunk and began pulling myself up to our fort housed in the branches above.

"Aly, are you crazy?" Jared asked, full of concern and worry, though there was an undertone of laughter in his words. "What if you fall?"

I hiked myself up one more step and looked down at the beautiful man staring up at me. The man I trusted with my life. "Then you'll catch me."

Something so perfect transformed his expression, a look of devotion so sincere it was enough to fuel all the hopes I had for this life. "Yeah, I will," he mumbled, so quietly I was sure he was only talking to himself.

I climbed the rest of the way up and settled onto the decaying wooden floor. Those large branches grew tall, stretching toward the sky. Jared hoisted himself up onto the old sheet of plywood in one swift motion. He scooted up beside me and rested his back on a thick branch that helped to support our fort, this place made of fairy tales and hopes and dreams.

They all came crashing back to me now.

Vibrant. Brilliant. Finally within my reach.

Jared pulled me against his side, and I nestled my head on his shoulder and sank into his warmth.

Our breaths were just barely visible in the cool air.

We stared up through the barren branches of the tree. Stars blinked where they dotted the sky.

Everything slowed, my heart contented.

Jared's arms were the best place to be.

His gentle gaze slipped all over my face. A caress. "I love you, Aly Moore. You know that, don't you?"

I reached up and cupped one side of his face. His fire burned my skin, the connection we shared greater than anything that should be possible. "Of course I know that."

I knew it long before he knew it himself.

TEN

Aleena

Anxious hands kneaded the steering wheel, the numbers stamped across Jared's knuckles prominent, his fingers bristling with unspent energy. He sat in the driver's seat of my car, cautious as he made his way through the heavy afternoon traffic on the freeway. He cast me a sidelong glance.

That same stirring of excitement I felt in my stomach danced all over Jared's gorgeous face, but it seemed amplified a thousand times, this carefree hope so evident in the searing blue of his eyes.

And the man was beautiful, but there was just something about seeing a smile on his face that made me weak in the knees. He tugged his bottom lip between his teeth, obviously trying to hide something behind his grin. He ran his thumb over the back of my hand that he had tucked on his lap.

Warmth spread over my skin, igniting the exhilaration I felt simmering in my blood.

"Are you going to tell me where we're going?" I asked for about the twentieth time, my penetrating gaze burning into the side of his playful expresssion.

He freed his grin, letting it spread. One side of his mouth twisted up with the secret. His big hand tightened on mine. "Nope. I already told you, it's a surprise."

I huffed. "This isn't fair, Jared. We're not supposed to keep secrets from each other," I said, making a last-ditch effort to get it out of him.

He slanted a knowing eye in my direction and released my hand long enough to tug on a piece of my hair. "Ha . . . nice try, Aly Cat. This is not a secret. It's a surprise. There's a big difference." He cocked his head with a smirk.

I shifted in my seat, trying not to fidget but unable to stop the rush of nerves firing in my system. The truth was, I had a pretty good idea of what his surprise would be. We'd been online, looking at apartments for a little place of our own, someplace to start our family together.

Judging by the direction Jared was taking us, I thought that was what it had to be.

But I pushed it down, not wanting to get my hopes up.

More than two weeks had passed since he came back to me. We'd settled into some kind of routine. Every morning he'd get up early for work, off to his job with the same construction company he'd been working with before. Only now, his duties had changed. He was giving orders rather than taking them.

Instead of leaving me with a tattered note like he'd done all those months before, he'd whisper the sweetest words to my temple as I traveled just on the cusp of sleep, feelings he'd been too fearful to say aloud before, these beautiful words that breathed our love into my ear every morning and pumped the deepest joy into my spirit.

After he left, I got up and went to class, and I'd done a few short shifts at the restaurant, even though Jared kept telling me it wasn't necessary.

He wanted to take care of me.

I knew he was making good money at his job. But I knew his meaning went deeper than just possessions. Jared wanted to provide and support.

Trying to contain my grin, I snuck a peek at him, my eyes caressing along his sharp jaw, his pouty lips pronounced in his strong profile as he focused his attention on the road in front of us.

I squirmed a little, thinking of the nights . . . the nights Jared and I were just a tangle of limbs, neither of us able to get enough of the other. Our hands constantly searched and our mouths sought, desperate to make up for that tortuous time when we'd been apart.

But we would never make up for that time because neither of us would ever get enough.

Still, Jared seemed perfectly content with giving it a try.

He looked over at me. One eyebrow lifted as his eyes narrowed, his interest piqued, as if he'd caught the blatant desire on my face. Heat pooled in my stomach. Guess I didn't mind it so much, either.

Chuckling, he turned his focus back to the road and lifted our entwined hands to his mouth. He brushed his lips over the back of my hand, didn't say anything, just let this joy radiate from him as he carefully wound his way off the freeway.

Happiness had taken us whole, our days spent together like a normal couple that I'd never been brave enough to hope for.

But I also understood the truth in what I'd told my mother on Thanksgiving. Things would not always be easy with him.

Nightmares continued to plague Jared. Not one night had

passed without panic and fear sucking all the air from my room. Jared would jerk to sitting, drenched in sweat and gasping for the breath the night had stolen from his lungs, his eyes wild and speaking of more pain than any one person should ever have to bear. Almost frantic, he'd gather me up in his arms and lay us back down, exhaling his relief into my hair when he realized he was in bed with me and not still stuck in the nightmare of a past he would never be able to change.

I'd tried to talk with him about it, to get him to open up to what he kept buried inside, but he would always force a smile, murmur against my cheek, *Don't worry*, promising he was sleeping better than he had in years.

I'd nod, even though the show of acceptance was nothing but a lie.

How could I not worry? It was impossible. I loved him so much, and all I wanted was for him to find a way to heal, to be whole. No, I didn't want him to forget. Forgetting Helene would be a tragedy in itself. I just wanted him to find peace.

But I knew for now I had to let it go and accept he wasn't ready.

Or maybe it was my own nightmare coming into play, my greatest fear that one day I would push him too far and push him away. It was like clinging to a quickly fraying rope. One day the burdened weight Jared carried on his shoulders would cause it to snap and both of us would fall.

I just didn't know where we would land.

Secure and whole and in each other's arms.

Or shattered.

I knew in my heart the impact would crush us both and neither of us would survive.

Jared took an exit in Chandler, one of the areas in Phoenix that had been built up over the past handful of years.

I made a vain attempt at sitting still while he made a couple of turns, one off the main road and then down a street that ran alongside a small neighborhood. But I couldn't. I was pretty sure everything I was feeling was fed directly from Jared. Because his excitement had shifted. It was still there, but a thread of disquiet had woven into his demeanor, restless and unsure.

He kept stealing glances at me, searching, reading, as if he were again trying to latch onto my thoughts. But my own thoughts were obscured because I was so unsure of where we were heading myself.

Jared turned right onto a narrow neighborhood street. He flashed me a nervous smile and ran his hand over his short hair. "So . . . uh . . . you don't have to take this, Aly. It's a complete disaster and it's going to take a ton of work to get it in shape."

Instead of taking me to an apartment complex like I'd anticipated, Jared pulled to the curb and came to a stop in front of a small house.

It was a typical newer tract home, a cookie-cutter frame with tan stucco walls and an arched roof, fronted by a two-car garage. A concrete sidewalk led up to the little overhang that protected the front door.

A *For Sale* sign had been yanked from the ground and tossed onto the sparse brown lawn. The place was obviously run-down from neglect. It appeared to have been sitting vacant for years.

But it was cute. Homey.

That stirring of excitement inside me whipped into a fury.

"Jared, is this . . ." I glanced toward him, my words trailing off as I looked back to the house.

I was so thrilled by the idea of Jared and me finding our own place, something that just belonged to us, where we could build memories and our future. But I never thought of it as being anything more than a stepping-stone. Maybe a little one-bedroom apartment that one day we could move up from, expand and grow as our lives stabilized.

I was almost scared to voice it . . . to hope for this.

Jared climbed from the car and came around and opened my door. Taking me by the hand, he helped me out, his eyes intense as he steadied me on my unsure feet. Doubt riddled his face, although there was no mistaking the underlying hope. His voice was soft, full of question. "It is if you want it to be."

I swallowed, peeking over his shoulder at the little house, my imagination running wild, too far and too fast into our future.

"Just don't say anything yet, okay?" Jared shook his head, shutting down the questions fighting for release on my tongue. "I wasn't joking when I said it's a mess." He glanced behind him, before he turned back to me. "Actually, saying it's a mess doesn't come close to doing justice to what's going on in that house. It's a fucking disaster, Aly, so be prepared."

He tugged at my hand and started us up through the unkempt lawn, if it could even be considered a lawn. I stumbled a little over the uneven ground, trying to keep up with Jared's long, impatient strides. "We need to get inside before it starts to get dark. The electricity is off."

He dug into his pocket and drew out a key ring that held a single bronze key. At the door, he looked back at me with a fading trace of hesitation before he turned to press the key into the lock. Metal scraped as he slipped it in, and the knob rattled as he twisted it free. He pushed on the door. It creaked from disuse as it swung open to reveal what was hidden within.

Jared released my hand and moved behind me. He placed his hand at the small of my back, his warm breath at my neck as he nudged me to enter ahead of him. "Go on in, baby."

Tentatively, I stepped inside the torn-up little house.

I stood in the entryway to an open living room that extended off to the right of the front door, facing the street. It wasn't huge, but it was plenty large enough for a comfortable couch, and a fireplace was tucked up against the right wall. The living room opened to the dining area and kitchen that took up the entire back portion of the room, the dining nook on the left and the kitchen to the right. Between the two was a large sliding glass door that led out to the backyard.

And Jared wasn't kidding.

The place was trashed.

All the carpet had been ripped up, concrete exposed, and the kitchen had been gutted. The only things left in it were cheap cabinets with half the doors hanging from their hinges and dingy Formica countertops. A few holes had been knocked in the walls and everything had about five months' worth of dust coating it.

But none of that was what I really saw.

My eyes slipped along the living area, up to the high ceilings and across to the large windows that allowed the late-afternoon sun to filter inside. The house was open and warm and inside it had to be about the cutest little place I'd ever seen.

Jared fidgeted behind me. "Like I said, it's a total mess. It's going to take a lot of work to get this place into shape."

He stepped around me, facing me as he walked backward toward the kitchen. The apprehension he'd been wearing before evaporated, the excitement back in his eyes. "Baby, I don't know if you can picture it finished, but I think this place has a ton of potential." He turned and gestured to the run-down kitchen. "Obviously, all of these cupboards have to go. They gutted just about everything anyway, so we'll just rip all this shit out. I can do all that. It's what I do at work." He shook his head, seeming to get lost to the plans, to the ideas in his mind, mostly mumbling to himself. "Don't think there's much of anything to salvage here."

He pointed to the cupboards lining the back of the kitchen wall. "We'll replace all of these with new . . ." He lowered his hand, held his palm about an inch above the countertops that jutted out from the back wall and blocked the kitchen from the rest of the open room. He ran his hand over the length. "Thinking we tear out this countertop and put in an island with some stools right in the middle?" he said, seeming to test the idea out in his head, to see the way it tasted as it left his mouth.

He looked up to the cupboards attached to the ceiling directly above the countertops he was already tearing out in his mind. "We knock all of this out . . . open the whole thing up . . . make it one big room."

He finally turned to look at me where I'd edged into the middle of the room. "There's some granite at my job. It was supposed to be used for one of our rehabs, but it was cut wrong . . . think I can get it to work for the kitchen. It's really pretty, too, mostly black with some flecks of gold and silver in it. Think you'd like it."

I nodded, trying to keep up with the flood of ideas pouring from Jared, trying to picture all of this through his eyes, where this passion I'd never witnessed before burned.

"Jared . . ." I blinked in confusion. "How?"

Jared smiled a little, reading my simple question for what it was.

He shrugged. "At lunch today, I was talking with my boss about us wanting to find our own place. Told him I was looking for a good apartment in a nice area, and asked if he knew of any good places to rent. Told me he was looking to get this place off his hands." Jared looked around. "He picked it up with the intention of flipping it, but the construction jobs have been too busy and it's just sitting here. He tossed me the key and told me to go check it out . . . said he'd carry the loan for us if we wanted to buy it. And we can get the house at a great price."

Something like pride filled Jared's face. "He said he considered it incentive to get his best guy to stick around."

My attention darted around the little house, unable to grasp that this could be ours. Really ours.

Jared grabbed me by the hand. "Come on, I want you to see the rest." He tugged me down a short hall off to the left of the family room. We stepped into a room probably twice the size of my room back at the apartment. "This is the master . . . and there's a bath. It needs to be updated, but it's functional right now."

Here too, the carpet had been ripped up, but again, the room was open with a large window running along the back, facing the yard. An arch to the left led into an en suite bathroom. For this little house, the bathroom was huge. A countertop with double sinks lined one wall. Opposite it sat a garden tub that was so large I could swim in it, and a separate shower was tucked in an alcove behind it. A walk-in closet was through a set of sliding doors at the farthest end.

I was pretty sure my mouth had to be hanging open as Jared hauled us out of this room just as fast as he pulled us into it. He towed me along, my hand wrapped snugly in his, and I held on to his wrist with my other hand, securing myself to him in an attempt to keep up with the man who had had something awakened in him.

My heart beat hard and my mind worked faster, trying to process what Jared had put in front of me.

I just want to take care of you.

He had to have said it at least a hundred times over the last two weeks, but I had no clue what that meant to him.

He rushed us back through the main room and into the hall that ran down the opposite side of the house. He ducked into the first door on the right, into a small room with a window that faced the street. "This can be the baby's room."

Expectation gusted through me, the fiercest squall of wind that whipped and stirred.

And I was feeling it, all that Jared imagined sinking into my consciousness.

Jared was higher than I'd ever seen him, tripping along with some kind of euphoria that overflowed with ideas and inspiration, burning with the need to create. I recognized it, because I felt it when I had the impulse to draw, the compulsion that I *had* to press a pencil to paper.

And there was nothing artificial about it, nothing synthetic clouding his mind, nothing destructive bounding through his veins.

This was him . . . something beautiful that had risen up in this beautiful man.

"Jared, this is—"

"Wait," he interrupted, his smile wide. "You haven't seen the best part yet."

He led me back out, pointing out a basic bathroom across from the baby's room as we passed. He didn't even stop for me to explore it, just mumbled through a low chuckle, "Yep, this bathroom needs to be redone, too. No surprise there."

He came to a stop at the end of the hall in front of a closed door. Gripping my hand a little tighter, he opened the door and led me inside a room that was larger than the baby's, but about half the size of the master bedroom. The carpet had been torn

up in here, too. One of the walls was busted in, and the sliding
closet doors had been knocked from their tracks.

But to the left was a huge bay window that opened up to the
backyard. Muted sunlight bled inside as twilight edged across
the darkening sky. Shadows played along the far wall of the
room as the last rays of light were cast inside, danced and
meshed with the anticipation beating from Jared's heart.

I inched toward the window and stared out into the backyard. It wasn't huge, but it was larger than I expected. A covered patio off the sliding door in the main room gave way to
what had been a lawn long since dead in the winter, unmain-
tained in the many months this house had sat vacant. Just outside the window, planters sat barren where flowers had once
grown.

A high block wall rose up around the entirety of the yard to
guard privacy.

Right now it looked like nothing, but with Jared and me, I
knew it could be beautiful, that we could care for it and nurture
it and bring it to life.

"And this . . . this room would be yours," Jared murmured
behind me.

Slowly I turned to face him. Confusion twisted my brow.
"What do you mean?"

"Where you can draw . . . set all your stuff up in here." He
waved his hand toward the window. "Look at the lighting in
here, Aly. You could work in here all day, looking outside. It's
big enough that we can put a couch up in the corner where you
could sit with a sketch pad on your lap . . ." Soft laughter rolled
from him, feeding me a picture I knew he saw so clearly. No
doubt, it was the way he saw me when he caught me drawing,
my sketch pad balanced across my crisscrossed legs.

"It'll give you enough space for a desk and whatever else you need."

I reeled, struggling to make sense of what Jared was saying. An upheaval of ideas flitted through my mind, all the dreams of my childhood clashing with reality. "Jared, I don't—"

"Yes, you can," he cut me off, his voice hard. His eyes flashed with something that almost looked like anger. Then he softened and closed the space between us. He pressed himself to me, one hand tangled in my hair and the other held firm across my back.

He whispered into the top of my head, "Yes, you can, Aly."

Emotion squeezed my chest, my heart too full. I melted into his warmth, shuddering through the breath I tried to draw into my lungs.

He pulled back. The force of his blue eyes bore down on me. "That night . . . when I came back and you finally showed me what you kept hidden in your sketch pads all those years . . ."

Jared brushed his knuckles down my jaw. A rush of chills skated down my spine.

"Other than this face, I've never seen anything more beautiful, Aly. You see things the way no one else can and you somehow make it come to life on paper." His tongue darted out to wet his lips, and he frowned, searching for an answer. "And I don't know what or exactly how to make this happen for you, but you can't settle."

He brought both of his hands to my face, holding me tight, breathing his own belief into me. "I can't fucking stand the thought of you settling. Not for one second. Not for anything." He blinked rapidly, hard and insecure. "And if this house is settling, I want you tell me and I'll find something better. I will, Aly, I'll make it right. I promise. You just have to be honest with me."

Emotions slashed the deepest lines into his face, fear and

doubt and that lingering shame. And I knew what he was thinking, that a part of me was settling by being with him.

It gutted me, him believing for even the flash of a second he wasn't worthy of me, when this man had been created for me.

He crushed my face in his hands, almost painfully, his fingers digging into the skin behind my jaw, silencing my own insecurities on my tongue. "Can you picture it, Aly . . . us here? Raising our family? Together?"

And I could. I could picture the perfection. Blood bounded through my veins, rushed to my head and tingled in my fingers. I stepped back, pressing my hands over my heart, feeling overwhelmed by the moment, by this man who knew me better than anyone, who saw the desires hidden in my heart when I'd never even spoken them aloud. "Can we afford it?"

He smiled a little, nodding slowly. "Baby, I already told you . . . it's yours if you want it. I still have a ton of money saved up from back when I was working in Jersey and I'm making enough now that keeping up the mortgage on this place will be no problem."

"Is this what you want? To rebuild this place?" I asked.

And I already knew the answer, but I needed to hear him say it. Wanted him to feel it. And I felt certain it wasn't just this house. There was so much inside Jared waiting to be freed, to be discovered underneath all that self-hatred, more beauty in this man than I could have ever imagined.

I suppressed the emotion that pricked behind my eyes, watching as Jared struggled through the shame that was always there, as he fought against the chains holding him down.

He took one tentative step forward and pulled me back into the safety of his arms. His hold was soft, and he rocked us slowly in the middle of the room. "Aly." I felt the weight in his swallow, the hard beat of his heart where it thundered against mine. "I didn't think I'd ever get this. Any of it. One day spent with you is a dream . . . a gift. Living here, with you . . ." He tightened his hold. "I want it more than I could ever tell you. Nothing would make me happier than building this for you, building this for my *family*." His voice cracked on the word, as if saying it aloud could curse him and steal it away.

I clung to him, silently promising that was never going to happen.

"Then I can't imagine a better place to spend my life with you."

ELEVEN

Jared

I dipped a roller into the pool of beige paint that lapped in the tray. Mine butted up against Aly's as she hurried to dive in, trying to beat me to the punch, launching us into a latex-fueled tug-of-war.

"I was here first." I nudged hers back and my roller disappeared deep into the thick pond.

Aly giggled and vied to take position. "And I picked the color, so I win."

A wave of contentment and a thrill of excitement played a contradictory beat on my heart.

I didn't think Aly had stopped smiling since I brought her to this wreck of a house more than two weeks ago.

And God, if I didn't love seeing my girl happy.

With one last playful prod, Aly straightened back up, pushing her roller up the length of the wall, crisscrossing it as she smeared a coat over the textured surface.

Doing the same, I peeked over at her, watching her while she worked. Her hair was piled on her head in the messiest knot, pieces falling all around her. Streaks of paint coated a few errant locks where she'd been careless and brushed up against the wet wall.

A couple of them were compliments of me.

I just couldn't resist, messing with her, seeing her get all flustered and trying to fight back. Like she could ever sneak up on me, mark me in the paint marking up our walls.

But this girl sure as hell had marked my heart.

A wide smudge of paint was branded across my chest.

Yeah, I'd let her get one in. Just because I wanted to see her victorious smile, the way she'd giggled and run away as she anticipated my retaliation.

So fucking cute.

And that's what she did to me, turned me to slush, liquid on the inside.

Megan, Aly's best friend since high school, and Christopher had shown up early this morning to help, and the two of them were across the room working together, chatting and laughing and pretty much making more of a mess than they were helping with. Megan painted in a slow sway beside Aly's brother, dancing to the music that pumped from the small radio that sat on the floor.

Lowering my voice so they wouldn't hear, I sidled up to Aly, our strokes keeping time. "I still don't think it's a good idea for you to be painting."

Sure, it was the same complaint I'd given her about a thousand times. Didn't make it any less valid.

Aly scoffed. "Jared, how many nurseries do you think pregnant women have painted over the years?" Lifting on a challenge, her eyebrows disappeared behind her bangs as she waited for my answer.

My voice dropped even lower. "Well, maybe those men didn't care about their women as much as I care about mine. And this isn't a nursery. . . . It's a family room," I pointed out, as if that was going to make any difference.

Of course she'd picked out paint for the small bedroom down the hall, too, and I was pretty sure there was no chance in hell I could keep her from painting it.

I knew I was stretching, grasping at nothing because it seemed just about impossible to get Aly to concede.

But fuck, a man could try, couldn't he?

Maybe it was irrational, but I wanted to erase anything that could possibly harm her, anything that could harm the baby.

"What if it's like one of those news stories?" I continued, dipping my roller back into the paint and bringing it back to the wall. "Like when they release a new miracle drug that's going to save the world and find out five years later it's burned a hole in your heart."

And, yes . . . stretching. I knew it. Aly did, too.

She rolled her eyes, but amusement played all over that gorgeous face. She leaned in and pecked my lips. It was just an innocent little kiss, but it was enough to awaken the desire lurking in the deepest places inside of me.

I could have Aly every second of every day and it still wouldn't be enough.

"Stop worrying," she commanded on a whisper, her nose brushing mine. "I'm pretty sure my mom painted my room when she was pregnant with me." Aly stepped back and lifted her arms out to her sides, putting herself on display. "And I turned out just fine."

My eyes raked down her slender body and back up to meet those green eyes. I lifted an appreciative brow.

Uh, yeah, I'd have to say she turned out just fine.

But I sure as hell didn't have to say I wouldn't worry.

Couldn't help it, and there was no chance I could stop it.

These two were the only things I did worry about.

Obviously Aly caught my thoughts, and she huffed out a little breath. "You're kind of ridiculous, Jared."

I cocked my head. "And you're kind of stubborn."

From the other side of the room, Christopher laughed, all raucous and like the asshole he was.

Fucker was a disaster, paint all over his shirt and splattered in his hair. A river of it coated his pant leg where he'd spilled the can. The drips that hadn't clung to his clothes dotted the cement floor.

Thank God the new carpet didn't go in until tomorrow.

Christopher dunked his roller into the tray, sloshing paint over the side. "I seriously don't know what's wrong with you, little sister. You have a perfectly good excuse to cop out on all this work, and here you are, making arguments to be a part of it."

Aly pointed her roller at him. "That's because I'm not a lazy-ass like you."

Wounded, Christopher smacked his hand over his heart. "Are you really calling me lazy when I got up at the butt crack of dawn on a Saturday to come and help turn this dump into something halfway decent?"

"And it had nothing to do with me bribing you with free beer?" I asked, teasing, unable to stop from jumping in with my girl.

"Oh, I'd make bets that has a whole lot to do with it." Megan didn't even look over her shoulder, just kept her body rocking with the motion of her roller.

"Fuck you, guys," Christopher said, laughing under his breath. "This was one hundred percent out of the goodness of my giving heart. This shithole would be nothing without all my self-less efforts. But since we're talking about beer . . ." He dropped his roller to the tray. Kicking off his paint-laden shoes, he headed toward the kitchen in his socks, dodging droplets of wet paint.

I laughed, outright and loud, and Aly giggled, watching her brother with all that affection pouring from her, that goodness radiating from her as she looked around the room that was taking shape, this slow transformation turning this shack into a home.

When I first brought Aly over to see the little house, my nerves had wound me tight. I had wanted her to see what I saw when I first walked through the door, the pure potential that lay in wait.

I had seen a home.

Dread had struck me hard when I first pulled up in front of it with her and realized she might not. I couldn't stomach the idea of letting her down. All I wanted was to provide for her and the baby. To give them something good when I didn't have all that much to offer.

But I should have known better, should have known she would see what was buried beneath the rubble. And I thought maybe Aly had seen even more than I had. Deeper, further and farther into the future, imagining the things that were still so hard for me to see.

Hope. It'd shown prominently in her eyes.

She'd been the only one who'd ever been able to give that to me.

Now the place was hardly recognizable.

My crew had worked their asses off the past two weeks, heading over in between jobs, tearing shit out and installing new. We hit the kitchen first, knocking out all the old cupboards and countertops while we waited for the new ones to be delivered.

Aly had picked out almost black wooden cabinets. And damn, if my girl didn't have good taste, a natural eye for beauty, for flow and continuity.

I had been right about the mis-cut granite. It had fit perfectly and looked even better. Pair that with the brand-new appliances and the kitchen had turned into some kind of gourmet's retreat or some shit.

Aly had actually cried when she saw it. She blamed it on hormones, but I knew her better than that. She was just fucking thankful and overwhelmed by the drastic change in everything.

Slowly everything had begun to come together. There was still a lot of stuff to do. The carpet was being installed tomorrow, thank God. The huge task of laying tile in the kitchen and bathrooms awaited me. But mostly I was itching to sink my fingers into the finishing details, things that would make the home unique, adding the depth and character and beauty it'd lacked when we started.

But other than that?

Pride simmered around the edges of my consciousness as I took a glance around the little house that was becoming our home.

Yeah. The place was turning out better than I ever could have imagined.

We hadn't really meant to, but Aly and I had moved in. I'd been here working so late every night that one night a week ago, Aly had shown up with an air mattress. She pumped it up in our bedroom and we'd slept on it ever since. She said she couldn't stand falling asleep without me, couldn't take one more night of me crawling into bed with her not long before dawn, exhausted after I'd spent hours getting this house ready for my family.

I didn't even try to dispute it. I'd missed her like crazy, all those nights here alone, without her. Still, I'd been all too happy to sacrifice that time, knowing what I was working toward.

Turned out I'd just accomplished getting Aly into the new house a little earlier than I anticipated.

Christopher ducked his head into the brand-new fridge.

"Bring me one of those," Megan called, ticking up the music a little louder.

"Grab one for me, too." I knelt down and saturated my roller.

"What do I look like, a fucking maid?" Glass clanked as he dug around, pulling out three beers.

"What you look like is a fucking disaster," I tossed back, laughing under my breath.

"Ha! Have you looked at yourself, lately? Pretty sure you have zero room to talk, my friend. I don't know how my sister can even stand looking at you."

"Oh, I have no problem looking at him." Aly's voice was all tease, dripping with innuendo.

Somewhere along the way, making her brother uncomfortable had become Aly's favorite game.

"So gross," Christopher muttered. But he was all grins when he sauntered back into the family room. He divvied out the beers before he slid down to the floor, leaning against the front door. He twisted the cap, drained half his beer while he surveyed the room. "Not half bad," he said in slow appreciation, turning to meet my eye, like maybe he got just how much fixing up this place meant to me.

I looked around the room.

No, not half bad at all.

Two hours later, Aly and I walked Megan and Christopher to the door.

Christopher clapped me on the shoulder. "Take care, man. I'll come by tomorrow after class and help you get the furniture moved in."

"Thanks. I appreciate it."

He wrapped Aly up in his arms. "Didn't know I could miss you so much, little sister. The apartment is boring as fuck without you there."

"Well . . . thanks," Aly drew out, all sarcastically offended as she squeezed him back.

Christopher cracked a smile and stepped outside. "What? Here I was thinking you were nothing but a complete pain in my ass, and it turns out I kind of liked having you around."

"You are such a jerk."

He winked, and a true smile curved his mouth.

Aly smiled back. "I miss you, too, Christopher."

Christopher eyed Megan, who was hugging me good-bye. "Well, since I'm so lonely, maybe Megan can come over and keep me company tonight." The edge of his words and the gleam in his eye reeked of suggestion. The asshole couldn't stay serious for more than two seconds.

"Not on your life," Megan shot back. Laughter rumbled around in her chest as she hugged me closer, wishing me good-bye.

"Oh my God, don't you dare go there, Christopher." Aly waved a scolding finger in his face. "Do you know how many times I've had to warn our little brother to keep his hands and thoughts to himself? Both of you lady-killers had better keep the killin' away from my best friend."

"Says the girl who's shacking up with my best friend. And *lady-killer?* Come on, Aly. You can do better than that. I'm a lady *pleaser* . . . believe me."

Aly smacked him on the back of the head. "Whatever you are, just keep your dirty away from Megan."

Christopher laughed and pinched Megan's side.

She squealed and swatted him away. "Oh, I don't think so. No touching, dirty bird."

Christopher hooked his arm around her neck. "I'm just play-ing, Megan." He dropped a kiss to the top of her head. "I don't want anyone who's slept with my sister."

This time, it was Megan's turn to smack him.

Megan stepped up and hugged Aly hard. "The house is beautiful, Aly. I'm so happy for you."

Aly's attention jumped between Megan and Christopher. "Seriously, you guys, thank you so much for coming over and helping us out."

"Of course," Christopher answered kind of soft, like his sister was crazy for even considering it a burden. Christopher had been there for her when she was at her lowest. He'd be there for her in the good times too.

"I've got nothing better to do unless I'm doing Megan here," he added with a smirk.

"Ugh . . ." Aly groaned.

Megan just shook her head and muttered, "In your dreams."

I laughed. Dude was such an asshole.

They waved and headed down the sidewalk.

Slowly, Aly shut the door and locked it, turned around to lean up against it. Contentment etched into every line on her face.

God, she was so beautiful.

I edged forward, pitching my head to the side as I slowly took her by the waist. "Thought I was your best friend, baby," I whispered low as I sought out the skin of her neck.

The softest moan slipped from her mouth as she lifted her face toward the ceiling, before she nudged me back a fraction, her head rocking on the door as she met my face, her expression se-rious and severe. "No, Jared, you're not. You're my everything."

I tore my shirt over my head as I walked through our bedroom door, heading right for the shower.

I was late.

Aly'd texted me earlier, saying Christopher wanted us to meet him out, to grab a few beers and maybe play a round or two of pool. Apparently he was bored out of his mind. He didn't know what to do with himself since Aly had moved out, since she'd become a permanent fixture in this home I was building for us. It'd only been three days since he and Megan had been here, lending a hand to get these walls painted.

Not a night went by that he didn't call, check on Aly, ask her how she was doing. Then he'd make some wiseass joke and act like she was wasting his time.

I chuckled low as I tossed my shirt to the hamper just inside the bedroom. I knelt down, unlaced my work boots, heeling them off before I shucked the rest of my clothes from my body and headed toward the bathroom.

I wouldn't be surprised if one of these days I found Christopher's sorry ass sleeping on the couch. God knew he had plenty of friends and even more acquaintances, not to mention an endless string of girls clamoring over him for their chance to keep him company. But apparently spending time with his sister was much more appealing.

I couldn't agree with him more.

Swinging open the bathroom door, I crossed the threshold. I stumbled, my feet nearly giving out. Regaining my footing, I froze in the doorway, my mouth dry.

Every last one of my muscles jerked and my heart sped, pounding the blood that beat through my veins. One glimpse of the girl and I just about came undone.

Motherfucking trigger.

She stood at the bathroom counter, leaning over it, inclined toward the mirror. Jaw slack, her mouth drifted open, her attention entirely focused on the job at hand as she applied a coat of mascara she most definitely did not need. Long lashes, just as dark as her hair, framed the intensity of her green eyes.

The only thing covering that delicious body was a towel, the tiny scrap of material wrapped under her arms. It came to her thighs, but since she was bending over the counter, it just skimmed the bottom of that glorious ass.

And those legs . . .

Those legs.

So fucking long and every kind of sexy. I wanted to live in them, wrapped up in them, lost in them.

God, she was impossible. A miracle.

And just like that, I grew hard, standing there in nothing as I looked on my girl from across the steamy room.

Moisture clung to the walls, her skin dampened from her shower, her hair wet and dark and clinging to her shoulders and back.

Through the mirror, Aly caught my eye. Her gaze drifted down, me standing there watching her, her watching me.

Need vibrated my body.

Pretty sure I would be content to spend the rest of my life coming home to this.

Exactly this.

My girl standing there. Ready for me.

I stalked up behind her, my hands impatient as they found her waist. I tucked my hips against her ass, my cock trapped between us.

I placed a gentle kiss on her spine right between her shoulder blades, that gentle action at complete odds with the intense urge I had to devour her.

Chills started there, beneath my mouth. A rush of goose bumps lifted on her back and spread in a slow blaze across her skin.

"What do you think you're doing?" Aly accused softly, hoarsely. Her hand trembled as she set the mascara aside. She stared at me through the mirror, a flame of desire lighting in her eyes.

I smoothed my hands up her sides, back down to grasp her by the hips. I yanked her to me, making her squirm against the force of my erection.

"I think the better question would be, what do you think you're doing?" I buried my face in her hair, nudging the locks aside with my nose, and whispered close to her ear. "Teasing me like this . . ." I splayed my hands wide across her ass. "Do you have any idea how temping it is finding you standing here like this . . . knowing what's hidden under this flimsy cover?"

Knowing how good it was going to feel when I uncovered it.

"*I'm* getting ready to go out . . . not teasing you. You do re-member we're supposed to meet my brother, right?" Aly was shooting for indifference, I knew, like she could brush me off, pretend I didn't affect her every bit as much as she affected me. But her voice wavered and cracked, deepened and dove as I pulled her closer to me.

"I have to disagree, Aly," I murmured low, my hands explor-ing the front of her thighs, my thumbs teasing up under the fabric. "I think you knew exactly what finding you this way was going to do to me."

Just her being in the room was a tease.

Torture, really.

Desire throbbed, twisted and curled.

And right then, all tight up against Aly's body? Any plans we had became nothing but a distant memory.

"I might have blanked on meeting up with your brother, baby," I said as my fingers continued their journey, sliding around to brush along the back of her thighs where they met the

curve of her perfect ass. "Pretty sure Christopher will understand if we're late."

Aly giggled through a moan as I pressed myself to her back.
"Jared," she whispered on a sigh.

"Do you feel that, Aly? What you do to me? I didn't even
have to touch you . . ."

Because the girl managed to touch me from across the
room.

I slipped my hands around her front, over the tiny bump on
her stomach. She'd just begun to show, the smallest hint of the
child that grew within her, a subtle widening below her belly
button. For a moment, I cupped it, my fingers spread wide.
Something like pride filled me, awe and fear and devotion. My
pulse stuttered when I met Aly's unfailing gaze in the mirror,
her thoughts matching mine as they played through her trusting eyes.

We were doing this together. All of it.

My family.

A bolt of fiery energy hit me, all these thoughts burning
through my veins. All the things I wanted for our lives. The
man I wanted to be.

Aly made me that way. Different. Better.

Lately I'd almost been feeling like him, like who I wanted
to be. Providing for my family. Taking care of them. Protecting
them.

I'd be doing it for all my life, because I didn't have one without this girl.

A spiral of need twisted through me like a raging storm,
passion and desire and lust. It wound with the commitment I
had for her, like they were one and the same, this consuming
hunger that made Aly everything.

I had to have her.

My palms pressed in as they roamed up, her ribs prominent where I caressed them with my firm hands. I palmed her breasts over the plush white fabric.

Aly whimpered.

I released the little knot, baring them, all that creamy flesh exposed.

"Shit, Aly, you're beautiful. So fucking perfect."

Aly took in what was captured in the mirror, the portrayal of perfection, the way I saw her every time I looked at her.

A soft moan rolled from her as she watched me, as she watched me dip down and kiss the side of her neck while I flicked my thumbs over the taut peaks of her nipples, while I plumped the heavy weight of her breasts in my hands. I brushed my lips along the shell of her ear, never leaving her eyes as I showered her in adoration, as I kissed and sucked, my mouth at her jaw, at the side of her mouth, at the cap of that sexy shoulder.

Through the hazy glass, her eyes flitted up to mine. A tremor of need rocked through her. "Jared, you don't . . . You have no idea what you do to me. How badly I want you . . . every day."

Aly'd braced herself on the counter, her palms flat. Mine wandered, sliding up over her shoulders, all the way down to her hands. I took her by them, shackling her wrists as I urged her up against the wall next to the counter. I flattened her chest against it, pinned her arms above her head.

Her hair was all in my face, her cheek pressed to the wall. "Jared." It was a whimper, a moan, a plea.

I groaned.

Taking her wrists in one hand, I let the other trail the contours of the endless expanse of soft skin, back over her breast, down the slope of her side, to her full hip. My fingers sank in. "Baby, I need you."

"Always," was her answer.

I took my dick in my hand, positioned myself behind her. I wedged my knee between her legs, forcing them apart, nudging her feet back.

Goddamn . . . she was gorgeous, the deep curve of her back jutting out that glorious ass. Hair fell all around her, tumbling over her shoulders and down her back.

Coconut.

Fuck, she always smelled like coconut, like girl and good and everything in this world that meant anything.

Voracious, I wanted to consume every inch of her, have all of her.

I brushed my fingertips between her legs, the folds slick and wet and scorching hot. I edged forward, poised at her eager center. I let my aching head slip into the welcome of her warmth.

Aly fucking shook.

Shit.

This girl was too much, every time, every second. There was nothing I could do to control the way she spun me up and strung me out, stretched me thin.

"Aleena." I rocked into her, hard, giving it all.

Taking it all.

A rigid gasp shot from her. She fisted her hands in my un-yielding hold. I kept her pinned to the wall. My free hand drifted, exploring every inch of her body, smoothing along her front, her muscles flexing and bowing as I filled her fast and deep. Again and again. Clutching her hip, I kneaded the soft skin, the creamy flesh, my fingers an anchor as they burrowed in, staking this claim that had overtaken my heart.

The girl was mine.

I took her hard, making her moan and writhe and beg my name. My hips jerked, coming flush to that perfect round bottom every time I buried myself in her.

Pleasure fisted my stomach. My mouth came to her ear, my voice fierce and desperate as I drove into her. "One of these days I'm going to make that sweet little ass mine," I warned, sure it was true. Damn, I wanted all of her. Every inch. To somehow be everywhere. My skin and her flesh, a vain attempt at satisfying this hunger that would never be sated.

As if there would ever be a moment when I'd gotten enough. Never.

Aly whimpered, tilting her hips back, granting me more. "All of me . . . it already belongs to you."

A growl ripped up my throat. I gripped her tighter, took her deeper. "Fuck, Aly." She shouldn't tempt me like that, because I'd be inclined to make good on it, and I figured that kind of shit needed to wait until after this baby was born.

Aly threw her head back on my shoulder, whimpering. "More. *Please.*"

I released her arms. She sagged against me. One arm was braced below her breasts, keeping her from falling, her legs weak as I turned her to face the full-length mirror hanging on the back of the door.

"Look at you, Aly."

Aly met my eye as I fucked her from behind, as I drove her higher, just as high as she was steadily driving me. I splayed my free hand across her stomach, swept it down, all of my attentions going to that sweet spot that had her legs trembling under her unsteady feet.

She watched me touching her, loving her, the green of her eyes dark, consumed, filled with need, burning with outright desire.

Her mouth dropped open, her arms coming up to hold me by the back of the neck.

And she was all spread out, fucking perfect in every way.

"Come for me, baby," I demanded at her ear.

Aly convulsed, tightened on my cock as she bowed back, her hair and her face and fucking delicious skin sending me right over the edge.

The knot of pleasure snapped, a consuming burn exploding from me and pouring into her.

Aly collapsed in my hold, her knees completely giving way. Her breath was strangled as she struggled to draw it into her lungs.

And I stood there, just holding my girl up, watching the one who trusted me with her life through the mirror. My arms were around her, the sickness of my own flesh wound around her waist, the evidence of my sins this stark contrast to the flawless span of hers.

But Aly . . . she stood between the consequences of them, blocking the wicked mark that marred my heart, like a shield to the truth of who I was. Like her presence cast a light on my darkness. Her spirit so pure, it was enough to chase the horrors from mine.

To silence them.

Extinguish them.

They might haunt me in the night, but here, in this light, she was the only thing that could be seen.

Aly clung to me, and I held her up, refusing to let her fall. "I love you, Aly," I murmured into the soft locks of her hair.

I loved her so much.

So much more than I should.

Sleep pressed in as an oppressive weight. Darkness crawled along his flesh, holding Jared down. A prisoner bound in its chains. Searing heat burned him from the inside out. It was quiet. Too quiet. And he didn't want to look because he already knew what he would find.

Against his will, Jared's head lolled to the side, seeking out her face. His vision blurred with tears that could never be shed, her face streaked in blood and her smile taunting him with a peace he could never find.

That smile wavered in fear.

It slammed him—her fear. It splintered through him, becoming the most excruciating pain.

A scream locked in his throat. "No!"

But it would never come and all he wanted was to reach for her. To stop it. To take it back.

And she whispered, "It'll be okay."

It'll be okay.

I jerked to sitting, my legs twisted in the sheets. Sweat drenched my forehead. It slicked down the back of my neck like the most frigid ice. Frenzied, my heart thundered in my tightened chest. I struggled for air when there was none, searching for breath in the darkest recesses where death harbored its hate.

I gripped my head in my hands.

Shit.

Nausea hit me and my stomach clenched. Beside me, Aly slept. So peaceful, her hair spread out all around her. Soft breaths parted her lips, the faint glow of the moon caressing her face.

The good.

I closed my eyes, trying to block it all out.

Still, she was there.

Guilt swam through the murky pit of my spirit.

I rammed the heels of my hands in my eyes, wishing for anything to blot it out, anything to take it away.

God.

I looked back down at Aly. How could anything I had with her be wrong?

Slowly, I unwound myself from the covers, careful not to

disturb her. I kept my feet light as I crept out of our room. Blindly, I fumbled for the pack of cigarettes I left on top of the fridge. Cold air hit my exposed chest when I opened the sliding glass door. I flinched when I stepped outside onto the concrete patio on my bare feet, my heart still beating a riot against my rib cage.

Brilliant. Outside in the middle of the night in December, wearing nothing but my underwear. No one mistook me for a genius, that was for hell sure.

Still, I welcomed the cool reprieve from the tortured fire raging inside me.

I dropped to the ground and rested up against the hard stucco wall. Lighting a cigarette, I drew in, holding the smoke in the well of my shallow lungs. Slowly, I blew out the smoke toward the winter sky that cradled the endless canopy of stars. It curled and rose, fading away into the nothingness that I'd always believed was my fate. The submission to the call. Surrendering to my due.

I don't get to have this.

I never meant to disrespect her memory, to take what I wasn't supposed to be given. And God, I loved my mother so much. Missed her more than imaginable.

Shame burned in the deepest place inside me when I snubbed out my cigarette. Anxiety pushed me to my feet. I opened the door.

"I'm so sorry," I whispered back out into the night. Sorry I couldn't give her more. Sorry I didn't know how to make amends.

Inside, it was dark, so dark I could barely see.

Urges screamed through my veins, begging for that balm.

The moment's euphoria.

But this craving? This craving could only be satisfied by one person's touch.

This hunger was fed only by the girl and the good.

I stripped my underwear from my legs as I crossed into the darkness of our room, shrugged them from my feet as I crawled over her.

She was all twisted up, lost in the abyss of sleep, in dreams that were pleasant and pure. Ones without the stench of rancid memories. Ones that weren't tainted by the sting of death.

I slid my hand into her panties.

Aly jumped, gasping as she was jarred awake. Her fingers bolted into my shoulders where I hovered over her like a sinister wraith in the shadows of our room.

"Cold," she whimpered. Chills skated her skin as my freezing fingers caressed over her warmth, searching, seeking, slipping inside.

I buried my nose in the sanctuary of her hair. "Got to feel you, baby." Coarse, jagged words grunted from my dry throat.

And I wanted.

Needed.

Craved.

Her mouth moved softly at my ear, a promise, a call I never believed I could heed.

"I am yours," came out from her on a ragged breath.

And I took.

I took what was mine.

TWELVE

Jared

The next morning, I stepped out the front door. The sun had just begun to rise, the sky a dusty gray. Took about all I had to drag myself out of bed and leave Aly sleeping there. I just wanted to curl back in her comfort, but workdays always began early.

I trudged down the walkway from our door and headed straight for where I had my bike parked in front of the garage.

I stumbled a little when I caught sight of the car parked up close to the curb in front of the house, came to a full stop when I noticed the window rolled down and Dave Moore sitting there, staring at me.

As soon as he caught my eye, he climbed from the car, never looking away as he shut his door behind him. Hostility vibrated from him, sending nerves tumbling through me. Mostly resentment. Asshole hadn't been over here once since we moved in, and it just pissed me off. I knew he hated me. Blamed me. I accepted that. But that didn't excuse him for treating his daughter like shit, acting like he didn't care what was going on in his daughter's life. Really I knew it wasn't that he didn't care. He just didn't want to know.

The air felt loaded, charged as he glared at me where I stood ten feet from him on the walkway.

"You're unbelievable," he finally said, his face twisting up in contempt. "Karen told me you up and moved Aly out of her and Christopher's apartment." It was an accusation.

I lifted my chin. "Yeah. With the baby, we're going to need a bigger place."

He flinched with the mention of the pregnancy.

Was I being an asshole? Doing it on purpose, rubbing it in, knowing that open wound would sting? Maybe. But shit, I refused to tiptoe around him after the way he'd been treating Aly.

He laughed, but it totally lacked humor. He cut his eye up to me, presumptuous, like he had me pegged. "You really think this changes things? You buy my daughter a house and all of a sudden you're worthy of her? Nothing could possibly make up for what you've done. Her life was all worked out before you showed up. She had it made . . . she had a good future, being a nurse."

Uncertainty poked me right in the center of my chest, and that voice howled through all my senses, asserting maybe he was right. I shoved it down and listened to what he really said. Because I was pretty sure he didn't know Aly at all.

"Her life was all worked out? Listen to yourself." It came out like pity. I realized that was really what I was feeling for him. "Your daughter told you flat out she never wanted to be a nurse. And here you are acting like she just gave up her lifelong goal."

He sneered. "And what, this is better? Aly quitting nursing school? All of this ridiculous bullshit about her going to art school? You should be ashamed of yourself, filling her head with fantasies, deluding her into believing there's any kind of future in that." He shook his head, whispered sharply out ahead, "What a waste."

What a waste? Anger twisted through my heart. For once this wasn't about me feeling unworthy. Didn't matter if I was or not. This was about Aly. About what she was capable of. "Did you come here to try to make me feel bad for encouraging Aly to go after her dreams? You want me to apologize for wanting her to be happy and believing she should chase after the things that make her that way?"

He blanched.

"Because I won't. I believe in her. She has an incredible talent and ignoring that is what would be a *waste*. The only thing I'm sorry for is you being too blind to see it."

I shook my head and headed toward my bike, just leaving him there because I couldn't stand to continue being in his presence. I paused and looked back at him. "I know you hate the idea of me being with your daughter. But I love her. And do you know what? I'm not ashamed of wanting to see her happy. That's all I want." My own disappointment poured from me. "I'd think you'd want the same thing, too."

Swinging my leg over my bike, I kicked it over. It rumbled below me. I rolled it back out onto the street, teasing at the throttle as I pulled up alongside him.

In shock, Dave Moore stared blankly ahead, like maybe he'd just been gutted by the realization of how amazing his daughter really was.

God, I hoped so.

Because I always hated being that wedge, separating Aly

from her family. But this was more than just about me. Even if I'd never come back to Phoenix in the first place and my coming had never changed the direction of Aly's life, I hoped she would have at least found *this*.

Because a world without Aly pouring out the beauty locked up inside her was nothing but a shame.

THIRTEEN

Aleena

Our breaths came short and hitched. Anticipation sucked the air from the tiny, dimly lit room.

Jared squeezed my hand, shifting in his chair.

"This is going to be cold," the woman said as she squeezed the gel over my stomach.

I jumped when it hit my skin.

Jared ran his thumb over the back of my hand, trying to calm me and provide me reassurance. But I felt him shake, his own nerves wringing him tight, like we were feeding off each other, the band of tension stretched taut between us a live wire, the connection that made us one.

A soft smile pulled at my mouth when I looked at him.

He raked his free hand down his face and bounced his knee.

The beautiful exterior of the man evidenced all of his anxiety. Jaw clenched tight. Rigid muscles flexing in his arms. It was obvious how difficult it was for him to sit still in the confines of this room with the walls close and the ceiling low.

But everything changed when our eyes met, as if maybe he found peace in what he saw in mine. Wistfulness touched his mouth and he gave my hand a reassuring squeeze.

"Okay, are you two ready to see what we have here?" the ultrasound technician asked, her voice soft with encouragement. She was young, her dark hair tied back in a tight ponytail, her expression easy. She had to be used to couples like us, two people completely on edge as they caught the first glimpse of their future, as they were given a taste of the mysterious, something that seemed such an impossibility.

New life.

The logic of it was incomprehensible.

I could see it as nothing less than a miracle.

"Yes," I rasped over the rough knot in my throat. Nerves trembled my bones.

God, waiting for this day to come had been nearly unbearable. Sleep had eluded me all of last night. I'd tossed and turned while Jared held me the entire time. He'd run gentle fingers through my hair, chasing away those bits of insecurity that tried to force their way in. The quiet, nagging worries, tangled thoughts that I would be told that this baby was not okay.

I just wanted to see.

Chair legs screeched against the hard linoleum floor as Jared edged up closer. The strength of his chest brushed up against my arm from where he sat staunchly at my side, despite his own insecurities, his own relentless demons that told him he didn't deserve the beauty of what we'd created together.

I wished he could somehow know what it meant to me that he came back to me, that he stayed. All of my fears of this pregnancy had been wrapped up in having to do it alone, without the one I loved to share something so momentous.

Jared cast me a restless smile, anxiety and hope and undeniable affection swimming in the blue ocean of his eyes.

She set the probe beneath my belly button. Together, we turned back, our attention glued to the screen. Blacks and whites passed in a fuzzy roll, completely unidentifiable.

Until an unmistakable image came to life.

My heart stilled.

Stopped.

Then it took off on a sprint, pounding hard. It surged with warmth, a flood that spilled over to expand my ribs. It spread fast, taking me whole, wedging in my throat and thickening my tongue. It swelled, filling my eyes.

Tears traced down the sides of my face and slipped into my hair.

There was nothing I could do to stop them.

I'd seen pictures of sonograms before, so I knew what to expect. The large, bulbous head, the body half the size, legs and arms tucked in close, the blossoming fetus swathed in the comfort of its mother's womb.

But this . . . this was my child.

Our baby.

What Jared and I had created, something so pure and innocent in the midst of all the uncertainty and pain that had surrounded our tumultuous beginning.

The tiny heart fluttered. So fast. So alive.

And a fist. Five fingers extended before flexing to a fist, held out in front of the distinct profile of its face.

I tried to swallow, to breathe through something so overwhelming I didn't know how to make sense of everything I felt.

I was shattered.

In the most amazing way.

By an overpowering love I didn't know how to manage, something new that rose up in the greatest wave before it crashed and swept me from my feet.

Yes, I'd already fallen in love with this baby. Anticipation and expectation had filled up the thoughts of my days and nights, ideas of what this child would be, a boy or a girl, the sound of its voice and the lilt of its laugh. What it would feel like in my arms.

But the magnitude of this came without warning.

Jared stood. Fingertips brushed down my face, capturing my tears. I turned to look up at him. He stared down at me, the blue of his eyes alight, on fire, caught up in his own inferno of emotion. Palpably, his pulse throbbed, his heart beating just as fast as mine. He pressed his mouth to my temple, kissing me softly, tenderly. "Look at that," he said so quietly, totally in awe.

Never had I felt more complete.

The technician continued, tapping her fingers on the keyboard as she took measurements, moving the probe to capture our baby's image, size and length in centimeters, while Jared and I just stared in awe.

She gave us the due date. That was the reason my doctor had sent me here earlier than what was typical. I didn't know the exact day of my last period.

"May sixteenth," she told us.

May sixteenth.

I turned the date over in my head.

I guess I'd always imagined this baby was conceived on that last morning when I'd felt Jared slipping away. Like he'd left a piece of himself with me when he subconsciously knew he was leaving. But no. This was conceived during one of those nights he'd come to me. When he'd cherished me and loved me when he didn't believe he knew how.

The woman left us with three pictures, a tiny image of our baby on each one.

The door slipped closed behind her.

Jared bent over my middle, his big hands stretched wide as he held our child. He craned his ear, leaning in close, like he could hear what was happening inside. He looked up at me from where he hovered over my belly. Completely wrecked. Undone. Like he would never be the same.

Just like me.

He drove us home. No words were said, like the two of us needed the silence to absorb the day. I settled my hand low on my belly, over the tiny bump that evidenced our child.

For both of us, I think it had finally become real.

Jared parked in front of our little house, and I climbed out onto my shaky feet.

I walked through the front door, and again, I was struck by this man, by what he'd done and wanted for us. Every inch of the house was beautiful. Perfect. Better than anything I ever could have imagined.

I still didn't think he could ever know what it meant to me, what it felt like every time I stepped through the door.

Like I was home only because Jared had come home to me.

I dropped my purse to the floor just inside the door. Images flooded my eyes and mind, and the innate impulse I'd always had to express my feelings in images hit me harder than they had in a very long time. My fingers twitched with the desire to create. I trailed my fingertips along the hallway, my steps slow as I headed for the place Jared had reserved for me, the place where he'd felt the power of inspiration that he wanted for me.

I nudged open the door.

It too had been completely redone, the walls repaired and the windows replaced. It was painted the softest hue of blue. My sketchbooks lined the walls on the shelves Jared had built next to a desk with drawers filled with supplies, a couch up to the side just like he'd promised when he first brought me to this place.

I loved it here.

I loved him.

And oh my God, I loved this baby.

In the middle of the room, I sank to the plush carpet with a large sketch pad balanced on my knees. I tucked my feet up close to my body, facing the window that looked out on the endless desert sky. The small protrusion in my belly jutted out into the cradle of my lap.

My hand brushed furiously over the blank canvas. Streaks of charcoaled black bled across the page, distinct lines and muted curves that I smudged out with the back side of my pinkie.

Tears streaked down my cheeks. I couldn't contain it all, this love that had bloomed too full. It had to be released, from my eyes and from my hand.

It came to life, this precious being I somehow already knew, something that forged the strongest bond and the deepest love. It was like I held my child while I drew, my pencil fierce as it sketched and burned and created the image of the face I could never forget.

It was what I saw. Not the two-dimensional image the machine had generated. But real. Full. Vibrant.

I felt the intensity of his presence behind me. It stole what little air was left in the room, like he was wading through the pictures of my imagination, the man a permanent part of it because there was no place he could go that I would not think of him.

He inched forward before he came to settle behind me. A

heavy exhale pushed from his lungs as he flanked my legs with his. He pulled me close to him. Over my shoulder, he stared, his breath in my face and in my soul.

His fingers fluttered along the picture of our child, his knuckles stamped with the year of his birth.

Life.

All I'd ever wanted was for him to experience it again.

He swallowed hard, his face buried in the back of my hair, his voice full of the deepest reverence. "Thank you," he murmured, the words hoarse, speaking of everything I wanted for our lives.

FOURTEEN

Aleena

I scrubbed down the kitchen, cleaning the gorgeous granite, my movements slow and fluid as I rinsed off the rag and squeezed out the excess water. Satisfaction thrummed a steady beat within every inch of my being.

I still couldn't believe this house was mine.

My ear tuned in on the other room where Jared worked. He fumbled around. A clatter of nails spilled to the floor. "Motherfucker," he mumbled over the commotion he caused.

I resisted a smile.

These evenings were my favorite.

I didn't know what it was, but I loved when it was just Jared and me. Christopher stopped by about every day, and Megan had dropped in twice this week. They missed me. And I missed them too.

Right now, though, I yearned for this time with Jared, to learn him and to let him learn me. Even though I knew him better than anyone in this world, and I knew his heart just as well as he knew mine, we were learning how to live together like a normal couple.

But deep within my soul I knew Jared and I were not a normal couple. We'd never be. Too many scars were scored on his heart. There was too much history and too much hurt.

My chest tightened and I fought for a breath.

And I knew, without a doubt, that I loved him too much.

It left us in this boundless bliss.

Yet vulnerable.

Volatile.

"Goddamn it." His voice rumbled from the family room.

I tossed the dishtowel to the counter and crossed the kitchen. I leaned my shoulder up against the wall and watched him from behind. On the floor, he knelt on his knees in front of the fireplace. Shirtless. Even though it was nearing the end of December, the winter days mild and the nights cool, a slight sheen of sweat coated his skin from the exertion he put into the job in front of him.

He ducked his blond head, dipping it low to carefully drag a pencil down the length of a piece of wood against a metal carpenter's square.

Shuffling around, he grabbed another piece of wood. He situated it next to the other on the clear piece of plastic he set out to protect the new carpet that now covered our family room floor. His jeans rode low on his hips. Strength bristled in his corded arms as he reached forward, his defined shoulders taut and straining as he moved. Muscle rippled down his back, a potent, slow dance of power beneath the horror of colors that swirled and bled across his skin.

Desire throbbed low in my stomach.

One thing I definitely knew was that body.

And God, did he know mine.

Jared took me places I didn't know existed, brought me more pleasure than should be humanly possible. One look and I shook. One touch and I came undone.

My gaze wandered in slow appreciation. He rose up on his knees and stretched out his long body to measure the height of the fireplace, verifying all his calculations were correct. Concentration edged his brow, his eyes drawn into a deep furrow as he studied his work, completely absorbed in it.

Not a moment existed when I didn't want him.

The crazy thing was I'd be content to stand here all day long and watch him work. I loved seeing him in his element. In the place where he appeared entirely free.

Here, his eyes never dimmed and his demeanor never shifted.

He never froze for a blink of a moment as he was overcome by a memory.

Never disappeared into the past where his spirit remained chained.

Never shook it off and continued on like he hadn't been slammed by an uprising of guilt, his body wrenched tight by a bolt of shame.

Jared hid those moments well. Pretended they didn't exist. He shoved them off faster than he thought I saw them.

But I did.

Because with Jared, I could never look away.

But here? In the midst of a project he was building?

Jared was lifted above what fought to keep him down.

"I can feel you staring at me," he muttered toward the floor, aligning two pieces of wood.

Fighting a smile, I crossed my arms over my chest. "You can, huh? And do you have a problem with that?"

From over his shoulder, Jared lifted his chin toward me with a cocky smirk. "Depends on what you're thinking about."

That smile let go, and I cocked my head, my eyes making another pass down the length of his hard body. I fastened him with a smirk of my own. "Wouldn't you like to know."

Jared scowled, blue eyes narrowed. "Goddamn it, Aly, I'm never going to get this fireplace finished if you keep looking at me like that."

I pushed off the wall, dodging a toolbox as I wound my way over to the couch. "And how am I looking at you?" I asked, playing his game, because there was no doubt what I was thinking, no question Jared was trailing those thoughts like a hound. Sitting down, I tucked one leg up to my chest, sinking into the comfort of the plush cushions.

Jared's eyes stroked over me, resting a beat longer on the back of my bare thigh. I figured I'd better wear my little sleep shorts as much as I could, the ones that Jared somehow both seemed to love and despise, before I couldn't fit in them anymore. They were getting snug.

Still, I felt incredibly sexy under the intensity of Jared's heady gaze.

Beautiful.

Because I knew that's how he saw me.

Blatant desire flashed in his blue eyes when they flew back up to mine. "You're looking at me like you want me to drop this hammer, throw you over my shoulder, and carry you to our bedroom. Or maybe you're just thinking you'd like me to take you right there on the couch." He inclined his head like he was deep in thought. Like the man could dig right through mine. "Yes . . . yes . . . that's exactly what you're thinking." His voice lowered, all indecent, making me squirm. "Definitely, the couch."

Heat flushed my body, from my ears to my toes.

"Pretty sure you just described exactly how you're looking at me," I countered, feigning disinterest, the pretense dropping from my mouth like a rock.

Throaty laughter rolled from him, and he shook his head.

He knew it, too.

As if I could really pretend he didn't have this irrational hold on me.

Jared rubbed his chin, something sweet taking over his expression. "Baby, believe me . . . whatever you're thinking right now doesn't come close to what I'm imagining doing to you. But I'm never going to get this fireplace finished if you keep distracting me."

"Distracting you?" It came as a flirty tease . . . because, yeah, that's exactly what I was aiming for, teasing him a little, loving that we were free to engage in it, that we belonged to the other and none of this was a secret.

Loved that we could play.

And Jared had taken to teaching me all kinds of games.

"You are in the room, aren't you?" he drew out.

I smiled, widened my eyes.

Obviously.

He bit out a smirk. "Then I'm distracted."

"Do you want me to leave?"

He turned back to his work. I caught the slant of his eyes as he stole another glance at me. "Uh . . . no . . . don't move an inch. Just sit there like the siren you are. Consider yourself motivation. Because the second I get this template laid out, I'll be taking my prize."

I blushed a little, fighting the girlish giggle that built somewhere in my belly.

God, how did this man make me feel this way, sifting through me with the heaviest weight and make me feel lighter than air?

"Hurry up, then," I commanded, biting my lip.

Of everything he'd redone in this house, this was what he'd been most excited about.

The fireplace.

He couldn't stop talking about it, the plans he had to design it himself, to transform the plain fireplace into something of beauty. To etch and carve and create. Three days ago, he purchased the thick cylinders of wood he would use. Wood he would bisect, cutting it in half to make two columns. Those columns would flank both sides of the hearth, and a heavy mantel would cap off the top.

And Jared would sculpt it all.

Jared had drawn out blueprints, plans to carve out these elaborate designs, an intricate pattern of petals and leaves, the stems twisted and twined, a snarled bouquet that perfectly flowed. Apparently he'd done some different woodworking jobs back in Jersey, but nothing close to the scale he was planning now.

No doubt, it would be stunning, accenting everything in this house perfectly.

A basic bench jutted out from the bottom of the hearth to create a sitting area. He had plans to cover that portion with flat, smooth stones, like a garden of rocks that would give way to the floral vines that would climb the walls.

Unadulterated pride had simmered all over his face when he first showed his idea to me.

It was one of the last projects he had planned for the house. It was almost complete, this house that was a dream, gorgeous and reflecting the true man Jared was inside. It shined from the walls, bore down from the ceilings, and radiated from the floors.

Since he had come back, I'd been struck by something I should have always known.

Jared was an artist.

I realized it when he first brought me here.

How could I not have seen it before? The way he'd been as a boy, constantly dreaming . . . imagining what we could create, taking us on journeys in his mind and doing everything he could to make them real.

Building.

Constructing.

Bringing the visions in his mind to life.

And his words . . .

God, the words that Jared wrote and the ones he whispered.

He was beautiful, that beauty formed within and pouring out.

A creator and a poet.

Maybe I'd only attributed art to my pencils and paper.

But Jared's craft encompassed so much more than that. It infiltrated everything he did, weaving through his thoughts and flowing from his words, the creativity forged by his hand left behind in everything he touched.

And all of it was stunning.

Jared had convinced me to chase my own dreams, too. I wasn't going back to nursing school this next semester. Instead, I'd enrolled at one of the art schools in town. I still wasn't entirely sure what I wanted to do with it other than draw faces the way I saw them in my head, but I hoped these classes would help me hone my skills and point me in a direction where drawing would become my career.

My phone vibrated on the end table, gave way to a shrill ring. I glanced at the screen.

"Who's that?" Jared asked offhandedly, settling back into his rhythm.

"Christopher. Surprised?"

"Uh, no. Asshole might as well move in."

"Well, I guess you kind of owe him," I pointed out, laughing under my breath as I swiped my finger across the faceplate to accept the call. Jared probably wasn't all that far from the truth.

Christopher was a constant, a mainstay.

I loved that he cared so much about me. Underneath all the brashness and banter was a man whom I'd come to deeply respect.

He'd been there for me when no one else had.

I'd never forget it.

It didn't mean I made things easy on him, because he sure didn't make things easy on me.

"Christopher . . . I was getting worried. I haven't heard from you in two hours." I winked at Jared, and he just shook his head in disbelief and crawled over the plans he rolled out. He traced his finger over them.

"Oh, was just thinking about my favorite sister."

"Your only sister," I corrected.

"That's what I said."

"You're such a jerk . . . did you just call to remind me of that?" I asked absently, because it took me all of about half a second to get distracted watching Jared tuck a pencil behind his ear. Slowly, he dragged his tongue over his bottom lip, then he caught it between his teeth, his focus intent.

Christopher laughed through the line, and I could almost see the smirk climb to his face, the mischief in the green of his vibrant eyes. "Nah . . . not this time. I was calling to find out what you guys have planned for Tuesday night."

New Year's Eve.

Right.

I just wanted to stay here, on the couch, curled up with Jared.

"Timothy's having a party," he stated.

Shocking. Timothy was always having a party. Memories of this summer flooded me, the night Jared finally snapped and gave in to what had been chasing us for so long, the first time his mouth met mine.

Fireworks.

There was no other way to describe it.

Jared paused his work, slanting his narrowed eyes up toward me. "Tell your brother I said not a chance." He shook his head and situated another piece of wood.

Pulling the phone a fraction away from my mouth, I frowned in question. "You don't want to go?"

Jared shook his head. "No . . . we're not going." A faint smile rimmed his mouth. Still, I could tell he was dead set, staunch, completely serious in his resistance.

This wasn't meant as a taunt to Christopher, not another rib to get back at his friend.

That frown deepened as I looked down at Jared, who sat back on his haunches, all of the focus that had been on his work now directed at me.

Christopher caught Jared's words. "Tell that asshole best friend of mine he owes me. He already stole my sister from my house, I'm not about to let him rob me of New Year's with you."

I held the phone out into the middle of the room for Jared to hear. "I don't think he's going to take no for an answer." I laughed a little, listening to Christopher's rant flooding the room, demanding we both be there.

Jared crawled toward me and snatched the phone from my hand. He pressed it to his ear. "Dude, you should know by now you can't sweet-talk me like one of those bitches you keep hidden away in your bed. Words aren't going to work. I told you no yesterday. What do you think has changed between now and then?" Jared challenged, grinning over at me, trying to contain his laughter when Christopher went off on him, piling more unsound reasons on top of the ones he'd already given.

Blue eyes remained locked on me as he listened. He shook his head. "Sorry, man, but no." Jared eyed me, something mischievous and secretive playing all over his face.

Butterflies took flight in my stomach.

Or maybe it was the baby, I couldn't tell. I'd just begun to feel it, this fluttering within me. The first time, it stole my breath, sucked all the air from the room, left me light-headed and reeling.

Either way, I adored the feeling.

"No, I wasn't joking. We have plans," he continued.

We did?

Those butterflies rioted, a rumble of nerves and excitement and an unknown thrill.

Jared winked at me while he humored my brother, listening to him carry on about the great injustice our absence would cause.

The question formed in my mind formed on my lips. "We do?" I mouthed.

So maybe I cherished the thought too much. That idea that Jared thought of me above all else. That he wanted to surprise me and cause me joy.

I looked around the house.

The last surprise he'd given me had been just about the best of my life.

I ran a tender hand over the small protrusion of my belly, my smile soft as I glanced down. Well, maybe not the best.

But close.

"Yes, we do," Jared whispered back, holding the phone away from his ear. He spoke toward the receiver, to me, to Christopher, like he was letting it be known. "It's just me and Aly Tuesday night, Christopher. Sorry, dude, no offense, but there's absolutely nothing you can say to change what I have planned."

My heart swelled, throbbed and pulsed and raced.

How much did I love this man?

I bit my lip, trying to cover up the huge smile that worked to break free from my mouth.

Christopher cracked some joke I could barely catch.

Jared rolled his eyes my direction. "Whatever, man."

Jared laughed, listened, shook his head.

"Your brother's such a dickhead." Jared staged the whisper, just loud enough for Christopher to hear.

Christopher scoffed, lifting his voice and shouting into the phone so I could hear. "Fine, Aly, choose this asshole over me."

"That's because she's mine," Jared shot back. "Get over it."

I giggled because it felt good, the two most important men in my life fighting over me, their banter light and full of ease. Contentment glowed bright.

I loved my life.

I felt complete.

Whole.

Jared softened, nodding at whatever Christopher said. "All right . . . yeah . . . of course I will . . . okay, I'll talk to you later." Jared paused, his ear craned toward the phone, but his attention entirely trained on me. A smile lit his face. "Yeah, you too, man. Thanks . . . bye."

Jared ended the call and tossed my phone to the cushion beside me. He crawled the rest of the way over. Kneeling in front of the couch, he grabbed me by the outside of my thighs and pulled me to the edge.

"What was that, what Christopher just said?" I asked, searching his face.

Jared's teeth clamped down on his bottom lip. The skin blanched. Ice blue eyes glimmered with the unknown.

Waves of warmth skimmed along my skin.

"It was nothin'," he said, too low and too severe for it to be true.

Jared edged back a fraction. He ran the back of his hand down my face, palmed my neck as he stared at me, searching. His thumb ran the length of my jaw, somehow shaky and unsure. "Is that okay, baby, that I made plans for us? I don't want to do all that party shit. I just want to spend the night with my girl. Alone."

Rapidly he blinked, and I watched the thick knot in his throat bob as he swallowed hard.

I brushed my fingers through the short length of his hair, then dragged them down his rugged face. For a flash, Jared's eyes dropped closed. I let my fingers linger on his full lips. "I can't think of any better way to spend the New Year. Just you and me," I murmured.

He slowly opened to me, accepting my answer for the truth it was.

Gently, Jared kissed the tips of my fingers, the softness of his tongue flicking out to meet my skin.

Jared slipped his hands down my sides and found the hem of my tank. Intently he watched me as he nudged it up a few inches, exposing our tiny bump. He trailed circles on my flesh. Goose bumps flashed, and I trembled.

Leaning in, he pressed the softest kiss to my belly, his voice hoarse.

"Good, because I wouldn't have taken no for an answer."

Below us, the deep valley was lit up in the city's glow, a bed of twinkling lights stretched out as far as we could see. Above us, a shimmer of stars blanketed the impenetrable, darkened sky.

Somehow, Jared and I seemed suspended in an unknown world lost somewhere in between.

Cold air gusted in. It lashed at my hair, stirring up the long strands. They thrashed at my shoulders, whipped at my face, uncontrolled, just as uncontrolled as the thundered pulse battering my ribs.

I was pretty sure Jared had staged an assault in my heart.

Yet I felt so safe.

Nothing in this world could touch me. Nothing. No one.

No one except for the man holding me in the haven of his arms.

He managed to pull me a little closer. "Are you cold, baby?" he whispered from behind. We were nestled on the bed of blankets he made, the two of us completely cocooned in a thick comforter. Unyielding, he held me tight, firm and unwavering, his body a rock of support behind mine. He tucked his chin over my shoulder and feathered a row of kisses on my jaw.

His heavy breaths panted out into the night air, filling up my senses as I drew him in. As I rested in his warmth.

"Mmm," I managed through a small moan. "Perfect."

So maybe I was a little cold.

But I wouldn't trade this moment for anything.

Like he'd just read my thoughts, he bundled us tighter in the blanket to deflect more of the cold.

"I can't believe how beautiful it is up here." I'd told him before, the first time he brought me to this place.

I guess I shouldn't have been surprised we'd return, that this was the spot Jared had chosen for us to ring in the New Year.

South Mountain.

It overlooked the breathtaking expanse of the sprawling city below. But more important than that was the fact it was the place that had meant so much to him as a child, an integral piece of those memories.

The same place he had ventured to bring me all those months ago.

Again, he wanted to share it with me.

Of course, we had to sneak up here tonight. Jared had parked my car off the side of one of the dirt roads at the base of the mountain where it was being developed, the main park closed off for the night.

I'd felt light as he'd wrapped my hand in his, both of us giggling and feeling so free as we stole our way up the mountain to find the deserted path Jared had scoped out a few days before. I loved knowing we'd be completely alone, loved the feeling of Jared whisking me away to a place he'd reserved only for us.

I ran my fingers over the backs of the hands that held me close. Night had taken hold, deep and dark, the half-moon barely enough to illuminate the sharp lines of his face. "Do you remember the last time you brought me up here?" I asked.

He snorted a little. "How could I forget?" He snuggled closer, his nose weaving through my hair as he breathed me in, as if it was the breath that sustained his life. "You on my bike . . . those legs wrapped around me . . ." I felt the affected grin push to his mouth. "One of the best fucking days of my life. God, Aly, I wanted you so badly I thought I was going to lose my goddamned mind."

I rolled my head back on his shoulder, looking up at him. His eyes glinted in the faint light, all soft and affectionate, lost to those days that had been so unsure.

"You had me the next night."

He nuzzled my temple, chuckling beneath his heated breath. "Now *that* was the best fucking day of my life."

I giggled and snuggled closer.

"I never stopped wanting you . . . not for a second . . . never gonna stop, either," he mumbled out on a flood of words he whispered against my skin.

Tingles spread.

I bit at my lip, a rush of joy speeding through my veins, infiltrating every cell. "Good, because I'm not going to let you go."

A sharp bite of cold air blew across the desert rim, and he hugged me, like he was affirming the statement I'd just made. Silence overtook us, the extreme beauty of the night not coming close to the beauty Jared and I shared.

A roll of agitation curled through Jared. "I wanted to bring you up here for a reason, Aly. So much has changed since the first time we came here." He shook his head against all the doubts. I could feel them, like an unseen plague, festering. But as strong as they were, I could feel Jared fighting them. Fighting for us.

"God, I was so confused. Always in this fucked-up war with myself, hating what I felt for you. Trying to pretend like you and I weren't meant to be together. All I knew then was I needed to see you in this place. Some of the best memories of my life were made here and I somehow wanted to make you a part of it. Now I know why I needed to bring you here the first time."

His chin dug further into my neck, his face pressed right up against my jaw. He ran his cold nose along it. Chills slipped down my spine. Comfort and unease. Like I could feel it, the inundating well of emotion that had built inside of Jared.

I knew he was getting ready to pour it out on me.

And I ached for it, for more, for him to press his mouth there instead, to lay me down and to love me under the stars.

Mostly I ached for his words, for him to open up to me, to show me more.

I knew the man still hid so much pain inside.

I clenched his hands in mine, clinging to him, begging him silently to continue.

"There was no stopping it . . . the way you worked yourself right into my heart. You took it over, Aly. You made me feel something real again when I believed all I could feel was hate." Jared's tone shifted just the same as his demeanor, almost desperate in its emphasis. "I can't live without you, baby . . . can't sleep without you . . . can't breathe without you."

My pulse escalated with the palpable rise of his. His heart beat erratically where it pounded against my back. He sucked in a shaky breath and unwound himself from the blanket. Cautiously, he stood, never releasing my hand. He looked out on the blackened horizon, over the vast sea of lights. "It's getting close."

An uproar echoed from afar, horns and the faint shout of voices, the pop of small fireworks being lit from backyards, the rise in excitement.

Jared helped me to my feet, making sure to keep the blanket secure around my shoulders. Wrapping me in his arms, he brought us cheek to cheek and turned to face us out over the city that harbored so many of our memories.

The place where we were building more.

Jared dug his phone from his pocket and swiped the screen.

The countdown rolled on, this past year that had changed the direction of my life coming to an end.

He gathered me up tight. His voice came as a soft rasp, like a promise at my ear. "Five . . . four . . . three . . ."

With each number that fell from his tongue, his voice dropped lower, the tone twisting through me with a frenzy of anticipation. With all our hopes and dreams.

"Two . . ."

Jared dropped his phone to the ground. He rested his forehead against mine and framed my face in his big, gentle hands.

"One."

I jumped with the loud boom.

I was sure I felt it all the way in my soul, the flare of firework colors that flashed, climbing toward the sky. The ripples of energy vibrated all the way to my bones the second Jared's mouth overtook mine.

He kissed me passionately, with all of him, demanding all of me. Lips tugged at mine, suckling at the top before turning to the bottom, making a firm pass over the top again. He just teased me with his tongue, the faintest whisper of wet.

Jared's hands held fast.

The sky lit in a barrage of color that reflected against our skin, beating at the lids of my closed eyes, like flashes of our future, like a vow had been spoken between us.

Jared pulled back, still holding my face. Fiercely. Fervently.

"Are you going to marry me, Aly Moore?"

Hopeful blue eyes looked down on me.

I froze with the shock. The question collided with my spirit. Flames of hope blazed within me. Tears welled, and I blinked through the blurriness, praying Jared really meant what he asked.

"Jared?" It scraped from my throat with all the love I had for this man.

He dropped to his knee.

My hand shot to my mouth to cover the sob that gathered in my tightened chest. The blanket fell free and pooled at my feet.

The fiercest squall of wind gusted in. Cold lapped at my skin while I remained submerged in the warmth of Jared's unflinching gaze. The faint moonlight illuminated the contours of his face, the sharp angles and planes, all that coarse beauty staring up at me.

He wet his lips, and slipped his hand in his pocket. He shook when he withdrew the treasure he had hidden inside.

Light glinted on the diamond set at the center of the ring.

And I was sure my heart would explode because he'd filled it so full.

Burst.

He took my shaky hand in his.

On the wind, Jared whispered his praise.

"Aleena . . ."

I watched him swallow down the emotion that thickened in his throat. "Tell me you want to spend your life with me, and I promise to give you mine."

"Oh my God . . . Jared . . ." Tears streaked down my face, hot and fast and hard. They dripped from my chin as I nodded. "Oh my God, yes. Yes."

Yes.

How could I want anything else?

Jared slid the ring onto my finger.

A rattled sob escaped my mouth, something like relief and shock and this undying love that I kept for this man.

I was overcome.

Slowly, Jared stood, his movements slow but sure. He lifted me from my feet and into his arms. I clung to his neck, and I buried my face in the warmth. Slowly he spun us, loved me in the slowest dance, my feet dangling two inches from the ground. His mouth was at my ear. "Won't ever let you go, Aly. I promise, I won't ever let you go."

FIFTEEN

Jared

I was never going to let her go.

I turned right onto the narrow neighborhood street. A ramble of older houses sat close to the road, barely a breath between them, the road cramped with what had to be a hundred cars lining each side. Timothy's house was lit up like a Christmas tree, white twinkle lights strung up everywhere, a haphazard jumble strewn in the trees and across the face of the house. People poured out the front door and onto the lawn, undoubtedly because they all couldn't fit inside. Hands boasted red cups and bottles, too loud voices and too loud music thumping against Aly's little car as we slowly passed by.

"You sure you want to go in there?" I asked, trying to untwist the frown that took a deep seat between my eyes.

New Year's Eve on a college street.

Now that was just a straight-out mess, a disaster waiting to happen.

No, thank you.

But it hadn't taken her much to get me to head over here.

When we got back into the car after climbing the short distance back down the mountain, Aly had inspected her ring in the overhead light for about five minutes straight.

Then she'd called her mom. Guess she figured her mom would still be awake on New Year's Eve, and if she wasn't, Aly didn't seem all too worried about waking her up. It'd been crazy listening to Aly talking to her, the thrill in her voice and the tenderness in her words. The joy.

Karen had asked to talk to me. She told me thank you, told me she already considered me a son. Her statement came like a double-edged sword, like fucking torment as it cut me through, then washed over me like some kind of astonishing consolation.

I cut my gaze to Aly. She looked over at me with a huge-ass grin owning that gorgeous face.

Once she'd stopped crying, she hadn't stopped smiling.

Joy lit a frenzy in my chest. The girl made me insane with it, a fray of nerves that clashed, all this fucking ecstasy and fear and need that all added up to her, added up to her happiness and everything I wanted to give her because she'd given me everything.

After tonight, after the promise we made, I hated the thought of taking her through that door. I didn't want to be here.

At. Fucking. All.

The only thing I had on my mind was getting this girl home and getting her laid out on our bed.

But I got it. Aly wanted to announce it to her friends. To her brother. Part of me wanted to scream it, too.

I mean, fuck.

I raked an uneasy hand through my hair.

Why the hell did I want that ring on her finger in the first place? I already knew she was mine. I just figured it was about time the whole damn world knew it.

A rash of memories stirred through my spirit, my mother's voice a warning in my ear.

I was a fool if I thought that was all. I knew what it meant, me asking Aly for forever.

My mom had been pretty open-minded, did her best at teaching me not to judge, to be tolerant and let people live out their lives the way they saw fit. But she taught me that some things were special, too. Sanctified. That marriage wasn't a fucking joke like so many treated it. It wasn't something to be wasted, wasn't a test or a trial, even though she made sure I knew marriage would be full of them.

I wanted that.

"When did you turn into a crotchety old man?" Aly teased, brushing a soft hand down my arm, all flirty and full of this excitement that radiated a glow from her smooth olive skin.

And goddamn, how badly did I want her?

I shoved down the shot of lust that fisted me in the gut and grinned at my girl as I lifted a surly brow, because apparently that kind of grinning was infectious. "Crotchety?" I tossed it out, daring her to say it back as I turned the car around in the middle of the street and wedged it into an open spot on the opposite side of the road.

"Yes, crotchety," she threw back with a small giggle. "You never even want to leave the house."

I smirked. *For obvious reasons.*

"I'm way too excited to go home and sleep," she said, anxious as she looked at the house lit up across the street.

Apparently she didn't realize sleeping wasn't exactly what I had in mind.

She chewed at her lip, stole a glance at her ring for about the five millionth time since we climbed down the mountain and into the car.

Green eyes gleamed when they met with mine; then she softened, like she recognized the resistance there.

A small, understanding smile pulled at one side of her mouth, and she cupped my cheek. She leaned forward and placed a swift kiss to my lips, innocent and sweet. Still, it lit a fucking raging fire inside of me.

"Give me a half an hour. I know you wanted tonight to only be the two of us, but I want to wish Christopher and Megan a Happy New Year. Then we're out of here." She cracked open her door, climbed out, then ducked back inside and wiggled her fingers in front of my face. Her ring glimmered in the glow of the cabin light. "Oh, and I want to show this baby off."

I chuckled at this girl, crazy good and full of life. As if I didn't know her showing off that ring was the only reason we were here.

I got out, came around, and dragged her into my arms. My mouth found the shell of her ear.

Aly shivered.

"We'll stay as long as you want, baby, just not so long you think you want to fall asleep the second I get you home."

"I wouldn't dream of it."

We crossed the street, dodging all the drunken assholes littering the front yard, half of them barely able to stand.

It wasn't even funny how many times I'd been that asshole.

I kept hold of Aly's hand, leading her through the masses. She stopped to say hi to a couple people she recognized, not spending much time with any of them, her destination clear.

Maybe that's why being here made me so uncomfortable, all these faces Aly knew. It made me all shifty and ill at ease, this piece of Aly's life I didn't know. Guess the best way to get over that obstacle was to jump it head-on.

I swung the front door open without a knock.

A horde of bodies overflowed the small house, all of them gathered in groups or huddled in corners, a mass of them loitering in the center of the room. Music thrummed into the muted light in the hazy room. Loud conversations and raucous laughter filled the air, but there was no chance to hear what a soul was saying with all of it mixed together.

Well, except for one.

"Holy shit . . . look what the cat dragged in," Christopher shouted as he wove and pushed his way through the crowd with his attention locked on me.

I laughed and pulled Aly in front of me. "Aly Cat," I teased beneath my breath, wrapping her up in my arms and tugging her back to my chest.

This girl who'd always held me in the palm of her hand.

"You two are such jerks," Aly mumbled only to me. Still, she melted into me, folding her hands over mine that held her around her front.

I felt her heave a breath of contentment, while I drew one in, all that coconut and good and girl.

This girl I was going to make my wife.

Christopher stumbled out and into the open area at the front of the door where Aly and I stood.

Should have known he wouldn't be hard to find.

A drunken smile morphed his face into a sloppy welcome. What had to be the tightest pair of black skinny jeans I'd ever seen covered his lanky ass. He wore a black, long-sleeved button-up shirt, wrinkled and untucked, the cuffs rolled up his forearms. Three buttons at the collar were undone, exposing a glimpse of the new tat he'd just had inked on a couple weeks before. Under it, clear color was sprawled out across the entirety of his chest. Fisted in one hand was a half-empty bottle of Patrón. He lifted both arms out to his sides, stretched out like a broken offering.

Dude looked like he just stage-dived into the crowd after playing in a three-hour show.

As Christopher approached, I lifted my chin. "Hey, man, Happy New Year."

Surprise flitted all over his face. "What are you two doing here?" Tequila sloshed when he lifted the bottle to his mouth. He took a swig as he eyed me with flat-out amusement. "Thought there wasn't a thing I could say that would make you change your mind." He mocked an insult through his grin, his throat bobbing as he swallowed hard.

"Right you are, my friend. There wasn't anything *you* could say to get me to change my mind." I squeezed Aly more, enough to just barely lift her off her feet as I buried my face in the soft flesh of her neck, hooking my chin over her shoulder as I pinned him with a frivolous stare. "But it seems your sister here does have the power to sway me."

Christopher laughed, drove a hand through his unruly hair. "Aly Cat does have a way about her, doesn't she?"

I could feel her cheeks heat with that bit of shyness I hoped to God Aly always had.

"Yes, she definitely does."

Christopher smiled. "Guess that power was in my favor, so I can't complain."

I sobered a little, watching my oldest friend over my girl's shoulder. "Aly was actually on a mission, coming here. She has something she wants to tell you."

I nudged her forward. Nervous laughter stuttered from her, and she tottered toward him, her smile sweet and timid with all that dark hair billowing around her. She fell into her brother's arms. "Happy New Year, Christopher."

Christopher wrapped her up, held her tight, the bottle dangling from his fingers at her back. He looked at me, those green eyes keen. He was obviously not as fucked-up as he had initially appeared to be.

I swear to God, he played that shit up, acting too loud and too appealing, indifferent and unmoved. No one knew how to make sense of him. I was pretty sure that's exactly the way he wanted it to be.

"Happy New Year, little sister," he said seriously as he pulled back and looked down at her. His attention jumped between us. "So what is so important that you managed to get this asshole to come out and celebrate the New Year with me?"

Aly lifted her hand, twisting it out to show Christopher the diamond glinting on her finger.

Then she squealed.

She fucking squealed and bounced and almost screamed, "We're getting married!"

And damn, if I wasn't smiling just as big as her, this entirely overwhelming feeling throbbing from every cell in my entire being.

Aly glanced back at me over her shoulder, the same expression I was sure I was wearing evidenced on her face.

God, I loved her.

Shock lanced lines into Christopher's forehead. But his eyes sparked with something meaningful when he looked over at me. Then he turned back to his sister and hugged her again. "So happy for you, Aly. Honestly."

She pulled back, holding him by the forearms, her voice filled with emotion. "Thank you."

A shriek lifted above all the noise in the room. "Aly!" Megan came barreling through the small room, paying no mind to the people she mowed down to get to us.

"I thought I heard you were here!"

Megan wore about the shortest skirt I'd ever seen and a pair of boots that went up past her knees. She threw herself into Aly's arms. The two of them hugged and rocked each other in this awkward little dance. Tipsy and overzealous, Megan almost tossed Aly from her feet. "Ahh . . . Happy New Year! I missed you!"

Watching them I chuckled. Obviously, Megan was trashed, her eyes all glazed over and her words slurring. Aly returned the wishes, her face alight as she pulled back and waggled her hand right in front of Megan's face. "Look what I have," Aly sang.

Megan grabbed her hand and studied it closely. "Holy shit." Her jaw dropped and she turned her wide blue eyes on me. "Did you rob a bank or something?"

Self-conscious laughter rolled from my tongue, and I shifted, rubbing at my chin, but I couldn't stop from smiling at Aly's best friend.

Okay, so it wasn't the biggest rock in the world.

It also wasn't the smallest.

The second I saw it, I knew it belonged on Aly's finger. The entire platinum band was covered with beveled inset diamonds, four rows of them that wrapped around to create the band. A huge rock sat prominent in the middle, set above the others.

Classic and beautiful.

Just like Aly.

"Only the best for my girl," I said, watching the reaction take hold on Aly's face, the way she looked at me as if she somehow saw me the same way I saw her.

Megan's palms slid to Aly's belly. Something reverent played out on her face, her words a whispered awe. "I can't believe my best friend is getting married and having a baby. It's just . . . crazy. And I get to be an auntie." Then her stark blue eyes grew wide, slammed with a thought. "Oh my God, think of all the work we have to do . . . have you picked a date yet? Before or after the baby?" She rambled on faster than I had time to make sense of her words, asking Aly about all our plans, what our budget was, where we wanted to have it, and a ton of other shit that made my head spin.

But I definitely got the gist.

A tingle of apprehension slithered down my spine and twisted somewhere in my stomach.

We sure as hell hadn't gotten that far. So what if I thought a quick trip to Vegas and the best fucking suite I could get for my girl sounded like a little piece of heaven? Making her permanently mine, without all the bullshit that normally went along with it?

Sounded like a solid plan to me.

Redness flushed up Aly's neck and settled as an ethereal glow on her cheeks, all this excitement and a jumble of elation and disquieted nerves playing out on her face.

Abject terror filled Christopher's eyes when he turned to stare across at me, the two of us frozen by just the thought of all the horrors involved in planning a wedding. Then his mouth twisted up in overt satisfaction and I was pretty damn sure the asshole was picturing me in a suit.

He pointed at me. "Dude, you are screwed. You surrendered your balls the second you put that ring on Aly's finger."

"Hey," Aly shot out. She scowled. "Do you have to be a jerk every second of your life?"

"What?" Christopher's shoulders rose to his ears, like he was innocent of all the asshole. "Just telling it like it is."

I scratched my head, fighting the chuckle brewing somewhere deep in my chest, fighting my impulse to agree with Christopher.

Because there was no doubt the girl owned me.

And there was no doubt I was going to be dealing with all the wedding bullshit.

But for Aly . . .

I looked at her as she beamed up at me from over her shoulder, radiating joy and happiness. She knocked the breath from me every time I stopped to take her in.

Anything.

I would do anything for this girl.

Truth was, I wouldn't even take the time to consider it bullshit. I'd do it with a grin on my face and a fucking skip in my step because it meant I got to make her mine.

Knowing laughter spilled from Christopher when he caught my expression.

I just shook my head, wrapping Aly back up in my arms.

Aly turned to Megan, all her hair getting up in my face when she rested her head on my shoulder.

"Don't get ahead of yourself, Megan." Aly squeezed my hands splayed protectively across her stomach. "This guy barely got up the nerve to propose an hour ago, so we haven't had a chance to talk about the details yet." It whipped from her tongue like a tease, and from behind, I could feel the force of her smile. "You should probably cool it before you send my man running."

I rocked her, tucked her close, my mouth tracing a path at the hollow under her ear. "Not running anywhere, baby."

Megan stepped around Aly and hiked up on her toes to throw her arms around my neck. One of my arms released Aly so I could hug her back in an awkward one-sided embrace that the three of us seemed to be partaking in.

She crushed me in her hold. "I'm so glad you came back to her," she whispered almost urgently, like she was sharing her darkest secret with me as she slanted an eye in Aly's direction. "You two deserve each other . . . to be together this way."

God, I wanted that. To actually deserve her. To be good enough to even stand in her presence.

Guess I was one lucky bastard that she was giving me her all.

Megan staggered back. "I think I need another drink."

My brow rose. Pretty sure she most definitely did not.

"Can I get either of you anything?" she asked.

Aly shook her head. "No, thanks. I'll grab us something in a minute. I haven't really gotten the chance to say hi to anyone else. I'd better make my rounds."

Megan nodded and backed away. "All right . . ." She pointed between the two of us. "Don't you dare leave without finding me and saying good-bye."

"Of course not," Aly promised, giving Megan's hand a quick squeeze before she released her.

Christopher wandered off behind her, and Aly spun around in my arms.

She touched my face. Worry struck across her features when she looked up at me, like our connection was alive, something that existed on another level, and she'd just experienced every single one of the questions that had run through my mind in the last ten minutes. Every fluctuation of my mood and every roil of my spirit.

And God, the girl was just that way, in tune with me, like she knew everything I continued to bury beneath all the shit that would forever plague my life.

That scared me a little bit, too.

She stepped closer to me. She slid her delicate arms around my waist and made herself all comfy against my chest. "Are you okay with all of this?" Her whisper was tinged with fear.

Again, Aly was already ahead of me, and she tipped her head back further to accept the gentle kiss I brushed across her forehead. "I'm fine, baby . . . don't mind being here at all."

And really, I was, because Aly was at my side.

"You know that's not what I meant. Everything that Megan was asking about." She chewed at the inside of her lip. Cautiously, she eyed me from where she had her head nestled on my chest. "Don't think I didn't feel you cringe when she started talking about wedding plans." Those eyes narrowed as she searched, waiting for my reaction.

Laughing low, I gathered her hand, twisted it up between us, and brushed the same kind of kiss I'd just adorned her forehead with on her ring. "I don't question this . . . not at all. But you have to know all the rest of that shit is going to make me nervous . . . I'm not exactly a dress-up kinda guy."

Her bottom lip blanched when she clamped down on it.

Damn, this girl was too much. I tugged her a little closer.

"I was surprised by this," she said honestly. For a second, she buried her face in my shirt, before she turned her gaze up to me. Trust and devotion and all this love glimmered in her eyes. "But I was hoping. I wanted it so much."

I exhaled softly. "Ever since I came back, I knew you were my life, Aly." I cupped her cheek. "You shouldn't have questioned this was going to happen."

She rocked up on her toes and pressed her mouth to mine. "I know . . . but it doesn't mean I'm not completely thankful for it." She settled down with a smile. "Best New Year's resolution ever."

Amusement twitched my mouth into a smirk. "Resolution?"

She stepped back, keeping hold of my hand as she pulled us deeper into the party filling up the walls of this tiny house. She glanced back. All the heaviness was gone and a sweet sexy grin that did crazy insane things to my heart was set firmly in its place. "Yep. You and me . . . It's going to be difficult but it's going to be worth it. Only the best resolutions are."

I struggled to keep up with her, tugging her back against me as she wove through the suffocating crowd. I let my hands wander down her front, knowing it was too dark for anyone to see much of anything. And hell, anything Aly and I had going didn't come close to touching on the brazen debauchery half the people in the house were partaking in.

"You think we're going to be difficult, huh?" My palms pressed flat into the top of her thighs, my fingers wandering for a flash in between.

Aly's breath caught.

"I thought things had been going pretty damn *easy*," I said.

"Oh, things are definitely *good*, Jared," she purred back with her face pressed all the way up under my jaw. "I'm just committed to seeing it through."

I was feeling playful, set free in the ease of Aly's touch, in the strength of her words that together were about the most powerful thing I'd ever experienced.

And a whole lot aroused.

I groaned, wishing we'd skipped stopping by after all.

"You need to stop," I warned, because while Aly might not expect it, I wasn't better than dragging her down the hall and finding a place to hide us behind a closed door.

A husky giggle wobbled up her throat and passed through those full lips. Aly let her hands do a little wandering of their own.

"You are evil," I accused, burrowing my face in her neck.

"I'm evil?" she mumbled through mock offense. Demanding
fingers made their way up to scrape over my head, twisting and
tugging at my short hair.

"In the sweetest possible way," I promised.

Aly stopped to chat with a few people she knew.

And did the girl ever like showing off her ring. She was
damn near giddy, flicking her fingers around, catching the cut
of the diamonds in the faint shimmers of light.

I tossed out some pleasantries when she gave introductions,
doing my best not to feel uncomfortable under all the scrutiny.

Most everyone had heard about us, had heard about the
baby, knew Aly's life was heading in an entirely different direction than the rest of her friends. It was kind of strange having
her here, too. Most of us were about the same age. Now there
was something that separated us, defined us as different, set us
apart.

One choice had changed everything. My decision to come
back to Phoenix had shifted the course of Aly's life and granted
me a new one. That one action changed it all.

If I hadn't have come, Aly would still be just like the rest of
her friends, focused on college, getting her degree, instead of
working on making a family.

Was it wrong?

I wasn't blind. I caught the looks, the outright shock when
we ran into a few of Aly's acquaintances who'd somehow missed
the gossip and hadn't heard she was pregnant. The eyes that
scoured my skin, then turned back to Aly like she'd lost her
mind. But Aly wasn't ashamed, not for a second, and I knew
without a doubt she wanted all of this, too.

She leaned in for a quick kiss, patted me on the chest. "I
think you've earned yourself a beer."

"Thank God."

She grinned, leading me by the hand into the kitchen, where the music wasn't so loud, where the secrets we whispered didn't have to be delivered on a shout.

"See, this wasn't so bad, was it?"

I roughed my hand over my face. "Nah . . . I love all your friends wondering what the fuck you're doing with an asshole like me." Sarcasm dripped from my tongue.

Playfully, Aly smacked me on the arm. "Ha . . . all those girls were wondering what you were doing with a girl like me. I don't know how we didn't slip on all the drool as we made our rounds. I think our announcement broke half the hearts in the room."

I shook my head, because sometimes my girl was ridiculous. "You are completely blind."

Soft fingers touched my face. "Twenty-twenty."

I grabbed those fingers, brushed my lips across the tips. "Love you."

"Love you back," she said.

Smiling, she turned away, leaned over to dig into an ice chest, giving me a good look at that sweet little ass.

Not a soul here could blame me.

Aly was just exquisite. Her ass and those legs were wrapped up in a pair of dark jeans. Jeans that were progressively getting tighter by the day, and goddamn, for Aly, pregnancy had managed some really fucking miraculous things.

I didn't think it was possible for this girl to get any more appealing, but each day, I only wanted her more.

Beer in hand, Aly spun back around. Her brow shot up when she caught my expression.

There was no denying the need stamped plainly on my face.

She sauntered up, pressed the beer into my hand. "Twenty minutes." She murmured the promise, knowing full well I was about to toss her over my shoulder and drag her the hell out of there.

I twisted the cap, flicked it into the garbage, and took a deep, satisfying pull. Ice-cold liquid took a freezing path down my overheated insides. I smacked my lips as I pulled the bottle away. "Fifteen," I corrected, cocking my head.

Incredulous, she laughed and shook her head, busying herself by grabbing a bottle of water. "Fine," she mouthed, passing by me with a wink. At the fringe of the crowd, she spun on her heel. She walked backward to keep an eye on me. "I'm going to find Calista before we go. I haven't seen her in forever. Can you stay out of trouble for that long?" she challenged, all playful like the tease she was.

She knew I loved it, too, how she got me all hot and bothered by that body. She also knew if I trailed her around this house I'd be pestering her until the moment I talked her out the door.

"I think I can manage."

Okay, probably not. But Aly wanted to be here, so I'd make do.

Leaning up against the wall, I kept a keen eye on her as she moved about the room, never far enough that she stole her presence from me.

I relaxed into it, into the atmosphere and the beat of the music and the smile on my girl. I nursed my beer. Contentment glided through my veins.

Christopher eventually made his way over. He bumped my fist. "Hey, man, how's it going?" He'd exchanged his bottle of death for a bottle of beer. "Figured you were standing over here suffering through some sort of mortal pain. You know, having to come out into the real world, and all."

I sipped at my own. "Nah, I'm good. Think Aly really needed this."

She stood across the room, talking to a girl I'd never seen before who was about a foot shorter than her with a crop of short brown hair. Aly was showing off her ring. Again.

"Just because my sister's probably the coolest chick in the world doesn't mean she doesn't get off on all this girly shit."

My gaze locked on her. Like she felt me, Aly turned a fraction, catching my eye. Affection swelled on her face and swam in her eyes, something lush and whole and sweet emanating from her skin.

I rubbed at my chest.

God, this girl made me insane.

A small frown pulled at Christopher's mouth. "So why didn't you tell me you had this planned? You could've let me know so I didn't go through all that shit trying to convince you to come tonight."

I shrugged. "Wanted Aly to be the first to know."

"I get that, I guess."

Standing there, Christopher let his gaze wander, appearing all easy and nonchalant. But I felt him twitch. A loose thread of strain trickled from him, and the muscles flexed on his exposed forearms.

"So what's up with all of this?" he asked out into the room, although he was talking directly to me.

Lines creased my brow, and I looked across at him with a scowl gaining in intensity. "What do you mean?"

He shook his head a little. He blinked, calculating, adding it up. "The house . . . and now that flashy ring . . . seems to me like someone is trying to prove something."

A blink of agitation lifted in me. There was nothing I could do to stop it. I fisted my hand, doing my best not to lose my shit with my best friend. What the fuck was his problem? Little more than a month ago he was demanding my loyalty, telling me to get my stuff and go if coming back wasn't permanent, and now I was taking things too far?

"All I'm doing is trying to take care of my girl . . . to take care of *your* sister," I punctuated with a hard emphasis. "Now all of a sudden I'm doing it wrong?"

"Didn't say that."

"Then what the fuck are you trying to say?"

His gaze shifted to the statement scored across the knuckles of my left hand.

2006.

He pinned me with sharp, green eyes. "Seems like a hell of a lot of demons chasing you, Jared. You sure you left all of them behind in Vegas?"

Goddamn it. I rubbed my jaw, doing my best not to lose my cool. Aly was always trying to drag this shit out into the open. Couldn't deal with Christopher doing it, too. "I'm fine." It grated from my throat.

"You sure?" It wasn't a question, but an accusation.

A heavy breath shot from my nose. "I'm not trying to prove anything to anyone. I just want to make her happy."

From across the room, I watched Aly. Her voice was completely washed out by the throb of music and the clamor of the crowd. But on her lips was ease and joy. She stole a furtive glance my way. Her gaze caressed over me. Gentleness danced at one side of that sweet mouth. Peace and a cleansing calm. Like she'd finally caught the breath she'd been dying for when she looked over at me.

I covered all my displeasure with a tender smile.

Christopher scoffed and took a swig of his beer. "Pretty damn obvious you've already accomplished that. But what about you? Are you happy?"

"Of course I am." I said it without hesitation.

"I'm not talking about being happy with Aly. Not talking about the way she makes you *feel*. I'm talking about my friend who disappeared when he was sixteen because he had his world shattered around him. What about him? You think I don't know he's still in there?"

Silence fell between us, amplifying the tension stretching us tight. Suffocating. I swallowed around it and forced the words from my gravelly throat. "You've got a lot of fucking nerve to talk, man. Don't think for a second I don't know there's something not right in that warped heart of yours."

"Yeah." He didn't even stop to deny it. "But I've got absolutely no one relying on me." He drained his beer. "Don't you get it? The way Aly looks at you? That's a fucking gift, man. No one has looked at me that way in a very long time. That's what you have to protect. But what scares me is the way you look at her . . . like you don't deserve to be in her life but would still do absolutely anything it takes to stay a part of it. *That* is dangerous."

Christopher pressed on, plowing right through the dread that built up in the center of my chest. "The house and that ring? All of it is good, Jared. I'm not implying it's wrong. Not for a second." He shook his head. "Marriage and a white picket fence . . . you two should have that. But I've known you a long, long time and building up the perfect exterior isn't going to be enough."

"Aly will always be enough," shot from my mouth as my only defense.

Because that's what she was. My shelter. My balm.

"But will you?" He looked over at me. Dark eyebrows almost touched he had them drawn so tight, concerned lines cutting all over his worried face.

Pretty sure I preferred the asshole over all the psychoanalytical bullshit.

"What do you want me to say, Christopher? I can't change

anything that happened in my past." All I was doing was trying to build a future.

He blinked like he didn't know how to break through to me. "You need to stop pretending that past didn't happen. One of these days you're going to have to face it."

Stark images of the family I'd destroyed flashed.

My mother.

My father.

My sister.

Christopher might as well have kicked me in the gut.

A harsh breath rushed from my nose, and I slammed my eyes shut, shoving it all back down, lost to the darkness somewhere deep inside. "Just drop it, Christopher." My voice was hard. "It's done. Over. I love her, and that's all that matters."

I had to believe that.

Christopher tapped his empty on his thigh. His expression turned grave. "I'm not worried about how much you love my sister, Jared. I'm worried about how much you hate yourself."

My throat thickened, and I rushed a shaky hand though my hair. Agitation prowled like a beast in the pit of my stomach. I felt caged. Blips of that old rage battled for a resurgence.

Shifting, Christopher blew out a heavy breath. "Sorry, man. . . . You have to know I'm not trying to attack you. I'm just worried. That's all." He yanked his fingers through the tousled mess on his head. "Probably could've picked a better time and a better place to approach you about this." Self-contempt flowed from him. "Apparently I'm not so great at keeping my thoughts to myself, especially when it has to do with the people I care about." Christopher's regard jumped all over the room, skidding from one indistinct face to the next. "God knows there aren't many of them," he said almost too quiet for me to hear.

My attention cut in his direction, trying to make sense of

him. Resentment flickered on the outskirts of my consciousness. It struck up a war with the margin of truth he spoke. I got it, knew exactly what he was saying because he was speaking straight to those sins I would never outrun.

But he was wrong when it came to Aly.

She *was* enough.

When she touched me, all those scars didn't hurt so bad.

Christopher cracked a smile, the wiseass set firmly back in place. "You should take it as a compliment."

Interest widened his eyes, his gaze suddenly distracted. It aimed somewhere over my right shoulder. "Oh, you're going to love this."

I jerked my attention to where he looked. It landed on Aly, like it was trained to seek her out. Then it wandered to the left.

Possessiveness surged, darkened my sight like the coming storm. My pulse took off at a sprint, pounding blood so hard through my body I could feel it in my ears.

I forced myself to breathe.

Gabe stood in front of her. He dragged his fingers through the flip of brown hair hanging in his pompous face. He smiled like an arrogant jackass when he brushed it back, intruding on the conversation Aly was having with the tiny girl.

That girl hugged Aly quickly and waved a good-bye as she gave up her spot. Dickhead didn't hesitate to take her place.

His lips moved with unheard words as he edged forward, that cocky smile planted on his face when he pulled her into an overbearing hug. Aly hugged him back, her face disappearing somewhere in his body.

My jaw clenched.

He seemed reluctant to release her, but for his own safety he finally stepped away. Still, he kept hold of her hand, letting their arms swing between them. The same hand wearing my ring.

Dickhead didn't even notice.

He just stared at my girl, eyes tracing her with hunger, murmuring something I couldn't hear.

Fuck no.

I was most definitely not okay with this, not okay with him. My leg bounced with the nerves prodding my anxious feet.

"Dude, you should see your face right now." Christopher's voice cut into the upheaval brewing up chaos in my mind, the words offhand but his eyes narrowing just as tightly as mine.

Aly nodded, her mouth moving slowly as she answered whatever Dickhead said. I could feel it radiating off Aly, too, this shock of discomfort that had chased away all the ease she'd been wearing before.

I knew he'd texted her, that he'd sought her out in the months I'd been gone. Knew he *wanted.*

I also knew the asshole had trouble taking no for an answer.

There was no question now he'd ever give up on the fascination.

She ran her free hand tenderly down her stomach. That bright smile again resurfaced on her face. Her shirt hugged the little bump. Aly cradled it, talking while she showed it off.

Then she tugged her hand back, not hard enough that he let go, but enough to draw attention to the ring on her finger.

Blatant shock rocked his expression.

Fucker had apparently missed the memo.

He dropped her hand like a stone. I watched him squirm in discomfort. I couldn't help but get some kind of morbid satisfaction out of it.

Still, he stayed, talking to her. Aly blinked, and I was doing my best to decipher their conversation, because I couldn't imagine one thing Aly needed to say to him.

What it was about him, I didn't know, except for the fact he wanted my girl.

Hell, half the guys here wanted her. I knew it. I could see it written all over their faces, the way their fingers would twitch and their throats would bob whenever she came near.

She was a fucking knockout.

Gorgeous.

I doubted there was a guy here who hadn't had thoughts straying that direction.

But something about Dickhead made me crazy with jealousy.

Just because he hadn't gotten that far didn't mean he hadn't been anywhere. And the thought of anyone else's hands on Aly made my blood boil. His mouth had been on what was mine. He'd touched and explored and hoped he'd have half a chance with her.

I bet the asshole spent half his time stroking his dick, thinking about her.

"What a douche bag." Incredulous, Christopher continued, watching them as closely as I was. "The guy is more shameless than I ever gave him credit for. Aly with a ring on her finger and a baby in her belly, and he's still looking at her like he wants to eat her."

Yeah. And I'd knock all his fucking teeth out.

Christopher laughed. "You'd better go on and get your girl before you crawl right the fuck out of your skin. Last thing I need is to drag your ass out of here after you incite a brawl."

I smirked back him. I was already on my way.

I slinked past a group of girls who crowded the way. Rounding around the back, I inched up behind her. My hand slipped around her waist, all too hasty to flatten my body to her back. Pulling her close, I met his eye from over her shoulder.

Hatred flashed on his face, before Dickhead reeled it in. Then he tossed me an arrogant smile. "Hey, man."

"How's it going?" I lifted my chin in my own silent sneer.

That's right, asshole.

Mine.

And fuck, I didn't pretend not to know what I was doing. Claiming her. Marking her.

Unease shifted his feet and flared his nostrils.

Dickhead deserved it, too, making me squirm that night months ago when he'd been locked up behind her door, driving me straight out of my goddamned mind, not knowing what was happening or what was being said. He'd come looking to reconcile, wondering what had gone wrong between the two of them. Aly had taken him into her room to talk. Him being alone with her had driven me crazy. At that time, Aly and I had been messing around, touching, feeling, kissing. No sex. That had been the rule.

But that night I'd snapped. Tripped.

Right into ecstasy.

It was the night I finally accepted there was no stopping what was happening between Aly and me.

It was the night I'd taken it all. Aly had given herself to me. Gave me what no one else had ever had. Sarcastic laughter caught in my throat. Guess I should be thanking him for pushing us over the edge.

Dickhead shrugged it off, like it didn't matter at all. Like he could pretend none of this mattered anything to him.

But I saw it all there, witnessed it where it was written across his face.

"It was great to see you, Aly. I'm sure I'll talk to you soon," he said with a nonchalant lift of his shoulder as he backed away. His eyes made another pass down the length of her body.

"Yeah, I'll see you around," she returned.

Darkness shrouded the room. I stared up at the shadows on the ceiling. I'd been awake for hours. There was nothing I could do to settle or quiet my mind. Couldn't still the agitation twitching all the muscles in my body.

Wind howled. Branches screeched along the outside wall, and a faint rim of light flicked shadows through our bedroom window. Winter battered the desert city on cold gusts of air, the sky inky and clear. There would be no rain or snow. No relief for the dried-up ground.

And there would be no relief for what haunted me tonight.

Aly stirred at my side where she slept. A soft breath of air parted her lips. All that silken hair was strewn out on our bed, a single bare shoulder exposed where she rested on her side, facing me. I looked down at her angel face. I traced the sharp cut of her chin and across the defined angle of her high cheekbones.

Yet everything about her was soft.

The hardness of me always seemed a contradiction.

But still we always seemed to fit.

Doubt fluttered into my consciousness and mingled with the guilt.

Christopher's concern had gotten under my skin. Gabe's presence had irritated it like a little piece of sand.

In the shadows, I lifted my hand, stared at the numbers stamped on my knuckles. I fisted it, wishing for a way to erase it.

A way to erase who I was.

God. I just wanted to be free.

To forget it all.

Aly burrowed into my chest. Her naked flesh burned into

mine. She singed me. Made me forget my name and made me lose my mind.

Allowed me escape.

A way to shun the pain and neglect my shame.

That was what I had to hold on to. Not the fucked-up questions brewing in my head, the ones Christopher had planted there.

A blink of light lit up on Aly's nightstand. A silent text illuminated her phone.

I smiled a little to myself.

Had to be Christopher. At half past three in the morning, no less. He'd probably gotten himself into trouble. I was betting my phone would ring in about fifteen seconds with him asking me to come bail him out of whatever he'd gotten himself into.

Instead Aly's lit again.

Then again.

Unease twisted through me. Carefully I stretched over her to retrieve it. I sat up in bed, careful not to disturb her. She just shifted to her stomach and turned her head the other direction.

I flicked my thumb over the faceplate.

Not Christopher.

And I knew I was intruding, reading Aly's texts. But fuck, I couldn't stop myself.

Can't stop thinking about you after seeing you tonight.

Hatred flared like a sickness clawing at the inside of my stomach.

Instinctively, I scrolled through the feed.

What are you thinking, Aly? Is this really what you want?

I crushed her phone in my grip.

You can't want that, Aly. That life? That guy? What happened to you? What happened to the girl I knew? We had a good thing and you're wasting it on him? I should never have just walked away. I'm sorry I didn't fight harder.

My vision clouded.

I know you have to feel trapped. I promised you a long time ago I wasn't giving up on us. I'm still not.

I swallowed the lump wedged in my throat. Shaking. Fucking shaking. The good-guy act perfected, playing me out to be the bad guy when he knew nothing about how much Aly meant to me. Fucking asshole. What did he think? That I'd let him have her? Give her up? Not a fucking chance.

I scrubbed my palm over my face, trying to break up the nerves, trying to clear my narrowed sight.

Another text came through.

The baby thing, it's weird. I admit it. But I can get past it. Just call me. Let me help you.

The baby thing? He could get past it?

Rage simmered in my blood. A steady build that just about hit an all-out boil. I ground my teeth as I squeezed Aly's phone in my hand, the other fisting tufts of my hair as I fought with the impulse to throw her phone against the wall, and I had the sudden undeniable urge to hear glass shatter. I tried to shun the compulsion to jump to my feet, did my best to ignore the desire to seek out a release, the moment's reprieve I'd find in the destruction, my fists lost in a fury as I buried them again and again in the wall.

Or better yet, buried them in his face.

I swallowed hard, staring at the screen as I tapped out a return. My hands trembled, and my fingers fumbled across the plate.

Shit.

Stay the fuck away from my girl. I won't ask you twice.

I gritted my teeth as I pushed send.

Minutes passed while I sat there seething, waiting for a response.

Daring him for one.

The coward gave me none.

Her phone sat silent while I struggled to breathe.

Did it make me an asshole that I read her messages? I mean, I wouldn't think twice about Aly picking up my phone. I had nothing to hide. She already knew every distasteful blemish tainting my soul.

Still, I found myself going through and deleting the messages from Aly's phone.

And I felt like shit, like a bastard for taking the coward's road, too.

But I couldn't stand the idea of Aly reading this.

Not from him.

Not when she was my all.

I would do whatever it took to protect that, to keep her away from anything that would threaten to steal her away.

I wouldn't let it happen. Couldn't.

Urges hit me hard. I wanted to forget. Needed her touch and her hand, her soft whispers that seeped like a tonic through my veins and poured directly into my soul.

I dove my fingers and my nose into her hair. Coconut filled my senses, that fucking trigger lighting me like a match.

Aly moaned, an incoherent fluttering from her spirit easing from her mouth.

Led, she rolled onto her back, like she was just as powerless to this need as me. Dependent.

Addicted.

Her eyes flew open to the deepest night. She looked at me hovering above her, confusion in the depths of her searing green eyes. A lick of fear. A rush of desire.

I nestled between her thighs.

A deep groan rumbled from my chest as I rocked into her with one deep thrust.

And I took.

Rough. Hard. Demanding.

The sick part was she seemed just as desperate to give it to me as I was to take it from her.

Aly whimpered and in seconds shattered around me. Her nails cut into my skin. Pain pricked at the surface, and satisfaction rolled deep.

"You," she whispered as she tipped up her hips to meet mine, driving me right to the edge sanity.

I felt it slip.

I roared when I came. "Aly."

Frantically I gathered her in my arms. "I won't ever let you go. Never," I promised. It sounded too close to a threat.

"Never," Aly assured. Soft fingers gentled through my hair.

Never.

SIXTEEN

Aleena

Rays of late-afternoon sun shined through the window, lighting up the small room. It glowed on the pale yellow walls, wrapped it in luminous warmth that I felt all the way to my bones.

I rubbed the fuzzy fleece blanket between two of my fingers. A smile lifted the edge of my mouth as I pressed it to my cheek. Anticipation hummed in my spirit.

"This room is going to be perfect, Aly." Megan sat on the floor behind me, folding a pile of blankets and miniature pieces of clothing I couldn't resist buying. Yesterday, I'd gone on some sort of pregnancy-brain-induced shopping spree, filling my cart full of small things that I wouldn't need for another four months. This morning, after I'd washed it all, I'd texted Megan a proud picture of the heap in the middle of the floor. I'd captioned it *My Tower of Tiny Treasures.* Megan showed up unannounced about an hour later with a grin splitting her entire face, proclaiming *I want to play.*

Apparently baby clothes had some kind of compelling force over women of any age, because I was now hosting a family dinner tomorrow night because my mom wanted a good excuse to come over and *play*, too.

"Do you think so?" I asked. I cast an appreciative glance around the room.

Jared and I had painted the room over the last weekend. I'd picked a soft yellow color that showered the room in calm and peace. White crown molding capped off the room with a luxurious feel. It flowed perfectly, both comfortable and elegant.

Jared had surprised me by bringing home the white sleigh crib I'd been eyeing. It fit so perfectly into the room it appeared to have been cut from it, the carving almost an exact match of the molding cradling the walls overhead.

I leaned forward and placed the blanket in the crib, then glanced back at Megan.

Her ponytail bounced around as she shook her head like I'd lost a little piece of my mind. "Uh . . . yeah . . . I know so. What kid wouldn't want to grow up with this being their room? It's gorgeous. Hell, I'd move in if you'd let me." She pitched an exaggerated wink in the direction of my ever-expanding belly. "That is if Itty Bitty wouldn't mind sharing a room with me."

Tiny teddy bears covered the onesie she held up in front of her. Carefully, she folded it into a little square, then reached for another one. We still didn't know if this was a boy or a girl. And we wouldn't. I didn't want to. When I met my child for the first time the day he or she was born, I wanted it to be without expectations. All except for the one that I loved him or her with my entire heart.

"I wouldn't make offers like that if I were you," I warned with a sly smile in her direction. "A built-in babysitter is really kind of tempting. You'll end up here at night watching this little thing instead of hanging out with Sam."

"Ha. I'm going to have to force you out of this house once the baby is born. My bets go on you not wanting to let Itty out of your sight. I'll be on my hands and knees begging for auntie time." She offered a revealing smile, replete with widened eyes. "And believe me, I won't be missing out on anything by losing time with Sam. What I was all spun up over that guy about, I have no clue."

I piqued a curious brow. "Bored?"

She shrugged. "Bored . . . annoyed. Tired of him not showing up when he says he's going to. I'm so over it. I deserve better than that."

And I kind of wanted to pump my fist in the air. So I did. "Uh, yeah, you do."

He'd been stringing her along for months, making promises the jerk was never going to keep.

Megan giggled through an uncontained grin. "Half the time I think he just shows up to some of the places I invite him to because Gabe is hoping you're going to be around."

I groaned. "Ugh . . . that guy is clueless. I mean, seriously . . ." I flashed my ring that Jared had placed on my finger three weeks ago. "You'd think this would be enough to convince him I'm not into him." I flung my hands down, gesturing my annoyance toward my stomach. "And if that isn't enough, then at least this is. I'm thinking these two scream *spoken for.*"

Megan's giggle transformed into an outright laugh, loud and uncontrolled, and she listed to the side as she clutched her stomach. "You know he thinks you two are soul mates."

"What?"

"Yep, that's what Sam told me, anyway."

"God, what an idiot."

"Yep," she said again, like I wasn't saying anything she hadn't thought.

I turned back to tucking the sheets into the crib mattress. My voice lowered. "Jared would lose his cool if he knew that. You should have seen him New Year's Eve when Gabe showed up . . ." I shook my head. "If looks could kill and all that," I said with a shudder.

Or if tension could strangle.

I was pretty sure if Gabe would have remained standing in front of us any longer, Jared would have snapped. And by snapped, I mean snapped Gabe's neck. Five seconds after Gabe had walked away, Jared had hauled me out of the house and into the night. He'd seemed desperate to touch me. He always did, really, but this had been . . . different. Jared had woken me several times during the night with the same intensity, in some sort of aggrieved frenzy. Like he was somehow trying to shed his own skin and seep into mine.

That night it'd been the worst.

"Well, if anyone could shoot deadly daggers, it'd be Jared." Megan laughed quietly below her breath, so low she had to be talking to herself. "God, that is one scary man."

"What?" I asked, because I suddenly heard her words in a way I never had before.

Megan's head snapped up and her eyes went wide. "Oh shit, Aly. That came out wrong. I'm sorry."

Rapidly I blinked, shaking my head. "It's fine, Megan. I'm not mad."

Because on the outside, I knew Jared appeared a little bit scary.

A frown cut across my forehead and tugged at my mouth because I wasn't entirely sure the exterior was what Megan was referring to. "Do you really feel that way, though? Are you afraid of him?"

She shrugged and busied her hands with folding. "No, I'm not *afraid* of him. It's just . . ." Her attention cut toward me while she seemed to weigh a way to say what she was thinking. "You know I've always thought he was different . . . thought he makes you different. He just makes me uneasy sometimes."

She lifted her face. Honesty shined in her wide blue eyes. "I don't know what it is, Aly. And please don't get me wrong. I like him. I really do. He loves you like crazy and treats you like a princess. Who doesn't want that for their best friend? But there's something about him that sets me off kilter. I try to ignore it . . ." She cringed, then blew out a concerned breath. "But there's a pressure in the room when he's there. It's like there's a silent warning radiating from him. And somewhere in the back of my mind, I keep waiting for a bomb to go off."

I nodded and tried to swallow over the sudden fear that crawled to my throat. The thing was, it wasn't really all that sudden. I wasn't immune to that pressure, either. Of course I felt it.

Over time, it'd only increased.

"He *is* different, Megan."

Stilling, she fully turned her regard to me. "Does it worry you?"

I occupied my hands by placing the stack of tiny receiving blankets into the crib, where I was storing them until I got a dresser. Turning around, I leaned up against the crib. "Am I afraid of him or worry he'll hurt me?" I shook my head. "No." Not physically, anyway. "But I know what you're talking about."

Fidgeting, I looked to my feet before I lifted my gaze to her. "I love him so much, Megan. Too much," I clarified, because somehow I really needed to voice it. "He's still in so much pain. But he's trying to ignore it. To pretend like everything is okay when it most definitely is not okay. He dreams . . ." Slowly I shook my head as I trailed off. "It's awful, Megan. He wakes up shaking . . . so scared and angry. It's almost like he's disoriented and he's not sure where he is."

Sickness flipped my stomach inside out. Those nights hurt me so much because I knew he was hurting. They also scared me. It was when anxiety wrapped him so tight he almost couldn't be touched, even though in the moment he was so desperate to feel.

It'd been getting worse since he proposed. He always seemed on edge. Or maybe it was that Jared was the edge. The sharpest blade. Ready to strike down everything and anything that threatened to expose the pain he harbored inside.

But he'd kept it sheathed, covering it up as he dove into our relationship, pouring everything into us—into this house and me and work and plans for the baby—without regard for everything that happened in the past.

The entire time, that edge had been sharpening.

"Every time I bring it up, he shuts me down. He just wants to focus on what's good in our lives right now." I waved my hand around the room. "And we have so much to be thankful for. We do, and I love it and I love him . . . and there is no question that he loves me. But it's like he's hanging on to me so tightly, I'm worried he's going to squeeze the life out of us."

Wringing my hands, I shifted and stared down at my friend, who watched me with sympathetic understanding. "I just want to help him, Megan, help him heal and finally forgive himself."

Her brow creased. "You don't think he forgave himself before he came back? I figured that was the only way he returned."

I shook my head, sure of this truth. "No. He shunned it. He wanted me so much he was willing to live with the guilt in order to stay with me."

But I knew, in my spirit and in my heart, that would never be enough.

The next evening, Jared barreled through the front door. At the counter in the kitchen, I stood facing out the window that looked over the backyard, furiously chopping the vegetables for the salad. Over my shoulder, I glanced at him.

Jared bit back a suggestive smile as he stalked forward. He pressed his body to my back. My entire body sighed.

"Damn, baby, it smells delicious in here. What are you making?"

"I made homemade meatballs . . . my family is coming over tonight for dinner. Remember?"

And by my family, I meant everyone, my father included.

What had brought on the change, I didn't know. I'd fretted the entire day about it. Part of me wanted to reject the idea of him coming here, to denounce his attempts at reconciling our injured relationship. The truth was, I'd been shocked, stunned by my father's actions. Above all of that, I'd been hurt. But I'd never been one to harbor hate, and I knew I at least owed him the chance to make his intentions known.

"Of course I remember," Jared murmured at my neck. His nose lifted a flash of goose bumps where he nuzzled my sensitive skin. "Anything I can do to help?"

"No, I've got everything set. I just need to finish up this salad and everything is done. Why don't you go grab a shower?"

He pecked me against the cheek. "Is that your way of telling me I stink?"

"Mmhmm . . . maybe," I teased, turning my head to catch him at the throat, my nose and my mouth and my smile pressed there. He smelled of dirt and wood and hard work. His soft, stuttered breath was minty, mixed with the lingering hint of cigarettes. Not for a second was it unappealing. Everything about Jared screamed *Man*. One delicious, gorgeous man.

I hummed.

A knowing chuckle reverberated at my back, and he held me close. "I love you, Aly Moore."

Playfully, Jared rocked us. "When are we going to change that name of yours, anyway?"

I giggled and lost myself in this Jared, the one who was carefree and whose words flowed with ease and eyes shined with light. The one who chased swarms of butterflies through the fields of my belly, stirred them up with the steady stroke of his hand and the tempting tenor of his voice.

"Don't you want to wait until I don't have to waddle down the aisle?"

Jared scoffed. "Waddle? You are insane. You still have no idea, do you? How absolutely stunning you are?" Jared palmed the front of my thighs. "*These legs*." This time it was Jared's turn to hum. "No . . . I don't want to wait . . . just want to make you mine. Forever."

"I already am yours," I contended, grinning, letting him know I was playing even though I was one hundred percent serious. I'd told him again and again. Jared held me in the palm of his hand. Eternally.

Of course, that didn't mean I couldn't wait to be his wife.

Mine and Megan's conversation from yesterday intruded my thoughts. I shoved it down. With Jared here . . . like this? I didn't want to be scared, didn't want to be afraid of what he had the power to destroy.

"It's beautiful in March . . . maybe sometime in the middle?" I suggested through the bundle of emotion that made itself known right in the center of my chest.

"March," he reiterated on a murmur that was utterly profound.

Jared and I had just set our wedding date.

He left me with a searing kiss before heading into our bathroom to get cleaned up for dinner.

Half an hour later, the doorbell rang.

I dried off my hands, tossed the hand towel to the counter, and ambled to the door. I opened it to my parents and Aug.

I did my best to ignore the unease that so clearly clung to my father's being.

Instead, I set my attention on my mom. Her hair was sleek and straight, blonder than the last time I saw her. She wore a pair of skinny jeans and heels, topping it off with a cream-colored sweater and a deep plum infinity scarf twisted snugly around her neck.

I stepped forward and threw my arms around her. She squeezed and rocked me.

"Are you trying to make me look bad?" I asked when I pulled away.

She rolled her warm brown eyes. "Hardly." She let her gaze slide down to my belly while she talked, not hesitating to place her hands on it. "I would've killed to look like you when I was pregnant. I was a house. Ask your father." She hooked her thumb over her shoulder. "He slept on the couch for the last two months each time because my stomach took up the entire bed."

He grumbled behind her, although his mouth hinted at a smile. "I think you need to check your memory, Karen, because it had nothing to do with the size of your stomach. You complained the entire time that I was hogging the bed. You ran me off."

She waved offhandedly. "Semantics."

Laughing, I stepped back and widened the door. "Come on in, you guys."

Mom came in, stalling in appreciation in the middle of the room. "Oh my God, Aly . . . this place is . . . unbelievable."

She hadn't been over for a couple of weeks. Not since Jared had added all of his elegant touches. Everything had come together cohesively and seamlessly. Jared had turned what would have been a simple, comfortable house into something memorable and unique.

It truly was gorgeous.

"It is, isn't it?" I murmured.

Aug came inside and gave me a less than stellar one-armed hug. I tugged his headphones from his ears and slugged him in the arm. "Hey, can't you take these out long enough to say hi to your sister? And give her a real hug?"

He shrugged with a dimpled smile and wrapped me up in one of his bear hugs. "Of course I can."

"Much better."

With a smirk, he stepped back, working a single ear bud back into his ear while he spoke. "And believe me, I could hear just fine. I should have turned it up . . . the last thing I need to hear are the words *Mom*, *Dad*, and *bed* in the same sentence."

Mom rolled her eyes again. "You're so dramatic, Aug, and you have no right to talk. If I have to watch you get *that look* on your face while reading a text ever again, I might puke. Don't think I didn't notice that on the way over here."

Guilt colored my brother's face, and he shifted through his laughter. "I swear, you're some kind of freaky ninja spy." Exasperated, Aug glanced at me. "She has to have eyes in the back of her head or something," he said as he wandered the rest of the way inside.

Mom lifted a telling brow. "Keep it up, and you can make it ninja assassin. How I ended up with two boys who don't understand the meaning of virtue, I'll never know. You and Christopher need to start taking some pointers from your dad before you send your poor old mother here to her grave."

Mom and Dad had been together forever, and I knew she was none too impressed with my brothers' romantic hijinks.

The worst of them rumbled up in his truck. Christopher pulled to the curb in front of my house and hopped from the cab. Raking a hand through his messy hair, he sauntered up to the door on his long stride. "Hi, Dad." He clapped our dad on the shoulder, angled around him to place a quick kiss to my temple. "Hey there, little sister."

"Hey, you. Glad you could make it."

He crossed the threshold and went straight for Mom. He dropped a kiss to her cheek. Then he sniffed the air. "Holy shit, Aly, did you magically learn how to cook since I left earlier today? It smells like a fucking gourmet restaurant in here."

Like always, he made himself at home. He walked directly into the kitchen and ducked into the fridge for a beer.

"Don't act like I didn't spend the last two years cooking for you."

He stood up and twisted the cap from his bottle. "Ha, bringing home *to-go* boxes from the diner does not count as cooking."

Shaking my head, I laughed. "Watch yourself or I'm going to make you eat the leftovers that have been sitting in the fridge for the last week."

"Not on your life. I have dibs on firsts . . . whatever you're making, my mouth is watering."

Reluctantly, I turned from the lightheartedness of the rest of my family to my dad, who still hovered in the shadows outside. He shoved his hands deep in the pockets of his pants and rocked back on his heels. Agitation billowed from him in waves.

I stepped outside and closed the door behind me.

Never in the nearly two months that Jared and I had lived here had my father stepped foot inside our house. And I could count the number of words that had been spoken between us . . . on my right hand. A quiet hostility and an outright sadness had clouded all the moments we'd shared, which had been few and even farther between. I hadn't seen him since Christmas morning. I'd gone for the shortest time, reluctant to leave Jared on the holiday but drawn to my parents' home all the same.

I'd asked Jared just to forget what my father thought. To go. For me. But that request was good for only one redemption. He still felt he was honoring my father's wishes by staying away, even as, at the same time, he was proving him wrong by taking care of me.

Going to my parents' house without Jared had stung. He was my family. I'd gone only to save my mother from the hurt she would feel in my absence. She'd even attempted to convince Jared to come, but he wouldn't have it.

Now I wasn't exactly sure what had drawn my father to my door today. What had changed, if anything at all? Perhaps my mother had shamed him into being here. If so, then he could just go. I didn't want him here out of obligation, and I sure as hell didn't want him here because of guilt.

The only explanation good enough was that he truly wanted to be here.

Swallowing down all the anger I still felt, I took a tentative step deeper into the burly shadows of my father.

His eyes dropped. I thought to his feet. But no. I realized he was doing his best not to look at my stomach.

Resentment flared. It clashed with the truth of how much I missed my father. "Dad . . ." I choked saying it, not wanting it to sound like a plea. "Do you have any idea how happy it makes me you're here? I've missed you so much."

Moisture filled my eyes. I swiped it away and stood my ground. "But I need to know you're here because you want to be . . . because you care about me and my family and you want to be a part of it. I don't want you to come inside if you're just here because Mom made you come or because of any other reason than you came here to support me and Jared."

Dad rubbed his hand across his mouth. Disquiet shifted his feet. "How have you been feeling, Aly?"

I blinked, trying to make sense of his question. I frowned, and frustration poured from my mouth. "Are you really going to stand there and try to change the subject? After everything that's been said? I asked you to tell me why you're here and I want you to be honest with me."

He exhaled heavily, and lifted his chin toward the door closed behind me. "I wasn't joking when I said your mom chased me from bed when she was pregnant with you kids. She was miserable the whole time. God, I worried about her. For nine months, I ran around, trying to take care of her, making sure she was as comfortable as she could be. It made me sick that she was sick. Nervous, too. I was always worried something would go wrong, and I did anything I could to make sure that didn't happen. I drove her crazy." He paused, blinked toward his feet before he lifted his face back to mine. "I've always been protective of the people I care about. To a fault. To the extent that I can't see past what I think is best for them."

Understanding dawned. It blunted the surge of anger that had pushed me out my front door to confront my dad. Still, it didn't make what he'd said before to Jared okay.

"I know you care about me, Dad. That you love me. But you also have to know that isn't enough."

His gaze glided down to the ring I nervously twisted around my finger. For a beat, he stared, and I saw his throat bob when he swallowed. "You're going to marry him?"

I fisted my hand over my heart. "Yes."

He nodded and his eyes glistened. He blinked it away. "You wanted to know why I'm here? I'm here because I miss you. Because when I lie down at night, I can't close my eyes because

I know things aren't right. My daughter will barely talk to me . . . barely look at me. That kills me, Aly."

"I'm not the one who's responsible for that."

His own frustration bled into his words. "I know that. Yes, I'm here because of you and because I want to set things right between us. But I'm also here because it's high time I apologized for the way I reacted on Thanksgiving. I had no right to do that. There is no excuse for the things I said."

Dismay twisted into his expression. "I was scared for you, Aly. Shocked. Blindsided by it all. One minute I think you're going to school . . . happy . . . working toward the career you want, and the next you're *pregnant*?" His voice dropped low and transformed into something that sounded like an accusation. "You gave me no warning, Aly, no indication of any of it."

"The school thing . . . I'm sorry," I said. "I should have told you a long time ago it wasn't really what I wanted. I've always wanted to draw, and I thought it was impossible. But Jared showed me it wasn't." In one of my classes with a mentor, I'd been working on drawing families, working on photographs, images that captured emotion in time. That was exactly what I wanted, the direction I wanted to go, to pour myself into faces of families, making them come alive in an image that would become a family treasure. "But you know this isn't really about what I want to do for a living, Dad. This is about me being with Jared."

Looking down, he shifted. "And I'm not going to lie to you and tell you I'm not still scared for you, because I am. You're my daughter. Of course all I want is the best for you. But I also accept how unfair I've been to Jared."

He dipped his head, shook it in remorse. "He was always a good kid. Super smart, but kind, too. Then after what happened with his mom, a switch was flipped inside him. A destructive trigger there was no stopping. None of us could get through to him. Even though I cared about him, I was much more terrified he would lead Christopher down the same road. I was relieved when they sent him away. I kept a lot of guilt for a lot of years for feeling that way."

A flash of regret hit me. Yeah, I'd hidden Jared. For many years. Maybe I should have given my dad some sort of warning. But the truth was, I'd kept Jared a secret for this very reason, because of the way my father had treated Jared during that time. Within our house, he'd made Jared's name a dirty word. Nothing but taboo.

My father's chest trembled with the admission. "It was wrong, and I knew it. But when you showed up with him at Thanksgiving dinner and I saw the way you two were looking at each other, it took five seconds for that same fear to take hold of me again. All I could think was this guy was going to hurt my baby girl. Then when you announced you were pregnant, it flipped my own switch. I lost it. I couldn't control how angry I was at him. At you," he emphasized. "Even at your mother. I knew she had to know something was going on between the two of you and she'd never once let on. I felt like a fool . . . like a lesser part of the family. Like I'd been shunned from all the important pieces of my daughter's life."

He scrubbed his hands over his face. When he looked back at me, his green eyes were pleading. "I regret that reaction so much, Aly. I handled it about the worst way I could. And again, I was laying all the blame on Jared. All of my reactions have always been controlled by my own fears and insecurities. Feeling threatened by the things I can't control. It's a personal flaw I've had to deal with all my life. I know it. All I can do is ask you to forgive me for it."

My lids dropped closed as I absorbed my father's admission.

Slowly, I opened them. "Dad, I don't blame you for being disappointed or worried." The words cracked over the sob stuck in
my throat. "I completely get it. But I don't think you understand
the kind of guilt Jared carries over his mother. If you did, you
could never have said those words to him. It's not me who you
owe an apology to." Lines creased my brows and my head tilted
in supplication. "You owe one to Jared."

My father blew a breath toward the sky and spoke toward
the night. "I already gave him one, Aly."

Confusion took me aback. "What?"

My dad heaved a sigh. "I texted him this afternoon and
asked him to meet me when he got off work. I figured I needed
to ask him for forgiveness before I could ask you for it."

A torrent of relief swept through me. I realized how burdened I'd felt by this dispute with my dad. I hated it. Hated that
he thought badly of the single most important person in my life,
hated that distrust had wedged a separation between us.

I felt the distance collapse.

With a step forward, I narrowed the gap between us.
"Thank you." It tripped from my mouth, fast and hard.

In surrender, he pulled his thumbs back from his jeans in a
conceding shrug. "I was wrong. I can admit when I am." His
green eyes flashed in the porch light. "It doesn't mean I'm not
worried about you. I talked with Jared for a long time this afternoon. And you already said it all. I don't understand the kind of
guilt Jared carries over his mother. At all. I can't fathom that grief.
And I honestly don't know him anymore. But I'm betting you do,
and that guilt was pretty glaring when I talked to him. That's a
lot of baggage to deal with, Aly." It slid from him as a warning.

I bristled, but I forced my tongue silent.

A gust of wind rushed in, pressing along the desert floor. I
hugged myself against the sudden cold. Dead leaves whipped up

from beneath the barren tree that protected my home, beat and stirred.

I lifted my chin for him to continue, trying to ignore the swell of defensiveness I felt at his admonition. As if he wasn't saying anything I didn't know. As if I didn't know the risk. As if Jared wasn't worth every bit of it.

He lifted his hand in a telling gesture to the house behind me. To my sanctuary. My home. Somehow I felt as if I was standing in guard of it. Defending what Jared had built for us with his bare hands inside.

My father's tone shifted, laced with remorse. "It was also pretty glaring that he loves you, Aly. I can't question that or his intentions with you anymore. I believe him when he says he's doing everything he can to make this work and he'd do anything to protect you." He chuckled a little, though it seemed completely lacking in humor. In discomfort, he scratched at his jaw. "Apparently Jared and I have something in common, after all."

His voice lowered, although his expression hardened. He pinned me with the intensity of it. He ground his teeth. "I just have to know you're happy. *Really happy.* That this is truly what you want and you're not doing it because you think it's the right thing to do."

I clutched both my hands to my chest. I just wanted to find a way to make my father understand. But I realized that was impossible. Because what I felt for Jared went beyond understanding, deeper than the rational. I explained myself the best way I knew how. "Dad . . ."

My voice quavered. "I love him so much. With all my heart. I always have," I admitted quietly. "I would do anything . . . give up anything to be with him." Tenderly, my hand slanted over my belly. "And this baby . . . I love it more than anything in this world." As much as Jared. But different. In a capacity I couldn't quite grasp. "Never in my life have I been happier than I am now."

Sadness swirled through the depths of my father's eyes before acceptance took hold. "That's all I really needed to know." He chanced a tentative step forward. And for the first time in months, my dad hugged me. "I'm sorry, Aly. Please tell me you'll forgive me for the way I've treated you."

"How could I not?" I whispered into the collar of his shirt, clutching him to me. All my resentment floated away. In its place, I just felt grateful. The only thing I'd ever wanted was for my family to be whole.

Jared missing from it had left such a stark void. And he completed me in ways no one else could.

Now, with my father coming back to me, everything would finally be perfect.

Pulling away, I wiped the wetness from under my eyes. "Would you like to come inside?"

Slowly, my father gave me one resolute nod. "Yeah, I'd like that."

I fumbled with the latch and opened the door.

Mom, Aug, and Christopher lingered around the island in the kitchen, catching up. Out of the corner of her eye, Mom cast me a knowing glance.

She'd been telling me everything would turn out okay.

And she'd been right.

Without missing a beat, she turned back to Christopher, who was filling her in on his classes, the last he'd have before he graduated in May.

As I stepped inside, Jared rounded the corner from the short hall that led to our room. His hair was all wet, deepened a shade, his clothes fresh. He hadn't taken the time to shave the coarse layer of stubble coating his jaw.

Need turned me inside out.

God, it didn't matter when or how many times I found him

this way. It was always the same. He struck me with a bolt of energy, somewhere deep inside, in that place I'd always kept for him.

When he caught sight of us, he came to a full stop. His eyes were soft as he traced over my face, softer when they met with my eyes. A flash of doubt sparked in them when they hit my father, before he lifted his chin in acceptance.

The two were calling a truce.

Biting my lip as an uncontained thankfulness flared, I rushed to Jared. I squeezed him around his middle, whispered too low for anyone else to hear, "You didn't tell me."

A soft breath left him, and he brushed his full lips across my forehead, over my closed eyes, to my ear. "Whatever you and your dad talked about tonight needed to be said between the two of you . . . without me getting in the middle of it. I never wanted to get in the way of your family, Aly, to put pressure on it. I'm just glad he's here and you both can forgive the bad blood I brewed between you two."

My father's presence weighed heavily behind me. Like he was an unwilling partner to the embrace Jared and I shared.

As I held Jared closer, a frantic murmur of truth expelled from my mouth. "You are my family."

Relief hit him hard. Palpably. His heart beat erratically, and I held on tighter. Jared shed his own truth at the tick of a pulse throbbing at my temple. "You're the only thing I have."

Pride simmered through my consciousness as Jared showed my father around our house. He was so knowledgeable. So capable. Even still, I could feel the flickers of tension coming from him. His movements were subtly uneasy. Of course I noticed it. He was on edge. As if he felt he was always being studied, judged. Not only by others, but by his own self-contempt. It didn't mean his pride didn't tug at one side of his perfect mouth when my father complimented him, or that he didn't go into detail about the kitchen, how much work it had been, and how happy he was with the result. Of course he'd played up my part in it, as if I'd had any bearing on the outcome of that impressive room.

When the oven buzzer chimed, my family gathered together at our little dining table. A couple extra chairs were squeezed in to make it suitable for six. I scoffed when they all went on about the meal, touting that it was one of the best they'd ever had. It clearly was not.

But it didn't stop the affection that buzzed in the air.

I couldn't contain my smile.

Christopher was no-holds-barred tonight, rambling on in constant entertainment, as if this moment was his ultimate calling.

Jared razzed him, and Aug laughed too loud, smacking Jared on the back. My mother played along with amused tenderness while my father settled into the fray, content to observe us all with a quiet calm.

It felt so good. Amazing.

Bliss shivered along my skin. I hugged myself, wishing I could hold on to this feeling forever.

Jared squeezed my leg under the table, like he innately knew what I was experiencing, his head cocked as he smiled over at me.

My heart fluttered haphazardly in the confines of my chest. It was warmth. It was joy.

I loved him.

I smiled back at him, my hand stretching out to embrace one side of his face.

God, I loved this man with all my life.

And I would never stop.

SEVENTEEN

Jared

I stood off to one end of the couch, a step behind it. On the fringe of the family room, like maybe I was the outsider. Which made no fucking sense since this was my house, but all of Aly's family had descended on it and I didn't quite know what to do with myself.

I lifted the half-empty bottle of beer to my mouth. Cold liquid slid down my throat. Swallowing, I sighed and let my gaze wander over my girl. She sat on the hearth beside her Mom, in the *garden*, as she liked to call it. An indulgent snort escaped my nose. How fucking cute was that?

I'd build this girl a thousand gardens if she wanted me to.

My attention drifted around the dimly lit room. Dave Moore sat in the overstuffed chair under the window. Christopher and Aug had made themselves at home, all sprawled out on the couch with their feet propped up on the coffee table, facing

Aly and her mom. In the fireplace behind them, flames crackled and jumped, igniting the warmth on the walls.

I still couldn't believe the way the house had turned out. Pride gave a firm tug at my spirit. Every square inch of it was perfect. Because it was perfect for Aly.

God, she looked like she was made to be sitting there on the smooth, flat stones. Dark hair twisted up in a messy pile on top of her head, pieces falling down to frame her face.

All of this I'd done for her.

She kept laughing, loud and carefree, listening to her brothers tell stories. That throaty lilt of her voice twisted through me like a summer breeze. Both she and her mom kept calling them out on their bullshit, reining in their tales that were stampeding out of control.

Another roar of laughter died down, and Karen sighed, sipping from a mug of hot tea Aly had made her. Her eyes traced the room I'd just been appreciating. She locked her gaze on me. "You have done such an amazing job with this place, Jared. I hardly recognize it since the last time I was here."

A shock of self-conscious gratification stunned me. It unsettled me. My entire adult life had been spent fighting against anything inside myself that hinted at good. All these desolate days offered as penance while my soul sought destruction—my identity given to the dead.

"Thank you." I had to force it out. Shame twisted through me on a gale-force wind—flashes of my mother's face, what I had done. They all clashed in a violent fury against the love I'd found in this life, in the light that was Aly.

My hand tightened on my bottle, just as tight as my chest.

God, all I wanted was the light. To stand in it. Bask in it.

Awareness gathered on Aly's features. She was so in tune with me. She cocked her head.

Are you okay?

She was the only one who understood. The only one who got me, as much of a fucking nightmare as I was, my moods manic, surging from one extreme to the other.

They'd been worse lately. Brewing. I could feel it. Like my demons were staging an assault, staking their claim. With each night, they dug their fingers deeper, spindly tendrils taking hold.

I wasn't fool enough to pretend like I didn't know why.

The first month back in Phoenix, I dove headfirst into making a life for me and Aly and our baby because I'd had the intense urge to *build*. To create something good in the chaos that ruled my heart and mind.

If I could just have one goddamned thing in this world that I did right, it'd be me doing right by Aly and our kid.

But it was like as soon as the year flipped, so did I.

I watched the calendar crawl, speed, and blur, dreading for the day to come and begging for it to pass.

All I had to do was get past it.

On its own accord, my hand fisted. The ink on my skin flexed as it burned, the imprint promising me I would never forget.

2006.

In a week and a half, seven years would have passed since the day I stamped out the good, since she'd sucked my soul into the nothingness where she'd forever beg in the bowels of my brain, where she cried out for atonement in the night.

But my spirit had rebelled against those chains. Now I somehow felt as if I was living in the light in the day and running from the darkness at night. Suspended somewhere in between. Fighting as hard as I could for what my heart wanted while my wicked feet took me down those same haunted roads.

But I refused to walk them.

Not a fucking chance.

I just needed to make it through that day and I would be *okay*.

Out of the corner of her eye, Aly continued to watch me. Worry crested her forehead, her eyes landing on mine almost hesitantly.

I swallowed hard, pushed all of that shit back down where it belonged. A reassuring smile pulled at the side of my mouth, my head tipping with it, letting her know it was all going to be fine.

With a frown, she wavered, before she let her own smile whisper at her mouth. This smile was meant only for me. Her own reassurance. That dose of encouragement that kept me going every fucking day.

Because I was living for this girl.

Slowly, Karen climbed to her feet, standing to take in the warmth of the fire. She seemed to rock as she let her attention pass over the few pictures Aly had added to the mantel. There was a family picture of theirs, all five of them smiling at the camera in a staged cheesy pose. In another, Christopher had his arm slung around Aly's shoulders when she was all dressed up in her cap and gown to graduate high school. She was already beautiful then, all her childhood days behind her and a woman taking hold.

The truth was, she'd always been beautiful. She'd just affected me differently, made my heart crazy at every age because she'd always belonged to me.

Different, but still the fucking same.

It didn't take a whole lot to admit my favorite was the grainy one snapped back when Aly had to be the cutest fucking kid around. Her two missing top front teeth weren't enough to stop the undaunted force of her trusting smile as she grinned right at the camera. Behind her, Christopher was midjump, acting like the monkey the asshole always was. Off to the side, I stood with my arms crossed over my chest, wearing a knowing smile like I was observing it all.

We were out in our empty field. Happy and free.

And fuck if I didn't like to be reminded of those days, just the overwhelming heat of the summer sun and the excitement bounding through our veins.

"I remember this day," Karen murmured. She looked over her shoulder at me. A wistful smile pulled at her mouth, full of sadness and outright affection. "Your mom and I had been sitting out back, listening to you kids play."

I blanched with the casual mention of her.

Karen slanted an accusatory brow in Christopher's direction. "I don't think you all knew that's where we'd sneak out to when you'd run off to play. We knew we had to keep an ear on you in case you needed us. Christopher was giving Aly a hard time . . . again . . . telling her it was past her naptime and she needed to go home. Of course she was six years old and she hadn't had a nap in years."

With a delicate snort, Karen shook her head, glancing at Christopher with a knowing gleam in her eyes. "You were always trying to embarrass your sister. . . . chase her off." She shifted and pinned me with a look that had me itching, wanting to run and desperate to hear what she had to say all at the same time. "But Jared was always there to stick up for her."

My hand shook as I roughed it over my head. Why did Karen have to pick a moment like now to bring this up? Audiences weren't exactly my thing.

But it was like Aly's entire family had settled into the memory, too.

Christopher chuckled low, but without all the asshole he usually injected into everything. He cast a repentant smile at his sister.

"You told Christopher to *shut it,*" Karen continued with a tender laugh, "and it wasn't Aly who needed a nap but him because he was the one who was always acting like a baby."

She bit at her trembling lip, fighting some kind of raw emotion. "Your mom climbed onto the storage box we had pushed up against the back fence." Wistful, she let her gaze travel over us all. "Bet you didn't know how much we spied on you kids to make sure you were staying out of trouble." She shook her head and looked back to the picture. "I grabbed my camera and climbed up beside her."

I swore to God if she started to cry I was going to bolt. I didn't talk about my mom. Ever. It'd been my rule for years, and it'd been a damn good one. Only one night had I ever faltered, the night I'd ripped myself open and told Aly what happened the day I'd taken it all.

Of course it was Aly.

It'd always been Aly.

But I sure as hell learned my lesson that night. Had gotten my fill of baring my soul. It amounted to no good, just ushered in the torment and shame, flamed the guilt that had chased me out Aly's door and into the three fucking most miserable months of my desolate life.

Aly had talked about her the night I'd returned, too, spoke secret words about drawing her, about my mom somehow crying out to her.

That was an idea I couldn't fathom. Refused to. All I knew was Aly'd been the one who'd partnered with fate, that piece of fate that kept me chained to this world, what kept me tied to this girl. That was all I needed. The rest I rejected.

After that, Aly had attempted to bring her up, subtly, tiptoe-ing around the subject I consistently shut down.

But not Karen.

She just jumped into it like she'd opened the pages of a his-tory book that was meant for everyone to see.

"She was giggling when she asked Aly if she liked playing with you boys or if she wanted to come in and hang out with us girls."

Picking up the picture, Karen caressed her thumb over the black wooden frame that housed the image, like she could some-how touch that day. "This right here?" she said, tapping it. "This was Aly telling your mom you were her very best friend and she wasn't leaving your side."

That rock of unspent emotion at the base of my throat throbbed.

Fuck.

I tried to maintain my cool, doing my all not to lose my shit. But damn it all, Karen Moore just had that way about her. Like she was a direct portal to the past, kicking up stones with every step she took. Stones that were better left unturned.

Still, my heart fluttered, because Aly beamed across at me before she looked up at her mom, like the memory had just sailed into her consciousness. "I forgot about that . . . I was digging through old pictures at the house a few weeks ago and found it." Aly glanced at me, love pouring free. "I knew I wanted it on display . . . now I know why."

My chest tightened.

She'd brought home a picture of my family, too. She seemed almost sad when I came in and found her in her little room, sitting on the floor. She was floating in a sea of photos, lost in all the memories spread out around her. She'd looked over at me as if she was in some kind of pain. Softly, she beckoned me to her side, where she had so many moments of our past set out on display.

In her hand she held a picture of my family. It was from when I was little and could barely remember my baby sister, who my mom had propped up against her chest.

But my eye had been drawn to the middle of the floor, where Aly had laid out a picture of my mom. She was by herself, just fucking smiling at the camera with all that light that had surrounded her.

"I think we should pick one of these to put up on the mantel," Aly had whispered, carefully, quietly. And God, I'd wanted to be pissed off at her, lash out at her for even suggesting something so obscene. Putting my family up there like I felt pride when what I'd done to it was my greatest disgrace.

As if I had the right.

It'd taken everything I had not to mangle them up in my hands, to destroy them like I'd destroyed everything else. Instead I'd looked at Aly, choked over my demand. "Don't . . . I don't ever want to see those again."

I knew she'd tucked them away somewhere in her studio, within the drawings bred in her mind and born of her hand, somewhere in the places where she kept my mother's face on the pages of her sketch pads.

Nostalgia billowed through Karen, her movements saturated with it as she carefully set the picture back on the mantel. Then she turned to the fireplace and ran her fingers along the ornate carvings. "And this . . . this is unbelievable," she murmured in distinct awe.

Pride made another rush on me, boosting me to a level where I didn't belong.

My head spun.

Shit.

It was like I was being forced up the shore on a swelling wave. At the same time I was all twisted up in the undertow, losing footing, losing ground. Once again, it was Karen Moore yanking me from one extreme to the other.

But this . . . this was what I was most proud of, what I'd poured myself into. Working on it, my hands had twitched while my imagination soared. I'd been *compelled*. That was the only way to describe it. The design for the fireplace had spiraled through my brain, urging my fingers to create. I saw it so clearly the first time I walked through the door of this house.

Even before I brought Aly here.

The idea of rebuilding this house had just come to me the first time I walked through it, like all the pieces had stacked together and become clear. But at the center of it was the fireplace. How this single structure would become something unique to mute out all the bland, how the rest of the layout of the house would flow from it, each room distinct on its own, but still tied to the creation Karen was currently tracing with her fingers.

I'd finished it only two days ago. After dinner, Aly'd been all too excited to build our first fire in it, to show it off. Immediately everyone had been drawn into this room, settling right into its comfort.

Karen's fingertips gently caressed the lines, curling through the vines and up to the petals that stretched out, twisted, and twined as they merged into the gnarled bouquet that stretched across the top.

"Just incredible," she whispered, her touch fluttering over the intricate designs as if they told a story. She looked across at me, sincerely, but with something so powerful it cut me to core.

A tremor of unease shook me. Because I realized she was

having some kind of secret conversation with me, as if she thought I should know something I didn't. Suddenly I felt like I was struggling to catch on, to catch up, when I was pretty damned sure the smart thing to do would be to step away.

"You know I have it?" she asked.

A frown formed, set deep between my eyes. Misunderstanding I shook my head. "I'm sorry?" I asked, wishing I hadn't, because something sick plummeted into my stomach, the hint of a heavy memory that had disappeared a long time ago into the darkest corner of my consciousness sinking like a stone.

Karen Moore wrung her hands, tilting her head, searching. "Before your father moved away . . . he . . . he brought me a bunch of her stuff . . . he said he couldn't handle taking it with him but he couldn't stand the thought of someone having it who didn't know her."

Cold crawled under the surface of my skin. Freezing me from the inside out. *Stop* got stuck on my swollen tongue, because that's all I wanted her to do. I just wanted her to stop.

I could sense the concern rise up in Aly. Palpable. Like it was pushing out from her and reaching for me.

Like she was desperate to shoulder some of my burden.

And God, I hated being this way. Karen couldn't even mention my father without me losing my shit. But goddamn it, didn't she understand? Didn't she know that dredging up old shit was just asking for trouble, bringing stuff out into the light when it was meant for the dark?

Didn't she understand what I'd done?

Karen just pressed on. "The jewelry box," she clarified.

Every muscle in my body seized. Because that hint of fear that had plummeted in my gut manifested into something whole.

Nausea rolled through me.

Lines etched into her forehead, and her head jerked for the

shortest second toward the fireplace. "It is the same, isn't it?" Her words came with caution, with a quiet love for her friend, all of it tempered with compassion.

Still, they stole every fucking last drop of air from the room.

Or maybe it was the sharp breath I sucked in that pilfered it all.

I slammed my eyes shut, squeezing the bottle in my trembling hand so tight I was sure I'd crush it, that it'd crack. Shatter. That it'd break and I'd bleed.

Because all I wanted in that moment was the pain. To release the spark of aggression that flamed, singeing my insides, seeking a release. Something physical to prevent the memory from finding its way back into the light.

But it didn't fucking matter if I tried to block it, it all came flooding back.

"It's exactly the same as you left it." Karen began to stammer, almost pleading as she spoke over strangled words. "It's still rough and unfinished. The design is every bit as beautiful here as it is there."

Fuck. What did she want me to say? That I was fucking happy that she had it stowed away somewhere? When I'd forgotten it'd existed?

Awareness constricted my chest, pressing in, crushing.

Because I knew somewhere inside me I hadn't really forgotten.

Drawn, I let my eyes glide open to the girl. She slowly stood. Warily, she watched.

As if she knew the fire had been lit.

"You did this for her . . . for your mom?" Karen asked, confused, looking back to the fireplace that I'd carved out as a sanctuary for Aly in our home.

When in reality it'd been some sort of fucked-up shrine.

Still, I denied it. "No." I shook my head, which only spun. "I did it for Aly."

I did it for Aly.

Karen straightened herself and brushed off the single tear that slid down her face. "Oh, well . . . I guess I misread it." She forced a smile, sniffled once. "You do beautiful work, Jared. You always have."

I just nodded through the unease, fighting the desire I had to rip the wood from the wall. To hear it splinter as I tore it free.

I just wanted to watch it burn.

Hatred flared. God, I was an idiot. A fool. Thinking I could outrun *her*.

She was fucking everywhere, taunting me, mocking every move I made.

For about three minutes, we all suffered through awkward conversation, no one immune to all my bullshit.

"We'd better get going," Karen finally said.

Christopher clapped me on the back as he headed out, his expression pained but pointed. His thoughts obviously went straight back to the conversation we'd had on New Year's Eve.

Karen came up to me and hugged me good-bye. "I'm sorry," she whispered.

"It was just a misunderstanding," I mumbled back, even though we both knew I was lying.

She just squeezed me tighter and murmured, "It's yours when you're ready for it."

My skin was crawling by the time Dave shook my hand and followed the rest of his family outside.

Aly locked the door behind them and slowly turned around. In silence, she stared across at me. Sympathy edged her eyes, creasing with lines, her green gaze begging me to tell her what the hell was going on in my mind.

But how could I tell her? That what I'd been most proud of creating for her had really been created for my mom.

Long ago.

Before I'd trampled her spirit, stamped out her light.

"Jared . . ." Aly pleaded, taking a step forward.

Backing away, I shook my head. "I'm going to go out back, get some air."

Aly nodded. Her expression turned pained, but she knew me well enough to know when I needed space.

With my head hung, I went into our room, grabbed a pack of cigarettes from the dresser, fumbled around through my old bag for my journal.

When I came back out, Aly was standing in front of the fireplace, staring unseeing into the flames. Awareness slipped through her, but she didn't turn to look at me. It was like she was promising to give me time and telling me she was there for me when I was ready for her.

I escaped out back. The night was thick. Stars stretched across the inky dome that sagged low on the city. Suffocating.

Still it felt fucking cold, the crisp winter air clashing with my heated skin.

I sank to the cool ground, propped my back up against the hard, stucco wall. I banged my head against it, wishing to blot it all out, to erase all the bad.

How could I ever leave it behind when it was always there? Lurking. Threatening my sanity and the world I'd worked so hard to build for Aly. For our baby.

Goddamn it.

I gripped my hair in my hands.

I just wanted to scrape it all from my consciousness. To purge it from my mind.

To take it back.

I shook a smoke from the pack and tilted my head down as I lit it. I drew it deep into my lungs. The faintest calm seeped through my veins, and I slowly blew it toward the sky. Curls of smoke rose upward, twisting as it spiraled toward the heavens. It dissipated, faded into the nothingness.

Bitter laughter rolled from me.

Didn't matter what I did, *she'd* always be there.

Pulling me back into it.

I grabbed my journal and flipped through the worn, tattered pages. Scrawled across the pages was my darkness, all that I held so fucking deep inside. I wanted to pour it all here and pray it would stay, that it'd be done, that I'd have paid.

Fuck.

All I wanted was to be able to breathe.

EIGHTEEN

January 2006

Dust billowed up in Jared's face. He fanned it away. Sweat soaked the back of his shirt. The collar stuck like glue to the back of his neck.

It wasn't even all that hot out, the temperature mild in the middle of January. But it felt muggy in the confines of the closed-up garage.

Jared had turned it into a makeshift shop.

He leaned in close and blew away the sawdust that coated his handiwork. Another puff of dust flew, adding to the haze hanging in the thick air.

A hand squeezed his shoulder. Jared jumped. He jerked his head around.

"Dad," he gasped over the surprise.

He'd been so absorbed in his work he hadn't noticed his father creep up behind him.

His dad grinned with casual amusement. "You're getting jumpy in your old age, Jared." His smile widened with the tease. "You'd think I just caught you sneaking out your window in the middle of the night."

Of course on any given night, his dad probably wouldn't have been that far from the truth.

Jared smirked and rolled his eyes. "Nah . . . just thought you were Mom there for a second."

Laughter rolled from his father, his eyes gleaming. "And you'd better watch out for her, too. She was pestering me for answers last night. She's dying to know what you've been up to out here."

Jared smoothed his hand over the design he'd created just for her, across the delicate carvings that represented everything his mother meant to him.

Jared hadn't been the best kid lately. He knew it. Shame always hit him when his mom looked at him with a fading trace of disappointment. She knew it, too.

She'd been talking to him a lot lately. Nagging him, really. Always telling him to make good choices. To be careful. Cautioning him against getting into situations so deep he wouldn't be able to climb out of them.

"There are some things you just can't take back, Jared," she'd warned him on more than one occasion, though she always said it with complete understanding. Like she knew and accepted he wasn't perfect.

Under his breath, Jared scoffed.

Far from it.

Jared knew he'd been treading dangerous water. All the drinking. Getting high. The girls.

He'd been messing around a lot. Two weeks ago he'd finally just taken it, had sex because he really just wanted to experience it. He didn't even like the girl. She was annoying and whiny.

For the better part of the week after, he'd felt guilty, because his mom had always told him not to waste himself that way. To make it matter.

Funny that guilt didn't even cross his mind when he'd hooked up with another girl he'd never even seen before this last weekend.

It was like once he started, he couldn't stop. But honestly? He didn't want to. Who knew fucking could feel so good? Sure as hell felt better than his hand. After he had a taste, he had no desire to go back.

"Your mom's going to love it, Jared," his dad mused from behind him, breaking into his thoughts. "I'm real proud of you, son. That's some talent you have there. Not many people can pull off something like this. That's art."

Pride heated Jared's cheeks, and his chest felt a little too full. "Thanks, Dad."

His dad rumpled his hair, like he used to do when Jared was just a boy. If Christopher would have seen it, he'd have given him shit for days. But Jared didn't care. His dad was cool—good to him and his sister and most of all to his mom.

His dad's expression shifted. His eyes narrowed, intense and serious. "I mean it. You are a good kid, Jared. Don't know many boys getting ready to turn sixteen who'd spend all their afternoons slaving away in a hot garage making a birthday present for their mom."

A satisfied smile forced its way to Jared's mouth, mingled with the disagreement at his dad's assertion. His mom's birthday was two weeks after his. Just three weeks from now. With all the garbage he'd been getting himself into lately, he wanted to make sure she knew she was far more important than all of that. He wanted her to see the way he saw her.

He was almost finished. All he needed to do was perfect the pattern, deepen the lines, shave to shadow, then stain the wood the dark color his dad had gone with him to pick out.

Jared took his chisel. His lips pressed into a thin line as he focused hard. The blade cut into the wood, carving a defined curve into the intricate floral pattern that graced the top of the jewelry box he'd crafted entirely of his own hands. Each piece had been cut to fit perfectly to build the box. Then he'd set to work to etch the same beauty he found in his mother into the soft wood, her stamp set forever in the elaborate design.

An intricate pattern of petals and leaves, the stems twisted and twined to curl across the top to create a snarled bouquet. A single rose was pronounced in the middle.

The symbol of the greatest beauty.

On the bottom was her inscription.

Helene Rose ~ beauty and light.

NINETEEN

Jared

I'd never had the chance to give it to her.

Did she even know, the way I saw her?

I dropped my head into my hands.

God, I just wanted to breathe . . .

That breath was sharp as I sucked it into my rigid lungs.

Because Aly . . . Aly was my breath. My light.

I rushed to get to my feet, desperate for her touch. Need flashed through me. It blazed as it clashed with the cold.

She was my balm, her fingers the calm I craved, the one drug that would finally take it all away.

I opened the sliding glass door. Who knew how many hours I'd spent alone in the darkness? All the lights inside had been turned off. All except for the single one she'd left on in the kitchen over the stove to guide my way.

And my way was to her.

Cracking open the bedroom door, I snuck inside, my quickened footsteps silent as I stole through the darkened shadows.

Aly lay as a silhouette across our bed. The covers were all twisted around her middle, covering up those legs that I was dying to have wrapped around me. One arm was turned above her head. She jerked, restless where she was lost in the abyss of sleep. Unease twitched through her muscles.

My heart pounded so fucking hard, I was sure it would jar her from sleep, fucking call to her the way she sang out to me. My perfect siren.

Everything I needed.

I climbed onto the bed on my knees. I rushed my hands up her sides.

Aly jumped, then moaned in her sleep. Disoriented, her eyes blinked open. My mouth descended on hers, desperate for the reprieve only she could offer.

"Jared," she mumbled against my lips. Her sweet breath fanned across my face, stirring that insanity inside of me.

I felt crazed, sick with need. Frantic, I shoved the covers away from her, tugging them free from her legs. She only wore a tight white camisole and a pair of panties. The tiny shirt hugged all her curves, the evidence of our child protruding out from that perfect body.

I dove in, kissing her jaw while I gripped her hips, roughly tugging her against me.

"Jared, wait," she said.

"Please, baby, need you . . . need to feel you."

My hands trailed, and Aly lifted to them, accepting their touch, because she needed me, too. Her hands were in my hair, and she kissed me, her mouth so fucking wet and warm and perfect.

I sat back, my hands clamoring for the panties that hindered what I needed most.

Her hands went to my wrists. "Wait," she said again, her voice a strained command.

She searched me in the shadows. Her chest heaved with indecision, and I could barely make out her face, the sharp lines and her pouty, full lips. Still, she was all I could see.

"We can't keep doing this," she pled through a pained whisper.

Palpitations rocked through my heart, and I released my hold on her panties and rushed to move over her, my hands on either side of her head. "Please." I pressed the word to her neck where my mouth met the sweetness of her skin. I kissed a path upward and nipped at her jaw. "Please."

She lifted her chin, allowing me access. A whimper rolled up her throat, because she needed me, too.

"Aly, baby, I love you so much. So fucking much." I burrowed deeper. Seeking. Pleading. "You feel so good. So good."

"Talk to me," she begged through a pant as I devoured her flesh, the softest hands working back through my hair, nudging me back, still holding me close. "Tell me what happened tonight."

A gush of air punched from my lungs, and I stilled. "There's nothing to talk about."

Aly pushed up to sitting. I snapped back to find the sadness in her face, this girl who could undo me in five seconds sinking her fingers into my skin. Literally. She clutched my hands. Green eyes flashed. "You can't keep doing this, Jared. You think I don't know that something is killing you right now? You think I don't know it's been getting worse for the last month?" Pain laced through her tone. "These nights when you wake me up in the middle of the night . . . your eyes . . . they're so intense. But hollow, Jared. Like you don't really see *me*."

Rejection slammed me, wound with a spike of remorse.

All I ever saw was her.

Her.

Didn't she know that?

I felt sick as I pushed away, because there was no chance I could deal with this shit right now.

Aly dug her fingers in deeper, refusing to let me go. "Don't you dare walk away from me right now, Jared. I know you, and I know what you're thinking right now. *I want you.*" Hoarsely, it trembled from her throat. "Always. I love you more than any-thing in this world and I know you love me. But I also know whatever my mom was talking about tonight shredded you."

Her expression softened, and she released one hand to cup my face. It singed me, her touch always fire, always comfort.

With it, my eyes dropped closed.

"I know you're hurting. I'm here for you. You can talk to me. You can *tell* me."

Bitter laughter broke into the night and I blinked back at her in disbelief. Was she really asking me to do this again? Did she not remember?

"The last time you told me that, Aly, I lost you." The words flew from my mouth, harsh and hard, with all the crushing pain of living those months without her. "I refuse to ever let that happen again. Nothing is ever going to come between us. All this shit . . . none of it matters. None of it. Not when I have you. I keep telling you to let it go."

"You can't just keep pretending, Jared."

"I'm not pretending. I'm just trying to find a way to live."

To find a way to live when I knew I really shouldn't.

Aly's eyes pressed closed for the longest time. Agony pinched up her expression, before she opened to me, those green eyes falling over me with all this love and affection.

My heart steadied, pounding hard.

She took my face between both her hands. "All I want is for you to live. To be free." Fear cut into the tenderness of her affection. "But I know you better than anyone else in this world. Anyone, Jared." She leaned forward and gently placed her palm over the punctuated throb of my heart. "And I know there is still a huge piece of this that is dead."

I swallowed hard with the strike.

Her voice lowered, filled with all the understanding of what she really didn't understand. "You have to talk to someone, Jared," she pressed on. She shook her head as if she was trying to grasp the right thing to say. "Find your father. Do something. What happened tonight? Do you think I missed the expression on your face? Do you think I didn't know how deeply my mother hurt you just with the mention of your family? You are not *okay*."

Anger surged and anxiety spun. "I told you to let it be, Aly." It slid from my mouth as a hiss.

Fuck.

She was going to do this now? "I warned you, told you I would never outrun all the shit in my life. You accepted that."

Aly lifted her chin. Her throat bobbed heavily as she swallowed. A tear slipped down her cheek, and God, if it didn't hurt watching it.

I didn't want to hurt her.

Ever.

But she had to know I wasn't going there.

Her voice was soft in surrender. "You also told me you wanted to be better."

I squeezed my eyes closed.

Goddamn it.

My fingers twitched because part of me wanted to destroy. To give in to the destruction. Because that's what I always did.

I looked back her, at this girl who'd shattered all of my beliefs. Cupping her precious face, I lost myself in all that love. "Baby, it's you . . . you that makes me better."

Aly's face tipped away, and she took in a shuddered breath.

"Please," I said as I inched forward. "I need you to let this go." Cautiously, I folded her up in my arms, careful as I laid us down in the middle of our bed. My hand slid down her delicate neck and flattened on her chest. "Please," I whispered again.

Aly curled onto her side. She pressed her face to my neck and whispered her own plea. "Please, let me help you."

But that's what Aly didn't fully understand. She couldn't grasp that she'd brought me back from the dead. Yeah, a piece of me died when my mother did. But what was left of my heart and soul belonged to Aly.

She clung to me, like I'd been clinging to her earlier. "I can't lose you," she said.

I brushed my fingers through her hair, wound a lock in my finger, the words hoarse. "You won't."

She couldn't.

Because she was the only air I could breathe.

TWENTY

Jared

Aly stood at the island in the kitchen. Completely absorbed, her focus was intent on whisking the creamy mixture she had billowing up in a silver bowl.

Affection pulsed through me. Hard and defined.

With my shoulder leaned up against the short hall wall just outside our bedroom door, I watched her.

How could I stop?

Quietly she hummed to herself. Black hair fell down around one shoulder, her attention fully absorbed in the task at hand.

It hurt a little looking at her. It seemed impossible one woman could make me feel this way, that one girl held my heart with a single string. The one that connected us, this unseen bond that wound us so fucking tight sometimes it felt like it was squeezing the life right out of me.

Like I couldn't breathe.

But really, it was that I couldn't breathe without her.

Shaking my head, I glanced around the open room. Our house looked like it'd blown up. Balloons and streamers were strung up everywhere, all of them black and silver with dots of hot pink.

I chuckled a little.

Aly knew her friend well, and I was pretty sure these decorations were spot-on.

Today was Megan's twenty-first birthday.

And that shit was going down here.

Yeah, Aly'd offered.

It was no secret she glowed with pride over this house, and any chance she got, she showed it off. Not that I minded. It felt fucking good, this house, knowing what I'd created for my family.

I pushed from the wall. Aly looked up when she heard me approach. She dragged one side of her bottom lip between her teeth, biting at her smile as I rounded the island and edged up behind her.

"Mmm . . ." She hummed as she leaned back on me, still whisking while she fell into my hold. "You smell good."

A soft chuckle rumbled in my chest, and I buried my nose in her hair, all coconut and good and fucking delicious girl. "Not nearly as good as you smell, baby."

I snaked my arm around her, quick to dip an impulsive finger into the bowl of white frosting. I sucked it into my mouth. "And not even close to how good this tastes."

Aly giggled and swatted my hand away. "Keep your fingers out of the frosting."

"What? I just had a shower." I wiggled my fingers out in front of me. "Clean . . . see." I slanted my mouth to her ear. "But I can think of all kinds of ways to get them dirty again."

"Oh, you can, huh? Like what?" Aly made a valiant attempt

at appearing flippant. Unaffected. But I felt the shiver. The flutter of nerves that moved through her.

I bit back a satisfied grin, and dove in again, this time with three fingers. I brought out a soft mound and smeared it at the corner of one side of her mouth. Over her shoulder, I leaned in, my tongue and lips stroking across the soft flesh. "Like this," I whispered.

A little whimper left her. The sound pierced me in the pit of my stomach.

Damn, this girl made me insane.

I swiped a single finger into the frosting again. This time I dipped it into her mouth. "Or like this."

With her head tipped back on my shoulder, Aly sucked it clean, those green eyes watching me watching her.

Lust twisted me in the tightest knot.

I groaned and Aly smiled, a little victorious and a whole lot sexy.

What had this girl done to me?

"I think you'd better stop. Megan will be here any minute and this cake should already be finished." She uttered the warning with a shot of playfulness. It wasn't close to being enough to cover up the need that thickened her voice.

I reached for the bowl. Megan could wait.

"Don't you dare put your fingers in there again," Aly mumbled through laughter, her hand clenching my hand to stop me. "You've already stuck your fingers in there enough that I should probably dump this out and start over." She turned a little, nudging me back by pushing on my chest, though her fingers lingered a little longer, twisting a bit into my black tee. Her eyes gleamed with mirth. "Don't you think you've contaminated it enough?"

"I doubt very much I've ever eaten a cake that someone didn't snag a little taste of first. It's expected."

Aly cocked a challenging brow. *Really?*

"Okay, maybe under different circumstances." I grabbed her hand, pressed it to my face, kissed her palm. "I say we just cancel the whole thing and see how creative we can get with this since I've already *contaminated* it."

"Ha. Not a chance." She smirked, and shook her head with a laugh. "Do you really think Megan would let us get away with that? She'd be over here banging our door down. You only turn twenty-one once. And the one thing my best friend asked me for was a party. So she gets a party."

"Yeah, yeah, yeah . . . I know . . . today is Megan's day," I said, relenting. Never had a chance in the first place. My eyes made a pass over my girl. But hell, it was worth a try.

Caution transformed Aly's expression, and she dropped those green eyes that always saw so much, that watched me and knew me and spoke to me.

With just the look, my chest tightened.

She chanced peeking up at me. "We have so much to celebrate, Jared. Not just Megan."

Fear and anger collided. I forced them down, doing my best to keep my voice even. "Please don't, Aly."

Tuesday was my birthday. Four days away. It loomed like this omen I couldn't shake.

And not a good one.

Aly gasped when I grabbed her around the waist and set her on the island countertop. I settled between her thighs, my cheek pressed to the rapid beat of her heart.

I knew what she was doing. What she wanted. But she kept asking for fucking impossible things. And God, I wanted to give her everything. Anything. But not this. "I won't ever celebrate that day, Aly," I mumbled into her shirt, away from her face where she couldn't see me, close enough that she could understand. That she could feel. "You have to stop doing this to me, suggesting this shit that isn't going to happen."

Aly stilled in my firm hold.

Since I turned sixteen, my birthdays had come with destruction. I'd drown myself in the deepest bottle I could find. The day always ended with bloodshed, whether it was my own or caused by my hand. It was like I was called out into the night, seeking chaos. It was never hard to find. So many assholes were out there looking for the exact same thing.

But fuck, this year was going to be different. It had to be. This one would be spent with the girl, with the one who'd injected her light into me. Things had changed so drastically since she lit up my life.

But I sure as hell wasn't going to be celebrating it.

All I could do was pray for it to pass, and when it finally did, that it would take all this fucking agitation that'd been simmering in me with it.

Aly shifted back to look at me. Compassion wove into her expression. She brushed her fingers through my hair that had gotten way too fucking long. "What do you say we just celebrate today?"

I reached out and held one side of her head. My hand covered most all of it, the silk of her hair weaving through my fingers the same way as she'd woven herself into my heart. I kissed her, softly, just a brush of my lips. "Yeah, let's celebrate today." I moved my hands to her belly. She was getting bigger now. Really showing. And damn, I'd been right. It was just a ball low in her stomach, the rest of her lean and long and fucking sexy as all hell. This girl just kept getting better and better. "Like you said, we have so many other things to celebrate."

Aly set a hand over mine, pressing my hands a little firmer against her stomach. Tenderness spilled from her. Hopeful, she glanced up at me. "Do you feel that? The baby's moving like crazy right now."

I stilled, strained. Longing pulled at my heart. God, how badly I wanted to. To know my child. To see his or her face.

I smiled at her and slowly slid a single hand upward to the center of her chest. "No . . . not yet . . . but I can feel your heart beating."

Redness settled on her cheeks, and I dropped my forehead to hers. For a few minutes, I lost myself in her.

The doorbell rang.

I groaned and Aly giggled. "It's party time," she sang with an obnoxious waggle of her eyebrows that was about the cutest fucking thing I'd ever seen.

Aly tipped her head to the side. "Go answer that. I'm putting five bucks on Megan and I need to get this cake frosted before she sees it."

I helped her down from the counter, making sure she was steady on her feet. Impatiently the doorbell rang twice in a row.

Striding toward the door, I glanced over my shoulder at Aly, who was slathering the remnants of my burst fantasy all over the waiting cake sitting on the opposite counter. "Stall her," Aly mouthed, smiling proud.

God, I loved her.

I swung the door open to Megan. She was all dressed up, her blond hair set in these long, wavy curls, wearing jeans and heels and probably the biggest fucking smile I'd ever seen the girl wear. "Happy birthday, Megan," I said, pulling her in for a quick hug.

"Hey, Jared." She patted me on the shoulder. "How are you?"

"Pretty damned good."

Aly's voice bellowed behind us. "Happy birthday, Megan! Don't move, I need to get this cake done and you're not allowed to see it until I'm finished."

Megan laughed and waved her off. "Pssh . . . I won't look, I swear. Why don't you put me to work instead?"

Megan tossed her purse to the couch.

Aly smiled across at her. "Fine . . . but no peeking. But I can use some help. There are some veggies and dip and chips and stuff that need to be set out. You want to handle that?"

"On it," Megan said. She smoothed out her shirt and stood tall, like she'd just put on her work face.

Laughing a little, I grinned across at my girl. "What else do you need done, baby?"

"Just the backyard stuff."

I crossed into the kitchen and dropped a swift kiss to her forehead. "Is that your way of trying to get rid of me?"

"Never," Aly said at the same time as Megan said, "Yes."

A short giggle escaped Aly, and she hiked up on her toes and planted a playful kiss to my lips. "I think we just need some girl-talk time before everyone else gets here. And outside work is"—her eyes widened in emphasis—"man work."

My head cocked. "Man work?"

"What, do you want your pregnant girlfriend hauling wood and lighting fires?"

"Pregnant fiancée, almost wife," I corrected. "Big differ-ence."

She squeezed my jaw. "Fine . . . Do you want your *pregnant fiancée, almost wife* hauling wood?"

I wrapped my arms around her expanding waist, rocked her in the middle of our floor, kissed her a little deeper than was entirely appropriate for a witness.

But hey. She was asking for it.

Pretty sure she was begging for it.

"No, I definitely do not want you out hauling wood." With a smirk, I stepped back. "I'll just leave you two to the kitchen."

Megan beaned me in the head with a baby carrot.

"Ow!" I lifted my arm to shield myself from the next that flew through the air as she pelted me again.

Megan was grinning hard. "You'd better be watching yourself there, Jared Holt. That's some hot water you're dipping your toes into. Didn't anyone ever tell you not to mess with a pregnant woman?"

"Yeah," Aly shot back in defiance, doing her best to muster a look of offense, as if the girl could be angry for a second of her life.

"Fine, mama bear," I baited through the smile pushing to my mouth. I dipped in for another kiss. "I'll be outside. You let me know whatever you need me to do."

Soft affection passed between us as I slid open the back door.

I escaped outside, narrowly missing whatever gossip began to spew from Megan's mouth.

That's really what the backyard had become.

An escape.

I came out here when my thoughts got too thick. Out back here, in our small patch of desert, I could work through them, sifting through all the bullshit.

Crazy thing was those thoughts always ended up in one place. On the girl inside.

Tonight the air was cool. Twilight stretched its fingers across the sky, light blues and a stark white hanging on to the horizon as the sun disappeared. Faint stars began to blink high in the sky as it deepened to dark.

I finished stocking the coolers with beer. I broke up little pieces of wood into kindling, and piled them into the fire pit I'd installed off to one side of the yard.

I got to one knee, my head craned over as I flicked my

lighter against the wadded-up pieces of newspaper I used as a starter. Instantly, a flame consumed the paper. I blew on it, urging it to spread.

The back door slid open behind me.

"Hey, man, what's up?"

I looked over my shoulder.

Christopher stepped out with a huge-ass grin on his face. He dove a hand through his hair, then shook the mess free as he closed the door behind him.

"Just getting this started . . . supposed to be chilly tonight."

He laughed, though it sounded too low. "Playing with fire. Always fucking playing with fire."

I glared at him. Fucking smartass.

Pissed me off he was always treading so close to the truth. I gestured to the woodpile I had stacked up against the back wall. "Make yourself useful and bring me some wood, would you?"

"Not a problem."

Christopher crossed to the far end of the yard, stacked a few pieces of wood in his arms, and lugged them back over to the fire. He dropped them unceremoniously next to the pit.

"Thanks." Sarcasm lifted my brow as I grabbed the smallest one and wedged it over the growing flames.

He cackled, all raucous and loud. "That's what I'm here for."

"Asshole," I mumbled the slur, unable to stop my smile. God, this guy. Didn't know how I got through all those years without him around to razz my ass. He'd started to feel like a necessity, like something fundamental would be missing if I didn't have him there to give me a hard time.

Laughing, he traipsed over to the cooler. "Want a beer?"

"That'd be cool."

I poked at the fire, stirring it up. Flames took hold of the splintered, dried wood and rose up to hug the log.

Glass clinked behind me as Christopher dug through the cooler. Five seconds later, he handed me a beer. "Here you go."

"Thanks." I twisted the cap and tipped my neck to Christopher's.

He flopped down into one of the chairs surrounding the fire.

Taking a long pull, I stared into the dancing fire.

"God, I love this kind of night," Christopher said with a heavy sigh. Lifting his bottle to his mouth, he settled back, stared up at the unending sky. "So fucking quiet. Calm. Like nothing else in this world matters."

My eyebrows climbed toward my hair, though I was feeling so much the same. "Dude, when did you get all sentimental on my ass?"

He laughed, scrubbed a hand over his face, his own taunt muting out the seriousness. "Apparently when you knocked up my little sister."

I grinned. "You aren't ever going to let me live that down, are you?" It was said as if it were a minor glitch. As if Aly and me colliding hadn't shifted our worlds. Like that baby growing in her hadn't become our lives.

"Uh, yeah, probably never," Christopher said pointedly with a shake of his head, snickering below his breath as he lifted his beer to his mouth.

Movement caught my eye behind me. I looked through the windows to where the house was all lit up within. The front door opened, and the first of Megan's guests poured into our house.

The house slowly filled up. Voices began to echo from inside and out back. Night slowly took hold on the city, a mild chill pressing down from above. When inside finally maxed out on capacity, people began to overflow into the backyard, where Christopher and I watched over the growing party. We kept the cooler stocked and the fire stoked, letting Aly and her friends do their thing.

Didn't mean I didn't keep glancing at Aly or that Aly didn't keep glancing at me. Our attention was always on the other while she made her rounds and entertained her guests. But it was like we revolved around the other, gentle brushes of hands and deeper connections of eyes.

I could never get close enough.

She spun me up, wrapped me tight, left me completely undone.

That smile . . . that smile kept slamming me, hitting me right in the center of my chest every time she cast it my direction.

It took Christopher about half an hour to find his next pawn in whatever fucked-up game he played. This girl was tall with huge tits that I was pretty damned sure were real, all wrapped up in a gorgeous face hidden behind a shy smile.

I wondered how pissed off he'd be if I warned her, told her to get the hell out of here before she fell victim to his prey. She looked way more unsuspecting than the type of girl he usually went for, and something about that just didn't sit right.

Night deepened and wind gusted in. People gathered around the fire, laughing and messing around as they vied for a better position to keep them warm.

I put a couple more logs on it, figured if I was going to build it, I might as well do it up right.

Flames licked up, popped and cracked, glowing warm against our faces as the fire grew higher, stretching for the sky.

"Ah, now that's a fire," Christopher called from where he sat, the blonde perched on his knee. She held her palms up in front of her, glancing back at him with a timid smile when he squeezed her thigh.

"I aim to please."

Laughter mingled through the conversations in our back-yard. The party was easy. Voices grew louder as the night progressed and more drinks were consumed, the party coming to fruition as the mood heightened.

Megan laughed hysterically when Aly came outside bearing her cake, twenty-one tall pink candles blazing, matching the beat of the fire.

"Oh my God, that is the best cake ever!" she squealed. Megan had definitely been living it up tonight, doing rounds of shots with her friends while Aly watched on with an amused smile. Megan just kept getting tipsier and tipsier by the minute.

Everyone gathered around the small table where Aly carefully set the cake.

They all belted out "Happy Birthday." Half the backyard sang off key, their voices discordant. Whistles rang out and Megan ducked down and blew out her candles, wished for whatever desires she kept hidden inside. She doused them in one swoop. With a sloppy grin shot in the direction of Aly, she pumped her fist in the air and yelled, "Woohoo . . . no more lame boyfriends for me!"

Aly laughed outright, loud and free.

Off to the side of the crowd, I smiled a little, brushed my hair back, sipped my beer.

I went back to tending the fire. Feeling fucking good.

Even with my own birthday looming just days away, I felt good.

Joy swelled around the edges of my heart.

The reason for that joy wrapped her slender arms around me from behind. "There's my man."

Peace pumped like the beat of blood through my veins.

She nudged her head under my arm and poked around my

side to face the fire. With a short chuckle, I wound my arm over her shoulders. Both her arms were wrapped tightly around me, held snug at my front, the two of us in this awkward embrace as we swayed in front of the fire.

"You having fun, baby?" I asked.

Aly smiled up at me, tacked to my side, exactly where I wanted her to be. Green eyes sparkled, dancing in the fire. "Yes . . . I love this . . . everyone here . . . at our house. It just feels . . . good."

I squeezed her. "Yeah, it does, doesn't it?"

"Aly, I need to talk to you."

The voice broke into our comfort.

A chill slicked down my spine. My muscles got all twisted up and I hugged Aly closer.

No fucking way was I going to let his happen.

From across the yard, I heard Megan raise her voice. "I did not invite you here, Sam . . . you and Gabe can just turn around and leave. You don't have any business being here."

"I'm not here for you," Sam hissed low.

"Aly," Gabe urged again.

Aly's arms loosened, but I kept my hold. Slowly, I turned us around. With my arm still around her, I edged her behind me, shielding her from the asshole who stood three feet from me.

"What do you want?" I asked him, my voice flat and cold.

Gabe shifted on his feet. Nerves rocked through him, but he held his ground, glared at me while he spoke. "I wasn't talking to you. I was talking to Aly." He inclined his head, trying to coax Aly from where she peeked out behind me. "Come on, Aly, all I'm asking you for is five minutes."

Oh no.

Dickhead really thought he was going to come stir up problems in *my* house?

Fucker had another thing coming.

Aggression spiked. I itched, hostility begging to break free. My hands fisted, and I was doing my best to keep it all in check.

His brown hair had been cut short, cropped. It shaved away all the boyish innocence he normally wore like some mask, revealing all the asshole he always had lurking inside. Arrogant prick.

Never trusted this guy.

Not once.

Sure as hell wasn't trusting him now.

"You've got a lot of fuckin' nerve coming into my house thinking you're going to talk to my girl."

He scoffed through caustic laughter. "What, you're not going to let her talk to me now?"

His attention turned to her. "What the hell, Aly? Do you let this guy own you? Tell you what you can and can't do? What kind of bullshit is that?"

Bullshit?

Nah. I was just protecting my girl.

"Back the fuck off," I hissed.

Morbid interest rumbled through the yard, bodies drawing near to get a better look at what was going down.

I hated all this shit. I just wanted to give Aly a normal fucking life. Was that too much to ask for? But it was like it chased me, the destruction, the bad blood that simmered through my veins, calling out to the rest of the assholes of this world.

That asshole took another step forward. "Is that why you didn't text me back on New Year's? Because this asshole won't let you talk to me? Because he's worried I'm right?"

He lifted his chin with the insult, the last part directed at me.

Violence skimmed my skin, and I sucked in a ragged breath.

Behind me, Aly stilled. Confusion emanated from her in waves. Flustered, she wound out of my hold, taking a step out beside me. Her eyes narrowed with the question. "What are you talking about?"

"I sent you like five texts on New Year's Eve." He glared over at me before turning his rabid attention back to my girl. "Trying to talk some sense into you . . . to tell you I'd be there to take care of you . . . no matter what. Figured since you wouldn't text me back, I'd just come to you. I told you a long time ago I wasn't giving up on us . . . and I'm not."

Aly's confused eyes blinked over him before she looked at me. I saw the second realization set in. Disappointment twisted up her face. Everything in her was trained on me, like Gabe didn't exist, which was a fucking good thing because that guy was about three seconds from getting his ass beat if he didn't get away from her.

But right then, he didn't matter at all.

Not for a second.

The only thing that mattered was the hurt written all over Aly's face.

"Baby," I said, trying to temper my voice, to keep it from shaking. "Listen to me."

She ignored me while she drew her phone from her back jeans pocket. Swiping her thumb across the plate, she clicked into her messages to find the last one Dickhead sent her.

And that was the fucking thing, he'd been texting her all along, fucking laying seeds of his own destruction, trying to claim what could never be his, steal from me the one thing that had ever truly belonged to me.

This girl was mine.

She'd always been.

Aly stared at the glowing screen. "Thanksgiving," she said quietly. She eyed him like she really didn't care to see him, but was much more interested in what he had to say about the situation.

I fucking squirmed.

"The last text I have from you was on Thanksgiving," she reiterated.

"I texted you a bunch of times on New Year's Eve . . . after I saw you. It was late." He watched her as he confessed, gauging her reaction, waiting for her to take the bait.

Aly turned to face me and shoved her phone in my direction. "Did you delete messages from him?" she asked. Disbelief poured from her. Tangible hurt.

"Baby, I'm sorry. Listen to me . . . I did . . ." I roughed both hands over the top of my head. "I know I shouldn't have, but it was in the middle of the night and you were sleeping and fuck . . ." I gripped the back of my neck. "I thought it had to be Christopher, so I looked. And I'm sorry for invading your privacy, but this dickhead was texting you and talking shit that I just didn't want you to hear."

"Because it's the truth," he tossed out.

"Fuck you," I spat, my attention jerking toward the little twit who was about to get torn limb from limb. I pointed at him. "I already warned you to get out of my house. I meant it. The next time I turn around, you'd best be gone."

I turned back to Aly. Fear rolled through me, all this regret burning up my insides. But shit, what else was I supposed to do? Let this guy wedge himself between us? "No good can come of him trying to get mixed up in us," I pled, trying to get her to understand where I was coming from. "We've got enough shit to deal with."

Lines pinched up that gorgeous face. "Do you think I care if

you look at my phone, Jared? Do you think I want to keep secrets from you?" She stepped away from me. She lifted her
hands, palms up and out to her sides like an offering. "I have
nothing to hide from you. What I care about is that you think
so little of me you feel the need to erase messages. That you
don't trust *me* enough to talk to him."

"I do trust you, Aly."

I trusted her with my life.

Desperate, I pushed toward her, trying to erase the space
she put between us. "Who I don't trust is him."

Aly blinked at me. I watched her swallow and fight through
some unwelcomed emotion. Her voice dropped, pained and
wounded. "No, Jared, I think who you don't trust is yourself."

I could feel all the eyes on us. Prying into our business.
Discomfort prickled at the back of my neck.

I hated all this shit, standing out there on display. But all of
that disquiet paled in comparison to what it felt like having Aly
look at me this way.

Sadness wove into her words. "This is that part of you who
still thinks he's not good enough for me, who thinks he doesn't
deserve how much I love him."

"He's *not* good enough for you." Gabe's voice cut into my
mind, into the truth of what Aly spoke.

Rage brimmed and spiraled.

Everything flashed, and I was in his face. I rushed him,
shoving him in the chest. "Get the fuck out of my house."

My hands met his skin, that skin I'd been dying to take out
for so long. Hatred burned, feeding the darkness.

This was the asshole who was stupid enough to think he
was supposed to be for my girl.

The one who wanted to take.

He shoved me back. "Fuck you. You think I give a shit what you think? What you say? You're nothing but garbage. Look at you, you fucking freak. I have no clue what she sees in you."

Blackness pressed into my sight. A frenzy of madness lit.

Somewhere in the murk, I heard Christopher's low voice, "Oh, shit, this is not gonna be good," in the same second I lunged forward.

"Jared, don't!" Aly screamed. Her voice pierced through the hatred clouding my mind, and I forced myself to stop. Shaking with rage, I looked back at her pleading at me with her eyes.

I took a step back. And as I turned aside, I felt his fist connect with my face.

Pain split my consciousness.

Stunned, I stumbled. I touched my mouth and pulled back my fingers. Blood coated the tips.

Motherfucker.

Dickhead just sucker-punched me.

He swung another fist that connected under my jaw. My head rocked back.

Fury exploded with the splintering pain.

And God, I so desperately wanted to hold on to sanity. To the light that Aly had injected into my life. To listen to her pleas.

But I felt it all slipping away.

The dark rose up, glowered from the depths, and took over my senses.

All that fucking agitation that had built up for months raced through every inch of my being. The muscles in my back and arms flexed and jumped, spurring me on. My hands fisted as they gave in and sought out the flesh.

Because this fucker was trying to take my girl. He wanted to take from me the one good thing I'd ever been given.

And there was no chance I was giving her up without a fight.

The crunch that landed on his jaw resonated all the way to my bones.

A second to his cheek.

Skin split and poured blood.

And I knew, knew I didn't deserve her. Because I couldn't stop. I just pounded into him, landing blow after blow, feeling this sickening satisfaction take me over as I gave in to the darkness I'd been fighting every single day since I came back into Aly's life. "Stay away from my girl. Do you understand me? She is mine . . . she's always going to be mine."

A fist landed on my temple. But this blow was delivered by another hand.

Sam.

It nearly knocked me cold. Still I clung to consciousness, not about to give up this fight.

Sam rammed a sharp fist into my ribs. Breath gushed from my lungs.

Christopher's face flashed as he descended in a blur of color, blinded with a fury of his own.

It took about five seconds until the four of us were a pile of limbs and fists and pathetic anger brawling in the dirt.

And I could hear Aly screaming, begging no. But I couldn't stop. I had to beat all this aggression out of me, to take it out on the one person who'd been stupid enough to fuck with me.

Frantic hands tried to restrain us. Voices lifted.

Only Megan's horrified voice was enough to get through. "Aly, oh my God, Aly."

Aly.

I fought to get to my feet while a shot of dizziness attempted to knock me back down. I blinked, trying to make sense of the scene. A couple of Christopher's friends restrained Gabe and Sam, hauling them back toward the house, and Christopher scrambled to his feet. Blood trickled from a gash on the side of his head, his green eyes just as wild as mine.

Everyone had backed away, making a wide circle. All except for Megan, who was on her knees in front of the fire.

Crying.

Fucking crying over Aly, who was curled up in a ball on the ground next to the fire. She had her hands on her stomach and her knees curled up. Protecting herself.

My heart seized before it took off at a sprint. "Oh my God, Aly, baby . . . baby, are you okay?"

I rushed forward.

Megan's arm flew out to stop me, and she whipped her head around to look at me. Tears streaked down her terrified face, and she shrieked, "Stay away from her. You're fucking insane."

Dread knotted my stomach. I stumbled back.

Christopher tried to approach, and she lashed out again. "All of you. Just stay away from her."

My eyes fixed on Aly. Megan helped her sit up.

"Are you okay?" Megan whimpered, touching her face, her stomach, her arm. "Tell me where you're hurt."

Aly winced. "It's just my arm."

Megan pulled it away from her body.

Redness flashed up the underside of her wrist.

Burned.

I clutched my hair. "Aly," I whispered.

She looked up at me with tormented green eyes.

Somewhere in my consciousness, I heard Sam's urgent voice, talking to the piece of shit who was trying to tear apart my family. "Come on, man, let's get the fuck out of here. Told you this shit wasn't worth it."

Gabe glared at me. He spit a glob of blood from his bleeding mouth, his jaw clenched as he knocked into me as he limped toward the back of the yard. The asshole was stupid enough to ask for another round.

I didn't even fucking care.

The only thing I cared about was her.

I'd thought maybe . . . maybe I could change. That I could shove it all down. Hide from it.

But it always just came looking for me.

Didn't matter what I did, I ended up on destruction's path.

I always ruined the good.

Livid blue eyes flashed as Megan sneered in their direction. "I don't ever want to see you again, Sam. You or Gabe. I'm not joking. This was it. I can't believe you used my birthday as an excuse to come here and cause trouble."

She turned back to Aly, murmuring soft words as Gabe and Sam jumped the back wall.

"Get him out of here, Christopher," Megan demanded with her back to me, though it was completely clear who she was talking about.

Christopher hesitated, before he tugged at my arm. "Come on man, let's get you cleaned up."

I shook my head. "I'm not going anywhere."

"Just go," Aly forced over the sob in her throat.

"Aly . . ."

She squeezed her eyes shut. "Please, just . . . give me a few minutes. I'm fine. I promise."

But I knew she wasn't fine.

I let Christopher lead me into the house and push me into the guest bathroom. He locked the door behind us.

I paced the small space, ripping at my hair.

Shit. Shit. Shit.

What did I do?

"Hey man, calm the fuck down. That wasn't your fault out

there. That piece of shit backed you into a wall. He deserved to get his ass kicked. Everyone saw what he did. Everyone knows."

I flopped down onto the lid of the toilet, sagged down as I rested my elbows on my thighs.

Christopher ducked under the sink and grabbed a couple washcloths. Turning on the water, he wet them and wrung them out. "Douche bag has had it coming for a long time."

He tossed one to me. Unseeing, I caught it, balled it up and pressed it to my bottom lip. "Yeah, he did."

I doubted Aly was going to see it that way.

Gritting his teeth, Christopher dabbed the cloth to the cut on the side of his head, studying himself in the mirror.

"You okay?" I asked.

"Yeah, man, it was nothing. Believe me, both of them are hurting way worse than we are."

I turned to stare at my feet. "Thanks for having my back."

He laughed, the sound all kinds of inappropriate and brimming with the same kind of satisfaction I felt at finally beating Dickhead's ass. "All too happy to. Besides, you saved my ass major tonight. If it hadn't been for your temper, I'd probably be stealing that sweet little girl back to my apartment right about now. Now that was not going to end well."

He tossed the cloth into the sink. "I'm going to go check on things out there." He stretched out a placating hand. "Just stay in here for a while. Cool the fuck down before you go out looking for Aly."

He cocked his head, his eyes calling out the fucking moronic mistake I'd made by deleting those messages. "You probably need to give my sister some time to calm down, too."

"Shit . . . I didn't mean for her to get hurt, Christopher," I whispered over the pain that flared when I thought about her on the ground.

"Was it you who hurt her, Jared?" he asked, his voice twisting with contention. "Or did I? Or that asshole who showed up where he wasn't welcome? Or how about his asshole friend who decided to jump in and make it an all-out brawl?" He raked an uneasy hand through his hair, looked at the wall. "And God, my sister doesn't know when to sit things out. Always trying to break things up."

I frowned. If it was anyone's fault, it sure as hell was not Aly's.

Christopher pegged me with his stare. "Tonight was fucked-up, but this isn't all on your shoulders, so don't go getting all emo on me, asshole."

I scoffed and he laughed.

Christopher curled and uncurled his fist slowly. He flinched a little, obviously in pain. The skin on his knuckles was all shredded, flaming red.

"Just . . . lie low," Christopher said seriously—a warning. "Let me go check on her and make sure the house is cleared out."

Subdued voices came and went as the front door opened and closed, all of Megan and Aly's friends flocking from what was supposed to be a good time for Megan. I climbed to my feet, paced some more, staring at myself in the mirror.

My eyes were too wide. Unfocused. Blood had begun to dry on the tiny cut at the corner of my bottom lip, and my eye was beginning to swell.

Damn it. I rubbed my palm over my mouth, trying to settle my rioting nerves.

I just needed to know she was really okay.

Bitter laughter climbed up my throat. *Okay.* What the fuck was okay? This bullshit I always got myself into?

That was most assuredly not fucking okay.

I forced myself to sit and give her the space she asked me for.

About ten minutes later, two knocks sounded at the door.

Christopher poked his head in. He looked me up and down, judging my mood, before he edged inside. His voice was muted in a fierce whisper. "Aly's fine . . . the burn wasn't that bad. She's pretty shook up, though. She said she really just wants to be alone, and Megan's had way too much to drink for us to cut her loose, so I'm going to give her a ride home, then I'll stop back by to check in."

He gestured to the door. "Think you'd better give Aly some time to process this all. I can't tell if she's more pissed off about the texts or the fight." His expression lightened. "You did what you thought was right tonight, Jared. Don't go beating yourself up about it." A smile cracked his face. Humor glinted in his eyes. "Besides, it looks like Gabe did plenty of that for one night."

I stared up at him from where I sat on the lid of the toilet. Always such a punk. I forced a smile before I dropped my face in my hands. "Go on, Christopher. Take Megan home. We'll be okay."

Fucking *okay*.

Never was gonna be.

"Yeah, man, just give me a call if you need anything. I'll be back by a while later."

I nodded understanding, listened to him retreat. The soft sound of Christopher's and Megan's voices filtered into the bathroom before I heard the final click of the front door behind them.

With a heavy sigh, I stood, my hands fisted at my side as I pushed out into the hallway.

It was dark. Quiet. Too quiet.

My feet shuffled forward.

Embers glowed from the fire that had been built in the fireplace.

That fucking fireplace.

Bitterness crushed the joy of it within me.

Drawn, I inched toward it. Unsteadily, I pressed my hands

up against the mantel, used it as support as I dropped my head and tried to catch my breath. Just for once, I wished I could be a different person.

But nothing was ever going to change. Knew it now.

I felt her searing presence behind me. Like shock waves.

I lifted my head. Regret flooded from me as I looked over at her, my arms still bracketed to the mantel.

At the edge of the room, she stood. Her arms were crossed protectively over her chest, hugging herself. A bandage was wrapped around her wrist, blocking out another piece of her skin that I had marred.

Another fucking sin.

I shuddered, my voice scratchy as I murmured over the pain, "Are you okay?"

She nodded, but tears slipped free.

I pushed away from the mantel, and turned to face her. Anxiety crawled beneath my skin, hate and fear and this sense of fading hope. Like the bleakest blackness was taking hold as I looked at the girl I'd only ever wanted to protect but just kept hurting.

"Aly, I'm sorry . . ." With the confession, my face dropped toward the floor. "It was stupid, erasing those messages." I lifted my chin, imploring, "But I can't lose you. I can't stand the thought of another man touching you."

Green eyes narrowed in pained disbelief, and she shook her head. "Do you really think there was any chance of that? Of me letting another man touch me? That Gabe texting me would have changed one single thing between us?"

She fisted a hand out in front of her, fighting through all the disappointment she felt for me.

Agitation ratcheted higher, twisting me tighter. I hated her looking at me that way.

In emphasis, her lids dropped closed. "Gabe is delusional, Jared."

She blinked them open, her eyes swirling with all this doubt I didn't know how to make sense of. "All of this is about us, Jared. About your fear. Don't you see it? What you're doing to us?"

My attention dropped to the bandage on her arm. Yeah, I fucking saw what I was doing to us. What I was doing to *her*.

She took a desperate step forward. I could see the bob of her throat, the hard swallow as she approached me. "Don't you see what's going to happen to us if you keep ignoring everything inside you?"

Dread barreled in. My heart started pounding so fucking hard I could feel it in my ears.

"You have to get help, Jared. Talk to someone. Find a way to face the demons inside of you." It was no longer a request. I could feel it. It was an ultimatum sliding out of my girl's mouth.

Aly shoved her fisted hand out in front of her and turned it over. She slowly unfurled her fingers. In her palm was a wadded-up piece of paper, small and yellow and square. Still it shouted out like some harbinger of war.

I blinked in confused distress, and took a step back as the dread increased.

"Take it," she pled, inching forward.

And I didn't fucking want to, but I was helpless to tell this girl no. With a shaky hand, I reached out to take the crumpled paper from her hand.

When I did, something like horror lashed across her face and settled in her eyes. "Please, know I didn't want to do it this way, Jared. I never wanted to back you into a corner." Misery twisted her face, and she clutched her chest. "I love you more than I could ever tell you. And I'm scared because I feel you slipping away. Every day it feels like another piece of you is stolen from me and one day I'm going to lose you. I can feel it, Jared. All the hurt you keep hidden inside is going to wreck you. Wreck us."

Panic hammered at my chest. I smoothed out the paper, trying to comprehend what Aly had written on the sticky note, knowing whatever it was I definitely didn't want to see.

And I was thinking of all these fucking terrifying scenarios. All of them led back to her writing her good-bye.

But no.

It was an address. In California.

Los Angeles.

Something vicious curled in my consciousness.

With it pinched between my fingers, I stared at her, my eyes narrowed as I searched her face, as I fought against the nausea that bound my stomach into knots and raced up my throat. It lodged right at that ball of unspent emotion, throbbed and pulsed and pled with the sorrow that could never be shed.

"What is this?" I forced out.

Hesitation thickened her tongue. She wrung her hands and whispered, "It's your father's address."

I felt as if I'd been punched. How many fights had I fought in my life? How many hits had I taken? I had no clue. The only thing I knew was this hurt was worse than any physical blow that had ever been inflicted.

"You looked up my father's address?" I demanded through the betrayal.

I gripped my head. I didn't want to believe it. How could she do this to me?

Aly stole forward. She stretched her fingers out toward me, fucking calling out to me like she did.

I backed away.

"Please don't be mad. I never wanted to give it to you like this. I . . . I started looking for him a couple weeks ago. I was going to talk to you about it, Jared, encourage you to find him because you *have* to. You can't move on and never look back when your soul is tied to the past. You need your family."

Bullshit.

She was supposed to be my family.

I crumpled up the little piece of paper and hurled it toward the wall. It didn't go far. It dropped fast and tumbled across the floor.

"What the fuck, Aly? You just go getting in my business?"

She blanched like I slapped her and staggered back. Confusion flitted all over her face. Her mouth trembled. "Your business?" Hurt saturated the words. "Anything that has something to do with you is my business."

"Not that!" shot from my mouth. "I asked you to leave it the fuck alone."

One fucking thing I'd asked from her.

One fucking thing.

I'd given her everything else.

"Why do you have to go digging up ghosts? It's done, and there's not one single thing I can do to change that."

"Ghosts?" Disbelief flashed all over her face. "You think I'm digging up ghosts? Well, guess what, Jared." Aly jabbed her finger toward the floor. "Those ghosts live right here. Haunting you . . . every move you make. And those ghosts are going to *ruin* us if you don't turn around and acknowledge they're there." Her angry eyes softened. "You have to find peace with what happened to your mom, Jared."

Peace?

Images burst behind my eyes. All that fucking blood and that scared smile, my mother's voice a fading echo in my ear. That fucking dream that set me on fire every night, singeing as it seared, cutting me deeper and deeper.

It'll be okay.

Red veiled my sight. I crammed my fists into my eyes.

I ruin everything I touch.

Anger surged, saturating every cell. Sickness clawed. I spun, and my fist connected with the wall to the side of the fireplace. Plaster and paint splintered, giving way beneath the rage that curdled my soul. Pain throbbed up my arm, and that sadistic satisfaction burned through my wicked spirit.

Aly screamed.

Ruin.

I cocked my arm back and rammed it again, tearing through the false security I'd erected around us, as if these walls could protect her from me.

Coals continued to smolder, the darkest red in the pit of the fireplace.

Burning to dust in that fucked-up shrine.

Enraged, I raked my hand through the row of pictures displayed on the mantel. Frames flew across the room and crashed to the ground. Glass shattered as another piece of me was destroyed.

It incited something inside of me.

I hated.

God, I hated.

Gritting my teeth, I dug my fingers into the edge of the carved wood that hung over the fireplace. That mantel. Sweat beaded on my forehead as I tore at it, like pebbles of vile blood excreted from my spirit.

It began to splinter and the seal broke free from the wall. I grunted as I tore it completely away, and I lifted it above my head and threw it against the stones, desperate to rid this house of anything that was my mother when it was supposed to belong to Aly.

Aly.

Blood seeped from my fingertips as I dug them behind the wood that had been mounted on each side of the hearth. The thin pieces of wood carved with the bouquet splintered. I frantically ripped and tore and rid this house of what never should have intruded into this place.

My mother was never supposed to be here.

In this place that was ours.

It was supposed to be for her.

Aleena.

Aly gasped. Wounded cries broke free. "Jared . . . don't." Fear saturated her tone.

I dropped the wood to the ground. Panting, I watched horror take her over. The girl I loved stared back at me as if she didn't recognize who I was at all.

But this was the darkness. The part of me she was always trying to coax out into the light.

The part of me I hated with everything. The part that I would never escape no matter how badly I wanted to.

Because there was no peace.

Aly backed away. Wetness soaked her face. Pain twisted her expression into heartbreak.

"Aly," I whispered, wishing there was some way to take it back, to bury it all back inside where it belonged. Hidden from her.

She set her hand protectively across her belly. She choked over the words, all this hurt pouring from her. "Is this how you want to live our lives? You putting holes through walls when I say something you don't want to hear?" She took another two steps back. The corner of her mouth trembled. "Tearing our house apart because it hurts?" Aly bit back a sob. "I refuse to live my life like this, Jared, refuse to raise our baby this way."

Hurt lanced through my nerves, splaying me wide. That

place I always kept hidden magnified, the void bloated with the truth of who I really was.

I wanted to be better.

"I will love you forever, Jared. Nothing could ever touch that . . . and no one could ever touch me the way you have." Pain tripped her voice. "But this?"

Hopeless, she looked around the room that I had just ruined.

Sabotaged.

Because I didn't know anything else.

I would always be the same.

The wicked tainting the pure.

"Look at this place. At what you built. At what you *created.* Look at how beautiful it is." She stumbled over the emphasis. "And look how easily you destroyed it."

I destroy everything I touch.

I stepped toward her, wishing I could go back to this afternoon when I was kissing her and she was kissing me, when we were free. "Aly—"

An injured cry erupted from her throat and she held her hand up to stop me.

It stopped me short, left me standing in the middle of the war zone I'd created in our home, in the middle of the chaos that was ripped from the walls and scattered across the floor.

The chaos that raged through my heart and mind.

Because I knew we hadn't been free. We'd never been.

I'd felt it building for weeks . . . building since the moment I came back, really.

My mother's face flashed.

It'll be okay.

And I knew it'd never be.

Aly's eyes slammed shut, as if she couldn't look at me. Fucking broken. "Please, go. If this is the way you want to live, then I need you to go."

Swallowing, I dropped my head. Crushing pain seared through me. Slowly I approached her and set my hand on her face. My thumb brushed away her hot tears, and I kissed her cheek, feeling something die inside of me.

Because I loved her. I once believed it impossible.

But there was no denying it was real.

Just like there was no denying I would never be good enough for her.

Turns out Dickhead was right.

"I love you, sweet girl," I murmured at her ear. Pulling back, I looked on her with the saddest smile, crushed by the torment staring back at me, torment begging me to stay, to be different from the person I was always gonna be.

Then I turned and walked out into the night.

TWENTY-ONE

Aleena

Softly, the door clicked shut behind him, a complete contradiction to the violence that had claimed him minutes before.

Silence swallowed the room, a deafening stillness that screamed of all my fears.

Excruciating pain bore down on my chest. Squeezing. Suffocating. I couldn't breathe.

I pressed my hand over my heart, as if it could somehow hold it together.

But my knees went weak and I buckled.

Body and soul.

I backed into the wall to catch myself from falling. Clutching my stomach with one hand, I pressed the other over my mouth and tried to hold myself up in this world that had finally beaten us down.

Jared.

Outside, his bike rumbled to life, roared to a thunder as he took it to the street.

Regret and anger and loss spiraled through me.

What did I do?

What did he do?

Oh my God.

It hurt. God, it hurt, and I wanted to take it back. I wanted to chase him and beg him not to leave even when I knew voicing it would be the biggest mistake I'd ever made.

Worse than the one I made when I cornered him, shoving the past he'd been running from in front his face without any warning.

Guilt throbbed deep, tangling with the overwhelming fear that I might truly lose this man.

I'd wanted him to know I searched for and found his father because I *loved* him, not because I wanted to hurt him. I wanted him to know I looked and pried because he deserved to get back that piece of his life that was stolen from him that fateful day.

But I should have done it all differently. Handled it with the care he deserved. Gave heed to this fragile situation that I knew could so easily crack and shatter into a million pieces.

Despair clogged my throat as I looked around the room.

Shattered.

All of it.

This gorgeous house that had been created by his hand brought down by the same.

This heart that loved him through every frantic beat.

The faith he'd had in me.

But what else could I do?

I'd been backed into my own corner.

Because it was true. I couldn't live this way. Waiting for the next explosion to be set off.

After what happened tonight with Gabe, I'd sat alone in our room, fisting the scrap of paper in my hand, coming to terms with what I had to do.

I knew I had to give it to him.

It was time. I couldn't keep ignoring the way he suffered. Night after night, I watched Jared splintering, frantic and lost when he'd wake me from sleep. Like he was begging me for help but didn't know how to ask for it.

Finding his family was the only way I knew how to help him.

The address wasn't given as a manipulation, not as a way to coerce this man who I knew loved me with all of his tortured life into doing what I wanted. All I'd ever wanted was for him to heal, for him to find a way to forgive himself for what he'd done, for him to finally come to terms with the mistake that had stolen so many years of his life.

The same mistake still robbing him of his freedom now.

Never would I dangle that hope I held for him over his head.

But I'd felt this coming. A storm brewing in the distance, a steady buildup of destructive energy, a force that could not be contained.

Tonight was the culmination of it all.

I just never expected how vicious it would be.

Sorrow squeezed my spirit. Part of me felt as if I had failed him. I'd let him go when I promised to always stand by his side.

But his reaction here in the living room? The madness that had taken him over with the mention of his father's name?

Even with how much I loved him, I refused to be partner to that kind of life, to raise my child in a house where violence reigned, madness triggered by words that evoked his fear.

In his parting expression, I knew Jared would never want us to live that way. He'd rather remove himself than subject the ones he loved to his rage.

My heart had to believe he didn't want to live that way, either.

He just didn't know how.

Drawing in a ragged breath, I crossed the room. I climbed to my knees, careful to dodge the shards of broken glass, nails, and splintered wood, and I began to clear away the mess that had been simmering for weeks.

My body ached, for him, for myself.

Tonight, I'd stumbled into the fray, too slow to get out of the way while I'd begged him to stop. My voice never had a chance at penetrating the rage that had taken over his heart and mind.

He'd lost control, and while I knew Jared would never willingly put me in danger, I wasn't sure he knew how to stop or fully grasped how dangerous the anger he harbored inside really was.

But *I* did.

I had to be strong and fight for our family when he didn't have the strength to do it himself.

Even if that meant letting him go.

The thought terrified me. Jared out there on his own. Alone. It broke me because all I wanted was for him to be here. Safe and protected from the ruin. Away from everything calling him back into destruction.

Sifting through the rubble, I brushed away the glass from the picture of us when we were kids. My heart swelled. I loved him. So much.

There was never any chance of letting him go, no breaking free of the bond we'd forever share. I couldn't live without him any more than he could live without me.

I fumbled over a gasping sob.

I needed him.

And I prayed, breathed the belief I always had in him into the night. Whispered his name. Begged him to find a path that would lead him back to me.

The front door opened and Christopher froze when he stepped inside. His face fell. "Oh, Aly, come here, sweetheart."

TWENTY-TWO

Jared

Sunlight blazed from the barren blue sky. Too bright. Blinding. Air heaved in and out of my lungs, jagged and coarse. A growl rumbled at the base of my throat. I hated every fucking miserable second of the day.

I lifted the handle high above my head and brought the shovel down with all the strength I could muster. Metal clanked when it met with the hard, ungiving ground. Still, I fought with it as if I could overtake it. Like I could find a modicum of control when I'd lost all sense of direction. My teeth ground in my ears as I lifted the shovel and slammed it down again and again.

I barely made a dent.

The muscles in my arms flexed and bowed, burning with exertion. The sins forever etched into my skin mocked me, the color stretched taut with the bristle of my flesh. Sweat gathered on my neck and trickled down my spine. It soaked through my dingy white T-shirt and clung to my overheated skin.

Only in Phoenix could I sweat my ass off at the beginning of February.

Or maybe I was just burning up from the inside out.

Incinerating.

Soon all that would be left would be ashes.

But that's what happens when you play with fire.

Thinking I could live a normal life. Give Aly and our baby one.

Harshly, I shook my head, hating myself a little bit more. Just fucking stupidity and greed. That's all it was. I knew I didn't get to have that kind of life, yet I'd taken it anyway.

Grunting, I rammed the shovel into the dirt, feeling myself coming unhinged.

Ripping apart.

Gasping, I stopped my assault on the ground, propped the shovel up, and leaned up against the handle. I dropped my head and tried to catch my failing breath. I lifted the bottom of my shirt to my face, attempting to wipe away the sweat and grime, to blot out all the misery that chased me into the exhausted days.

A wave of dizziness hit me, and I squeezed my eyes.

Damn it.

Three days.

Three days of nothing but torture. Three days of unending regret.

God, I missed her. I missed her so fucking bad I couldn't sleep. Couldn't eat. Couldn't think.

My gut told me to split, to hop on my bike and put as much distance between me and this insufferable place as possible. I couldn't be here, feeling her everywhere. Knowing I was only minutes away from what I wanted most. It was the worst kind of anguish. I felt like I'd been pierced. Crucified.

But my spirit kept me rooted here.

How could I just leave?

My pregnant girl was sleeping alone. I knew in my heart she was scared. I knew even deeper that she was missing me just as much as I was missing her. And even if I was too fucked-up to be welcome in her space, that didn't mean I wasn't going to take care of her. Provide for her. Be there to protect her when she needed me.

I wasn't going anywhere.

My hands shook with an old urge, that gnawing impulse that clipped through my nerves, the desire to slip into a moment's oblivion. To dull and distort.

Because God, this fucking hurt.

I pressed my face deeper into my shirt.

But those urges had nothing on how badly I wanted Aly.

"You doing okay there?"

I dropped my shirt and jerked my head up. Kenny, my boss, stood in front of me, squinting at me through the rays of light.

"Yep. Perfect." I faked a smile.

He frowned at the nonexistent hole I'd been pounding out for the last hour. "Doesn't look like you're making much headway over here." His brow lifted in question, calling me out on my shit. Things were obviously not perfect. "Why don't you check on your crew . . . we can get one of the Bobcats over here to dig that hole because I'm pretty sure that shovel's not going to cut it."

Kenny rarely checked up on me. He trusted me with my crew, sought me out for advice, put me on tough jobs he knew I'd find a way through.

It was like the guy could read me, see exactly what I was capable of.

Apparently it didn't take all that much for him to pick up on when I was unraveling, too.

I tossed the shovel to the ground. "Yeah, that'd be good."

I began to turn when he set his hand on my shoulder to stop me. "Hey, if you need anything, you know you don't have to hesitate to ask? If something's eating at you, just say it."

"Nah, man," I said, shucking my gloves. "It's nothing you can change. I've just got to deal with some shit right now."

Internally I scoffed. *Deal with*? How the fuck was I dealing with this? That was the problem. I wasn't dealing. Not at fucking all. I was just wallowing because I didn't know how to fix this.

I wouldn't go back, not when all I would do would be to end up hurting her.

Not for a second did I blame her for cutting me loose. After what I'd done, I wouldn't have stayed. Aly deserved so much more than that, that perfect girl who loved and gave and fucking believed in me when I was nothing but a monster lurking in the shadows.

And I hated the monster in me.

The part that was vicious and vile. The part I couldn't control, no matter how desperately I wanted to.

But the truth was, I was a little bit pissed at her, too. Her betrayal throbbed, cut me straight to the core.

I wanted to claw my eyes out because that little piece of yellow paper with the address on it was all I could see. It'd been ingrained deep in the recesses of my mind, seared into my memory, glaring and clear.

Like Aly'd managed to set the man I ruined right in front of me.

Another reminder of what I'd done. Another life I'd destroyed. Another heart I'd broken.

He'd loved *her*, and I'd stolen his world.

He'd loved my mom the way I loved Aly. I knew it. And the thought of losing Aly that way. Nausea turned my stomach and I squeezed my eyes against the thought. I couldn't even imagine.

Now I could feel his eyes watching me, judging me like he'd done the night I'd stolen the Ramirezes' car, when I'd had the intention of ending it all but instead Aly had been there, saving me from my own destruction. He'd stood over me in that hospital bed after I'd been arrested, staring down at me with condemnation and outright hate.

I'd never hated myself more than in that moment, when he'd looked down on me like the piece of shit I knew I was.

Then he turned his back and walked away.

Somewhere inside me I'd harbored the idea that one day he'd try to find me. The fucked-up thing was that for a long time I'd longed for it. I'd just needed to hear him say he forgave me.

But never once had I heard a word. Not a sign of life from him.

Because I knew I'd stolen his too.

Kenny squeezed my shoulder, his expression genuine. "Just . . . if you need something, say it, okay?"

I swallowed hard. "No, I'm good, I don't need anything."

Biggest lie ever. I needed Aly.

He frowned and turned to walk away.

In the distance, a pickup truck approached, the roar of the engine cut above the high whine of power tools. I glanced over my shoulder to catch the dust flying as it barreled onto the work site. Edging off the dirt road, it came to a sudden stop on the other side of the barricades.

Christopher was here.

A blink of fear flashed through my entire being.

Aly.

I fisted my hand in my hair. My mind rapid-fired, flitting through every possibility. Ones where Aly was hurt and I wasn't there for her when I was supposed to be.

Then I caught sight of Christopher's face when he jumped from the cab. He slammed the door shut behind him. Fury ignited his path as he flew around the front of the truck and made a beeline for me. Black hair stuck up every fucking which way, and he was wearing tattered jeans and a wrinkled printed tee.

There was nothing casual in his posture.

He was pissed. Fucking livid.

Aggression radiated from him, sucking all the oxygen from the air. He kicked up dirt as he tore across the lot. Nearing, he only picked up speed. He didn't slow when he launched himself at me. He rammed me in the chest before he reached for my shirt and fisted it in his enraged hands. He shoved me back. His face contorted with some emotion I'd never seen him wear before. "You fucking idiot," he seethed.

I stumbled. My work boots skidded over the rocky ground. I popped back up, catching my footing. I shook myself off and spread my arms wide in invitation. My mouth pinched up in a sneer, just fucking begging him for it. For him to give me all he had because my body ached to take it, to feel the pain of what I'd inflicted.

I was never one to deny what I deserved.

Hostility vibrated through his bones. My oldest friend bounced on the balls of his feet, visibly shaking with disgust. He pointed at me. "You promised me. You fucking promised me you weren't going anywhere."

Guilt squeezed my lungs. I'd been spewing that shit for so long, making promises I should have known I couldn't keep, I'd convinced myself into believing they were the truth.

But that was the problem. I wanted them to be.

"You think I left because I wanted to?" I shot back. "I left because that's what your sister wants."

And because it was best for her.

He scoffed. "You think this is what my sister really wants? For you to take off again? She's fucking miserable without you,

Jared. Worried sick. She wants you home. But what she doesn't want is some loose cannon who'll lose his shit at the drop of a dime and tear his house apart."

Shame beat at my heart and pulsed through my veins. Agitated, I shifted on my feet and roughed a hand over the top of my head. That rock tightened in my throat. "But I *am* that guy. What happened Saturday night was just proof of it. I'm no good for her, Christopher. You and I both know that."

"Huh," he huffed, like he was completely confused. Ridicule flashed in his eye. "Funny how for months you've been working your ass off to prove you were good enough for her."

Our conversation from New Year's Eve echoed in my ear.

"Guess you were right," I whispered through a pained breath. "It made me dangerous."

"Don't go twisting my words, Jared. You know that's not what I said."

"Doesn't mean it's not true."

Christopher's eyes made a pass over the job site. I could feel my crew behind me. All of them were on edge, at the ready to have my back. "So where've you been hiding your pathetic ass while my sister sits at home terrified you're going to jump off the deep end?" he asked, all blunt and like he had the right to know.

I gestured to one of my guys who'd taken up my right side, about ten feet away. A friend, I guessed, the only other person I knew to call when I found my ass without a place to sleep. Not that I'd been doing any of that. "Crashing on Kurt's couch. Sound familiar?" It came with a sneer.

"Sure does." Christopher crossed his arms over his chest, bristling with contention. "Does he have a little sister to keep your dick warm at night, too?"

Bitterness thickened my tongue. My chest squeezed. "Fuck you. I won't ever step out on Aly."

The thought of someone other than Aly touching me made me physically ill, and Christopher suggesting it just pissed me right the fuck off.

Green eyes narrowed on me. "You aren't ever going to step out on my sister? And how is this any different? Leaving your pregnant girlfriend, the one you're supposed to *marry*, alone? Are you really going to stand there and call that devotion?"

"What else am I supposed to do?"

"Maybe what Aly asked you to. Get some fucking help, man. Talk to someone."

I backed away. No way was I going there with him.

Frustrated, he threw he hands out to his sides. "So what? That's it? You're just going to walk away?"

My heart skidded at the notion. Every last cell in me screamed no. Of course it wasn't. It couldn't be. There was no letting Aly go.

Christopher's demeanor shifted when he saw the panic in mine, and he dropped his voice. "Damn it, Jared, look at you. You're just as messed up as my sister." He gulped over a hard swallow, asked on a heavy exhale, "Do you really think this is what your mom wants?"

With the mention of my mom, my insides curled, turning me inside out. Exposed and raw. I struggled for a breath.

"You think she'd really want Aly alone and scared and missing you? That she'd want her grandchild not to know its dad? Do you really think you owe her that? That holding all that guilt inside is somehow going to make it up to her?"

He dropped his gaze to the ground. When he lifted it, all the sympathy was gone. "You need to grow some balls, man. Own up to your shit. For a guy who will take down the first asshole who gets in his face, you are nothing but a pussy. Making excuses with every turn you take." He flung his arms out.

"Look around you. My family, Jared . . ." He shook his head. "All of us . . . we love you. Care about you. Stop acting like you don't deserve that and fucking face the shit you don't want to. Quit being a coward . . . because all this bullshit about not being good enough?" He began to back away. His eyes narrowed with disappointment. "It's just that. Bullshit."

Then he turned and walked away.

Frozen, I stood there watching him go.

Jumping into his truck, he turned the ignition and the engine roared. He gunned it, dirt spewing as he flipped his truck around in the middle of the road and left the way he'd come.

I jerked my attention around to my crew who stood there gaping.

"What the hell are you all looking at? Get back to work," I yelled, hoofing it across the yard and toward the office trailer because there was no way I could stand out here for a second longer, couldn't bear this fucked-up world for a minute more.

I hated Christopher for everything he'd said.

Because I knew every word of it was true.

TWENTY-THREE

Jared

Noon held the sky captive, the sun sitting high in the center of the endless expanse of blue.

My pulse thundered just as loud as my bike, and I gripped the handlebars, my legs stretched out to prop up the rumbling mass of metal.

What the fuck was I doing?

Torturing myself this way?

But after Christopher left this morning, coming here felt like the only thing I could do.

I blinked to clear the haze. From across the narrow street, I forced myself to watch what I'd thrown away. The little house was quiet. But I knew she was there. I could almost feel her inside. Missing me. Swimming through the void that had taken over our lives.

How many times had I promised her I was done with all the hurting shit?

Movement fluttered at the window where rays of sunlight glinted and glared, blinding as they shined down against the glass. Still, I saw her, recognized that trusting face.

My heart clenched, just as tightly as my jaw.

God, I wanted her, to run to her and hold her and tell her everything was gonna be okay.

To take away the hurt I felt crying out from her now.

But I understood the separation.

The walls I'd erected.

The bridge I'd burned.

Aly pressed her palm to the window, her fingers splayed wide, calling for me, like she could reach through those barriers and pull me from the rubble.

Pain clawed up my spine and settled at the base of my neck. My head throbbed.

I didn't know if there was any way to reconstruct it, to re-build this fucking unbearable mess I'd brought down at our feet. Didn't know if I could *fix* this.

If there was, there was only one way.

That unspent emotion grew at the base of my throat. Pul-sating. Pressing out.

Watching the curtain drop closed, I sucked in a ragged breath.

For her, I would try.

How many times had I told her she made me better?

It was about damned time I proved it.

Cranking the throttle, I spun the bike around in the street and hit the open road.

Vibrations rocked through my body, and the roar of the engine overtook my senses, partnered with my spirit that thrashed and fought and warred, shouting out that I was a fool.

Beneath me the road blurred.

It took the rest of the world with it.

And I knew I'd either find it, or lose it all forever.

Bright city lights stretched on for what seemed forever. Each unbearable mile I put under me just ratcheted the foreboding higher and higher. Night closed in, this fucking ominous glow hanging too low from the bleeding sky. My muscles ached with fatigue from straddling this seat for the last six hours, though I felt completely strung out. Like I hadn't slept for days and was coming down from the worst kind of high.

Wasn't all too far from the truth.

Rapidly I blinked, gritting my teeth as I cut through the gridlocked traffic that overflowed with people fighting to make their way home.

Guess that's what I was doing, too. Fighting my way back to Aly. Even though the direction I was heading felt like a dead end. A trap. Still, that address was all I could see. Every part of me screamed to turn my ass around, tuck my bastard tail, and go back.

But I had nothing to go back to.

So I raced headlong, right into the eye of the storm.

I cut through two lanes, taking the exit to the route I'd memorized.

Here I was, throwing myself at the feet of a man who hated my guts. A man I'd fucking loved with all my heart growing up, a man I'd looked up to and respected. The man I'd prayed I'd one day grow up to make proud.

And for what?

I had no idea what I hoped to achieve, coming here.

What difference would it make?

It sure as hell wouldn't bring my mother back.

But truth was, no matter how far and for how long I'd run,

I always knew it'd come to this. That one day I'd have to stand in front of the man I destroyed. Maybe this was just fate taking another perverse turn, teasing me with ecstasy, tempting me with the girl when the whole time it'd been a ploy to push me toward this brutal punishment.

The question was, who would be punished tonight?

Seeing him was going to hurt like a bitch.

No doubt about it.

But him seeing me? What would it to do him, coming face-to-face with me?

Fear lashed and I pegged the throttle. I sped through intersections, diving deeper into the suburban city, my destination so unclear but set in stone. My head spun in this muddle of confusion and dread and the faintest flicker of hope.

I was scared to see him. I could admit it. Like Christopher said, I was nothing but a coward. I didn't want to witness what he'd become in the wake of my ruin.

The sound of him sobbing echoed in my mind, those nights that had been the loneliest of my life, when I'd begged for death while he wept for hers.

I'd broken his heart, trampled all the light from his life. Crushed it.

I'd taken the *good* and left him with *nothing*.

Shame gripped me by the throat.

I knew I shouldn't be here, shouldn't come where I wasn't welcome.

Still I surged forward. For Aly. For our life.

I turned right into a quiet neighborhood. Mature trees lined the streets, and manicured lawns stretched up from the road to the modest houses set close together. Lights glowed from within them, and I could imagine the stirring of families coming together inside as evening settled outside their walls.

I swallowed hard when I saw the sign proclaiming the street name that had haunted me for the last three days.

What am I doing? I asked myself for what felt like the millionth time.

And I could almost feel Aly's hand press over my heart, like she was giving me silent encouragement. A soft buoy to my spirit.

I was doing it for her.

I was doing it for my family.

My bike warbled low as I slowed. Inching forward, I approached the address.

Terror welled in my chest, stretching me thin.

But for Aly, I'd try. I'd fucking try. Because I couldn't live without her. And God, the truth was, I didn't want her to have to live without me.

I pulled off to the right side of the road, across the street and one house down from my father's.

Bright lights blazed from within, pouring out from every window. Red tiles covered the pitched roof, and the shutters and trim were painted a dark green. Wood columns jutted out from the roof to cover the front door in a cozy porch that was lifted two steps from the rock pathway. Flower beds ran the span of the house, and shrubs rose up to flank the freshly painted matching green door. Like the rest of houses in the neighborhood, the lawn was cut short, full and lush, extending from the sidewalk bordering the street to the flower beds blooming below the windows.

That rock lodged in my throat expanded, digging into my vocal cords, squeezing off my air.

Confusion clouded my mind.

What I expected coming here, I didn't know.

But this simple house definitely was not it.

Torn up, I guess I'd imagined. Crumbling and decayed.

Like our lives.

But no.

This house looked like a home.

A twinge of envy jabbed me.

I shook it off, nudged the throttle on my bike, and cut across the road to come to a stop right in front. I was shaking when I kicked the stand and stood. Tremors rolled through me, uncontrollable and harsh.

I gripped my head. Fuck, I just had to do this.

Sucking in a steeling breath, I stalked over the flagstone path, ready to face all the shit Aly'd been urging me into for months, the hatred and the shame. For her, I'd take it.

I'd take it for both of them.

On the porch, I stood in the hazy glow of the ornate hurricane lamp hanging on the wall and rang the doorbell, twitching while I waited.

Footsteps echoed on the other side. I listened to the distinct sound of sliding metal as the latch was freed.

The door opened a crack.

For the flash of a second, I pinched my eyes shut, not ready to face what was waiting for me on the other side. Finally, I pried them open.

A woman stood there, pretty but plain, probably in her mid-forties. Dark hair was pulled back in a loose ponytail. Her light brown eyes widened with unsettled surprise when they landed on me. Wary, her gaze made an analyzing pass down my body, along my arms to my hands squeezed so fucking tight they were cutting off circulation.

"Oh," blew from her mouth in what sounded like fear.

Agitation shifted my feet. I shook my head, blinked, began to back away. I felt like I was on the verge of losing my goddamned mind. I was pretty sure that fact was evident on my face. Pair that with the rest of me?

Bet she was wishing she'd taken a peek in her peephole before she'd so hastily opened her door.

In an effort to assuage her, I lifted my hands in surrender. "I'm sorry . . . I must have the wrong—" I started to say, edging away, before her mouth drew into a sharp *O*. Panic flashed across her expression.

"Oh m-m-my God," she stuttered. Her hand slammed down on the center of her chest like she'd just flatlined and she was trying to jump-start her heart.

A slow dread settled over my consciousness. It only made me move faster.

I was out of here.

"Wait," she demanded on a desperate exhale. "Please, don't go." She flung the door open wide. Keeping her eye pinned on me like she could tie me down, she frantically shouted, "Neil!"

The name sliced through me with a keening awareness, and that dread pounding at my ribs dropped like a rock into the roiling pit of my stomach. "Neil!" the woman hollered again, flipping her head around to look down a short hall that led into the house. "Get out here!"

But I'd already caught the bastard's face over her shoulder.

Frozen, he stood at the end of the hall. Shock dilated his dark blue eyes, and his chest heaved and he struggled for a breath. "Jared?" he managed, taking a step forward. Pain cut a river of lines across his face, and his mouth twisted in some kind of horrified confusion. "Jared?" he asked again, almost on a plea.

I was speared.

Gutted.

Darkness rushed in.

I couldn't see.

Sickness curled through my stomach. I stumbled back. Old wounds ripped open. Wide and gaping. Crippling. I gripped my head.

Oh fuck.

I shook my head harder, fumbling down off the steps that had led me to his door.

What the fuck did I think I would achieve coming here?

Redemption?

Closure?

All I'd earned was another slap across my mother's face, her memory disgraced.

My attention shot to the woman's hand still splayed across her chest, to his that hung limp like submission at his side, their matching rings a fucking mockery.

I slammed my eyes shut as if I could block it all. The same pleading voice ripped through the memories. I tore my eyes open. My father stood right in front of me. "Jared . . . please . . . don't take off," he coaxed. "Please . . . stay. Talk to me."

I took two shaking steps back.

He grabbed for my elbow. I tore it away, flinging my arm out at him in warning. "Don't fucking touch me."

Hurt flared in his eyes. "Jared, please."

His attention latched onto my knuckles, first the hand I hurled in front of his face. It shot to the other stamped with the year she died before he tracked it up the sins that marked every inch of my skin.

The deepest frown pulled at his brows, like he was processing the last seven years, like he didn't recognize me and he was seeing the son he shunned for the very first time.

Then it all registered.

He buckled at the middle, gripped his own head. "Oh my God . . . Jared."

What did he think? That I'd just moved on with my life? God knew I'd been trying to, to find some semblance of normalcy amid all the chaos, to let myself *love* when I'd stolen *his.*

I glanced up at his house. But that was exactly what he'd done. He'd moved on.

He'd rejected me and forgotten her.

I was just a kid.

The thought blasted through me, almost knocking me from my feet.

That rock of unspent emotion lodged in my throat burned with the burden, threatening to break free, cracking under the weight of the affliction I'd carried for all these years.

God, I hated him. Hated that he hurt me.

It was the first time I could admit it.

He hurt me.

Left me when I needed him most.

I fought against the emotion brimming within me.

I'd just needed him to tell me it'd be *okay.*

Tell me that he loved me even after everything I'd done, like he'd done when I was a little boy.

Just once.

He never had.

Now, he lifted his head and stared back at me.

Tormented.

Maybe he was just reflecting my own expression.

His wife had moved to the top stair. With her hand covering her mouth, she watched us. Tears streamed down her face, hot and fast. With some kind of twisted pity. Like she knew me.

She didn't know anything.

"Jared," he attempted again, taking a step toward me where I stood panting in the middle of their lawn while night crawled heavily across the sky, sinking down. Closing in.

I felt caged.

Fingers reached for me.

I held both palms up in warning, backed further away, repeated on a pained whisper, "Don't touch me."

I couldn't handle it right now, making sense of everything I was feeling. It was too much.

Turning, I jogged toward my bike, leaving behind everything that should have remained in the dark.

I told her . . . I told Aly again and again to let it go, to let it die, because there wasn't anything in this world that I could do to change the past.

Now even those memories had been defiled.

I was almost to my bike when frantic arms wrapped around me from behind, desperate as they clung to me. I flung around, ready to shove them off. But I froze with the long blond hair that was all over me, this girl burying her face in my chest, my tee soaking through with her tears.

"Jared," she exhaled through a sob. "It's really you." She squeezed me tighter. "It's really you."

My arms lifted away from my body while she glued herself to it. They encircled her with a hovering embrace. My heart pounded so hard I was sure it would hammer a hole right through my aching chest. Then these blue eyes looked up at me, holding more sadness than I'd ever seen.

This girl that was more like a women than a child.

"Jared, please, don't go. *Stay.*"

God, she looked so much like my mom.

My baby sister.

Fucking beautiful.

I was shaking when I tentatively wrapped her in my arms, touched her and felt . . . home and warmth and all these fucking emotions I'd so long repressed.

I didn't know her anymore.

Not at all.

Wasn't sure if I ever could.

But she felt so familiar and good.

Gently I pulled back and brushed a kiss to her forehead. "I'm sorry," I whispered at her skin before I set her aside and swung my leg over my bike.

Heartbreak flowed from her as she hugged her arms across her chest. Our father rushed up to take her side. Agony twisted his face, and he curled his arm protectively around her waist.

And it stung and bruised and bled, but still, I took some kind of comfort in it, knowing these two had somehow found their way back to each other.

At least one thing was the way it was supposed to be.

I kicked over my bike. The engine roared as I revved the throttle. For a fleeting moment, I sat there, submerged in the past.

I met my father's eyes and hoped he could see how truly sorry I was.

Then I turned and fled.

TWENTY-FOUR

Jared

Fatigue weighed down my body. Closing my eyes like a shield, I flipped the switch just inside the door. Light blazed against my lids. Reluctantly, I opened them to the desolation of the empty hotel room.

Cold sank all the way to the marrow of my bones. I'd ridden through the streets of the city for hours, mindless, without a destination. Finally I'd given up the fight warring in my mind and headed in the direction of where I'd come. Cold air beat against my skin as I'd opened my throttle and barreled into the long, silent night. When I could ride no further, I pulled off the freeway and checked into a crappy motel.

Motherfucking story of my life.

On a heavy sigh, I tossed the keycard to the small round table under the window and scrubbed my palms over my weary face.

God, I felt so lost.

I missed Aly more than I could ever imagine.

This longing was different, though. Different from those months I'd lived without her when I'd been wasting away in Vegas, when the days had blurred and bled and spun in an endless oblivion of pain. When I'd filled my veins so full of any substance I could get my hands on I'd believed it'd somehow have the power to erase her memory that had been scored into my heart and mind.

Difference was, I no longer wanted to forget.

No longer wanted to run.

For so many years, I believed I didn't belong anywhere.

Now I knew better.

I belonged with Aly.

I just didn't know how to get back there, how to love her the way she deserved, how to be that man I felt like I'd almost become.

Ghosts.

My humorless laughter ricocheted around the walls of the barren room.

Fuck, that girl knew me better than anyone. She'd been completely aware of what I was suffering all the while I was pretending the past couldn't touch me.

I'd run from it again, although in a completely different direction than I'd ever gone.

I'd run for Aly. Which was a really goddamned good place to be.

But I should have known it'd catch up to me.

I got why Aly had been pushing me. She knew where it was headed, and maybe she'd been clinging, too, doing her best to stop something that was inevitable.

I went straight for the bathroom. I didn't bother with a light. I just turned the shower as hot as it would go. Steam filled the small space. I shucked my clothes and stepped into the blistering heat of the relentless spray.

Waves of chills rolled through my body as it was pelted with the shocking warmth, a complete contradiction to the chilled air I'd sped into for too many hours. Sucking in a breath, I let my eyes fall closed.

Green eyes stared back at me, and the girl smiled, full of gentleness and affection.

With belief.

I leaned my forearm on the cold shower tiles and dropped my forehead to it, pinched my eyes tighter as all these images rushed me, this girl who had me completely undone.

And she was there.

Aly.

Like I could reach out and touch her. God, I missed her so bad. I didn't think I'd ever needed her as badly as I needed her now.

Every inch of me hardened, my body going rigid as my mind slipped into her hold, as I gave in to this girl who tore right through every wall I threw up.

She'd changed me. Touched me in ways no other person possibly could. Because she was meant for me.

Couldn't stop myself when I gripped my cock.

God, I just wanted to feel her.

Wanted to touch her. Wanted her to touch me.

My hand slipped up and down my length in a punishing rhythm, as if I could pump this need right out of me.

With every stroke, the need only grew.

The muscles in my stomach clenched, rippled and bunched, and a deep, guttural moan climbed up my throat.

Aly.

My mouth fixed in a wide, silent cry as I came.

I banged my forehead repeatedly against my arm resting on the wall.

What a joke. Like my hand stood a chance at substituting for my girl.

It didn't even scratch the surface of the need I felt for Aly.

It just left me feeling more vacant. Hollowed out.

Made me remember what I was missing and why I'd hauled my ass all the way to California, throwing myself on the mercies of a man I thought hated me.

I'd gone seeking answers. Instead, I ended up with more questions.

Exhaling, I scrubbed myself clean, turned off the water, and toweled dry.

Never in the million thoughts I'd had of him over the last seven years had I imagined that he would have moved on. It seemed impossible.

Wrong.

My chest ached because I didn't know what to do with the information now.

Didn't know how to process how seeing him felt.

In the dim light that spilled into the bathroom from the main room, I stared at the darkened silhouette of myself in the mirror.

So much anger lived inside me, day after day convicting me of this unbearable guilt.

Standing before him, I thought I'd feel ashamed.

Instead I'd just been shocked.

And sad.

Unbelievably sad.

Grabbing my phone from my jeans heaped on the floor, I shuffled back into the main room and flicked off the light. It plunged the room into darkness. Blindly, I flopped on my back in the center of the bed.

Aly held fast to my thoughts.

As if there was a chance of escaping her.

It was close to two, but I couldn't stop myself. I just needed her to know I was thinking of her because I couldn't stand the thought of my girl imagining I'd walked out with the intention of abandoning her and our baby.

Never.

I tapped out a simple message and hoped she understood it was my truth.

I miss you.

Almost instantly, my phone chimed with a message. I pictured her lying awake, too, thinking of me, tossing and turning in a vain attempt to find sleep.

I swiped the screen.

I miss you . . . more than you could know.

Two seconds later, another message came through.

Please. Find a way back to me.

Warmth spread through every cell in my body.

Still, I knew her words weren't an invitation for me to go running straight back to her, as much as I wanted to, like I'd done more than three months before. Without regard, without thinking about how messed up I still was inside. Using all that shit as an excuse to continue feeling the way I did, pretending like it wouldn't cause me to stumble.

Somewhere inside me, I knew I would.

And I did.

I fucked up the best thing I ever had in my life.

Sleep never came. For hours, I lay in the silence of the room, listening to the world passing me by.

Sunlight slowly climbed to the window. A thin strip of light bled through the small part in the heavy drapes.

The day dawned on my twenty-third birthday.

Sorrow spread, slowly taking me whole. Blood pulsed harshly through my veins, my body injected with a steady rise of fear.

Because Aly had been right all along.

It was time.

Wind gusted across the winter ground. Leaves whipped around my feet.

When I got back to Phoenix, I came straight here.

I struggled and managed to draw a lump of heavy air down my raw throat. Unbearable weight pressed against my ribs. Crushing.

Just like that day seven years ago.

The moment when my world shattered. When everything I loved was spoiled by my ruin. When I sat helplessly and watched her light dim in her blue eyes.

Screaming against the searing pain, I'd begged her to take me with her. It hurt so fucking bad, and all I wanted was to die.

That pain had followed me through the years, amplified in the moments when I closed my eyes, when my lids would flutter shut and the images would invade. When the memory drew so close it was all I could see.

All I could feel.

This same fucking pain.

Pressing my hand to my chest, I exhaled a jagged breath and forced my feet to move. My boots were silent as I treaded across what seemed an endless lawn. Nausea pooled low in my stomach, and sweat beaded on my brow.

I'd made a thousand promises never to return here.

The stupor of the day they laid her in the ground remained so distinctly clear, a photographic memory that somehow I hadn't been present for. Like my eyes had been pinned wide open, forcing me to see what I'd done. But it felt as if I'd witnessed it from afar, my ear acutely trained to every cry that rippled through the grieving crowd as I watched on from a distance.

At the same time, I could feel nothing.

Excruciating numbness.

Like I'd been removed from the mourning because I had no right to it.

And God, I'd wanted to cry. I'd wanted to cry for her so badly, but it'd just locked up in my throat, wedged there forever because I didn't deserve to weep for her when I was the one who brought all the tears to the endless sea of black surrounding me.

Swallowed by the pain of the crowd, I'd sat staring into the void.

Vacant.

Lost.

Lost in the spray of roses blanketing the shiny casket.

I'd been unable to look away. Like I was locked to the beauty getting ready to be left forever in the cold, hard ground, willing them to wrap me up and somehow take me, too.

It was the day I made a promise to her I would find a way to pay for the sin I committed.

Even through the numbness of that day seven years ago, I still knew the exact spot.

I slowed as I approached. Another wave of sorrow crashed into me. Overwhelming. Staggering. That physical hurt in my chest only intensified, and my breaths snapped in and out of my lungs. Weakness overcame me when I came to a stop in front of her stone.

Helene Rose Holt.

I sagged and dropped to my knees.

An intricate rose was carved into the marble behind the deep imprint of her name, a reminder of the beauty that had been my mother.

My fingertips brushed over the engraving.

Memorizing.

Guilt flickered around the edges of my consciousness, warning me I had no right to be here. But it was muted, nothing more than a fading burn replaced by an intense grief I'd never allowed myself to feel.

I missed her.

"Hey, Mom," I whispered so low no one could hear, but my heart felt it deep. That rock of unspent emotion flared. A tingling sensation ran the length of my throat. I swallowed down the saliva gathered at the back of my mouth.

I'd give anything for her to be able to respond, to talk to me and look at me with that smile that promised I was her world, for her to once again tell me it would be *okay*.

But she was gone.

Had I ever truly accepted that?

Slumping back, I sat, planting my feet on the ground as I wrapped my shivering arms around my knees. Nervously, I tugged at the front of my too long hair.

I didn't know if I had. All these years had been spent wrapped up in that one singular moment. The disastrous choice I'd made. For years, I'd been stuck there. A prisoner to all the shame, regret, and hate.

I never reached the point where I accepted I had to live in a world without my mother.

All the muscles in my body went rigid when I sensed the tentative footsteps approaching from behind. Maybe he didn't know if he belonged here any more than I did. I stole a wary glance over my shoulder.

My father.

Swallowing over the sadness that hit me at seeing him there, I turned my attention back to my mother's grave. "You followed me?" I asked on a quavering voice, not knowing if I wanted to cry out in some sort of fucked-up relief at the idea or run as far as my feet would carry me.

I stared at the date on my mother's grave and buried my fisted hands between my knees.

February 3, 2006.

It was the day I'd begun the run.

The race.

Sprinting toward anything that would usher in my destined destruction.

I'd been so strong, *so* convinced of that certainty. Of my conclusion. Paying for my sins with an empty life I could never truly give, hating each day I was forced to live.

But God, I was tired, worn down, weakened now in that belief.

I felt my father's presence grow as he advanced from behind. Slowly, his head drifted to the side, weighted by his own sorrow as he edged forward. Passing by me, he knelt and swept loving fingers across my mother's headstone, even softer as he brushed them over the sacred ground.

I cringed, thinking of the woman who'd stood gaping at me from their front door yesterday.

Nothing made sense, because looking at my father now, I was pretty fucking certain he hadn't forgotten about my mom.

Hurt dripped from his every pore.

I blew out a troubled breath, dropped my eyes because whatever passed through him now felt too private, too intimate for me to see.

Finally he stood and took a couple steps back. Exhaling heavily, he settled to the ground off to the left of me, facing into the stillness of my mom's silenced voice.

"No, I didn't follow you here," he finally answered. "Figured if you came to my door, it was about damned time I had the courage to show up at yours. Should've done it years ago," he admitted quietly.

I fidgeted, rubbed the back of my hand under my chin. Sure as hell didn't know what to do with that statement.

At one point in my life, I would have confided anything in him. Now he'd become nothing more than a stranger. I didn't know him any more than he knew me. And here we were, tiptoeing around all the shit we should've hashed out years ago.

His voice grew thoughtful. "As soon as you took off last night, Mary hurried inside to her computer and searched to see if she could find out where you lived."

A hard breath escaped my nose. *Mary.*

"Saw you had a house back here in Phoenix. Drove all night to get here . . . hoping you'd gone home after you left my place last night. Went straight to your house." He lifted his face in my direction and quirked a sharp brow. "Imagine my surprise when your front door opened and there stood Aly Moore."

Aly.

Just her name tightened my chest.

Soft, disbelieving laughter seeped from him. "Pregnant, too." He shook his head and looked off in the distance. "Would've made your mom real happy, the two of you being together."

I tucked my knees closer to my chest. "I heard something about that." I paused around the discomfort, sucked in a breath and forced myself to continue. "She always knew everything before the rest of us, didn't she?"

God, it felt like treachery, talking about her aloud. Voicing her had always seemed forbidden. Taboo. Like I'd overstepped my penance, illicit in my taking, dipping my fingers into the memories of the good when I'd been given over to the wicked.

"She sure seemed to," he mused softly.

His tone sobered. "I have to tell you when Aly saw me, it just about brought her to her knees, Jared. If I didn't know how badly I messed up seeing you last night, then I sure as hell found out today."

My eyes jerked toward him. Did he really have the nerve to come here and lecture me? Judge me? He had no clue what was going on between me and Aly.

He caught my exasperated expression, his own deflecting, his eyes flashing with regret. Nervously, he rubbed his hand over his mouth, cocked his head so he could see me better. "Aly didn't reveal a whole lot to me. She told me if you wanted me to know what was going on, then that was between the two of us to work out. But I could see how badly she was hurting."

He shook his head. "God, if that woman isn't ferociously protective of you. She was angry. No question about it. She didn't even try to hide her disappointment in me. But there was no missing her compassion, either. How happy she was that I came." He stopped for a second, lost in thought. "She was always that way, even when she was a little girl. She was always one of the sweetest, kindest girls. But she sure as hell never kept quiet if she believed someone was being wronged. Clear not a whole lot has changed." He smiled a little. "She loved you back then, too, you know. Obviously she never stopped."

My stomach twisted, tangled with all the emotions pushing out from the inside, vying for release.

For a moment we sat in awkward silence. Then he dropped his face in his hands, burying the desperation of his words in them. "God, I wish there was a way for me to make you understand the relief I felt when I saw you yesterday. Like the weight of this ugly world had suddenly been lifted from my shoulders."

I shifted on the hard ground, doing my best to keep my cool. To listen. To really fucking hear. Because a huge part of me wanted to unload on him. Pretty sure he didn't know the first thing about *burdens.*

He pressed on. "But then I saw the disappointment in your eyes when you made the connection that Mary is my wife. You looked at me as if I'd been unfaithful to your mother. It just about killed me, Jared. You took off without letting me get a word in and all that weight came crashing back. And I knew I didn't deserve a minute of your time . . . I still don't . . . not after the way I failed you. But I had to try. I'm tired of living with all this pain. That's why I chased you back here."

He stared at me, his gaze traveling all over me again, like he'd done last night. Only this time slower. Studying. Like he was reading the horrific story painted on my skin.

"Look at you," he said, the words laced with pain. "I didn't know it was possible for my heart to break any more. But seeing this?" He craned his head toward my scars, to the evidence of my sins exposed in vibrant color, all of them shouting out my guilt. His jaw visibly clenched.

"Don't pity me," I seethed, the old anger I didn't know how to rid myself of breaking free.

The shake of his head was harsh. Disbelief narrowed his eyes. "Pity you? I pity myself. I don't even know my own son. The boy I raised and loved with all my life is getting ready to become a father and I had no clue until I showed up at your door an hour ago. It makes me sick, Jared. *Sick.* Disgusted with the person I allowed myself to become. It took my son being man enough to come find me for me to be man enough to turn around and try to find my son. There's something majorly wrong with that picture."

Blood sloshed in my mind, and a wave of dizziness swept through me. I wanted to cover my ears, to scream at him to stop, while the little boy locked up inside me felt frenzied, frantic with the need to hear him say it.

To say what I heard bleeding from his voice.

His gaze caressed the stone, and his voice dropped, became slow and reverent. "No one saw things like your mother did. She had an insight about her like no one I've ever known."

He rubbed his forehead, seemed to waver on what to say.

"She loved you and Courtney so much. At night before we'd go to sleep, she'd lie in bed in my arms, dreaming about what the future would hold for you and your sister."

My heart squeezed.

God, this was unbearable and seemed vital all at the same time.

Incredulous, low laughter tumbled from his mouth, like it originated somewhere deep within him. "It was always you and Aly in those dreams, Jared. I thought it was ridiculous. I chalked it up to her having some romantic notion about her son marrying her best friend's daughter. I humored her . . ." He shrugged, like he'd always been as helpless to the connection he shared with Mom as I was to Aly. ". . . because how could I not? Aly was so cute, the way she followed you around. Turns out I was wrong about that, too."

Sadness fell over him, and he looked away, his eyes tracing over the letters cut deep into the stone that marked her grave. "Without your mom, we all lost our way. Every single one of us."

Shame bowed his head. "Jared, I need you to understand how much I loved that woman. I didn't know how to go on when she was taken from my life. Somewhere inside of me, I knew you and Courtney needed me and you both were scared and hurting, too, but I couldn't see through the pain to the other side. During that time, I couldn't feel anything but my own loss. Nothing else mattered except for the way I felt. With the trouble you started getting into, it was easier letting you take the fall for it than admit you needed help just as badly as I did."

He choked over a sob stuck deep in his throat.

I squirmed, staring down at my fisted hands.

"The night you stole the Ramirezes' car . . . I knew what you were trying to do, Jared." He lifted his face to the sky, his eyes squeezed tight.

Something rocked through his voice. "My last memory of you was in a hospital bed, escaping death for the second time in months. God, you were so messed up, Jared . . . your eyes wild . . . but I saw you under it. Saw someone who was suffering as deeply as I was, and I couldn't handle it. I just turned my back and walked away." He touched his chest. "I betrayed my own son because I hurt so bad inside."

That lump expanded. I choked over it. "I thought you hated me."

"For a while, I thought I did, too," he said, completely honest.

And fuck, it hurt, him coming right out and saying it. But I got it, understood being blinded by pain.

I'd been blinded by it for a long, long time.

Something heavy broke free inside of me. Sorrow gripped me tight. My eyes blurred. "I needed you," I whispered.

"I know," he said, his voice strangled. "I know that now."

Restlessly, he propped his forearms on his knees and wrung his fingers between them. "When your grandma passed, I had to pull myself together because Courtney had no one left. I packed up our stuff and headed to California, looking for a new start. But it didn't take me long to realize that start wasn't moving away. It was realizing how badly my child needed me. Those couple of years messed your sister up. Scarred her. She wasn't immune to any of it, either, and I knew it was time I was strong for her. But once I finally found that strength, I soon found I needed to be strong for myself, too. I was never going to truly get over your mother until I allowed myself to move on. Moving on was impossible, though, knowing you were out there. There's been a void inside me for years, and not just the one left behind by your mom."

I reeled, my fingers digging into the back of my neck as my head dropped.

"When I met Mary . . . she loved me through a lot of crap, Jared. She also helped me come to terms with what was missing from my life."

I crammed the heels of my hands into my eyes, trying to stop the emotion welling there. My fucking throat burned and tingled and throbbed.

"But I've been struggling with the guilt, not knowing how I had the right to ask you to become a part of my life after what I'd done. I had to find you, I knew it, but guilt kept holding me back. When I saw you yesterday . . . it was like looking at myself, Jared, seeing all the same guilt I've carried for years."

He huffed a heavy breath from his lungs. "I love my wife, Jared, but no one will ever replace your mother. She was the love of my life. My soul mate." He shook his head with a soft chuckle. "Didn't believe in any of that shit until the day I met her."

I smiled a little. Now that I could relate to.

"But I had to find a way to live again. Had to finally accept Helene would always be missing from my life."

Sadness deepened the line between his brows when he looked at my knuckles. "You've got to let your guilt go, Jared. You're almost there, son. I can see it. Feel it. I may not have seen you in almost seven years, but I recognize you. Recognize the boy who always made me and your mom proud. I can also see him clinging to the past, afraid of letting it go because it might mean letting your mom go. But guilt doesn't do anything but destroy what's good. Neither Aly nor your baby deserve that. You don't deserve it, either."

Tears gathered in his eyes. "I'm sorry, son," he said, the words raspy as he pushed them up his throat. "So sorry I left you to deal with what was never your fault. You were just a boy . . . a boy who made a mistake."

His admission tore through me.

Shit.

I couldn't tell if his words comforted or cut.

Emotion tightened his voice. "Don't ever feel guilty for loving someone, Jared. I have to believe your mom can see us now . . . have to believe she's looking down and sees the happiness returning to our lives. I have to believe it makes her glad and she wants that for us. That she knows she's getting ready to be a grandma and you're living the life she wanted for you. Don't let your guilt over what happened destroy that for her. Don't let it destroy it for you."

I felt pinned by the magnitude of his stare. "Don't repeat the mistakes I made. Fight for what you love. For what's important. Cherish it. Only a fool believes there's a good enough reason to let love go."

He climbed to his feet and gently settled his hand on my shoulder, spoke out into the distance behind me. "I know you can't forgive me overnight. I have a lot of years to make up for. But I sure hope you let me try."

That rock of unspent emotion raged like a ball of fire.

"Yeah," I whispered hoarsely. "I'd like that."

He squeezed me once before he turned to walk away.

I watched him make his way over the grass, his head hung low as he retreated.

My heart pumped hard. Too hard.

All the years of guilt and pain knotted at the center of my chest. It surged and spun, my mother's voice the softest echo in my ear. God, I'd loved the sound of it, loved the way she'd sit and listen and whisper her belief into me. I drifted on it, like I could feel her here, like maybe just like my dad had said, she was looking down.

Maybe she knew how lost I'd be without her.

Maybe she knew how much I would need Aly.

I lifted my face to the subtle warmth of the winter sky. Sadness twisted up my expression, but somehow it was still a smile.

And I felt shocked, almost horrified, when that rock of unspent emotion finally broke free.

Tears burned hot, dragging all the torture inside me finally out into the light.

Into her light.

And I just fucking sobbed.

Sobbed like a baby because it hurt so bad.

Because I missed her and I wanted her back and I wished I could change what I'd done.

But I couldn't.

Fuck, I couldn't.

But I also couldn't hang on to the guilt any longer.

I thought I'd gone to my father for mercy.

But he'd shown me that mercy was buried somewhere deep inside of me.

And I knew, just like I was sure my mother knew.

Just like Aly knew all along.

It was time I forgave myself.

TWENTY-FIVE

Aleena

I froze when I heard a key slip into the lock.

I stood at the kitchen sink, facing out the window into the backyard. Rays of late-afternoon sun slanted into the dimly lit house, and my arms were soaked with the dishwater I had my hands buried in, desperate for anything to distract my distraught mind. Over the last four days, I scrubbed every surface of the house, multiple times, knowing I had to keep my hands busy if I didn't want to lose my mind.

Or lose my nerve.

So many times I'd been close to begging him back, my finger poised at my phone in the weak moments when I was missing him so much that I'd take him any way I could. But I knew the error in that, knew I was only inviting the same trouble back into our home, and I had to wait for him to find his way.

And I knew . . . knew with all of me, Jared wanted to find that path just as fiercely as I wanted him to. So for the past four days, I continued to breathe belief into him, pouring all of my thoughts his direction, praying he would hear or that fate would somehow intervene.

That intervention had come in a tangible form to my doorstep.

Now my stomach twisted in anticipation, and I listened acutely to the rattle of the knob as it was turned.

God, I'd been begging for that sound, my hopes soaring on a boundless high ever since Neil Holt had shown up this morning.

Jared had gone to him.

I knew it the second I saw Neil's pleading eyes staring down at me—of course after all the shock had worn off at finding each other there, the two of us standing with gaping mouths for endless seconds. Obviously, neither of us were what the other had expected.

Then the strongest sense of pride had taken hold of every corner of my heart and swayed in the slowest dance with my spirit, because I knew Jared had finally taken the first step.

I also knew whatever meeting they'd shared had not gone well, and the man I loved with all my life had been hurt yet again.

It killed me, knowing Jared was out there alone, suffering through the anniversary of his mother's death, on his birthday. Being helpless this way was awful. But the waiting was even harder. I wanted to run to him, wrap him up and hold him and whisper I was never going to stop loving him.

Every single one of those assertions were the truth. Because I would never let him go, would never give up on this man with the tortured, beautiful heart. But I knew I had to wait until that heart was truly ready.

Ready for what being a family could mean for him again.

Somehow I knew that meant Jared beginning with his own family. Going back to where it all started.

I tensed, listening to the door creak open behind me. My knees went weak. I supported myself on the counter, my head dipped low between my rigid arms as I struggled to find a breath through the smothering tension that pulsed along the floor.

I could feel him standing there, watching me, his own disquiet palpable in his ragged breaths.

I could feel his want . . . his love . . . and there was no mistaking his own uncertainty.

God, how badly did I want to turn? To look at him? To set my eyes on the gorgeous face I'd been missing so desperately?

But I remained rooted.

Waiting on him.

Because this . . . that's what this had always been about—Jared finding himself beneath all the debris and pulling himself from it. This was about Jared finding his way. I always knew his destination would lead him back to me.

Subdued footsteps moved behind me, cautiously but with a distinct purpose. Drawing near. Edging forward. Each step he took sent a jolt of need straight to my failing heart. That need spiraled through me, settling in the deepest place within me, in that place that had always been reserved for him.

He paused behind me, hesitating, before he reached out and wound a single lock of my hair around his finger. Jared breathed out in relief.

As he anchored himself to me, his sweet breath seeped out against the skin of my cheek, lifting a shock of chills racing from the back of my neck and down my spine, and I was suddenly inundated with this perfect mixture of a man.

I released a staggered breath of my own.

"I missed you," fell from my mouth, because I just needed him to know.

I missed him.

So much it physically hurt. But I would endure a thousand days alone if it meant Jared had found a way to be truly free.

He twisted his finger tighter in my hair. The connection between us glowed. Years ago, this honest and pure gesture had begun so innocently, the bond between us so naively sweet. Yet the years had given us over to something deeply profound, this childhood affinity blossoming into the greatest love.

Nothing could keep us apart.

"Aly," he whispered urgently, and he spread the rest of his fingers out, threading them loosely in the long length of hair flowing down my back.

I shivered, and listened to his call. I tilted my face up, seeking out his.

Unprepared to find him this way, a sharp gasp rushed from my mouth. My gaze traced every line of his rugged face. His lips seemed so full and red against the backdrop of blond stubble coating his entire jawline, like he hadn't shaved since before he walked out our door four days ago. On its own accord, my hand stretched out to cup one side of his face, my thumb trembling as I brushed it along his bottom lip.

Shakily, Jared exhaled and his mouth parted.

His cheeks were red, almost blistered from the wind and sun.

Tentatively, I lifted my eyes to meet his fully.

This . . . this was what I had been unprepared to see.

Blue eyes begged back at me. They were puffy and rimmed in a striking red, his dark, heavy lashes framing the stark evidence of sorrow, leaving them bloodshot and misty.

Emotion overflowed from them, a flood of misery and love and devotion.

And hope.

My brows knitted softly and my head listed to the side, taking him in, him staring down at me while I stared up at him, this hardened man exposed in a kind of vulnerability he'd never shown before. Moisture gathered in my own eyes, and my thumb caressed just at the side of his mouth where it trembled, where all this emotion played out, visibly and without restraint.

Jared shifted to take my face between both his big, strong hands. They were warm, secure, almost fierce in their hold.

His voice was hoarse, his expression rigid. "I have made so many mistakes in my life, Aly . . . Won't make you one of them. Not ever again." His eyes softened while his hold increased. "You never were. You're a gift. A gift I didn't know how to truly receive." He shook his head, and mine followed the movement, locking onto him. "God, Aly, I pushed you away for the longest time because I couldn't accept the way you made me feel. But when I couldn't resist you any longer, feeling you became everything. And you felt so damned good I used it to cover up all the bad shit I didn't want to feel."

With a long blink of his eyes, he released a revealing laugh. "And God, I crave you, Aly. Need you. But I get it. I fucking get it. I can't fully belong to you if I belong to my past, too."

Jared's hands went to my waist. Gently he lifted me and set me on the counter, wedging himself between my legs.

Tender hands went right back to my face, and his fingertips brushed softly against the lobes of my ears, tickling along the backside of my jaw, before they kneaded the nape of my neck.

My tears broke free, slipping into the palms of Jared's hands.

Right where this man had always held me.

"Please, don't cry." He swept his thumbs beneath the hollow of my eyes, capturing all the relief spilling from me. "Don't cry. God, baby, I hate that I hurt you. Please, don't cry."

I ran my fingertips across his tense brow, down between his eyes, and across the dark bags shadowing his eyes, before I cupped all of his face in my hands, stretching my fingers out as wide as they would go, holding him whole. Praying he would understand. "Sometimes it's okay to cry."

Jared's eyes slammed closed, and he nodded against my hands that were all in his face, on his lips and his nose and pressing into the lids of his tortured eyes.

"It's okay to cry," I whispered again close to his mouth. "It's okay to miss *her* and be sad and wish she was here. You don't have to be ashamed of that."

Jared's eyes opened to me, the blue raging in intensity. Glassy and transparent.

Desperate but not distant.

Not like the nights when he woke me with fumbling hands.

He pulled me to him, holding me under my jaw as his mouth crashed onto mine.

Every last one of my nerves sparked. Wet heat slipped from his parted mouth. Coaxing. Pulling. Promising.

I opened to him and met his tongue with a tangle of pent-up need, with all the relief that flowed so freely and the desire that flooded my chest, expanding my ribs and slithering down in a hot wave straight to my core.

Tingles spread over every inch of my skin.

Little needy sounds climbed up my throat, encouragement and pride and joy. And all the honor I felt at giving my love to this incredible man.

Jared swallowed them down, kissing me harder. Demanding. Possessive as he led me through this passionate kiss.

I gripped his shoulders, drawing him closer. My legs wrapped around him, high up on his chest.

Jared dug his fingers into my hips, then stroked them down

my legs, caressing from my ass to my knees, dragging them back up again.

I wrapped him tighter, the burn of his stomach pressing right between my thighs, right where I felt frantic to have him.

God, he thought he craved me?

"These legs," he mumbled at my mouth, squeezing into my flesh, taking wild handfuls like he could never get enough. "You are a fantasy, Aly. Please tell me you'll let me spend my whole life here, wrapped up in you."

"You," I murmured. That was all Jared ever needed to know.

Suddenly he pulled back. His eyes flashed to me before he grabbed the hem of my shirt and yanked it over my head. He tossed it to the ground. I sat there with my chest heaving, Jared staring at me for a long beat before he set his hands on each side of my widening belly. He dipped down and placed a tender kiss below my belly button, like the sweetest embrace, like maybe he'd missed our baby as much as he missed me.

I melted.

Then fell a little further for this man.

Impossible?

It should be.

But in that moment I slipped deeper in love with him.

Jared wound his arms around my waist. He pulled me from the counter and against the strength of his body, and I wrapped him back in my legs, hooking them over his narrow waist. He looked at me, his hair a mess, his eyes filled with our future and swimming with his past.

That past he had found the courage to face.

And I could feel his heart, pounding at mine. It thundered in my ears and danced with my spirit, this man that was mine.

Volatile yet pure.

Corrupted yet worthy.

My beautifully broken boy.

Jared hiked me up higher. Neither of us looked away as he carried me to our room. The mass of my hair fell down around us, tumbling over my arms where my fingers were anchored in his shoulders.

Inside, the blinds were drawn, the room darkened, lit only by the late-afternoon sun seeping through the cracks. He crossed to our bed, keeping a firm hold on me while he dragged down the comforter and gently laid me back on the cool sheets.

I sighed, my eyes wide as I watched up at him watching down on me, climbing over me, hovering an inch away.

My fingers pushed through the length of his soft blond hair, and massaged into his scalp. He moaned and leaned into my touch, hungry for it, before he dipped down to kiss along my jaw. "Missed you . . . missed the way you taste . . ." He pressed his nose behind my ear. "Miss the way you smell."

I lifted my neck, my head pressing back into the bed as I invited him closer. I could feel him breathing me in, his chest expanding as he filled himself with a little more of me.

Jared nuzzled his nose against the lacy black fabric of my bra, slipping a hand under me to free the clasp, exposing me to the cool air.

My nipples hardened.

Jared groaned as he edged back, flicked open the button on my jeans. "So beautiful."

I almost cried when he pulled away.

Jared smiled a small, satisfied smile. "Don't worry, baby. I've got you."

Stepping off the bed, he pulled my jeans from my legs and took my panties with them.

Then he slowly began to undress himself. My eyes never left him, just trailed his movements, watched as he peeled his shirt over his head to reveal every toned muscle that rippled over his stomach and chest, his story screaming out from above it.

A story that had robbed him of so much.

But a story that had yet to tell its end.

I wanted to be a part of the rest of it. To add a million new chapters. Ones filled with laughter and smiles and soft caresses.

And an uncountable number of moments like this.

"I love you, Jared."

A soft breath left him, and he slowly climbed back over me, taking one of my hands with him. He pressed it over his hammering heart. "Since I was just a little boy, this has beat for you. Even before I knew what it meant. Now I know it means everything."

"You can't imagine how badly I missed you," I admitted, splaying my hand wide over the wilted rose.

Regret and blatant lust swirled through his longing eyes. His expression burned me, boiled in my blood and throbbed between my legs. His voice cracked. "I knew every second where I belonged. Nothing in this world is right unless I'm here with you."

He stared down at me, pain drawing his brow into a severe line.

I lifted my hand and smoothed it out. "Please, don't look at me like it hurts."

"Right now it does . . . looking at what I could have so easily let slip away. I can't do it, Aly. I can't run from any of it. Not anymore."

My heart swelled, overflowed in my chest.

Rejoiced.

But still I understood all Jared had to overcome.

Softly I nudged him. For a moment, he appeared confused, before he allowed me to lead him to roll onto his back.

I straddled him and dipped my head down to kiss along the outline of the rose, that piece of him that had died too soon.

He sucked in a strangled breath, before he twisted his fin-

gers in my hair, chills sliding over me as he caressed my head
and allowed me to pour all my love into him, all this belief I'd
held for him all along.

I leaned back. My gaze moved along the defined planes of
his body.

"You are beautiful," I whispered low as I reached down to
take his thick erection in my hand.

His stomach jumped, the muscles twitching as I gripped
him, softly, then tight. The smooth skin was hot, radiating heat.

I burned.

I leaned up on my knees and brought him to my center.

For the longest moment we just stared, drowning in a sea of
anticipation.

Jared's mouth dropped opened as I slowly sank down on him.

He was so big, it stole my last breath, his body searing into
mine, like he'd become the most prominent part of me. Spreading
me. Filling me so full it almost hurt. This perfect, pleasured pain.

I dropped my head back with a whimper, and Jared dug his
fingers sharply into my hips. "Goddamn," he grunted, shifting
under me to draw me deeper.

I planted my hands on his stomach, my eyes meeting his,
silently asking him to lead me.

He lifted me, guided me back down, his movements controlled. Slow and hard.

I got lost there, watching as his face washed in pleasure,
piercing blue eyes blazing into mine as he filled me again and
again.

"You scared me," I confessed on a murmured whimper, my
fears openly revealed, given to the man who held me in his hand.

Jared increased our pace, moving to take hold of my waist
with one hand while he let the other wander up to tangle in my
hair.

I met with the vulnerable truth revealed in endless sea of his open eyes. "I scared me, too."

Leaning back, my body arched, and I gave in to the heated tingles gathering low in my stomach. My walls grasped him as I slid up and down his length, meeting his hips as he rocked into me, straining as I coaxed the need from his body.

He just watched me.

Touched me.

He'd been the only one who ever could.

He brought the hand tangled in my hair to the side of my face, pieces woven through his fingers the same way he'd woven himself through every fiber of my heart while he continued to drive my body to the brink.

It all felt contradictory, the softness and the fire, the raging flames with Jared's soft glow, all of it merging, molten as it surged through our veins.

The connection between us was so profound I was sure I'd been created from a tiny piece of his soul.

Jared steadied me, holding me still as he continued to rock into me. Harder. Faster. My legs shook when he hit that spot inside me. "Oh, God," trembled from my lips.

"Let it go, baby," he whispered.

My breath hitched in my throat, my fingers grasping at Jared's skin when the pleasure broke free. I threw my head back, my eyes squeezed tight while I rode out the blinding bliss.

Jared jerked up to sitting, bringing us chest to chest. Both of his hands dug into my backside as he pressed me down, burying himself deeply in me.

So deep I cried out, shocked when I was slammed with another orgasm, just as intense as the first, but slower, languid as it lingered and spread out through every cell of my body.

I shuddered, shaking in Jared's arms. He pulled me down,

bringing us chest-to-chest again. He grunted and strained. With one last thrust, he went rigid.

Jared roared as he poured into me.

He let out a sharp breath, clung to me with all his life, his face pressed into my neck.

Panting, we both remained still, catching our breaths and stilling our frenzied hearts, holding on to what was precious.

Finally, Jared exhaled as one last tremor rolled through his chest.

He pulled me down at his side. I rested my head on his shoulder and trailed my fingertips over the rose imprinted on his chest. He shivered under my touch, but he didn't pull away. He just wrapped me up in his arms, and at the top of my head, he released a gush of air that sounded distinctly of relief, gentle as he buried his nose in my hair. We rested in the silence, in the calm of the darkened room, listening to each other breathe.

Finally I leaned down and pressed my lips to the green eyes he'd forever etched as a piece of himself onto his skin, that piece of me he wanted to live eternally in his heart.

I felt the words forming on my tongue, and I took a chance. "Happy birthday, Jared," I whispered against his skin.

He tensed below me, his fingers halting their lazy pursuit through my hair. Shifting, he blinked up toward the vacant ceiling. I worried I'd made a mistake before he finally spoke. His voice cracked over the hushed words. "I went to see her today . . ." His tongue darted out to wet his lips. "To her grave."

I hugged him tightly. Floored. I knew he'd taken a step in the right direction. I just had no idea the distance he'd gone.

God, what had he been through today?

I had no clue.

In the silence, I waited, supporting him through the heightened emotions that bobbed heavily in his throat.

"It took everything I had to go there. I swore I never would, but I felt drawn . . . like there was no way to resist it. Like she was calling me back at the same time all the darkness in me was condemning me for even considering it."

I snuggled closer into his side, urging him to continue.

He exhaled heavily. "All these months I've been running, trying to stay one step ahead of my past, because if I did, then I could keep it from catching up to me. And you . . . my sweet girl . . . you knew exactly what was happening. And like an asshole, I just kept shutting you down."

"You were scared," I contended through a murmur, my fingertips smoothing over his bare chest.

He seemed to debate this for a second in his mind before he admitted, "Yeah . . . I've always been. Fucking terrified, Aly."

He hooked his finger under my chin, forcing me to look at him.

Like I'd ever be able to look away.

"Baby, I can't . . . please . . . just don't give up on me," he pled. "I'm fucked-up. I told you a long time ago I was always gonna be. But I realized today it doesn't always have to be like that. And, yeah, I've got a long way to go . . . I know it, and I'm sorry that's who I am, but God, Aly, I can't do it without you."

He blinked rapidly, shook his head. "Maybe I could," he admitted, like it just occurred to him that he had to rely on himself too, that maybe he was worth the effort. "But I don't want to. I don't want to do it without you."

For a moment he held a breath. Then he blew it achingly between pursed lips. Tucking me closer, he uttered the statement at the top of my head.

"I need help."

His words sounded with a trumpet of deliverance.

And I repeated the ones he'd promised me so many times.

"I'm not going anywhere."

———

Faint rays of sunlight broke through our bedroom window. I blinked against them, slowly pulled from the depths of my rest-ful sleep. I awoke to an empty bed. I propped up on my elbow and swept my palm across the cool sheets beside me.

In the middle of it rested a folded-up piece of paper, washed out and worn, the edges frayed from where it had been torn from a journal.

I bit my lip as I reached out and snagged it. Slowly I pushed up to sitting and held the small treasure Jared had left.

He hadn't written me one once since he returned home just before Thanksgiving. Instead he'd whispered sweet words into my eager ear.

Carefully I unfolded the note. I just sat there, absorbing the statement he made.

When beauty breathes life back into the broken.

Without making a sound, I slipped from bed and tiptoed out our bedroom door.

In the early-morning light, I stood and gazed down on the man who held all my days. In the family room, he was kneeling on the floor with his back to me, facing the fireplace.

Pieces of splintered, broken wood were spread out around him, dragged out from where I'd stacked them in the corner after he'd torn all the beauty he created from its rightful place.

He sensed me, and Jared sat back on his haunches and shifted to look at me over his shoulder.

For a moment we just stared, before his mouth edged in the softest, sweetest smile.

Butterflies took flight in my stomach.

And I knew. . . . this was Jared's new start.

TWENTY-SIX

Jared

Darkness held heavy over the moonless sky.

I slumped back against the rough stucco of our little house, the pitted wall making its mark on my bare back. I dug my toes into the cool, damp grass where I propped my feet.

On a sigh, I lifted my half-spent cigarette to my mouth, balanced it between my lips as I let my head drift to the side, turning my attention back on the choppy, scrawled words that overflowed the dingy pages of the notebook seated on my lap.

My therapist had encouraged me on nights like this, the ones when I woke up gasping and begging for air from the aftermath of the horrors of that vivid dream, to do this.

Write.

I shook my head.

I had a therapist.

Never thought in a million fucking years I'd sit in front of one without it being court ordered. And when it'd been, those sessions had been nothing but a sham. Me sitting there like a punk-ass kid because that's exactly what I was, spewing inane bullshit at a group counselor, dodging questions and throwing back vapid words when they were required.

It's when I started pouring all this shit across these pages, at night in juvie when I couldn't sleep.

Felt like I'd been doing this for fucking ever.

The difference was all those pages had been inscribed with hate.

I raked a hand over my head, scratched at it as I tried to define what I wanted to say, because these pages were no longer filled with hate.

These were letters to my mom.

God, the first time I did it, I sat out here in the middle of the night and cried for hours. Because I felt her, somehow knew she was listening, somehow knew she was talking back to me through all these words that came bubbling out of me from some unknown place.

My thoughts had been disorganized, a ramble of words that didn't make a whole lot of sense except for the intense need I felt to tell her how much I loved her.

Slowly over time I opened up, revealing to her how I felt that day. How scared I was—how all that fear was for her.

I told her I was sorry.

Even though I'd come to accept she'd already forgiven me, in almost all my letters, there was an apology.

Now . . . now I was working on forgiving myself.

Some days were harder than others because I no longer blocked the misery, didn't close off her face or shun her smile or reject her good.

I submersed myself in it and allowed myself to mourn.

God, I'd gone through a lot of fucking pain to come to that

point, but I finally accepted I had the right to miss her. That I didn't have to feel guilty for it, didn't need to heap it up as another burden to bear.

I missed her.

It was part of my truth and I poured that feeling into these pages. No longer did I hesitate to tell her how much.

And damn, there were some moments when it just about brought me to my fucking knees.

But every time I got back up again.

I lived and loved with everything in me. Giving it my all.

She knew all my secrets, how much I adored my girl, just like my mom knew I would. She knew how terrified I was of becoming a father, all this anxiety of the unknown wrapped up in Aly's ever-growing belly. But she also knew how insanely anxious and proud and thrilled I was at the same time, that my heart beat a little stronger every time I felt our baby kick.

She knew it all.

I let my thoughts wander, back to when I was a boy, to the soft lilt of her laugh and the tender touch of her hand. God, she'd been beautiful. So good and pure. A mild breeze rustled through the deep, slumbering night, and if I held still enough, I could almost feel it, her fingers brushing through my hair.

My chest swelled.

I felt so close to her.

Like she was right here, still guiding me through all the moments of my life.

And I thought maybe . . . maybe she is.

I looked back to the page, and set my hand free.

Tomorrow I'm going to marry her. Can you believe it? I get to call Aly my wife.

God, Mom, I'm happy.

So happy I think I might be a little crazy, and all of this sometimes seems impossible. That girl steals my breath.

I lifted my face to the starry sky, my leg bouncing when I turned back to my journal.

I'd do anything for you to be there.

I hesitated with my pen poised over the paper; then I set it back down.

But I know in some way you will be.

I rocked my head back on the wall.

Yeah.

She wouldn't miss it.

EPILOGUE

Aleena

Loving someone is one of the biggest chances we ever take. I once considered it unfair because it's rarely a conscious decision we make. It's something that blossoms slow or hits us hard, something that stirs and builds gradually, or something that shocks us with its sudden intensity. And sometimes it's something that's been a part of us our entire lives.

But almost always, it's inevitable.

This . . . this was inevitable.

I slipped outside into the heavy night air. Dark, angry cumulus clouds gathered where they built high in the heated summer sky. Strikes of lighting illuminated the blackened heavens in quick flashes, and thunder rolled in the distance.

I hugged myself and lifted my face to the burst of stormy wind that blew in.

The monsoon was almost here.

It would always be my favorite time of year.

It would always remind me of where Jared and I began. As children out in our empty field. And again as adults when we embarked on a tenuous relationship filled with insecurities and questions.

One that grew into the strongest love.

He stood across our tiny yard, facing out over the wall, waiting for the start.

I paused in the sheltered shadows of the patio, silent as I watched.

My spirit shimmered with pride when I thought of what he'd become.

When I recognized everything he'd overcome.

My eyes traced over my gorgeous man, his profile so defined, his stance so strong, all this coarse beauty that shielded the kindest heart. He wore a fitted black tee and jeans, and my stomach did a little flip-flop and my pulse responded with a patter. Heat rushed to my cheeks.

After everything we'd gone through, you'd think he wouldn't still affect me this way.

But my need for him only seemed to grow.

From where he stood, his left side faced me. My attention trailed over the exposed skin of his arm. Years ago he covered it in blacks and grays that morphed into horrific faces. Those faces promised all his days were condemned to be served out in a tortured living hell.

Now a long-stemmed rose grew up between the faces, shedding light on the dark, a new birth when he'd once believed his punishment was death.

The bright stem twisted and turned through the statement of his self-loathing, growing higher and thicker before it blossomed into a vibrant red rose.

Life.

I always prayed he'd find it.

And he had.

The new does not blot out the old. Rather, it is an extension. A symbol of a life that ended much too early and the beginning of another that some would say began too soon.

Curling out from the rose were little spirals of vines. They wove into the most precious words.

Ella Rose.

Affection squeezed my heart.

She was curled up in a tiny ball, fast asleep on her daddy's chest.

It was her favorite place.

I could hardly blame her.

Slowly he rocked her, one hand protecting her little head, his arms secure around her little body.

He was a good father.

A good husband.

Jared was a *good* man.

I'd always seen it.

Now he finally accepted it—that he was a part of the *good*, and that without him our lives would never be so full.

He was *important.*

Needed.

He brushed his lips across her head, and I edged forward across the lawn, drawn deeper into the darkness.

Drawn to my family.

From behind, I wound my arms around his waist and pressed my lips to the center of his back.

A rumble of pleasure vibrated through him. "There you are, Mrs. Holt," he whispered low.

I felt the redness rush to my face. God, I loved when he called me that. And he did *a lot.* Apparently Jared liked the way it sounded, too.

"Where else would I be?" I asked as I flattened my palm to his taut stomach, the other latching onto a tiny foot as I peeked around Jared at our daughter.

Ella grunted, and her little head bobbed as she stirred.

I had become a mother six weeks ago. I thought I was prepared for the overpowering love I would feel. I'd really had no clue until the moment I held her in my arms, my precious black-haired baby girl with the deepest gray eyes. Those would be blue, I was sure, this perfect little mixture of her father and me.

Jared chuckled low, bouncing her softly as he shushed her. "You gonna wake up and watch the fireworks with Daddy and Momma, Ella?"

He dipped his chin, softly nudging our child. She squirmed and let out a high-pitched cry that sounded like a kitten's yowl.

The force of my smile was all-encompassing, the rush of love that filled every crevice of my heart overwhelming. Moments like this, I felt staggered. Overcome. My voice filled with awe. "I love her . . . so much."

"She's amazing, isn't she?" Jared whispered, falling into a slight sway as the two of us rocked our child together, this miracle that seemed so impossible, this tiny, perfect life.

I was so blessed to be able to stay home with her, so blessed to be able to draw. Just like Jared said I could. They were images like the ones I had kept hidden away in my sketch pads, although now people paid me to capture their treasured faces, their children, their spouses, their families. My mentor had gotten me started, so much sooner that I'd ever anticipated.

It made Jared proud, so extremely proud, and he told me every day.

But my proudest moment was when he sat with me while I drew a picture of a snapshot of him and his mother from when he was a small boy, clinging to her neck. The drawing was now displayed proudly on the wall above the mantel he had recon-structed, the mantel where the jewelry box he'd made for her had found its home.

I was so intensely *proud* of this man. He'd accomplished so much in such a short time. I hadn't been shocked in the least when he'd come home from work two months ago, pacing, ner-vous, unsure of what direction to go when his boss had asked him to become his partner in a new venture designing and cre-ating custom kitchens.

Christopher joined their business too as a partner, which was kind of funny, but completely expected, my crazy brother meshing with Jared, constantly bickering and never far from each other's sides.

Jared was also slowly renewing his relationship with his father. Neil, Mary, and Courtney had come to Phoenix to meet Ella the week she was born, and Courtney had plans to spend a couple weeks with us during her summer vacation from high school. Rebuilding those bonds would take time, but Jared was willing to put everything into them.

"Do you think she'll be afraid of the fireworks?" Jared asked as he turned his attention out beyond the boundaries of our yard.

"No . . . I think she's going to love them."

How could she not?

Soft laughter floated from his mouth, and he rocked her a little more. "Did you know one year ago tonight I kissed your mommy for the first time? She drove me right out of my mind that night. I had to have her." His voice softened. "Thank God I took her."

"You took me?" I teased, lifting our daughter from his arms. My entire body sighed in contentment, the feel of her, my heart so full I was sure it would burst.

Jared turned me around and wrapped us both from behind in his embrace.

It throbbed a little more, just a little fuller, just a little more. Always just a little more, because with Jared, I never got enough.

"Yep," he said, almost proudly at my ear. "Give me about a half an hour, and I'll be taking you again," he whispered through his deep voice. Soft laughter escaped my mouth. Like it was difficult for this man to get me into bed.

One look from Jared? Call me *seduced*.

Jared pulled us closer, and I listened to him murmur sweet words to our daughter, filling her tiny ears with the sound of her daddy's voice, with the beginning of our story.

But that night one year ago was far from our beginning.

A rumble in the distance stole our attention. We turned to watch the first explosion of color lift to the sky from afar. Still it was palpable, like the three of us felt it, the twines of color wrapping through us, weaving through our hearts and our spirits and the fabric of our beings.

Making us one.

Maybe a year ago was the first time we'd given in to it, to this unseen bond that had been bred in us.

But this . . .

I leaned back into Jared, letting him hold me up, this man who had thought himself so weak who had become my rock. The foundation of who I had become.

This . . . this had begun long ago.

This connection I would cherish for all my life.

One I would wake up each day and give thanks for.

This amazing love that began in a boy who grew up to be my man.

A NOTE FROM THE AUTHOR

Dear Reader,

Thank you for reading *Come to Me Softly*. I hope you enjoyed reading Aly and Jared's story as much as I enjoyed writing it. If you could leave a short review on Amazon.com or Barnesand Noble.com, it would help me so much! Those reviews are the best kind of support you can give an author. Thank you!

Up next in the Closer to You series is Christopher Moore's story in *Come to Me Recklessly*. Be sure you don't miss it!

TEXT "jackson" to 96000 to subscribe for important updates plus exclusive teasers and extras just for you!

Thank you for all your love and support—it means so much to me!

Wishing you love,

Amy

A. L. Jackson

A. L. Jackson is the *New York Times* bestselling author of *Take This Regret* and *Lost to You*, as well as other contemporary romance titles, including *Pulled* and *When We Collide.*

She first found a love for writing during her days as a young mother and college student. She filled the journals she carried with short stories and poems used as an emotional outlet for the difficulties and joys she found in day-to-day life.

Years later, she shared a short story she'd been working on with her two closest friends, and with their encouragement, this story became her first full-length novel. A. L. now spends her days writing in southern Arizona, where she lives with her husband and three children. Her favorite pastime is spending time with the ones she loves.

CONNECT ONLINE

aljacksonauthor.com
facebook.com/aljacksonauthor